THE FEARLESS
HIGHLANDER

AMY JARECKI

OLIVER
HEBER
BOOKS
GNARLY WOOL PUBLISHING
EST 2016

To my Mom and Moriah for their ever-present support and inspiration.

Chapter One

❧❧❧

The door of the surgery burst open and two sweaty dragoons scooted inside, straining to carry a Highland prisoner sprawled atop a canvas stretcher. Charlotte clasped a cloth between her hands and watched while the soldiers rolled the enormous man onto a cot and chained his leg irons to the metal footboard.

"Another one?" asked Doctor Munro, Fort William's army physician.

"Fevered just like the blighter yesterday and he smells worse than a heap of sh—" The soldier looked at Charlotte and cringed. "Apologies, Miss Hill, but this lump of rancid mutton stinks."

Charlotte's cheeks burned as she looked down at the cloth in her hands and nodded, her fingers twisting the piece of Holland so taught, fibers frayed. Her father's men could be overly insensitive when it came to the Scottish prisoners— and there she stood nodding in agreement. *Blast my shy streak, I cannot allow this heartlessness to pass.* "Truly?" She stepped forward. "And this man is so dangerous he must be chained to the bed? He's unconscious, for heaven's sake."

"I'd not be taking any chances with a blighter the size of Goliath." A gutless dragoon raised his palms. "Who knows what he'll do when he wakes?"

The physician held a kerchief to his nose while he bent over and examined the Highlander. "Why in God's name did you bring him here? He's half dead already."

The two dragoons inched toward the door. One carried the stretcher upright and inclined his head in the direction of the fevered man. "The prisoners made such a ruckus, hauling him to the surgery was the only thing to get them to shut their gobs."

Doctor Munro snorted. "So now we're allowing murderers and thieves to tell us what to do? Colonel Hill received orders to send the lot of them to the gallows—and in short order."

"No!" Charlotte snapped. "Papa is awaiting a pardon from the king."

The physician smirked. "You think the king cares about a handful of bedraggled Jacobites rotting in a remote outpost? Why let these criminals run free? A dead man cannot return and thrust a knife into your back."

A twitch of his eye was the only outward sign the Highlander may have heard Doctor Munro's caustic opinion. By the saints, he was unusually large. The soldiers had propped up his shoulders to prevent the man's legs from overhanging the cot. Oh yes, they were well formed, quite muscular legs at that.

Blinking away the image of the Highlander laying atop the cot like an effigy of Richard the Lionheart, Charlotte picked up the ewer and poured a stream of water into a bowl. "I daresay they were right to demand he be seen," she whispered, hoping no one could hear. So unpopular her point of view, any public expression of it would only invite a terse rebuttal. But her insides roiled with a tempest. How could they all be so unfeeling? Was she the only person at Fort

William who cared an iota about the living conditions of the poor prisoners? It wasn't the Highlander's fault he smelled a tad unpleasant. She'd continually asked her father to provide water and lye for the prisoners to bathe, yet he always responded with the same terse remark. *Dear Charlotte, you are too kindhearted. These men are convicts—animals. And Fort William is no bathhouse of luxury.*

The physician stood, and with brisk flicks of his fingers, folded his kerchief and replaced it in his sleeve. "You men are dismissed." He watched them leave, then turned to Charlotte. By the pinched purse of his lips, he'd overheard her remark. "If I may be so bold Miss Hill, you are too gentle to be tucked away in such a disagreeable outpost. In my opinion, a young woman such as yourself should not be exposed to foul lowlife akin to this man, or any of the other riffraff incarcerated in this prison. 'Tis just not proper."

"Oh please." She dared meet his gaze. She hated looking Doctor Munro in the eye because he always stared at her with the most intense expression—just as he did right now. Curse his gunmetal-grey eyes. But rather than shy away, Charlotte squared her shoulders. "You speak to me as if I'm but a delicate flower."

He stretched his fingers toward her cheek, but when she leaned aside, he quickly snapped his hand to his hip. "Oh, how delicate you are, indeed." He took a step closer. "Your father should have at least sought a post nearer to Edinburgh where *civilized* people reside. This outpost is no place for a lady as well-bred as you."

Charlotte regarded the bowl she'd just filled with water and bit the inside of her cheek. "Indeed?" After taking a hesitant look at the patient, she hastened for the door. The unconscious man could use tending, but presently she wasn't about listen to the physician utter another word about what he thought of her gentility. The man had been growing bolder with such remarks.

She took in a sharp breath. "Pardon me, but my father serves the king where he is needed, not where it best suits me." Besides, if Charlotte moved anywhere away from Papa it would be London—where she was born. Placing her hand on the latch, she curtsied. "I shall see you at the evening meal."

"Very well—" he said as she closed the door before he could utter another opinionated word.

At the top of the stairs, Charlotte stopped and drew in deep breaths as she turned full circle. Good, no one was about, as was usual in this part of the fort. Most everyone gave the surgery a wide berth, which she suspected was why her father allowed her to assist Doctor Munro. The physician wasn't too terribly horrible. Though he was teaching her to be his assistant, he watched her with too much intensity beneath his beetle brows. Of course it was only natural for him to scrutinize her closely. He was even somewhat amenable, except when it came to ministering to prisoners. There, his manner was decidedly stiff and insensitive.

She ducked behind the wood stack and waited.

As she expected, it wasn't long before the physician locked the infirmary and headed off. Doubtless, he hadn't taken a second look at his fevered patient. Doctor Munro had the same opinion about the prisoners as everyone else in the Government Army. They were all but wild animals locked in chains where they ought to be.

But Charlotte vehemently disagreed with them. For the most part, she kept her opinions to herself, except when it came to her father. Inordinately shy, she hated the way the soldiers looked at her when she spoke at all, let alone expressed her unpopular beliefs. Of course with Papa she knew what she could and couldn't say. The others? She shuddered. Merely speaking out came with great risk, and a charge of sedition would not only see her hanged, it would ruin her father's prospects for advancement. With civil war an ever-present threat across England, Ireland and Scotland, no one knew what spies lurked at every turn.

Fishing the surgery key from the purse at her waist, she waited until Doctor Munro's footsteps faded. On tiptoes she crept from behind the wood stack and peered in all directions to ensure she hadn't been spotted. Then she lifted her skirts above her ankles, and as fast as a rabbit, pattered down to the surgery and slipped inside.

With the lamp snuffed, the light was dim, and Charlotte stood against the door keeping her hand on the latch while she waited for her eyes to adjust. The Highlander's breathing wheezed. Her heart sped. Tightening her grip on the latch, she nearly fled. But the outline of the man became clearer. Lying on his back, she could see only his profile. A massive warrior, he didn't have a hooked English nose, but his forehead angled to a proud Norse-shaped nose—straight, noble-looking. Like all of the other prisoners, his beard was rather unruly.

The unfortunate soul. By the saints, Papa will send this man to the gallows over my dead body—and I will see to it he survives.

Taking a deep breath to still her jittery nerves, Charlotte lit a candle and placed it on the table nearest the Highlander's cot. She set the bowl she'd filled with water on the table and fetched a small cup of claret. Resting the back of her hand on the Highlander's forehead, she tested his temperature. The patient was afire.

After dousing the cloth, she cleansed his face and neck with swirling strokes. Once she'd cleared the grime, she stood back for a moment. He had a handsome face—rugged as the Highlands. His dark hair was the color of well-oiled leather, and he'd braided his moustache hair into his beard—to keep it clean, she supposed.

How wretched for anyone to be housed in the bowels of Fort William.

At the age of twenty, Charlotte had grown weary of biting her tongue and blindly accepting the brutal treatment of prisoners of war. Goodness, she'd been at Fort William for a month. How much longer must she remain silent? As far as she knew, they had done nothing wrong but fight on the losing side of a battle. The men sharing the dank hold were not common murderers or thieves as Doctor Munro had accused this man of being. They were warriors.

She studied him while curiosity fluttered in her breast. Of course, her concern for his wellbeing is what had her insides flittering about. Unusually captivating, he had lines etched into the corners of his eyes like a man of perhaps thirty. Was he married? Did he have a family? Would she be in danger if he weren't unconscious?

A colossal hand in repose atop his belly sported thin white scars. She'd seen such marks caused by nicks from the sparring ring. His fleshy fingers were long, artistic, but moreover, they looked so powerful, Charlotte had no doubt he could crush her much smaller hands without even a grimace.

Nonetheless, sick with fever and flat on his back, he did not appear too terribly dangerous. *Is he a murderer? No. By the stirring of my blood, I do not believe him to be.*

With an exhale Charlotte's gaze trailed lower. His shirt laces were open, revealing tufts of mahogany curls. Licking her lips, her gaze meandered down the length of the loosened laces. His chest rose and fell with his breathing. She dunked the cloth in the basin and wrung it out. He smelled better already, but she would cleanse that which she could reach.

"I'll run the cloth through your beard and over your chest," she said as if he could hear. Heaven forbid he wake and startle.

Charlotte's hand trembled a little after she moved from

his beard to his chest. The Highlander's flesh was nearly as hard as stone—far more muscular than she'd imagined a man would be—especially a prisoner.

Of course, she'd seen her father without his shirt, but at the age of two and sixty, Papa's chest was—well, it wasn't nearly as solid as this man's.

Clearing her throat, she drew her hands away. *That should suffice.*

As she turned to the bowl, the Highlander coughed.

With a backward leap, the cloth flew from her hands, over her head, and landed on the poor man's stomach. "A-are you awake?" Cringing, she tiptoed toward him and snatched the cloth away.

"Mm," the Highlander's deep voice rumbled, but his eyes remained closed.

"You're terribly fevered." Biting her knuckle, she glanced toward the door. She really ought to be dressing for the evening meal. Then she regarded the poor soul chained to the cot. It would be ever so cruel to leave without doing something to ease his suffering.

She picked up the cup of claret and placed one hand under the base of his skull. "You need to drink. I'll lift your head now." Goodness, merely his head weighed a stone. But she held him steady and moved the cup, tipping it up ever so slowly until the red liquid touched his lips. He opened his mouth just wide enough to take a small sip.

His Adam's apple bobbed. "More."

"How long have you been awake?" she asked, testing to see if he was well enough for conversation.

"Please," he grunted.

"Yes, of course." She offered another sip, and this time he took in a mouthful and swallowed it with a gulp. Charlotte eased his head back to the cot.

He sputtered and coughed. "Forgive me."

"You needn't apologize for being ill, sir."

Before she could draw away, his eyes flashed open and those enormous fingers wrapped around her wrist, squeezing so forcibly her fingers went instantly numb. Holy Moses, it hurt but Charlotte clenched her teeth and froze.

"Help me," he growled through his teeth.

"I-I'm trying to." She attempted to pull away, but his grip held fast.

Then as if Satan possessed him, his hand dropped and his eyes rolled back, shuttering his haunting stare with inordinately long lashes. By the saints, the color of his eyes gave her pause—treacle brown like liquid pools of unfathomable depth. How on earth a man as fevered as he could be so expressive with a look, she had no idea. In that moment when their gazes connected, aside from her heart flying to her throat, she'd read so many things. Without a doubt this prisoner had suffered inconceivable pain and hardship. But he wasn't a common crofter. Oh no, there was something special about this Highlander. If only Charlotte could put her finger on it.

❧

HUGH'S HEAD POUNDED LIKE SOMEONE HAD TAKEN AN IRON hammer and bludgeoned him to within an inch of his life. But God's bones, after enduring one year and seven months in the bowels of hell, this woman's voice soothed him as if she spoke with the sweet tenor of an angel. No red-blooded Scotsman could allow such temptation to pass without a mere glimpse even if he was close to death.

He willed his eyes to open. At first the fair-haired beauty posed a blur to him. With all the concentration his fevered head could muster, he forced himself to focus. His heart actually fluttered. Oh, Lord in heaven, such a gift he'd been given in these final moments of life. Her wide-eyed gaze expressed her surprise, almost as if she feared he'd do something ungentlemanly. No, no, no, never in his life would Hugh act out against a woman—especially one with bonny wisteria-blue eyes. He guessed with such an expressive countenance, she'd never be able to keep a secret—not with blues the size of silver coins.

If only he could enjoy such a morsel for himself. If only he could ask her to lie in his arms and succor him until he drew his last breath. Damn the unrelenting hammering against his skull. He smirked at the irony—Hugh may not trick death, but bloody Colonel Hill wouldn't have the satisfaction of putting a noose around his neck. Hugh hadn't heard much the physician had said, but the drivel about the false king not caring about a few miserable souls rotting in Fort William's pit rang true. Christ, he'd known he was doomed all along.

Through his hazy vision, Hugh watched the bonny lass. Wasn't a man entitled to a last request?

How long had it been since he'd held a woman in his arms? At two and thirty, he should be married with sons and daughters at his feet. But war had a way of stalling a man's plans for his life.

"What is your name?" she asked with a gentle coo that sent a shiver along his fevered skin.

"Hugh MacLeod," he replied with the same answer he'd given everyone else since his internment into Fort William's hell. If anyone discovered he was the heir to the lands of Glencoe, the bastard dragoons wouldn't wait to hang him. He'd lost count of all the sordid ways they could ensure he died within these walls. His entire body convulsed. *Death be damned.* He must fight to survive, not for himself but for his clan. Clenching his fists at his sides, he stilled his chattering teeth. "And you?"

"Miss Hill," she whispered, as if ashamed.

Hugh's eyes flew open. *Hill?* Blast his rotten, miserable, bloody luck. "The Colonel's daughter?" he croaked, hanging on to a shred of hope that she was of no relation to the sadistic governor of this ill-fated prison.

"Yes." She turned away and doused her cloth in the bowl.

A lump took up residence in his throat.

Earlier, Hugh had been remotely aware of her gentle ministrations—her lithe fingers upon his chest. He'd come to consciousness enough to consider asking her not to stop—to keep kneading her magical fingers all the way down to... *Boar's ballocks.* Now he knew her father was Colonel Hill, Hugh would immediately cease his errant thoughts. Absolutely nothing positive could come from befriending this lass.

He gasped when she placed the cold cloth on his forehead. She was the bloody daughter of Satan incarnate. Why the hell was she in the surgery? Had the devil put her there to tempt him in his last hours?

Damn, he would be far better off if he had no luck at all.

"Do you think you can take another sip of claret?" she asked. "Doctor Munro gives it to all the soldiers—says it will help them regain their strength."

Jesus Christ, did she have to sound so bloody bonny? With a voice like that, he'd offer to gulp down a draught of nightshade. His mouth dry, Hugh only managed to nod. But this time he watched her while she held his head and offered the cup. The fruity wine slid over his tongue, down his gullet, and instantly swam in his head as if he'd guzzled a healthy tot of whisky. Holy Mary, it had to be the most flavorful ambrosia he'd tasted since his capture at the Battle of Dunkeld.

"Why..." He eyed her well-tailored gown, cinched tightly at the waist. Though petite, she was full-bosomed, yet wore a lace modesty panel to prevent him from stealing a glimpse of the velvety white flesh swelling above her bodice. Just as well.

The last thing he needed was to be brought up on contrived charges for ogling the Colonel's daughter's breasts.

"Yes?" She regarded him, the expressive concern painted on her bonny face unwavering. Why on earth did the daughter of the devil have to have creamy porcelain skin and a smile that would melt the snow atop Ben Nevis in winter?

"Hmm?" was all he managed to utter as a wave of nausea clamped his gut.

"You were about to ask something?"

The pain eased. Ah yes, now he remembered. "Why does your father allow you in the surgery alone?" His voice sounded like he'd swallowed a rasp.

She glanced back toward the door. "He doesn't really. Since my arrival, I've been assisting Doctor Munro with simple tasks—rolling bandages and tending ill soldiers whenever necessary." She bit her bottom lip. Indeed, the lass shouldn't be alone with Hugh at all.

"Why doesn't he have a local woman assist him?" With his next shudder, chills fired across his skin.

High color blossomed in her cheeks. "Honestly, I needed something to occupy my time. One can only embroider and practice the violin so much in a day."

"You're a fiddler?" he asked through chattering teeth, willing himself to focus. Why couldn't she have a hooked nose with a wart atop?

"Yes, of sorts."

"I wish..." He shivered. "I could hear you play someday." God, he was daft. *Right. Ask the Sassenach lassie to come down to the pit and play a merry tune for the poor bastards as they wallow in their stench. Och, she could accompany the drummer beating the death knoll as he climbed the steps to her father's gallows.*

A bell rang in the distance. Miss Hill cringed and snapped her gaze toward the door. "I'm afraid I must go." She wrung her hands. "Will you be all right?"

Honestly, this cot was the most comfortable thing Hugh had lain upon since his arrival at Fort William. He regarded the chain securing his leg irons to the footboard and the pounding in his head resumed. But still he eyed her. "How about giving a dying man a last request?"

Standing, she grimaced as she rubbed her wrist. "What would that be?"

Hugh squeezed his eyes shut to block the pain. "The key to these bloody manacles for starters."

Chapter Two

❦

Hugh didn't move when the door to the surgery opened. By the heavy footfalls, his instinct to remain still was exactly correct. A skill he'd learned tracking deer in Glencoe and later as a Jacobite scout, he slowed his breathing and forced his body into a motionless trance as the man approached.

The footsteps stopped beside Hugh's cot. "Lived through the night, I see. Unfortunate. But the bloody flux will win. I've witnessed enough of it to know you have little chance of surviving." The man sniffed. "You're stinking up my entire surgery."

Hugh had suffered from the chills most of the night, but come dawn his headache had nearly cleared—and hopefully his fever. The previous day he'd been so ill, he wasn't certain he'd live out the night either.

Mayhap Miss Hill's kindness was the remedy I needed to heal.

"God forbid the thought of touching you makes my insides roil." Footsteps faded away. "Bugger it, I won't. Besides, if this doesn't rouse you, there's little hope you'll ever see the light of day again."

Hugh opened an eye to a mere slit. Christ Almighty, the physician hefted up a bucket. Hugh's mind raced. If it weren't for his legs being chained to the bed, he'd spring from the cot and overtake the backbiter.

Forcing his mind into a place of blackness, he readied himself.

"This ought to do the trick," the doctor growled.

A cascade of icy water splashed across Hugh's body, clothes and all. His mind might have been steeled to the shock, but an onslaught of fevered shudders resumed with a vengeance.

"'Tis as I suspected," said the physician. "With those chills you'll be dead by dusk."

Hugh barely registered the door opening, but he did notice a high-pitched gasp.

"Doctor Munro, what on earth happened?" Hugh doubted he'd ever forget Miss Hill's angelic voice.

"Had to douse him with a bucket of water to allay the stench."

"Oh, for heaven's sake, can you not see the man is chilled to the bone?"

"'Tis the bloody flux," the physician said as if he'd hammered the last nail in Hugh's coffin.

"Saints preserve us, it will claim the entire fort before father receives the supplies he's requested time and time again." At least Miss Hill cared about the state of this miserable fort.

"Either that or we'll all starve first," growled Munro.

"I sincerely hope not. Father writes letters requesting medicine and rations daily...Goodness, someone should light the fire in the hearth." Soft footsteps pattered across the floor and hinges creaked.

Bless her saintly soul, Miss Hill draped a blanket atop Hugh. He opened his eyes wide enough to give her a nod of thanks while his chattering teeth rattled inside his head. She tucked the blanket under his chin with worry stretched across her face. "We'll have you warm in no time, sir."

"He cannot hear you," said the physician. "You know as well as I there was nothing to be done with the last victim of the bloody flux. I'm surprised this one survived the night."

"But the last soldier was far older than Mr...um. Surely this man has a better chance of survival."

Hugh warmed a bit beneath the wool. Interesting Miss Hill chose not to repeat his name. *Hmm*. Doing so would indeed alert the doctor of her visit last eve.

"You are ever the optimistic one. 'Tis good to see your compassion, though I fear it is wasted on a doomed *Jacobite*," Doctor Munro spoke the word Jacobite as if it were blasphemous. "Come along. I'm riding north with your father and this is no place for you alone."

"I'd like to stay," she said in a firm tone—far more assured than Hugh would expect of a wee lassie as tender as Miss Hill.

"I do not think it wise," the physician whined.

"Only for a time. I-I'll light a fire in the hearth and then be on my way."

"Always wanting to help, are you not, Charlotte?" God's bones, now the physician sounded like a lovesick fool, cooing in an annoying voice.

Out of the corner of his eye, Hugh watched the man saunter toward Miss Hill and take her hand between his palms. Then he leaned forward and sniffed her hair—the lout. Bloody hell, he even hovered over her far too close as if he were planning to kiss the lass. Ballocks, if only Hugh could slap that lecherous grin off the man's heavy-lidded face.

Pursing her lips, she drew her hand away and rubbed it. *Smart lass*. Hugh applauded her. Munro was as ugly as a sow.

Worse, he wore his dark wig too high on his forehead, giving him the look of an ogre.

She bowed her head politely. God's bones, she'd most likely be polite to a dog begging in the street. "Why should I not help another living soul who is stricken with illness?"

Munro smoothed his hand over his unshorn wig. "Because he's not long for this world."

Shaking her finger, Charlotte's sleeve slid back and revealed a bruise around her wrist. "How can you say that when you know everything Papa is doing—?"

"I know—ever the hopeful one, are you not?" Jesus Christ, Munro grasped her elbows.

Hugh jerked up, only to be stabbed in the gut by miserable cramps. Damnation, if Munro was the cause of the bruise on her wrist, as soon as he was free from these blasted shackles, he'd strangle the bastard—even if it was his last act on this earth.

Charlotte twisted aside. "Leave me. I'll be but a moment."

The physician threw a glare Hugh's way, then sighed and brushed his grubby fingers across her cheek. "Very well. I'll alert the guard that you are within. However, do not tarry overlong. You cannot trust these Highlanders."

Hugh's blood boiled. If it weren't for his damned leg irons, he'd show Munro just how little he could be trusted when it came to men who took liberties with young maidens. Did her father know of the doctor's intentions? Hugh sincerely doubted it.

Charlotte stood with her hands folded while she watched Doctor Munro collect his hat and cloak. "I shall see you anon."

"Indeed," he said with a bow, then pushed out the door.

Charlotte looked to Hugh and touched her finger to her lips, requesting silence until the doctor's footfalls could no longer be heard. Then she walked forward, her taffeta silk skirts rustling as they brushed across the floorboards. "How are you feeling this morrow, Mr. MacLeod?"

Hugh almost looked behind him to see if someone else was in the surgery. Though he'd been using the name MacLeod, no one ever referred to him by it. No one ever referred to him much at all, unless dishing out an insult. He tried to sit up a bit. "Better, thank you. I believe your kind ministrations set me to rights."

She smiled. Lord in heaven, the surgery glowed as if a hundred candles had just been lit.

"I'd best set to lighting the fire so you can dry. 'Twas terribly callous of Doctor Munro to douse you as if you were nothing but a dog."

"I admit it was a wee bit of a shock." Hugh grasped her hand before she turned. The saints only knew why he'd made such a move, but now that he held her delicate fingers in his palm, he hadn't a mind to release them. Her skin was as soft as a sealskin pelt—just like the one he slept upon in his cottage in Glencoe. The smoothness of it sent tingles all the way up his arm—due to the fever, of course.

She gasped and looked at his hand, though she didn't try to pull away as she had with the physician. Like yesterday, their gazes met, yet this time the moment lingered. Aye, there was no steering around it. She had the most intoxicating pair of violet-blue eyes. Her dainty lips formed the shape of an archer's bow and a hint of rose flooded her porcelain cheeks. Though the curls framing Miss Hill's face shone like honey, her eyebrows were darker, giving her face an expressive quality. Hugh hadn't noticed the high arch to her brows yesterday, but now her bonny countenance had him bewitched.

He considered pulling her down to the bed so he could steal a wee kiss. Regrettably such boldness might send her scurrying for the door and yelling for the guard to haul him back to the pit. In a moment of sanity, Hugh released his grip. "Forgive me."

She snatched her hand away and patted her chest. "I daresay I must ask you not to be so forward again. Please do remember that I am helping you out of the kindness of my heart." There was a wee edge to her tone, dammit.

Now he'd proved himself as lecherous as Munro. Christ, Hugh had just done the same thing he'd mentally chastised the physician for. How could he have been so careless? Even if the lass was Colonel Hill's daughter, she was a lady, not some alehouse wench. "I have no idea what came over me. You have my word my hands shall remain by my sides."

"Very well, I shall hold you to your promise." She moved to the hearth and picked up a bundle of flax tow for starting the fire. "Where are you from?"

Hugh bit his lip and stared at the low ceiling. If he told the truth, he would betray his clan. He'd like nothing more than to be forthright, but circumstances as they were, he couldn't take the risk. "Up north—the MacLeods of Dunvegan." Now that was the boldest lie he'd ever told. Clan Donald included Hugh's sept, Clan Iain Abrach. They were bitter enemies with the MacLeods—had been since the beginning of time. As a matter of fact, Clan Donald started warring with the MacLeods before the loathed Campbells.

Using the flame from a candle, she bent down. For all that was holy, Hugh couldn't turn his gaze away from a pair of enticing hips so damn tempting, not even a fever could keep him from growing hard beneath the bedclothes. Any man would drool when confronted with such a sight, and Hugh hadn't had his hands on a woman for...*Jesus Christ*. The fire popped.

"Are you married, Mr. MacLeod?" Leaning toward the fire, she blew the flame to life.

Hugh let out a rueful snort. "I'm afraid Fort William is rather limited on its supply of eligible maidens."

"Oh dear, my question must have sounded heartless." She replaced the candle on the mantel. "I thought perhaps you had a family in...what was that...Dun-veee-gan?"

"Unfortunately, no."

"What, may I ask, is the reason for your...um...incarceration?" She used a set of tongs to place some coal on the fire, torturing him with those enticing hips again.

Hugh clenched his fists. "You're full of questions, are you not, Miss Hill?"

She faced him and cringed. "Goodness, I am ever so sorry. Curiosity always drives me to be overly inquisitive."

"Not to worry." He grinned, seizing the opportunity to exonerate himself. "The same thing made me reach out and grasp your hand."

She dipped her chin and twirled a lock of her hair around her finger. She wore her honeyed tresses with stylish feathery curls framing her face with a bun in the back held in place by a cowl net. Still, regarding the coy smile on her lips, if Hugh hadn't been flat on his back, he might have thought the lass was flirting. *Is she shy?*

Miss Hill dropped her hand to her side and squared her shoulders. "Are you hungry?"

"Famished." Indeed, he could eat an entire steer if offered. Now that he wasn't shivering like a leaf in the wind, the rumble of his stomach complained of being empty for too long.

She clapped. "I'll send for some toast and peppermint tea."

Oh no, that wouldn't do at all. Surely the daughter of Colonel Hill had some clout with the kitchens—even if food was scarce. "If you haven't brought a key for these manacles, a few sausages and eggs would serve to help build my strength, miss." The dragoon bastards fed the prisoners gruel twice a day—about enough to keep them alive and no more. Hugh's mouth watered at the prospect of eating real food. Then he'd press her for that blasted key before her father marshalled him up the gallows stairs.

She bit the tip of her fingernail. "I'm not sure that would be a good idea, given how ill you've been."

"I've not had a decent meal in over a year," he pleaded, testing the waters with the soulful expression that had always worked on his Ma.

By the blush spreading from her neck to her silken cheeks, his pinched brows did the trick. "Very well, I'll order a tray." She emitted a delightful giggle. "I'll tell the kitchens 'tis for me so they don't balk."

Och aye, he kept his pleading eyes in his arsenal for young maidens like Miss Hill. And if she stayed long enough, he just might convince her to give him that key. "You are an angel." Now that he'd won her sympathy Hugh didn't want her to go anywhere, but she promised to return as soon as she put in the request for food—then he'd pour on the charm for certain.

When later she walked through the door with a servant in tow, Hugh could have died a happy man simply by the fragrant aroma of cooked food.

Charlotte gestured toward the table across the surgery. "Please set the tray there."

"Aye, Miss Hill," the lad said in a Highland brogue. "Is that all?"

Hugh eyed the boy—Highlanders working for the government didn't sit well. *Must be a Campbell.*

"I believe so, thank you." She inclined her head toward the door. "I'll let you know if I should need anything more."

As the lad left, the lady regarded Hugh. "Can you sit?"

"Aye." He looked to his leg irons. "But I'm a bit tied up at the moment." *Unchain me and after I have my meal I'll be on my way—back to the Coe where nary a soul will find me.*

"How about if I pile some pillows behind you?"

"I'd prefer it if you could remove these manacles." The corner of his mouth ticked up.

She shook her head with an exasperated cough. "My father would lock me away for an eternity if I did such a thing."

Hugh sighed. "Och, lassie, you cannot blame a man for trying." His brows pinched again, going for the kill. "Is it true the king has ordered the prisoners to the gallows?"

"Papa has written to the king, the Privy Council and to the Master of Stair requesting a pardon."

"So it is true?"

Charlotte looked down with a nod. "I wish it didn't have to be like this." She collected pillows from the other two vacant beds.

"Me as well—most likely more than you."

"But I believe in my father's sensibility—and there hasn't been a Jacobite uprising in Scotland since Dunkeld. His argument is sound." Placing her hand under Hugh's shoulder, she leaned over him with the pillows. Lord in heaven, she smelled more alluring than a bouquet of freshly cut roses. Fire ignited deep in his groin—hell, there was only so much a man could do to resist temptation. If only he hadn't promised to keep his hands at his sides, Miss Hill would be in his arms about now. Oh, to sink his fingers into the supple flesh of a woman. He almost groaned.

Hugh sat forward as she fluffed the pillows behind him. Bless it, he couldn't help his sideways glance. Her breast was so close, if he leaned over a wee inch he could inadvertently brush it with his cheek. He started to incline his head when she straightened.

"Oh my." She grasped his shoulders. "Are you lightheaded?"

Taking in a deep inhale through his nose, he certainly felt light in the head. What miserable prisoner wouldn't be when cared for by a beauty such as Miss Hill? Charlotte, the doctor had called her. The name danced on the tip of Hugh's tongue. He liked it—feminine, yet sophisticated. He cleared his throat and sat squarely. "Not to worry. I'll be right as soon as I get a bit of sustenance into my gullet."

"Let us hope so." She moved the tray to the bedside table and sat on the stool. Her sleeve slid back revealing her injury.

"How did you get that bruise?" He leaned forward for a better look. "Are those finger marks?"

"You do not remember?" she asked with a wee chuckle.

"Pardon? I did that?" Hugh's gut turned over.

"You were fevered," she said as if it were nothing.

"Devil's fire, I would never knowingly hurt a woman."

She tugged her sleeve down. "Not to worry." The tip of her tongue snuck to the corner of her mouth as her gaze slid to his hands. "You're stronger than you think."

Hugh kent how strong he was—but that still didn't make it right. He folded his arms to keep from grabbing her again. "Forgive me."

"There's nothing to forgive. The mark will fade in a sennight." Who suffered a bruised wrist and then returned for more? This woman must be Saint Margaret incarnate. Charlotte picked up a knife and a tined implement and cut a piece of sausage.

"What is that?" he asked, pointing.

She held up the two-pronged stabber. "It's a fork. I always use them. My father purchased these in London from an Italian merchant. Says they're the latest fashion to adorn a well-set supper table."

Hugh shrugged. He'd not be soon adopting a new English

practice of eating with a fork. A knife had served him perfectly well all his life.

Miss Hill skewered another bit of sausage with the two-pronged implement and held it up.

Well, Hugh might allow her to feed him with a fork this once. After all, he deserved some pampering after having been locked in a dank pit by Charlotte's father for nearly two years. Hugh opened his mouth. *God's bones*, it was a good thing he wasn't standing because the burst of flavor would have made him go weak at the knees. "Mm," he moaned a bit too loudly.

Miss Hill grinned. Lord, she could nearly make him forget about escape with that smile. "You like the sausage?"

He glanced toward the plate wishing he could just shove both links in his mouth and savor them as the juice ran down his chin. "Delicious."

"You must eat slowly, otherwise it could come back up."

Hugh clenched his fists to avoid snatching the newfangled fork from her hand and helping himself.

Instead, he licked his lips and watched her carefully cut a piece too small for a bairn's mouth. "You didn't mention what happened to you." She looked at him out the corner of her eye. "I mean, why you are a guest here at Fort William."

He threw back his head and laughed. "Guest? Ah, lassie, you do have a sense of humor."

She busied herself swirling a bit of sausage in the egg yolk. "You don't seem like a vile criminal to me. I only sought to confirm my suspicions."

He cleared his sore throat. "You needn't worry about my character. I fought for Bonnie Dundee when the Jacobites won at Killiecrankie, and then had the misfortune of being captured in Dunkeld, wrapped in irons and marched to this miserable outpost."

Her hand stilled. "How awful."

"I'd be a mite happier if I could return home and resume my life."

She placed another bite in his mouth. "What did you do before...ah...the war?"

Closing his eyes, Hugh chewed and gulped his mouthful down. "Raising cattle, mostly."

"Beef?" Her lovely eyes brightened. "You must be well-to-do."

"Och, I wouldn't say that. We mind our own affairs, there's food aplenty for the clan, and sheep's wool for clothing. We just..." His eyes trailed aside.

"What?"

"We just don't care to be told how to live—or to have unfair tariffs levied against our wares because of our religion. We're Highlanders is all—equal in the eyes of God."

"I daresay I agree." Her shoulder ticked up. "There's even speculation King William might pardon all the Jacobites."

Just the name of the Dutch king sitting on the throne in London made Hugh's blood boil. He couldn't bring himself to look at Charlotte. She was one of them. Her father was the reason he'd suffered as a *guest* at Fort William for the past year-and-a-half. A bleeding pardon from a usurper? William and Mary could sail right back across the channel and stay there. Bring back King James VII, the true Stuart King of Scotland. Hugh didn't need to be pardoned for any of his actions. He'd acted for right—supported his king as should have everyone else in all of Britain.

"You've grown quiet." Miss Hill handed him a cup of tea, the whiff of peppermint clearing his congested head.

"Not much to say, really." He shrugged and sipped.

"Well then." She stood. "I'll put a bit more coal on the fire and I'd best be on my way."

Hugh's fever hadn't affected him so much he'd completely lost his wits. He eyed the fork and waited until Miss Hill reached for the tongs beside the hearth. With a sudden spike to his heartbeat, he slipped the fork off the tray and slid it beneath his thigh. "I do appreciate all you have done to help me. The tot of claret saw me through last eve. I'm certain of it."

Brushing off her hands, she turned and smiled. "'Tis good to hear." Och, it wasn't the lass's fault she was on the wrong side of this miserable war.

Hugh reclined against the pillows, doing his best to feign nonchalance. "I'll wager they'll send me back to the pit as soon as Doctor Munro returns."

She strolled toward him. "I could put in a good word with my father. Mayhap he'll see fit to release you."

Right, put a noose around my neck is more likely.

Hugh grasped her hand and met her gaze. "If only this were another time and place." He bent his head and placed a gentle kiss atop her silken flesh. With an inhale, he closed his eyes and committed her intoxicating scent to memory. "Thank you for your kindness, Miss Hill."

Blushing red as an apple, Charlotte curtsied, picked up the tray and hastened out the door.

Goodbye bonnie lass. I doubt our paths shall ever again cross.

Chapter Three

❦

Charlotte could scarcely breathe as she left the surgery. How on earth could a convicted prisoner—a Jacobite, no less—make the flesh on the back of her hand tingle? Goodness, it wasn't only her hand that tingled from his brief peck. Her entire body felt like it was floating. Yes, she'd been kissed on the back of the hand numerous times, but never had such a gesture turned her knees into boneless mollusks.

In that moment, her mouth had gone completely dry. Her lips had even puckered as if her betraying body actually wanted him to kiss her there. Heaven's stars, it was a good thing Mr. MacLeod had recovered his health, else she'd not be able to visit the surgery again. As it was, she should stay away until Doctor Munro sent him back to the hold.

Ascending the three steps to her father's house, she paused and clutched her fist against her stomach. To think poor Mr. MacLeod would soon return to the vile pit—a mere hole carved into the damp ground. Why on earth King William hadn't yet sent his approval to release the prisoners, she couldn't fathom. Things had been relatively quiet in Scotland since Viscount Dundee had been killed. His troops had disbanded, and with her father leading the government forces in the northwest, law and order had resumed. She believed the king to be a reasonable man—he should know hanging the prisoners of Dunkeld would destroy the trust Papa had earned with the locals. But waiting bore a risk for the Highlander.

I must argue for Mr. MacLeod's release with Papa as soon as he returns. 'Tis the least I can do. If only he could resume his life, he might find the woman he's been looking for and marry. Charlotte's stomach squelched. For some reason the thought of the Highlander finding a wife did not sit well with her. Of course she wanted him to prosper. The back of her hand still tingled.

She opened the door and headed up the squeaky stairs to her chamber. She really shouldn't care who Mr. MacLeod married. After her father released the Highlander from Fort William, he would head north to his family in Dunvegan, wherever that was, and she'd never see him again. Charlotte had come from London to Fort William on an ocean transport after receiving notice that her father was so ill he wasn't expected to live. However, the army had severely underestimated Colonel Hill's strength and by the time she arrived, Papa had resumed his place at his writing desk.

Now entrenched in the daily activities of the fort, so many things concerned her, especially the fact that Papa hadn't made a complete recovery. After all, the man had fathered her at the age of two and forty. Determined to ensure Papa no longer needed her before boarding a ship for home, Charlotte resolved to remain at the outpost until his color improved.

Of course, within days of her arrival, her father had mentioned that she might start thinking about marriage. Charlotte eventually wanted to return to London—find a husband *there*, not in Scotland.

She pushed through the door of her bedchamber and

shuddered. There wasn't an officer in her father's ranks who made her heart flutter the way Mr. MacLeod had managed to do even though he was abed with the bloody flux. No, her best chance to find a husband was to return to London where her aunt and uncle could introduce her at court.

❦

HUGH FEIGNED UNCONSCIOUSNESS UNTIL THE GUARD checked on him. Besides, his chances would be far better after dark. He slipped the fork from beneath his thigh and bent one of the tines. Bloody oath, the sickness had weakened him. That combined with being on the brink of starvation for months had taken his once well-toned physique and turned it into a pile of bones. True, he'd weathered incarceration better than most, but he needed a month of good meals with red meat to bring him back to rights. And he had no intention of facing the executioner's noose.

He felt a twinge of guilt using kindhearted Miss Hill's fork as a tool for escape, but then what Highlander would not take advantage of a wee bit of luck when presented with it? God bless her, she'd given him a gift of more than just a full belly. Yes, indeed, a newfangled fork might be useful after all.

He pushed the bent tine into the padlock and turned. When the metal hit the locking mechanism, Hugh twisted his wrist, adjusting the angle of the tine until the padlock clicked. Careful not to let it drop to the floor, once he'd released the chain between his manacles from the bed, he jammed the fork into the barrel-shaped lock of one shackle, then the other. Thank God, the tine was just the right length to trick all the mechanisms and act like a skeleton key.

He moaned aloud when the each iron manacle finally opened and dropped from his ankles onto the cot. Rubbing his skin alive, Hugh flexed his feet.

God save his wretched neck, he'd need every bit of strength he could muster.

Though the coals had mostly burned to a cinder, enough light remained to cast a dim glow through the surgery. Pushing the blanket aside, Hugh placed his bare feet on the floorboards. He leaned forward for a moment and tested his steadiness. Sickness had a way of knocking a man off balance, but he'd be damned if he'd lie back and wait for Doctor Munro to return on the morrow and declare Hugh fit enough to return to the hold.

Oh no, he'd paid his penance—not that he owed anything to anyone. He'd been stripped of everything except his kilt and shirt. Lord only knew how he survived last winter without his toes falling off.

Hugh stood and took a reviving breath. He could do this, damn it. Stealing across the floor, his toe caught on a chair leg. Before he could stop, it scraped the floorboards with a screech louder than a musket blast.

Hugh froze.

"What the bloody hell?" bellowed the guard outside the door.

Let the game begin.

As the surgery door flew open, Hugh darted behind it. The dragoon inched inside. His musket at the ready, the sharp bayonet affixed to the top passed a foot from Hugh's nose.

"Where the bloody hell are you, ye bastard?"

Hugh held his breath. *A bit further. Come now.*

With the dragoon's next step, Hugh lunged and grasped ahold of the musket barrel, sliding his hand toward the iron cock. If the bastard pulled the trigger, the entire company would be upon him in seconds.

With a grunt the redcoat jerked back.

The gun's cock hammered into Hugh's finger. Sharp pain

shot up his arm, but at least the musket hadn't fired. Gnashing his teeth, Hugh struggled to wrench the gun from the dragoon's grasp. In a fight of wills, the swine's grip finally released.

Hugh stumbled backward as a stool hurtled toward his temple. Ducking beneath it, he grasped the musket barrel and slammed the butt over the guard's head. The man dropped to his knees, sucked in a deep breath, then collapsed on his face.

Hugh bent over, rested his hands on his knees and panted. Holy hell, he'd lost so much strength, he'd nearly let the soldier kill him. As soon as his lungs filled with air, he went to work stripping the man. Coat, boots, belt, sword, dagger. He needed it all.

Pulling the boots off the lump proved more difficult than tugging a breech calf from a heifer. But Hugh wasn't about to give up. Not until he shoved his feet into one of the damned things and his foot stuck about halfway. What the blazes? Did the man have feet the size of a child? With a grunt, Hugh cast the boots aside. Turning in place, his mind raced.

Bandages.

He quickly wrapped his feet and tied the ends around his ankles. Then he hoisted the guard into his bed and locked the man's ankles in his old manacles—*best use of that set of iron cuffs ever*.

Slipping to the door, he held his breath and listened. In the distance, muffled voices chatted and chuckled. Had the physician returned with Colonel Hill, or were they gone for a bit? Hugh supposed it didn't matter. With luck, they wouldn't find him missing until the morning, especially since he'd made it look like he was still abed.

Moving through the shadows, Hugh wound his way to the main gate. Locked inside the fortress walls, he pressed his body into a corner and considered his options. He could climb up the stairwell and out onto the wall-walk. A jump from fifty feet shouldn't kill him—if he landed on grass or mud. He could overtake the guard and raise the portcullis. But then the last fight had almost killed him. He had about as much strength as a lad of twelve. At night he'd oft listened to the surf from inside the depths of the pit. Perhaps there was a sea gate.

Hugh didn't like a single one of his options, but a leap from the wall-walk had the greatest chances of keeping him from another altercation. Bloody oath, when he recovered from the fever it would be his pleasure to return and take on the lot of them...all except Miss Hill, of course.

As Hugh started up the tower stairs, a groan of chains resounded from the gate.

"Colonel Hill has returned," a voice boomed. "Long live King William."

Och aye, I can tell you what should be done with the Dutch king, and it has nothing to do with a long life.

Hugh ran his hands over the dirt and wiped it across his face. Then he crept into the shadows and watched the company of dragoons pass, trotting their high-stepping ponies beneath the portcullis. The sight of snobbish, straight-backed redcoats turned his stomach sour. Too many meals of gruel. Too many jabs with a bat, and too many malicious taunts had given him a bitter taste that would not soon ebb.

Doctor Munro brought up the rear. The pasty codfish was unmistakable with his brown wig curling down his back while he sat his horse like he had a ramrod up his arse. He'd be the first to receive a vengeful blow from Hugh's fist, especially after the bucket of water in the face. Och aye, Hugh would remember that transgression for a very long time.

Doctor Munro looked straight in Hugh's direction.

Every muscle in his body tensed. Had he been spotted?

But the contingent proceeded onward. The portcullis

started to groan again, but Hugh didn't move—not until he was certain Munro wouldn't spot him.

Once the physician turned the corner and rode out of sight, Hugh looked to the gate. Only a few feet from hitting the ground, the deadly iron teeth inched downward. If the chain didn't hold, they'd smash to the ground with the force of eighty stone.

"The prisoner has escaped!" someone hollered with the slapping of running feet.

Ballocks!

Clenching his teeth, Hugh took two racing steps. Right before he dove beneath the gate's deadly teeth, the iron tines boomed as the portcullis slammed into the ground.

He crouched on his knees, his nose inches from blackened iron. The fever had not only made him weak, it slowed his response as well. A fraction of an inch closer, and he would have been crushed in two—a more gruesome death he could not imagine. Hugh slunk back into the shadows.

A trumpet sounded from the battlements. Guards hollered while they raced for the wall-walk. With no place to run, his shoulders pinched as if he could feel a musket ball hitting his back. The next option? Hug the walls and pray.

Chapter Four

WHEN a trumpet sounded, Charlotte set aside her embroidery. A blast from a trumpeter after dark could only mean something terrible was a foot. Clutching her hands against her abdomen she stood and listened.

The door burst open. "Miss Charlotte, did you hear?" Emma, Charlotte's chambermaid bustled inside. "A prisoner has escaped!"

Her stomach dropped all the way to her toes. "Oh dear heaven, do you know who it was?" Charlotte needn't ask. A prisoner hadn't escaped the pit since her father had carved out the hole and dropped the first man inside. *Mr. MacLeod.*

"I've no idea, but there's commotion afoot for certain." Emma wore a linen coif atop her head and an apron to match. Married to Papa's most trusted Highland tracker, Farley MacGregor, she'd been Charlotte's only friend at this lonely outpost.

Drawing her hand to her head, Charlotte fought to hide her panic. Hells bells, she'd thought seriously about returning to the surgery with a key. But somehow Mr. MacLeod had

33

managed to free himself. Worse, if the poor man was caught, her father would want to punish him severely.

She moved her hand to her mouth and gasped.

Emma gaped. "What is it?"

"I think it could only be the man they brought into the surgery yesterday. He was terribly ill, but..."

"But?"

"I think he was feeling a bit better this morn."

Emma covered her lips with her fingers. "Oh, my heavens."

Loud footsteps clomped through the corridor. Oh dear, such a bold stride could only come from one person. Colonel John Hill pushed through the door and stopped in the middle of the chamber with fists on his hips. "Doctor Munro tells me you were the last to see the prisoner." Father wasn't one to mince words when riled. Though of an average height, Papa embodied the ideal of Colonel. His grey wig never had a hair out of place; his starched uniform never showed a wrinkle, and his face was stoic and battle weary.

Her guess had been right. Wringing her hands, Charlotte faced him. "Was I?"

"You tell me. Munro rode out with my company before the noon hour. Said he left you with a prisoner, God forbid. That pea-brained physician left my daughter with a *murderer*."

Charlotte cast a panicked glance toward Emma who was cowering beside the vanity, clutching her fists beneath her chin. A lot of support she'd give, but Charlotte had to come up with something intelligible and fast. "Mr. MacLeod isn't a murderer, Papa."

Father slapped palms, making a deafening crack. "Well if he wasn't before today, he is now."

Her mind raced. Mr. MacLeod had appeared so genteel. "'Tis dreadful."

Father threw up his hands and paced. "First of all, I

cannot believe the physician had the poor judgement to leave you alone with that vile beast. But I'll deal with Munro later. I now have a fugitive to track down and send to the gallows."

Hanged? Charlotte's head swooned. "I cannot believe he... did he kill a guard?"

"Nearly bludgeoned one of my dragoons to death."

"Nearly?" Was there a thread of hope?

"The soldier's fighting for his life—Doctor Munro is with him now."

Clasping her hands over her heart, Charlotte fought to steady her sudden dizziness. "The news grows worse."

Father stopped with his fists on his hips. "What I want to know is how did he manage to free himself from his leg irons?"

"I have absolutely no idea." She took in a deep breath and looked up—anywhere but directly at her father's angered stare. "When I left, Mr. MacLeod was still chained to the bed."

Papa shook his head, the powder from his wig making a faint cloud. "Did he touch you? Could he have taken one of your hairpins?"

She cast her mind back to the curious morning she'd spent in the surgery. "N-nooooo." Charlotte absently rubbed the back of her hand—the one Mr. MacLeod had kissed. Yes, he'd touched her hand twice, but never tried anything ungentlemanly. Of course he did take liberties by kissing the back of her hand, but that wasn't too excessively distasteful. The experience had been rather pleasant. She snapped her hands to her cheeks. At a time like this, she was thinking about Mr. MacLeod kissing her hand? "I fluffed the pillows for him and I did order some food."

"Oh, my dear girl, fluffing pillows for a criminal?" Then Papa clapped his hands again and pointed as if he had an idea. "What kind of food?"

"Sausages and eggs." She held up her finger. "But I fed him and promptly removed the tray when he was done."

"My word, your generosity extends all bounds of reason. That food is for the soldiers and we scarcely have enough to feed *them*."

She chewed her bottom lip. "The poor man was starving. Goodness. I'll go without the morning meal for a sennight if that will help replenish supplies."

"My word, Charlotte that is not the point! When this is over, you and I will have a discussion about consorting with prisoners." He threw up his hands. "Something must have happened when you were there. I am sure of it. And now we've one guard down and a prisoner on the loose. No one for miles will be able to sleep until we track the varlet down."

Charlotte couldn't speak. Truly, she was concerned for the guard and would pray for his recovery, but more than anything, she prayed with all her heart that Mr. MacLeod would run free. By the saints, the man was on death's door only one day past, and though he was sitting up this morn, he was still fevered. It was night, March and *cold* in the Highlands. If Mr. MacLeod didn't find help, he wouldn't make it alive. No one could endure the flux and suffer the elements and survive.

Papa sauntered forward. "Did he tell you anything about his family?"

Charlotte wanted to be sick. She couldn't lie—could she? Her shoulder ticked up. "He said his name was Hugh MacLeod. I asked him if he was married and he said no. I asked him where he was from and he said Dun—" She couldn't bring herself to utter the word. "Um, Dun-something. Up north. Didn't specify where exactly."

"Dunvegan perchance?"

Curses! Charlotte chewed her lip. She couldn't withhold information from her father if she had a barrel over her head.

The colonel drummed his fingers against his chin. "That's odd. The MacLeods are loyal to the crown. But this man is a Jacobite prisoner. Hmm. I suppose this is a war that pits son against father." He marched to the door. "Keep yourself locked within. I'll post a guard at the door. Emma—you'd best stay with Charlotte until my return. She could be in danger."

The maid stepped out of the shadows and curtsied. "Yes, sir, as you wish."

"Do you think the fugitive is still inside the fort?" Charlotte asked.

Papa regarded her over his shoulder. "Lord only knows."

Once the colonel left, Emma shook her head. "I didn't think it was a good idea for you to volunteer in the surgery, miss."

"Oh please, at no time did I consider myself in danger."

"That's even worse." Emma pattered to the bed. "I think you'd best retire early, Miss Char—"

"I have no intention of seeking my bed with a man fighting for his life." *Which somehow seems to be my fault.*

Emma wrung her hands. "You cannot be serious. Colonel Hill told me to stay with you until he returns."

Charlotte collected her cloak from the wardrobe. "Then you'll have to come along."

"Oh, my heavens. You're always so restrained, Miss Charlotte. What is it about this escapee that has your petticoats in a twist?"

Charlotte wasn't about to answer. "Make haste, Emma."

After they arrived at the surgery door, she couldn't recall ever being so relieved. The guard the Highlander had bludgeoned was sitting up on the same cot which had been occupied by Mr. MacLeod earlier in the day. Aside from being a bit pale, and a bandage wrapped around his head, he appeared to be in good health.

"Oh, praises be." Charlotte led Emma inside. "To hear my father tell it, I feared this man would not survive."

Doctor Munro stood from his seat at the table. "Miss Hill, whatever are you doing here this late—and with a fugitive about?"

"I couldn't live with myself knowing one of Father's guards had been injured."

"Miss Hill is a tad over-curious if you ask me," Emma mumbled from the rear. Charlotte could have ribbed the woman with her elbow.

"I assure you, I have everything in hand," said the physician as he bowed and grasped Charlotte's palm.

She tried to pull away, but Doctor Munro held firm, and clapped another sweaty palm over the top. "As you can see, Sentinel Blair has come to, and I do believe he will make a full recovery."

"Aye, thank you for your concern, Miss Hill," said the soldier on the cot. His teeth were stained brown as if he'd never cleaned them.

With a firm tug, Charlotte pulled her hand away and hastened toward the guard. "Pray tell, when did Mr. MacLeod —ah—accost you?" Her mind raced. *Where is he?*

"Not long after dusk." He pointed. "I heard that chair scrape across the floor and came in with my musket at the ready, but the mongrel attacked me from the side."

She wrung her hands. "My heavens, and him being so terribly ill with fever." *He could not have gone far.*

"Must have been of solid Highland stock, that one," said Emma with a hint of admiration in her voice.

Charlotte had no doubt Mr. MacLeod had been bred in the mountains. Even though he'd suffered the ravages of incarceration in that horrible pit, he still had an impressive physique—and proved it by overcoming one of her father's dragoons.

"Miss Hill, please allow me to see you back to the Colonel's house." The physician stepped beside her and clutched her elbow. "'Tis not safe for you to be about."

She leaned away from him, not yet satisfied with the information she'd gathered. "Do you think Mr. MacLeod is still nearby?"

"He could very well still be within the walls of Fort William. Aside from Sentinel Blair, nary a sentry heard or saw a thing."

"Goodness, this whole situation is ever so frightening." *Is Mr. Macleod still here?*

Doctor Munro smirked. "Not to worry. As ill as that blighter was, he won't make it far."

"And if I know your father, he'll bring him in afore the sun rises," said Mr. Blair from the cot.

That's exactly what Charlotte feared the most. If Mr. MacLeod fell into her father's hands, he'd be better off succumbing to the flux. Papa generally had an affable nature, but he was an ardent soldier of the crown. If anyone raised a hand against one of the king's men, Colonel Hill would ensure the man would pay a severe penalty.

Doctor Munro again grasped Charlotte's elbow. "Come now."

Her back stiffened and she drew her arm away. "I shall pray for your swift recovery, Mr. Blair."

The man grinned. "Thank you, miss."

Bowing her head, Charlotte glanced from the physician to Emma. *Curses. How do I slip away from two of them?* With a fugitive on the loose, there would be no talking the persistent doctor out of accompanying her back to the governor's house. She feigned a deep yawn. "Goodness, all this excitement has made me ever so tired. I suppose if I am not needed here, I shall retire for the evening."

Chapter Five

D ragoons shoving their bayonets into every crevice, Hugh found himself moving through the shadows at the top of the surgery stairs. Wracked by fever and body aches, he had no chance of fighting his way out, and even less of a chance of running. Already exhausted, he crept behind a wood stack and curled into a ball. God, he was chilled. If only he had one of Miss Hill's blankets, he might survive the night.

Ballocks to my miserable luck—I escape, only to succumb to the fever afore I can scale Fort William's walls.

When the surgery door slammed closed, Hugh peered through a gap in the wood. Doctor Munro climbed the stairs, leading the dragoon he'd bludgeoned. Shivering, Hugh's mouth watered at the thought of the cot and blanket he'd used—but camping in the surgery would get him caught for certain. He'd better make a move soon—give it an hour or two and he'd regain enough strength to attempt another escape.

The noise from shouting dragoons faded on the wind. With luck, they wouldn't come back around this way. What bloody fool would hide outside the door where he'd escaped?

Hugh wasn't only chilled; fatigue seeped through his limbs like they'd been wrung out with the washing. His eyelids refused to stay open. No matter how much he fought, they kept sliding down. He had no recourse but to wait until past the witching hour when most of the bloody bastards would be asleep—save he could manage to stay alive.

Curling tighter, he gave in to the fight to stay awake. *Only for a wee while—until 'tis safe.*

But sleep on a night like this didn't last.

Hugh's eyes flew open when a light footstep tapped beside him. Power pulsed through his veins as he steeled himself for a fight.

Another step.

The bastard wants to take me on himself? Hugh splayed his fingers. *Come just a bit closer.*

With his next breath, Hugh sprang up, grabbed the sneak by the throat and threw him to the ground. Scurrying on top of the blighter, Hugh jerked his fist back.

"Stop," a high-pitched voice peeped.

Hugh blinked. "Devil's fire!" His fist froze midair. "Miss Hill?" his whisper cracked. "What in God's name did you think you were doing sneaking up on a man without so much as a word?" Christ, he'd almost slammed his fist across her bonny face.

She stared at him, her eyes stunned, her breath coming in short gasps.

"Och." Rocking back on his heels, the chills resumed. "I could have killed you."

She sat up, brushing the outsides of her arms. "I whispered your name, but if I'd spoken any louder, I might have raised an alarm."

Hugh stared at his open palms. She must think him a monster. "Forgive me."

The lady nodded. "I thought you were too weak to flee."

"I am—though I figured I had them all fooled by now." He cringed. *She hasn't screamed yet—what's stopping her?* "Are you planning to turn me over to your father? Cause if you are, I might have to find a gag and a bit of rope."

Her eyes flashed wide. "You'd do that?"

"I want to go home, miss." He pushed to his feet and took a step back. "Is one uncomfortable night bound and gagged a fair exchange for nineteen months in the pit?"

"Please." She raised her palm to him. Though Hugh should look for a bit of rope and leave her there to take his chances leaping from the fifty-foot walls, he ground his back molars and pulled her up. "I came to help, you boar-brained Highlander. But by the strength with which you slung me to the ground, I'm not entirely sure you need my assistance."

"Apologies." He wiped the cold sweat from his brow. "Merely standing makes my legs tremble, but when faced with life and death, I suppose power surges through a man, no matter how fevered."

She folded her arms tight across her body and inclined her head westward. "Follow me."

He didn't budge. "To see your father?"

"No."

Hugh motioned for her to proceed, peering every which way as they stepped from behind the wood stack. "Keep to the shadows."

She flashed a challenging smile over her shoulder, her teeth sparkling in the moonlight. "I'm quite adept at slipping through Papa's garrison. Now stay close behind."

His head pounding with fever, chills firing across his skin, Hugh was in no condition to argue with the lass. He only prayed Miss Hill knew what she was doing with his life.

Taking his hand, she tiptoed between the buildings and skirted along the western wall where one lone guard had his back to them, watching out over Loch Linnhe. Hugh squeezed her hand and threw his thumb over his shoulder. "The gate is that way," he whispered.

"Did you expect to walk through the main gate? You'd end up with a noose around your neck before dawn." She mightn't have a clue where they were going, but Hugh liked her mettle. She tugged him onward until she pulled him down slippery stone steps, right into the bowels of the fort, stopping at an iron gate.

Water slapped beyond.

Hugh gestured toward the enormous padlock. "How the—"

"Sh." Charlotte pulled a key from around her neck, slipped it into the lock and turned it. The click reverberated like a strike from a smithy's hammer. No wonder she'd silenced him. They were standing in an echo chamber.

Pulling him through the gate, she pointed. "There's a skiff at the end of the pier. If I were you, I'd row straight out from the fort, and by all means do not let the guard see you."

Colonel Hill's daughter had led him to a boat? Hugh grasped her hand between his palms. "Your kindness exceeds anything I could have thought possible from a Sassenach lassie. How can I ever thank you?"

She squeezed his fingers. "Go. You must never come back."

Hugh licked his lips, gazing into the most enticing violet-blue eyes, made more iridescent by the moon reflecting off the water. "Most men I know have not an iota of your bravery."

"You deserve a second chance on life...ah...Papa knows you're from Dunvegan—you mustn't return there." Those lovely eyes turned liquid. Miss Hill cared enough to shed a tear for him?

Hugh's heart swelled, his blood thrummed beneath his skin. Before he had another rational thought, he pulled her into his arms and stole a kiss. He'd only meant to give her a peck and be off, but a feminine curl brushed his cheek. His eyes closed and her intoxicating scent showered him with the essence of a million rose petals. "Lord, I wish I could stay."

The lady took a step back and drew her hand to her lips. "Please—leave before someone happens past."

Yes. He had no other choice. With a bow, Hugh blew her a final kiss. "I'll never forget this."

AFTER HUGH TOOK UP THE OAR, LOW CLOUDS HUNG ABOVE, making Loch Linnhe inky black, and even better, Hugh's escape smooth and soundless. Thank God Colonel Hill thought him from Dunvegan. Not a soul in Fort William knew him as MacIain of Clan Iain Abrach, the most powerful sept of Clan Donald. His clan suffered enough scrutiny on account of their everlasting feud and power struggles with the Campbells. His father didn't need a host of dragoons befalling Glencoe. None of his kin did.

The icy gale across the loch blew cold enough to freeze his cods, and worse, the damned fever hadn't left him, but, by God, he couldn't allow himself to succumb to it. He'd been given a gift by an angel and he'd pull through this. His head throbbed with the force of a mallet pummeling his brain with his every movement as he rowed through the loch's choppy waves. Sick and chilled to the point of retching heaves, his teeth refused to cease their chattering. No matter how much he wanted to curl into the hull and hide from the frigid wind, he refused to stop. He'd face the gallows before going back to Colonel Hill's rat-infested pit, no matter how much he wanted to see Charlotte again. Bloody oath, he'd force that woman's bonny face from his mind, regardless if she'd helped him.

All night he rowed, growing numb to the agony in his shoulders. Raw blisters stung his palms, but Hugh continued on, forcing himself to endure the tears to his flesh. He must sail into Loch Leven and past the government lookout before dawn. If the regiment spotted Hugh, Colonel Hill would be alerted within hours.

The good news? Once past Captain Drummond's lookout, Hugh only needed to row the skiff around the bend and across to the mouth of the River Coe and he'd be on his family's lands. The mere thought infused him with strength. Though a son of the snowcapped Highlands, Hugh knew the waters of Loch Linnhe and Loch Leven as well as he knew *Gleann-leac-na-muidhe*, the mountainous site of Clan Iain Abrach's summer house.

If his luck had taken a turn for the better or if God had blessed him with good fortune, Hugh didn't know. He muscled through until just before dawn when, with his last shreds of strength, he rowed the skiff onto the sandy bottom of the River Coe outlet.

The bandages wrapped around his feet soaked clean through as soon as he stumbled over the side and tugged the wooden hull into a copse of trees and concealed it beneath the foliage.

Hugh was so close, he could smell the peat burning in the hearth. As dawn shed light upon the glen, the outline of Carnoch, Da's grand stone manse appeared through the mist like a dream. Bloody hell, his head swam as perspiration dribbled down his forehead. He reached out his hands as if he could touch home. Forcing his legs to continue, jagged rocks ripped through his bandages and punished his feet with their unyielding razor-sharp ridges. Hugh only had mere paces before he'd be sitting before the fires of Glencoe, sipping a pint of warm cider with Da and his brothers, Alasdair Og and Sandy.

The bottom of his foot sliced open on a rock. Grunting, Hugh stumbled and crashed to the ground. His head hit hard —another jagged rock cut his temple. Trying to push himself up, everything spun out of control. He eased himself back to the rocky ground and closed his eyes. *I'll be up in a moment.*

❧

HUGH SHUDDERED AWAKE WHEN A DOG LICKED HIS FACE. Christ, he'd nearly frozen to death lying on the soggy earth with water seeping through his threadbare plaid. An enormous, shaggy deerhound hovered over him. Then Hugh's heart stuttered. He reached up with all the effort he could muster and gave the dog's shoulder a pat. "Och, Cuddy, do not tell me you're still alive, old fella."

The dog whimpered and sat beside him.

Footsteps slapped the mud. "What have you found you worthless hound?"

Hugh would recognize Da's gravelly voice anywhere. He tried to sit up, but a volley of shivers coursed across his skin and his teeth chattered so relentlessly, he could utter not a word.

"Lord in heaven." Da dropped to his knees beside him. "My son has returned!" Da's big arms surrounded him.

"D-d-d-da," Hugh managed to utter. Devil's breath, unable to focus, the relentless pounding in Hugh's skull refused to ease.

"You're burning up—hotter than a pot over the cooking fire."

As consciousness slipped from Hugh's grasp, Da had hoisted him over his shoulder. "Come Cuddy, we'd best take this lad to his mother straight away."

❧

HUGH STIRRED TO A SOFT CLOTH BRUSHING ACROSS HIS forehead. "Och, you're a bonny lass, Miss Hill," he mumbled.

"Hill? And who might that be?" came a voice decidedly like Ma's.

He must have been lying atop a feather mattress, because he couldn't remember ever being so utterly warm and comfortable. He hadn't a mind to open his eyes, but he did so all the same. "Ma?"

The careworn face he'd adored all his life smiled. Blue eyes twinkled beneath a ruffled linen coif. "You've come back to us, laddie."

"Aye." His voice rasped. "I finally found a rabbit hole out of Fort William."

"By the looks of you, I'd reckon the escape nearly sent you to an early grave." She smoothed her hand over his forehead.

Hugh choked down a sticky gulp. "I came down with the bloody flux whilst inside—did a turn in the infirmary—escaped from there."

Ma patted her chest rapidly. "Oh, merciful father. I hope we won't have a mob of dragoons beating down our doors."

"Nay, Ma. They all think I'm a MacLeod."

She laughed out loud—the same laugh that had always filled the rooms at the chieftain's manse in Glencoe—had always made him feel loved.

When her laughter ceased, Ma cupped Hugh's cheek. Her fingers weren't silken like Miss Hill's. Ma's skin was rough and calloused. Aye, Clan Iain Abrach of Glencoe mightn't have a motte and bailey fortress, but their wealth came through the tilling of the land and the raising of cattle. Their walls were three thousand feet high, walls only rugged Highland stock could navigate. Nay, Ma need not lift a finger to work, but she forever busied herself doing something—spinning, embroidery, weaving—Ma even rolled up her sleeves and kneaded bread when she felt the leavening could use an extra bit of muscle.

Her expression took on a troubled frown. "What happened at Dunkeld? Your father never speaks of it—just says if it hadn't been for you, all of Clan Iain Abrach would be rotting in Fort William's pit prison."

Hugh took in a deep breath and let it out slowly. "That's about the gist of it, I'd reckon. At least I got off five good shots afore they cornered me."

A deep crease formed between her greying eyebrows. "I nearly strung up your father by his thumbs when he came home without you."

"Not to worry. You would have been proud to see him." Hugh chuckled at the memory of his fearless da. "He fought with the strength of ten Highland warriors."

Ma pressed on the cloth atop his forehead. "But he left his son in the hands of the usurper's men."

"Aye, there were too many of the Williamite bastards. If Da came after me, it would have been the end for all of us."

"You could have died in there."

"But I didn't." Reaching up, Hugh touched his fingers to Ma's weathered cheek. "And now I have your gentle hands to set me to rights."

"You'd best heal with haste." She gave him a stern Highland mother's stare. "Once you've risen from this bed I'll expect you to help your father with the livestock. The herd has grown so large we'll need to take some steers to market."

"'Tis good news."

"And then we'll need to find you a wife."

Bloody hell, Hugh had been conscious for all of five minutes and Ma was ready to send him to the altar. "No need to rush there."

"Did you ken Sandy married?"

"He did?" Hugh grinned. He always thought his younger

brother might end up married first—since birth the lad could win the hearts of every female within ten miles. "Who's the lucky lass?"

A nervous chuckle pealed through Ma's lips. "Sarah. She's the eldest daughter of Alexander Campbell of Lochnell."

With a spike from his heart, Hugh tried to sit up, then flopped back to the mattress. "You cannot be serious."

"You ken the way of it. One year we pinch cattle from the Campbells, the next they raid our lands and murder our sons and daughters. Well, 'twas time your father put a stop to it."

"But still, a Campbell, Ma?"

"That's the way of it." Her mouth formed a straight line with her nod. "One day you'll be Chief of Glencoe and the people will look to you for protection. What better way than to make alliances with our greatest enemies?"

"Had I not heard it from you, I never would have believed it." Hugh stared at the exposed ceiling beams on a sigh. "If Da wanted to make a Campbell alliance, why did he not go straight to Argyll?"

"Och, I doubt I'll see the day when the MacIains are making alliances with the *earl*. Lochnell was enough of a stretch." Ma's eyes twinkled. "Sarah's a nice lass—hard worker, too. I thought the news might come as a blow, but give her a chance. I think you'll like her."

Devil's fire, to hear his mother talk, she'd practically opted to forgive all past transgressions of the earls Breadalbane and Argyll. At every turn for centuries the pair of Campbell bastards attacked MacDonald lands with fire and sword—and with not a care for women and children. And what about Sandy, the poor sop? "Is he happy?" Hugh asked.

"Och, you ken your brother. He's content to watch the sun rise every morn. There's not a happier lad in all the Coe. Besides, Sarah's a sturdy lass—she'll give him many bairns."

He hoped to God Da kent what he was doing with the

wench. Hell's bones, Hugh would have preferred to slumber atop the feather mattress for another day before his mother bludgeoned him with the news they were now related to the Campbell Clan—a small sept at least. "Miserable bleeding hell," Hugh groaned.

"Promise me you will not do something rash," she said with a shake of her finger.

Right—as if Hugh would hop out of bed and kick Sarah's sturdy, child-bearing hips back to Lochnell. "I'll try to keep an open mind. But if she does anything to bilk or backbite my brother, so help me..."

Ma grabbed Hugh's hand and squeezed. "The lass is well aware I'll tolerate no nonsense on Clan Iain Abrach lands. Regardless, we must keep faith. I ken 'tis not an alliance with the house of Argyll, but 'tis a step toward harmony." Ma released her viselike grip. "And I hope they'll keep their grubby hands off our lands and off our wee beasties."

Hugh sighed with a labored breath. "Forever the peace-maker, are you not, Ma?"

"Wouldn't you rather have peace than to lay awake every night wondering if the Campbell bastards are planning to slip inside and run a dirk across your throat?"

Hugh groaned. "I've lived with that fear all my life—'tis what makes a MacIain tough and rock solid to his core."

Ma smoothed her hand over his cheek. "Give it some time. You've had a terrible ordeal. Once you're on your feet, take a wee hike up the Rannoch trail. The tranquility will calm your troubles away."

Chapter Six

Wrapped in a sealskin cloak, Charlotte stood atop the battlements and cast her gaze north, just as she had every day since last August when King William offered a pardon to all Highland Clans providing they took an oath of allegiance before New Year's Day, 1692. Finally Papa's letters had been heard and all surviving Jacobite prisoners had been released. Though at first Charlotte had hoped the king's pardon would lessen the tensions in the Highlands, it only served to make things worse.

Skirmishes between government troops and Jacobites broke out in every corner, and her father had been forced to increase the patrols, using second-rate sentries who carried out their duties with abject indifference. Indeed, civil war had been imminent until mid-December when news came that the exiled King James II sent word permitting the Highland Chiefs to sign their allegiance to William and Mary.

Charlotte's hopes for peace rose. On another note, as her father suspected, they hadn't located Hugh MacLeod at Dunvegan or anywhere on the Isle of Skye. True, guilt had made her stomach clench every time anyone mentioned the incident—but if given the chance, she would have done it again. Since that March night when she helped Mr. MacLeod escape, Charlotte had awakened each morning with an image of his striking face emblazoned upon her vivid dreams. She'd never forget the color of his eyes. And ever since he'd made her heart flutter with his fleeting kiss, she'd looked closer at every man she happened upon. Not a one sported Hugh's fathomless treacle brown. She was quite certain the color owed to Hugh MacLeod alone—if that indeed was his name.

Colder than usual, grey, ominous clouds hung so low, if she didn't know the peak of Ben Nevis existed to the east, she never would have believed it loomed so near, presiding over the township. Her nose continuously ran, complaining about the relentless wind. Blanketed in white, a hush muffled the entire village as if Jack Frost put all of Fort William and Inverlochy to sleep for the winter.

This year, Mr. Frost had also sent Charlotte's heart into seasonal slumber. Though Doctor Munro had been annoyingly clear about his romantic interest, she felt nothing for the man whatsoever. She'd been melancholy and unsettled, which wasn't like her at all. Perhaps something was wrong with her. It certainly made no sense to stand upon the battlements in the bitter cold, searching for someone who quite possibly was an outlaw in his own right—a menace to everything her father stood for. Mr. MacLeod could very well be a member of the thieving clans that infested the Highlands, preying upon and stealing from each other, all the while having no respect for the interred government that ruled them. Of course, those were her father's words.

Thus far, Charlotte had seen no reason to abhor the Highlanders.

Some plaid-wearing men served in her father's garrison—clans like Menzies, though they were oft regarded with more contempt than respect. True, they dressed in bold tartans that exposed their knees, and they mostly kept to themselves. Highlanders probably didn't mix with the others because there was no encouragement to do so.

Marching in place, Charlotte tried to stave off the bitter cold—rather unsuccessfully. The holiday season was upon them, and fewer travelers mulled through Inverlochy's streets, though in the past fortnight they'd been flooded with clansmen all accompanying their chiefs to pledge their fealty to King William.

"I thought I'd find you up here." Rubbing the outside of her arms, Emma hastened forward. "My, 'tis freezing."

"Where is your cloak?" Charlotte asked, opening hers and putting her arm around her serving maid's shoulders.

"Never mind that, Colonel Hill asked to see you straight away."

Charlotte's back tensed. Father usually saved their daily conversations for after supper. "Did he mention why?"

"To me?" Emma rolled her eyes. "Your father wouldn't tell me if the sky was falling."

"Oh stop. He isn't all that bad." They headed to the stairwell and down the winding steps.

"Mayhap not to you."

"He's an inordinately busy man."

Arriving outside the governor's door, Emma primped Charlotte's curls. "I know, and I'm ever so glad he employed me to look after you."

With a grin, Charlotte grabbed Emma's hands and squeezed them. "As am I."

Taking a deep inhale, she opened the door. "Good evening, Papa. You wanted to see me?"

The colonel rested his quill in the silver stand and stood from his writing desk. Though a fire crackled in the hearth, she could still see his breath. "Ah yes, Charlotte, my dear." He spread his arms and beckoned her into his embrace. "How are you?"

"Well."

His brows pinched together as he inclined his face down to look at her. "I've noticed you've not quite been your energetic self as of late. Is something troubling you?"

Oh Lord, if she told him she'd fallen in love with the man who'd escaped the surgery nine months ago, he would declare her completely daft. Besides, how on earth could she merely have a conversation with a man, lead him to safety, give him a hurried kiss and fall in love? Perhaps her mind was addled. Love at first sight only happened in books—and usually a princess had to kiss a toad to find her prince. "I think 'tis simply the season," she finally said. "I do miss Mama so very much." Honestly, she did. Mother had fallen ill and passed away when Charlotte was but ten.

Papa released his grasp on her shoulders and turned his head. "I must admit I do share your pensive feelings toward the season. Christmas should be a time of great joy, yet I fear my own mournful woes have had a profound effect on you."

"'Tis not that."

"No, I believe it is." He strode toward the hearth, scratching his chin. "And I have been ever so selfish in keeping you to myself. You see, you are the only bright rose in this wretched soldier's life."

"Oh dear, don't say that, Papa." She'd never considered her father might be lonely. Heavens, most of her life, he'd been away from home. Even after Mama passed, Charlotte had lived with her aunt and uncle in London while her father tirelessly served in the king's army. Her ten-month turn at Fort William had been the longest span of time she'd ever spent with her father. It seemed every day she grew to know him better. He was far more human and less stringent than she'd realized. Though an ardent soldier, he experienced emotions like any other person. Why Charlotte found that odd, she had no idea. Surely Papa had needs just like anyone else. "Do you...do you want to remarry?"

He faced her and chuckled. "You are a dear, forever thinking of everyone's needs but your own." He reached out and grasped her hands. "To be honest, I believe it is past time for *you* to wed."

Her heart stopped. Worse, her head swooned. They were three days from celebrating the New Year, and Papa wanted her to... "Me?"

"Yes." For a moment Father smiled like he used to when Mama was alive. "Doctor Munro has asked my permission to court you."

Her corset suddenly became too tight for her to manage a breath. To be courted by the physician? But she had no feelings for the man whatsoever. "Munro?" she said as if it were the first time she'd uttered the physician's name. Thank heavens Father hadn't already summoned the priest. She wouldn't have been inordinately surprised if he had. One of her first observations was that Colonel Hill always acted decisively. Once Papa set his mind on something, there was little chance he'd waver.

"Why, yes, you've made quite an impression assisting him in the surgery. He's a good man and well respected in Edinburgh. You'd live in a manse, have plenty of servants. My grandchildren would be well looked after." Papa rattled off the positives as if he were calculating sums.

Grandchildren? Father definitely spoke out of turn. Charlotte clutched her chest, straining to breathe. "I cannot—" Swooning, she toppled backward.

"Charlotte!" Papa caught her elbow before she collapsed to the floor. "What the devil?"

She fanned her face while he led her to a chair.

His thick, greying eyebrows drew together. "I thought you would be elated with this news."

Taking in deep inhales, she recovered her senses enough to speak. "The physician is very capable, indeed, but I do not *love* him." Honestly, over the past months she'd grown to like him less and less, coming up with excuses to avoid the surgery whenever possible.

"Love?" Papa ran his hand over her crown. "My dear child, what ideals you must hold in your fanciful head."

"I do...I-I-I—um." This was definitely not something she wanted to discuss with Papa. But she could not allow her tongue to tie while her future hung in the balance. "Shouldn't there be some sort of attraction? I-I mean, shouldn't my future husband be pleasing to the eye?"

He waved a dismissive hand through the air. "Fondness, love, allure—all that comes in time. In fact, I didn't marry your mother until I was one and forty." He took the seat opposite her. "But I would be remiss if I didn't ask if there is another officer who might be more to your fancy?"

Charlotte folded her hands in her lap and looked down. "No." *Just a braw Highlander whom I'll never again see.*

"Surely you've thought about marriage. I know I have been a tad remiss in my fatherly duties since accepting this post at Fort William, but do not all young maidens dream of the day a gallant man will ask for her hand? The physician is a learned man—definitely no slouch in anyone's eyes."

Papa hasn't seen him at work in the surgery. "He's not very pleasant when it comes to attending prisoners."

Father chuckled. "Nor should he be. If anyone is to blame for his lack of manners when tending thieves and murderers, it is I."

Charlotte tried another approach. "Let us hope with the Highlanders pledging allegiance to King William things will soon settle and we can return to London. If I am to marry, I think an Englishman would suit."

"Unfortunately we are a long way from London, my dear." Papa sat back and frowned. "I wouldn't raise my hopes about peace in the Highlands. There are still a number of clan chiefs who have not yet sworn allegiance. And mark me, the king will not be lenient with those who fail to visit the sheriff."

"I'm certain he will not," Charlotte's voice trailed off. In her one and twenty years of life, Charlotte had never witnessed leniency from the crown. Honestly, the amnesty offered to the Jacobites and the release of the prisoners from the battle of Dunkeld was the most lenient act she'd seen from the Williamite government.

Father reached out and grasped her hand. "I will grant my approval for this courtship. You will be chaperoned by either Mrs. Emma or a guard when Doctor Munro comes to call."

"But—"

He shook his head. "I ask only that you give this match serious thought. But keep in mind I will not be around forever and you will need a husband to see to your maintenance."

Still looking down, Charlotte nodded.

Papa cleared his throat. "Will you do that for me?"

"Yes," she whispered. She hadn't thought about how much of a burden she must be for her father. So many doubts swarmed in her head. Was she the reason Papa hadn't remarried? Could she be the cause of his unhappiness? The lines across his brow had grown ever so furrowed in the time he'd been at Fort William. Charlotte had always assumed the pressure from governing a fortress in the midst of the highest population of Jacobites and Highland rebels was the cause of his despondency, and the reason for the way he'd become curt at times...and the decreasing amount of time he spent with her.

I was blind to think his duties were the reason.

Papa moved to his writing desk. "If there is nothing else, I've some missives to pen before supper."

"Of course." Charlotte stood. "Is there anything I can do to help ease your burden?"

He straightened and looked her in the eye. "Well, I do believe we've just had a lengthy discussion about that, have we not?"

Chapter Seven

❧

After nine months of hearty eating and hard work, Hugh again felt like he could conquer the world—or lead Clan Iain Abrach of Glencoe against the backbiting Williamite army. He would not soon forget the hospitality shown to him at Fort William—bar one delicate morsel whom he'd never forget.

With the livestock turned out for the winter, he'd taken the opportunity to renew the thatch on his cottage roof before the snow got too deep. Though he'd grown up living in the great Carnoch manse, when he reached his majority he'd built a home up the River Coe near Signal Rock—the outcropping where he lit the cauldrons when his father made a call to arms.

He'd built the cottage sturdy with ample room—more than most of the crofter's shielings in the valley. At one time, he'd dreamed of marrying a Highland-bred lass who'd bear him sons and daughters, but those dreams always managed to be pushed aside by clan duty and war.

Hugh swung his ax over his head. With a heave, it came

down and spilt the log in two perfect halves. Then he wiped his forehead with his shirtsleeve.

Perhaps Ma had been right. Hugh needed to find a wife. The only problem? Nary a lass had made his blood run hot since he'd met Charlotte Hill. Blast, his miserable luck had continued to follow him. Take a fancy to a lass who not only was a Sassenach, her father was the bleeding Governor of Fort William—Colonel Hill embodied the hated Williamite government and all the tyranny that came with it.

Hugh reached inside his leather sporran and pulled out the fork Charlotte had used to feed him—the same tool he'd also put to use picking his locks. Funny how a Sassenach tool aided in his escape. *I wonder if she realized she'd left it behind.* He slid the keepsake back into his sporran and patted it closed.

Aye, he'd one day inherit the Glencoe title—if he outlived his father. A mammoth man of six feet seven inches, Hugh figured Da would outlive them all. True, Hugh had inherited his father's height for the most part, bar an inch. He'd inherited Da's temper as well. But he'd seldom met a Highlander worth his salt who didn't have a bit of audacious cheek in his swagger.

A dog barked, running toward him, clumps of snow hanging from his wiry coat. Hugh looked up and dropped to one knee. "Cuddy! What the blazes are you doing all the way up here?"

Thundering into Hugh with slurping swipes of his tongue, the deerhound yipped and looked back down the trail. Big as a mighty oak, Da marched up the glen wielding a sturdy walking stick. Da's long ginger beard may have turned white, but that only served to make him appear more menacing—just like the spiked moustache, the blue bonnet cockeyed over his long white tresses pushed back enough to expose the deep scar on his right cheek. His countenance alone was enough to give a man pause, but that combined with his enormous stature left no question as to who was chief: Alasdair Ruadh MacIain MacDonald, Twelfth of Glencoe. A true Highland commander, Da solely had the right to judge and condemn his own people, even to carry out the thrust of a dirk or order the swinging of a hangman's noose.

And no, the big chieftain had never done anything to cosset his eldest son. Though Hugh acquired rank and privileges by birth, Da had challenged him at every opportunity. From an early age, Hugh had to prove his valor and talent for leadership. He'd been beaten up and bloodied more times than he could remember—sent on cattle raids and led sorties against the Campbells—the very clan with whom Da was now trying to make amends. Bloody oath, if Hugh had not proved his grit on many a raid across Campbell lands, he'd be six feet under and Alasdair Og the heir. That was the way of the MacIain MacDonalds—the proud descendants of Angus Og who took the title Lord of the Isles. From their great ancestor's loins Clan Donald populated the Hebridean Isles by the Butt of Lewis to South Uist, from Skye to Jura and Islay. On the mainland, besides Glencoe they held Lachaber, Ardnamurchan and Kintyre. In Ireland MacDonalds filled the glens of Antrim. Och aye, they were the lords of Gaeldom no matter who tried to usurp them, be it king or neighboring Campbell.

Hugh marched toward his father and grasped him by the elbow in a firm greeting that meant so much more than a Sassenach handshake. "What brings you up here on this frigid morn?"

"I've a missive with the seal of King James in France."

Hugh's eyes popped wide. "You should have sent a runner for me, but now you're here, I've a kettle of cider warming over the fire. Come. Tell me more."

As they strode side by side, Hugh glanced over at his

father. "Either you're shrinking or I'm still growing." At three and thirty, he doubted the latter.

Da eyed him and grumbled under his breath. "I can still beat the likes of you any day."

Hugh doubted that too, but he no longer had a need to prove himself. Instead, he grinned. "'Tis why you're still clan chief and I'm living in the hills."

The big man thwacked him on the back with a hearty laugh. "'Tis good to see you've retained your sense of humor, lad."

Walking across the threshold, Hugh gestured to the bench and headed for the hearth while Cuddy curled up on the rag rug. "I suppose it disappeared for a bit—but never for long." He picked up the ladle and stirred the cider. "What news from France?" Hugh hoped to God King James had sent word of a full-blown attack with the French and Spaniards sailing their eighteen gun galleons across the channel to blow the Dutchman back to Holland.

The old man removed his bonnet and ran his fingers through his mop of unruly white hair. "King James hasn't been able to rally the French forces."

A lead ball sunk to the pit of Hugh's stomach. "Unfortunate. Now I've regained my strength I'm more than ready to ride against the government bastards."

With a glowering purse to his lips, Da pulled the missive from inside his buckskin coat and slapped it on the table. "Says we're to pledge the oath of fealty to King William, else risk annihilation."

"Bloody hell." Hugh squinted. "You mean to tell me James wants us to kiss William's lying arse? What about the money Breadalbane promised the Highland chiefs? Has anyone seen a farthing?"

"Not a penny has come from London's coffers." Da shook his head. "I'm more worried about the multitude of redcoats infiltrating the entire western shore. A man cannot ride north or south without meeting a company of bloody dragoons."

"The redcoats will be infesting the hills of Glencoe soon. And now King James is asking us to perjure ourselves and sign our support to a cutthroat usurper?" Hugh slammed his fist on the table. "Jesus, Da. I spent nineteen months of my life in the bowels of Fort William owing to my support for the true king—the man with the God-given right of sovereignty over Scotland *and* England."

Da tapped the missive with his forefinger. "I ken, son—our king asks us to be patient, and bide our time. Worse, John Dalrymple, the Secretary of State and Master of Stair is looking for any excuse to make an example of a clan such as ours." Da leaned forward with an intense blaze flashing in his blue eyes. "They're looking for any reason to march into the Highlands with ten thousand men and put us to fire and sword. And Colonel Hill has amassed enough backbiting dragoons to do it. The Camerons and MacDonalds of Sleat have already made their pledge. If I do not make haste for Fort William, we could find ourselves defending the Glen without an ally at our backs."

Hugh's gut twisted. "The news grows worse." He picked up the missive and read. "For Christ's sake, this is dated December tenth."

A tic twitched under Da's eye. "The runner said we were among the last to be notified."

"If you don't sign now, two days hence you'll have missed the bloody deadline." Hugh slapped the parchment on the table. "Devil's fire, there are three-foot drifts of snow out there."

Da snatched the missive and shoved it back into his coat. "Aye, that doesn't give me much time now, does it?"

The thought of a jaunt up to Fort William wasn't entirely unwelcome—though the reason for the journey made him want to slam his fist into the wall. Remembering the cider, Hugh placed a tankard in front of his father and sat beside him with a cup of his own. "When do we leave?"

"Oh no, *you'd* best stay here. Someone up at the fort could recognize you."

Hugh looked from his one shoulder to the next. "I reckon I've put on two stone of muscle since March—shaved my beard as well. I doubt a soul would peg me."

"Och, you think so?" Da leaned forward. "What about your height? Not many men on this earth are as tall as a MacIain."

Hugh picked up his tankard and drank. "I'll give you that. But I'm not allowing you near that place without my sword at your back."

"You're not *allowing* me?" Da's deep voice rumbled with a rueful laugh. "Next, you'll be muscling me aside and collecting the rents."

"I already collect the rents on your behalf."

"Och aye, you have a set of cods, lad." Da grinned. "A man bred from my own loins for certain." Da picked up his cider and drank it down. "If you're hell bent on riding with, be at the house afore first light. With the snow piling up, the going will be treacherous, mark me."

"All the more reason for me to have your back."

❦

THE EVENING OF DECEMBER 30TH PROVED TO BE MISERABLY cold and snowy as Charlotte perched in the corner of her father's study. For more than a week the weather had been dreadful, and this night had to be the worst of it with deep drifts formed by the howling wind. She inclined her embroidery toward the flickering candlelight, painstakingly making minute stitches in her effort to capture the hills below Ben

Nevis abloom with heather as they had been last August. How long ago summer seemed now.

Papa rigorously wrote missives to every person in Edinburgh and London he could think of who could possibly have some influence on the miserable state of affairs at Fort William. A payroll hadn't been received in three months. The only food stores were borrowed on the weakening credit of the crown, and the Highlanders in the surrounding towns were becoming less and less willing to part with supplies they might need to see themselves through the winter, let alone accept a promise of payment to part with their food in support of the four hundred hungry men stationed on the lonely peninsula jutting out into Loch Linnhe.

Entering with a rap on the door, the Captain of the Night removed his hat. "Governor, a Highland gentleman and his retinue has passed over the moat and through the main gate. He and his son now await an audience outside your door."

Charlotte cringed as she turned to look out the window. Though dark, snow had all but covered the panes. Indeed, the storm continued to usher in heavy snowfall. The gentleman's need must be dire for him to travel to the fort in such a squall. She lowered her embroidery to her lap as her father asked for the Highlander to be shown inside.

Heavy footsteps clomped upon the passageway floorboards until an enormous Highlander stood in the doorway. His bonnet, long white hair, and beard were covered with snow, as was the plaid wrapped tightly about his shoulders. His dark blue eyes shone proud over the fierce curl of his moustache. Yes, Charlotte had seen many a Highlander before, but none with such a commanding presence as this man. With bold strides he stepped into the drawing room, paying not a mind to the melting snow dripping around his feet while his large sword clanked at his hip.

Behind him, another man remained in the passageway.

The back of Charlotte's neck prickled, making her sit forward and strain for a better look. However, the Highland gentleman posed too great an obstacle for her to make out the man behind him.

Papa hastily stood. "MacIain MacDonald? What brings you all the way to Fort William in this abominable storm? You should be by the fire with your lady wife."

"I have ridden all the way from Glencoe to swear the oath." The man's voice was as menacing as his appearance. His gaze shot to Charlotte and his eyebrows arched as if noticing her for the first time. "Will you kindly administer it, that I may have King William's indemnity?"

"Me? I am but a soldier." Papa snorted ruefully and snatched a piece of paper from his desk. Holding it up, he pointed. "Why in God's name did you come here? Glencoe is under the jurisdiction of the Sheriff of Inveraray. Blast it man, you should know as well as I the proclamation states the oath must be taken 'in the presence of the sheriffs of the respective shires where any of the said persons shall live.'"

The man's blue eyes grew fiercer. "Aye," he grumbled. At his sides, his gloved fingers clenched into fists. "But you are King William's highest ranking officer in the Highlands. Surely you would not deliver me into the hands of my greatest enemies whilst a blizzard blows a gale strong enough to move Ben Nevis."

Papa threw the proclamation on his writing desk and faced the Highlander with bold sternness. "If only I were able, I'd set quill to paper immediately, but you *must* gain an audience with Sheriff Campbell of Ardkinglas."

The old man crossed his arms and tipped up his heavily whiskered chin. "Bloody oath, I cannot reach Inveraray afore the first. And every Campbell for miles will jump at a chance to throw a noose around my neck. You *ken* you're asking me to do the impossible."

Charlotte could have sworn she saw steam rising from the Highlander's shoulders.

The colonel backed toward his writing desk. "As I said before, I am unable to issue you the oath, but seeing as you have reached me by the prescribed deadline, I will write you a letter of passage, requesting that Ardkinglas receive you as a lost sheep."

Frowning, the Highlander took another step forward. "You mean to say you aim to make me turn around and ride seventy miles in a bloody *blizzard?* You're spewing a cock and bull story if I ever heard one. I've received rumblings they —*you* intend to put all who do not pledge the oath to fire and sword." He placed his big palms on the table. "Tell me these words are untrue."

Papa leaned in, challenging the Highlander's intimidating stance. "I pray to God this madness will not come to that. My letter should allay all doubt." The colonel reached for his quill with a trembling hand. "But you had best make haste."

"*Haste?* By God, I will not stand idle while you ride your backstabbing dragoons onto my lands!" The man's steely eyes shifted to Charlotte. "Och, forgive my vulgar tongue, Miss..."

"Hill," she said, holding out her hand.

"No one is planning a raid on your lands," Papa sputtered, however his stubborn frown didn't prevent him from gesturing Charlotte's way as the angry stare melted from the big Highlander's countenance. "If you hadn't barreled in here like a bull, I would have made the introductions forthwith." The colonel cleared his throat. "My daughter came to Fort William to look after me when I took ill. I'm afraid I've enjoyed her company too much to send her home to London, which I will do as soon as the winter snows melt."

Charlotte smiled. "I'm pleased to make your acquaintance, Chief MacIain MacDonald, is it? You must be chilled to the bone, after riding in this weather."

He took her fingers in his woolen-gloved hand while a bit of mischief now sparkled in his blue eyes. "Aye, lass. You're fortunate to have a fire to keep your toes from turning to ice."

When he bowed to kiss the back of her hand, Charlotte suddenly couldn't breathe. For the love of everything holy, Hugh MacLeod—the very man who consumed her dreams watched her from the passageway. She wouldn't have recognized him but for his stare. His eyes were even more intense than the old man's...but darker with a burning fire so fierce it nearly scorched. Mr. MacLeod didn't smile—showed no recognition whatsoever. The look on his face was hard, intense, and roused Charlotte all the way from the top of her head through the tips of her toes. Straining to steady her breathing, her blood ran hot, yet gooseflesh covered her skin.

She could not pull her eyes away from the magnificent Highlander, staring at her as if she might pull a pistol from her belt and fire it straight at his heart. But then his father straightened. The old chieftain's mouth quirked and he glanced over his shoulder. "Apologies, m'lady. I've not introduced my son, Hugh MacIain MacDonald—next in line for the Chieftainship of Clan Iain Abrach of Glencoe."

Her mouth suddenly dry, she could scarcely take a breath, let alone utter a word. So Hugh had given her a false name? Charlotte couldn't blame him—suspected as much. Given the circumstances, she might have done the same. Gaining a thread of composure, she curtsied. "Pleased to make your acquaintance, Mr. *MacIain*."

He bowed, keeping his eyes level with her face. "Miss Hill."

Though Papa cleared his throat, Charlotte ignored her father and stepped toward the chieftain. "Our stores are rather thin, but I would offer you a bowl of pottage and a warm drink before you head on your way."

"I'd be much obliged for your kind hospitality," Chief MacIain quipped. "Might just help the seventy miles pass a wee bit quicker, since your father is unable to issue me the oath."

"If you'll excuse me, I'll go see to it a table is prepared." After dipping into a curtsey, Charlotte sidled past the big Highland chieftain as her father took a seat at his writing desk.

"I'll escort the lass," said Hugh. Lord, his voice was even deeper than she'd remembered.

Charlotte's stomach flipped upside down.

"Very well," said the chieftain, rolling his R. "I'll join you as soon as the colonel writes his missive."

Stepping past him, Charlotte's shoulder brushed Hugh's plaid. Though she barely touched the man, the sensation sent shivers coursing up the side of her neck. "This way," she uttered, managing to keep her voice steady.

Chapter Eight

꧁꧂

Filling his senses with the tantalizing fragrance, Hugh not only followed, he floated after Miss Hill, breathing her in—rose oil mixed with a healthy dose of woman, Hugh's tongue snuck to the corner of his mouth as he followed Charlotte down the passageway. The lady's curls bounced with her graceful progression while the soft rustle of feminine skirts called to the deepest recesses of his heart.

His palms itched to touch her, but he clenched his fists at his sides to keep from doing so until they came to a window embrasure. In a blink, he grasped her elbow and tugged her inside. "I have a gift for you."

Her eyes wide as a frightened doe, she glanced down the passageway. "We mustn't tarry." Then she looked him over from head to toe with a squint to her eye. "*Mr. MacLeod.*"

Hugh cringed—well a half-smile, half-grimace sort of cringe. Surely she'd forgive him for assuming a name and slipping away when presented with the chance. "You cannot hold a wee fib against a prisoner of war. Do you ken what the dragoons would have done to me if they'd discovered who I am?"

A spark of anger flashed through her eyes. "But——"

"Clan Iain Abrach of the Coe is the most powerful and most feared mob of restless rebels in Scotland. Some say we're the most incorrigible and troublesome of the Gallows Herd lot."

She crossed her arms and tipped up that delicate chin. "It sounds as if you're proud of being a rebel."

"Proud? Mayhap I am. We're Highlanders—live by a code of respect and honor that few in the Lowlands can understand." Hugh threw his thumb over his shoulder. "And government men like your Da have moved onto our lands to force us to bend to their rules—their religion. They're trying to snuff out our Highland ways. And I'll tell you now, that's nay going to happen."

"Is that so?" She took a step back, biting her bottom lip. "You're even taller than I remembered. And now you've drawn me aside with no one else about. Should I be in fear of you?" Then she clasped her hands together just beneath a slender neck. "You must realize, if I let out even a hint of a scream, a hundred dragoons will fall upon you before you can draw that mammoth sword of yours."

"Nay, nay. I'm not trying to frighten you in the slightest." Hugh held up his palms to show his good intentions. Bloody hell, he'd had to boast like a braggart. Here he'd been presented with an opportunity to speak to the lass alone and he was making a mess of it. "You saved my life and for that, you will always have my protection."

"Protect me?" She looked to the ceiling and groaned. "Why is it every man in the Highlands thinks I need to be suffocated with protection?"

Hugh hadn't thought about that. But she did live inside a garrison with a company of soldiers—her father heading the lot of them. He nodded, buying time to collect his thoughts. "Regardless, I owe you a debt of gratitude." *And for nine miser-*

able months I've been unable to stop myself from dreaming about your bonny face.

"I thank you." She dipped her head in a polite bow, but her worried expression didn't soften. "Is it really true what they say about your clan? You raid wherever your fancy takes you—that the MacIains have no allies aside from the men you support? That you would steal a man's last meal and burn his home whilst you laugh, driving his livestock into your horde of plenty?"

Her words cut deep. *Sounds as if she's been listening to the Campbells for certain.* Hugh removed his bonnet and held it between his hands to keep from reaching out and pulling the bonny woman into his arms. "Och, you make us out to be a mob of heathens."

"Then tell me the rumors are untrue." The lass had a righteous streak when she set her mind to it. But by the saints, her lips pursed into the most kissable bow shape he'd ever seen. No wonder he'd lost his fevered head and kissed the lass so many months ago.

"Uh." Bloody hell, this conversation was nothing like he'd planned. If he didn't take charge now, Miss Hill might just inform her father about his escape. His shoulder ticked up. "Raids are rare, though I'll not say they haven't happened. Our lands are plundered by the Campbells and, in turn, we take back what is rightfully ours."

"So an eye for an eye, is it?" She bit her rosy bottom lip.

"Something like that." How the devil he thought he could turn an English lassie to the Highland way of thinking with a wee conversation was too much of a stretch—even from him. He needed a diversion afore the lass decided him daft.

She lowered her hands to her sides. "I don't think—"

Remembering his purpose, Hugh slipped a hand into his sporran and pulled out the fork. "I believe this lock picker is yours, miss."

Charlotte's lovely mouth dropped open with her sharp gasp. Then she snatched the implement from his grasp. "You mean to tell me you used my fork to..." She glanced up and down the passageway. "Pick your locks?" she whispered.

Having managed to disarm her, Hugh smiled broadly. "Aye, and I'll be forever in your debt."

"Oh my heavens, if my father should discover I unknowingly gave you a tool that you in turn used to...to...*escape*."

"But you helped me slip out of the fort."

She held her finger to her lips. "Sh. You must never, ever mention that to anyone."

Hugh could keep his hands idle no longer. Simply the pale white of her skin filled his chest with longing. He cupped her blushing cheek in his palm. "When I knocked at death's door, you gave me a new chance at life. Your kindness alone saved me, and for that I will always be in your service, m'lady."

Her mouth opened and formed an O before she spoke. "I-I...you were so ill and so...um...I don't know what to say to such a declaration of chivalry."

Hugh stared into her eyes for a moment, the torch on the far wall casting just enough light for him to appreciate the rich lavender he'd remembered from the surgery. "Not a day has passed that I haven't thought about you, your compassion, your loveliness."

"Oh please, Mr. MacIain. You cannot possibly expect me to believe you've thought of me that often. It has been *nine* months."

Hugh's heart skipped a beat as he leaned toward her and rubbed his thumb over her silken cheek. "Did you ever think of me?" God, he hoped so—the intensity that always connected their gazes could not have been felt merely by him, could it?

Charlotte shuttered her lovely eyes as she looked down. "Yes," she whispered. "I've thought of you."

His finger twirled around one of her curls. "It warms my heart to hear you say so."

"But you're a Jacobite." Charlotte had become soft spoken again, the color in her cheeks deepening.

Hugh couldn't again lie to her, though he'd never wanted to jump ship so much in his life. "Aye. I've fought for the Stuart king. Is that reason enough to allay our friendship?"

"It should be."

"But do you want it to be?"

She kept her gaze downcast while she shook her head. "No." The word was spoken so softly, Hugh barely heard. Then she placed a dainty hand on his arm, the warmth of her touch melting what little control remained. "We must move along before someone happens past."

Hugh stepped in nearer and slipped his hand to her corseted waist. "I've one more thing I need to do." God save him, Charlotte was just far too tempting to allow this opportunity to slip by. As he moved even closer, she backed until stopping flush against the wall. Her heavy-lidded gaze fell to his mouth and her tongue slipped out, moistening her bottom lip. Did she have any idea how enticing she looked? Hugh stood so near, her breath wound its way through the laces of his shirt while her bosoms rose and fell with every inhale.

"Sir?" She met his gaze, stunning violet eyes wide.

Hugh grinned as he slowly dipped his head. "I need to kiss you, lass," he growled right before he closed the gap and captured her mouth. Sliding his hand around to her back, he trapped her against the wall. Charlotte made no attempt to flee, but clearly by her stiffness, she'd never been properly kissed—oh no, a fleeting peck whilst fleeing didn't count. Aye, she needed a wee bit of coaxing. He kneaded his fingers up her spine whilst he brushed her satiny lips with his tongue.

Ever so slowly, she yielded to him until she opened enough for him to slip inside and taste her. Oh, blessed be the ambrosia of the gods, this woman was as pliable as unfired clay. With a winsome sigh, she succumbed to Hugh's encouraging hands and melted into his chest. All the silver in Edinburgh would not be enough to pull him from this moment. With her soft breasts titillating his chest, she did something totally unexpected. Her hands slipped around his waist. Lithe fingers kneaded the muscles in his back.

As his breathing sped, Hugh deepened his kiss. Lord Almighty, if only he could coax her to the next room, and show her exactly how much he'd been thinking of her—what he dreamed of doing with her—how much he wanted her to—

A footstep sounded.

Charlotte jerked away, hitting her head on the stone wall behind. With a gasp, her hand flew back, and then she froze, her eyes filling with fear as her gaze shifted toward the sound of nearing footsteps.

Hugh gave her a reassuring wink and adjusted his plaid before stepping into the corridor.

A red-coated officer approached, powdered wig, buckled shoes, stiff gait, sporting one of the haughtiest expressions Hugh had ever seen. "What in the devil's name are *you* doing here?"

Charlotte started to move, but Hugh shielded her behind him. "Miss Hill was just showing me to the kitchens."

"From the window embrasure?" The officer peered around him.

"I do not see where that is your concern, Lieutenant Hamilton," Charlotte quipped. Och aye, the lass had spunk.

"Lieutenant *Colonel* Hamilton. I daresay, I've been at Fort William a month. You should be well aware of my rank." The snooty man sneered as he looked Hugh from head to toe. "Are you in need of assistance, Miss Hill?"

"Not at all. If you must know, Mr. MacIain MacDonald

stopped momentarily to return a fork he borrowed some time ago."

Hugh had to bite the inside of his cheek to keep from bursting out with laughter. My, the lady did have some mettle, practically giving his tool of escape away.

The officer smirked, his gaze narrowing as if a deep seated hatred had surfaced. "What on earth would a Highlander do with a fork?"

Hugh shrugged. "Eat. What else would those flimsy tines be good for?" He stepped back and made a show of frowning whilst he eyed the Lieutenant Colonel. "I'd reckon a redcoat the likes of you would be far too tough to take on with a table fork."

Charlotte cleared her throat and curtsied. "Please excuse us, sir. I'm afraid Mr. MacIain and his father mustn't tarry." She grasped Hugh by the elbow and hastened him down the passageway. "That man makes me very uneasy," she whispered.

"Hamilton?"

"Yes. Repeat this to no one, but Papa fears he has come to do ill." She stopped and held up her finger. "You think my father is a threat to the Highlands?" She again looked both ways as if afraid the walls were listening. "Well, I've seen enough of the lieutenant to worry that the relative peace that Papa has managed to bring about may not last, and you and your father had best steer clear of him."

"Aye?" Hugh placed his hand in the small of her back as they continued on. "But then how am I to steal more kisses? Nay, a pasty codfish like Hamilton cannot keep me away from your bonny smile, Miss Hill."

Clapping her hands to her cheeks, Charlotte shook her head. "Oh no, kissing me is far too dangerous. We mustn't ever do that again."

"You mean to say you didn't enjoy my wee peck?" Hugh

watched her expression. High color flooded her cheeks like she'd spent an entire day with the sun's rays beating down on her face.

"Mr. MacIain, you are shameless."

He gave her a wink. "You enjoyed it—mayhap as much as I."

Chapter Nine

Wrapped in a cloak, Charlotte stood atop the battlements while angry snow and sleet whirled around her. Night came early in the Highlands. She could scarcely see Hugh and his father mount their garron ponies down below, their silhouettes dancing in the glowing torchlight from inside the gatehouse. Her teeth chattered as they rode off, their long legs thrust out from the stout ponies. Cloaked in furs and armed with muskets and swords, the MacIain clansmen followed, bonnets pulled low over their brows.

She could scarcely imagine riding seventy miles in a blizzard on a night as cold as this. Only the heartiest of men would survive such a journey. *God save them. If only Papa could have taken the chieftain's oath.*

Charlotte remained motionless, watching while the snow swallowed Hugh's fading outline until nothing remained but the icy flakes stinging her cheeks—and darkness.

Her lips still tingled from Mr. MacIain's kiss. When he said he wanted to kiss her she *should* have pushed him away—heavens he'd done it twice now. The only problem was his words made Charlotte's mind completely run amuck. One moment she thought she was in control and the next, his big hands slipped behind her back while he lowered his lips and joined them with hers. How on earth was a woman supposed to resist such a temptation as Hugh's puckered lips, his warm, spicy breath, not to mention his soulful eyes fanned by long, chestnut lashes? He'd gazed upon her with such fervent hunger—the same craving that had been simmering in the darkest recesses of her heart since the first day she'd laid eyes on him.

Her breasts ached with longing to again press against his solid chest—now even larger and harder than she remembered from his brief stay in the surgery. No man hath ever recovered with such vigor. Heaven help her betraying flesh. In no way could she allow Mr. MacIain to kiss her like that again. What on earth would her father say?

Charlotte swiped the stinging snow from her face. She must be content with the memory of his strong arms wrapped around her while his lips plied hers. That a man as robust as Hugh MacIain of Clan Iain Abrach could be so gentle surprised her as well. *Heaven help me, I must put him out of my mind.*

But I do not want to do so.

Charlotte stamped her foot. Why, with the fort full of available officers, did she swoon over a Highlander of all people? Hugh admitted himself that he had participated in raids—though as an act of retaliation. *What difference was that to Papa's soldiers when fighting the enemy? Truly battles are their own acts of retaliation against a perceived injustice.*

"Miss Hill? What are you doing out here in this terrible storm?"

Charlotte cringed and pulled her cloak closed tighter at her throat. The only person aside from Doctor Munro who she'd prefer not to meet when alone was Lieutenant Colonel

James Hamilton. She'd meant everything she'd told Hugh about this man and more. Worse, her father didn't trust him and feared the ambitious young officer would stop at nothing to push Papa aside.

Regarding James over her shoulder, Charlotte moved toward the stairwell. "Just a bit restless. This storm has had me cooped up in my chamber for days."

"I'm afraid you'll have to grow accustomed to long winter storms if you're planning to remain in the Highlands. I must say, this is the most squalid outpost to which I've ever been assigned, as are some of her visitors." He snorted, following her down the steps. "Case in point, those vile MacIains your father just sent on their way."

Charlotte stopped midstride. "Is it all Highland clans you disapprove of, or is Clan Iain Abrach of Glencoe particularly distasteful to you?"

"All Jacobite supporters should be snuffed," James said with a scowl. "You saw the chieftain. He shamelessly dressed in outrageous plaid trews and buckskin. He should be imprisoned for the lewdness of his attire. If you ask me, Alasdair MacIain MacDonald and his band of thieves are the basest rogues of the Gallows Herd."

"And what brought you to such a conclusion?" Charlotte clenched her fists at her sides. "Have you faced them in battle before?"

"'Tis common knowledge they raided Breadalbane before the blood stopped flowing on their way home from the Battle of Killiecrankie. Hell bent on claiming their pay from the Campbell coffers they were. The rogue you were speaking to in the corridor—Hugh MacIain—stole the Laird of Glenlyon's prized stallion in that raid."

"Did he?" Her gaze darted to the direction Hugh had ridden. Could Hugh be a heartless reiver akin to those she'd heard her father complain about? Charlotte had also heard of

Captain Robert Campbell of Glenlyon. A rogue himself, he had a reputation for gambling and drinking, gaming away every farthing his ancestors had passed to him. "Interesting Mr. MacIain rode a garron pony this evening."

"You are a smart-tongued lass, are you not?" The lieutenant followed her from the stairwell into the corridor that led to her father's house. "I doubt a member of Clan Iain Abrach would be bold enough to be seen with that horse. No, the stallion must be out to pasture with the mares to breed some height into those worthless garrons."

"But they do seem stout, and rather adapted to the rugged winters here."

"Charlotte?" Holding a lamp, Doctor Munro stepped from the house and closed the door. He'd started using her familiar name right after they'd begun "courting". "Is all well here?"

She tried to smile. "Yes, the lieutenant colonel was just seeing me home."

"It appears Miss Hill has taken an interest in some rather unscrupulous Highland renegades." Hamilton cleared his throat. "I found her atop the wall-walk not long after MacIain and his mob left for Inveraray."

The physician grasped her hand and knit his brows. "Is this true, my love."

Charlotte hated it when he referred to her as his love. She drew her hand away. "Not at all. I needed a bit of air after enduring days of this wretched weather."

The lieutenant colonel looked between them while the corner of his mouth ticked up. "Munro, if I had a morsel as tasty as Miss Hill to woo, I surely would not allow her out of my sight."

"I beg your pardon?" The doctor stepped between them. "You speak out of turn."

"Yes you do." Charlotte skittered aside and placed her

hand on the latch. "There is absolutely nothing wrong with taking a stroll atop the battlements, be it snowing or not, and given your demonstrated propensity for exaggeration, I would appreciate it if you would refrain from discussing this any further, *lieutenant*." Purposefully leaving off the "colonel", Charlotte opened the door and slipped inside before being forced to listen to another insulting word.

"Charlotte, are you well?" the doctor's voice resonated through the timber door.

"Yes, just a bit tired. Good night."

She could picture Roderick hesitating, trying to think of some way he could coax her to open the door. "I shall see you on the morrow, then," his reedy voice had a pleading edge to it.

She untied her cloak, breathing a sigh of relief. "On the morrow," came her half-hearted reply.

૬ৱ

HUGH COULD HAVE SWORN HIS CODS FROZE DURING THE long and frigid journey to Inveraray. Every other part of his body had turned to ice, too. His fingers froze in place around his reins. If he dared move them, he feared they'd shatter like ice on a loch. Och aye, he could weather the storms in the mountains with the most robust of Highlanders, but riding seventy miles in a blizzard was pure madness if not complete torture.

Worse, Sheriff Campbell of Ardkinglas had taken a galley across Loch Fyne to celebrate the holidays with his family. And that wasn't the half of it. Along their journey to Inveraray, Thomas Drummond's patrol of redcoats stopped them with their muskets unslung.

Da tried to be amicable and told his men to keep their weapons sheathed. He showed Captain Drummond Colonel

Hill's missive. A lot of good that did. By the time Captain Drummond thumbed his nose at the letter, a dragoon held a pistol against Hugh's skull. The MacIains were surrounded, with no option but to give in to the wiles of a cheating redcoat.

Giving no sound cause, Drummond ordered his guards to throw the MacIain men into the hold of Barcaldine Castle, thus ruining all chances of making it to Inveraray by the first. Hugh knew Drummond was laughing at his ploy, the bastard. It was another day before they were released. That morn, New Year's Day the year of our Lord 1692 had arrived and Da still hadn't pledged fealty to William of Orange—not for lack of bloody trying.

Though the old man looked like shite with lines of worry etched in his sleep-deprived face, he mounted his garron pony and led on. "I've Colonel Hill's missive in hand. And by the saints, the powers that be will soon learn of Drummond's backstabbing tactics from Edinburgh to London. Mark me, the Privy Council will not sit idle whilst I tell of the captain's trickery."

Fighting the cold and snowdrifts, Hugh rode in beside his father. He clenched his teeth as he hunched over in his saddle, one hand clinging tightly to the plaid around his shoulders. "Agreed. They cannot be allowed to get away with this. Christ, you've been trying to sign the oath for three bloody days. Nary a man would put us to fire and sword given your effort."

Da glared ahead and said nothing while his horse trudged forward, clouds from warm air meeting cold puffing through the beast's ice-laden nostrils.

By nightfall they skirted around the head of Loch Awe. Breadalbane's Kilchurn Castle rose like a grey snow-capped monolith, looming against a moonless sky, lonely on an islet surrounded by icy water. Icy like the earl's heart, which surely wasn't melting while he sat in the draughty hall and tried to warm his hands before his hearth. Not even a dragon-hearted earl could find warmth in this weather.

After five miles of trudging through deep drifts, they turned southward across the high hills to Loch Fyne. Heading down to the valley at dawn, the snow-covered paddocks blended with the sky. It was the second of January, three days after they'd left Glencoe for Fort William, and the garrons' muffled hoofbeats ambled silently through the Campbell capitol. An unnerving passage indeed, for no MacIain was welcome within twenty miles of Inveraray. Their forefathers had twice looted the township—retaliation in exchange for retaliation.

Here Campbell wealth and power could not be questioned. Hugh rode beside his father past the tall castle with the round turrets, the tolbooth and the courthouse, and finally Doom Hill where more than one MacIain man's life had been strangled from his throat.

Da led them down a narrow close to a discreet change-house. He wanted no quarrels or mishaps with any inebriated Campbells who still might be drinking in the New Year.

❧

HUGH NURSED A TANKARD OF ALE, SITTING AT A SMALL table at the back of the alehouse with Da. "We've been rotting here for three bloody days. Will the bastard never return?" he growled behind the pewter cup, his eyes constantly shifting. Christ, at any moment, Argyll's men-at-arms could come crashing into the establishment and put them all to the sword.

Da rocked back in his chair and put his feet up on the table, crossing them at the ankles. A cavalier move, even for

Da. "He cannot stay away forever. He's the bleeding sheriff. Law and order has to be served, even on Campbell lands."

"Och, I've had enough of sleeping with my eyes open and my boots on." Hugh reached for the pitcher and topped up Da's tankard and then his own. "For all we ken, the miserable Campbell reivers are riding to Glencoe to pay us back for the Killiecrankie raid."

"I doubt that, lad. With Alasdair Og and Sandy standing guard, no Campbell rabble will make it past Ballachlulish. And no one can stage a raid from the east. There must be thirty-six hands of snow piled in the Devil's Staircase by now." Da shook his head of gnarled white locks—a fearsome sight he made. "Our kin is locked tight in God's mighty fortress."

Hugh sipped his ale. "'Tis a fortress and a trap."

"Wheesht." Da spat over his shoulder to send evil spirits away. "Four hundred years past, our forefathers took the Coe by fire and sword and we've held it ever since. Not a man in all of Scotland would be successful against us. You ken as well as me."

"Aye, I do. But times are changing. There were far more soldiers at the fort than when I was there months ago—and they're better outfitted. I think we should be looking at our defenses."

"You ken I never go a day without training."

"Aye but we've no bailey walls surrounding Carnoch. No cannons. Mayhap 'tis time to think about improving our defenses."

One corner of Da's mouth ticked up. "Son, I do not think it a good idea to pinch the Campbell's cannons on our way home. Besides, they're awful heavy to drag through this miserable snow."

Though his gut was twisted in a knot, Hugh managed a wee chuckle. "I didn't say—"

"MacIain, sir?" A runner stepped into the alehouse.

Hugh pushed back his chair and stood, ready for anything. Da slid his fingers around his hilt. "Aye?"

"The sheriff's galley has been spotted."

"Och, I said he couldn't stay away forever." Da swatted Hugh's back with a hearty laugh. "I'll take the oath and we'll be sitting before your mother's hearth by the evening meal on the morrow."

"At least we do not have to spend another night in this unsavory establishment." Hugh pointed to the men. "See to it the ponies are ready to ride. We'll return anon."

He tightened his sword belt and walked beside Da to the courthouse. Not long and the sheriff entered, brushing snow from his cloak. "A man alights from his galley and told to head to the courthouse afore he's had a chance to light a fire in home's hearth. This had best be good, MacIain."

Da pulled Governor Hill's missive from his buckskin and slapped it on the board. "I've been six days waiting for someone with cods enough to take my oath to King William." He then went into great detail about Hill's refusal at Fort William and being unlawfully detained at Barcaldine Castle by Drummond's patrol. "To top it off, me and my men nearly lost our lives riding through the worst blizzard since God Almighty created Scotland. 'Tis a wonder I'm standing here afore you this day."

The Campbell sheriff frowned and stroked his fingers down his chin while he pored over Hill's missive. Then he sat back in his chair and casually tossed the parchment on the table. "I'm afraid 'tis too late to take the oath. The writ clearly states it must be sworn to before the first of January."

"Did you not hear a word I said?" Da took in a deep inhale, puffing out his chest. "I tried to swear the oath to anyone who would listen. Why Colonel Hill, the Governor of Fort William, could not administer it, I've no idea. Why

Captain Drummond saw fit to lock me in the hold against my will for an entire day is unforgivable."

"But 'tis the fifth of January."

Hugh's fingers itched to draw his sword and level it under the smug sheriff's chin. Why the hell was he stalling? Da had the letter from Hill explaining what had happened. Damnation, he'd held his tongue long enough. "You *want* us to fail, no matter that in good faith my father tried to take the oath afore the deadline."

"You, sir, have not been addressed. And had you been in *Inveraray* on the thirty-first of December and not *Fort William*, I might just be so inclined to issue the oath to your errant father, regardless of my profound distaste for the man."

Hugh thrust his finger at the codfish. "You see? You admit——"

"Silence!" Da bellowed loud enough to wake the dead buried in Glencoe's hills.

Even the "sheriff of the damned" jolted in his seat, his grey wig toppling cockeyed.

Da took a step forward, spreading his palms wide. "Please." His voice warbled like never before. "I've come to you in good faith. We've lain low and kept to ourselves. Administer the oath to me and upon my honor, I will promise that I shall order all my people to do the same. Those who refuse, you may imprison or send to Flanders as soldiers."

Hugh closed his eyes. *What words did Da have with the colonel when I was in the passageway with Charlotte? And after with Captain Drummond? Da's never been afraid of anything, but I ken fear, and if the tremor in Da's voice isn't downright terror, then I'm no Highland scrapper.*

Sheriff Campbell straightened his wig and looked up at the great chieftain's face.

"Please, I beg of you," Da continued. "I have endured

great hardship to stand before you this day. I've patiently awaited your return. I'd like nothing better than to head home to my lady wife and have this business behind me."

With his frown, the sheriff shook his head. "Boar's ballocks, my duty is but to record the oaths given in my presence. Come to me on the morrow and it will be done."

"Why wait until the morrow?" Hugh started forward to be met with Da's steely grip on his upper arm.

"One more day at the change-house, lad." Then Da looked to the sheriff. "My thanks."

Once outside, Hugh led his father off the path to a bench where they wouldn't be overheard. "Devil's fire, I've never seen you bow to anyone like I just saw in there. Bloody hell, Da. We're MacDonalds. Fearless in the eyes of God. Does that account for nothing?"

The proud old man's shoulders sagged while he swiped a hand down his face. "Bless it, son. Do you not ken this is all for you? All of it!"

Hugh's brow pinched. "I beg your pardon?"

"The Master of Stair is moving forty thousand troops to rain fire throughout the Highlands. He aims to snuff out those who do not make the pledge." A spark flickered in his eye. "And Drummond laughed in my face when he told me Glencoe was first on the master's list of upstarts."

Hugh shuddered like a snake had just slithered up his spine. "Christ. Will they never leave us be?"

Da grasped the plaid draped across Hugh's shoulder and twisted it in his fist. "By God, I will see to it that my sons thrive, and their sons, and their sons after. You *will* succeed me, and our clan *will* rule the Coe forever." His grip tightened until the plaid nearly split its woolen fibers. "Understand one thing. I'd drop to my knees and beg if it meant our kin would be free from King William's wrath."

Chapter Ten

✦✦✦

For the most part Charlotte enjoyed the officers' banter during the evening meal. She always listened thoughtfully, careful to keep her opinions bottled and corked, especially when her views didn't mirror the others'. Why they all managed to believe they were still at war with the Jacobites, she couldn't fathom. Not every clan had taken the oath, but most had—especially those thought to be a possible threat, and Papa expected little in the way of retaliation from the others who hadn't yet come forward.

In her opinion, the threat of war had never been so unlikely. Besides, the weather made any such improbable retaliation unlikely.

Charlotte cut her roast lamb with precise slices as her ears piqued. The generally lighthearted banter had taken a turn to matters at hand. Why soldiers oft insisted on making a stir just to agitate that which would otherwise be idle, she would never fathom.

"We need to make an example of the laggards to show all the Highlanders that disobedience will not be tolerated," said Doctor Munro, seated beside her.

Papa and Lieutenant Colonel Hamilton exchanged pointed frowns. "I daresay I agree," said Hamilton. "However, no small clan will do. The king's action needs to be on a grand scale—a statement by the army that ends any question to James' claims to the throne forever."

Charlotte swirled the bite of lamb and turnip in her mouth, contemplating what might happen if she spat it at the insensitive cur. Make an example of an entire clan? And to what end? To show the kindly Highland folk that the king's men could be the most immeasurable asses in all the world?

Papa leveled his eating knife in the young officer's direction. "Watch yourself, sir. There is a lady present."

She stopped mid-chew. Papa's rebuttal sent heat firing across the back of her neck. Did her father condone such an act of barbarity? Worse, the two men again locked gazes, communicating about something to which everyone at the table was obviously not privy. She rested her fork on the side of her plate. "Fortunately, the MacIain and the Cameron Clans have sworn fealty. Did they not pose the greatest threat?" she asked, dabbing the corner of her mouth. Surely the lieutenant colonel could occupy his time with things other than plotting against the local clansmen and women— or her father for goodness sakes.

Hamilton stabbed a turnip as if he were thrusting a dagger. "Alasdair MacIain was late to pledge the oath. Word came from Inveraray he didn't manage to sign until the *sixth* of January."

Charlotte took in a deep breath, straining against her corset, yet unable to capture the deep breath she needed to settle her trembling fingers. "Not for want of trying."

"He knew better than to come to Fort William," the blackguard continued. "Governor Hill could no more record his oath than I could."

"And why not, pray tell?" She leaned forward. "You are both high ranking vassals of the king."

"Enough." Papa reached for his goblet of claret. "I'm happy with the number of chieftains who pledged their fealty to William."

"Honestly, Governor?" Hamilton eyed Charlotte from across the table. "I think since Miss Hill inquired, it should be made clear no favors will be extended to men who are themselves criminals, living in a den of thieves."

For the love of everything holy, her stays had become two sizes tighter since the meal began. Though her head swooned, she would uncover the truth of Hamilton's abhorrence. "Oh? And why is it you have taken such a dislike to Clan Iain Abrach of Glencoe?"

The smirk on the young officer's face gave her pause. Oh, how hatred and prejudice twisted relatively attractive features into ugly darkness. If Hamilton's heart were the color of his features, it was black and compassionless. "I believe I've mentioned the rogues not only fought against us at Killiecrankie, they ventured home by way of the Glenlyon Campbells and all but ran Captain Robert into bankruptcy. The Laird of Glenlyon is a good friend of mine."

"Is that so?" Charlotte situated her fork and knife across her plate—busying herself to allay her urge to scream. "I understand Sir Robert is a gambler and a drunkard."

"Charlotte!" Da admonished. "You will apologize for that remark."

See what happens when I engage these men in conversation? Now I'm made out to be the muttonhead. "Forgive me." She folded her hands in her lap and glared at them. Clearly Hamilton harbored abhorrence for Hugh's clan. Be it a raid on a raider's lands, she had no idea, but something told her his prejudice delved far deeper than he'd let on.

"I daresay it was quite brilliant of Captain Drummond to

stall the old man on his journey to Inveraray." Hamilton held up his wine glass with a wry grin as if he'd won the battle of words. "Here, here to that."

"Here, here," repeated the men at the table, all grinning like a pack of mindless baboons dressed in red coats.

Charlotte couldn't bring herself to partake in such a heartless celebration of another's misfortune. Out of the corner of her eye, Papa frowned and swirled his claret. Something didn't sit well with him either. *At least there's more than one compassionate soul at the table.*

"Things in the surgery have been quite busy." Doctor Munro reached for the decanter and refilled his glass. "Now that I have the bloody flux under control, influenza is upon us."

Papa shoved a bite of bread into his mouth. "Bring it under control. I cannot have an entire battalion of men abed with fever."

"Aye, and 'tis terribly contagious." The physician shot her a pointed look. "Charlotte, I do not want you anywhere near the surgery until the epidemic is over."

She wouldn't mind that at all. In fact, she hadn't visited the surgery in sennights. "Very well. I've plenty to keep me busy now I've taken up mending uniforms."

He leaned toward her until his shoulder touched hers. "On a lighter note, I do believe the sentries have cleared away the snow from the wall-walk. Would you take a turn with me atop the battlements? After, we could warm our insides with some of Mrs. MacGregor's raspberry leaf tea."

If nothing else, Charlotte needed to clear her head and the physician seemed to be the most amiable officer at the table. "I do believe a spell of frigid air would revive the soul."

"Be careful not to stay out too long. With the influenza about, I do not want you catching a chill, my dear." Papa stood and took Charlotte's hands, giving her a peck on the cheek.

The physician stood as well. "One turn and then a warm cup of tea. I promise."

After donning their cloaks, Doctor Munro grasped Charlotte's hand and led her up the narrow stairwell. His hands were always clammy and cold. But it would be insensitive for her to pull away now.

"How long do you think the influenza outbreak will last?" she asked.

"Only God knows. But sure as the rain, we have an outbreak during winter every year which, on average, puts a soldier on his back for a sennight, with another sennight of sniffles, coughing and muscle weakness."

"How dreadful."

Doctor Munro stopped and took both of Charlotte's hands between his palms, holding them against his heart. "I meant what I said about staying away from the surgery until the epidemic is over, but what troubles me more is I haven't enjoyed the gift of your presence in over a fortnight."

She stared at their joined hands and felt nothing. Her heart didn't race as it had when Mr. MacIain held her fingers against his heart. Was she attracted to rogues and villains? Perhaps not entirely. Lieutenant Colonel Hamilton's blue-eyed stare did make her shudder—as opposed to the tingles that made her heart swell when she gazed into Mr. MacIain's eyes.

But she must face the fact that though she felt no abhorrence, she experienced no giddy heart pounding when the physician held her hands and gazed into her eyes. She truly wished he wouldn't be so familiar with her. Yet, wasn't that how a man was supposed to act when courting a woman?

What a dreadful state of affairs. If only I could return to London now and not wait until the snow melts. Why, it's so deep, it may not melt until July for all I know.

"I fear your thoughts are a hundred miles away." Doctor Munro's gaze drifted aside. "Have I done something to drive you away?"

She stared at his chin. "No."

"Then what is it? Do I displease you?"

"Oh, Doctor Munro—"

"Roderick."

Charlotte gulped. She could no longer pretend. "Forgive me, Roderick, but I must tell you it is unfair of me to continue this pretense of courting given my inattentiveness."

"Is it Lieutenant Colonel Hamilton?" The physician's brow furrowed. "He is quite a handsome gentleman."

"Most certainly not." She gave an exaggerated shake of her head. "I fear that man's heart is evil."

"He seems to be a most ardent soldier."

Growing suddenly warm, Charlotte pictured herself like a kettle with steam billowing out the top of her head. "With bloodlust as large as his love of advancement." Yes, she'd given a curt reply, but someone in this fort needed to call attention to the errant, power-loving wiles of that braggart.

A timid smile played across Roderick's face. "Though it is a relief you harbor no feelings for Hamilton, I want to strengthen our bond. Do you not find our friendship invigorating?" His eyes grew dark as he slowly lifted her hands to his mouth and plied them with a purse of his lips.

Charlotte tried to smile. But honestly, did he have to kiss her hands and look so miserably forlorn? And why couldn't she find it in her heart to love him? He was educated, from an esteemed family, and would always maintain a stately home. Life with Roderick Munro would be comfortable.

"What must I do to gain your adoration, my love?"

Grow ten inches taller, carry an enormous sword with which you would always vow to protect my honor and speak to me with a rolling Highland burr. Charlotte cringed. Was she so shallow, she could not see beyond all the things that attracted her to Hugh MacIain? For goodness sakes, she hardly knew the Highlander, and more than once she'd heard tales about his fierce battles. Perhaps if she could spend an afternoon strolling the wall-walk with Hugh, she'd discover his true self and discern if her unabashed attraction consisted of a foundation of stone or sand. Alas, she'd probably be sailing back to London before Mr. MacIain ventured to Fort William again, if he ever did.

"Charlotte?" Doctor Munro brushed her cheek with the back of his finger. "Are you deep in thought about my ardent love for you, or are you elsewhere."

She stepped back and cleared her throat. "Forgive me. Your question made my mind swarm. Please, if you need an answer from me forthwith, I must say no, for my feelings for you run no deeper than friendship."

His eyebrow arched. "'Tis said friendship is a delightful place to start a marriage."

Her stomach squeezed and not with a tingling sensation. It clamped with dread. Marriage? Of course courting led to marriage. And she wasn't getting any younger. If she didn't accept a proposal from Doctor Munro, she just might end up a spinster. "No," her lips blurted, seemingly governed by a force outside her body.

"Not ever?" The man blinked rapidly as if she'd slapped him.

Drawing a hand to her chest, she took a deep inhale. "I am not yet ready to speak of marriage, and it would be selfish of me to expect you to wait whilst my feeble mind tries to make a decision."

"May I suggest you defer to your father? He waited until

middle age to marry. He might be best to advise you, since *I* obviously am struggling to make you see reason."

Charlotte moved back and folded her arms. "You think I am unreasonable?"

"Not so much that, but I do think you need a mature person with whom you can consult." Roderick took her elbow and proceeded along the wall-walk. "Until then I am not planning to leave Fort William any time soon. I've another two years on contract with the army. I've nothing but time, my love."

With such selfless encouragement, Charlotte almost agreed—until a picture of Hugh MacIain shackled to a cot in the surgery soaking wet and shivering popped into her head. Doctor Munro might be genteel with her, but there were grave matters upon which they fiercely differed.

❧

A SCORE OF CLANSMEN AND WOMEN SAT IN DA'S DRAWING room, most on wooden chairs, some of the younger ones on the floor. Ma, Sandy and his wife, Sarah, occupied the overstuffed couch across from the hearth. As children, Hugh and his brothers used to fight for such a comfortable spot beside Ma when Da started in on one of his stories. But none of that mattered anymore. Hugh sat on a stool jutted up against the whitewashed stone wall.

Da took a long pull of ale from his prized drinking cup of French silver—a relic from his time in Paris where the sons of Highland chiefs were sent to polish their God given autocracy and pride. A place where honor and chivalry were a part of the curriculum, but only second to leadership and absolutism. Hugh had the honor of a term in Paris where he made allies with men like Donald MacDonald of Sleat, Iain-a-Chraggain Grant of Glenmoriston, and Kennan Cameron of

Lochiel—all young bucks like Hugh, and all men upon whom the good fortune of being the first born heirs of a clan chieftainship befell.

Sputtering, the old man, white with age, but still with a spine as straight as a plank looked out over the gathering, his blue eyes sparkling with good humor. "Never forget the land of the Coe sprouts the very roots to the MacIain sept of Clan Donald. It was the year of our Lord fifteen hundred when the greedy house of Argyll tried to evict our ancestor John of the Ilis from Glencoe. They viciously set upon us whilst they had the great chief Donald Dubh locked in their rat infested dungeon at Innischonnell..."

A story Hugh could recite in his sleep, Da continued whilst the peat in the hearth crackled and all eyes focused on their fearless chieftain. Indeed, if the day ever came when the stalwart icon of the family perished, Hugh would have very big shoes to fill, both figuratively and literally.

Nonetheless, Hugh loved to listen to his father ramble on about the history of Coe and clan, and how he'd fought to keep their lands from greedy Campbell fingers. Amusing, each time Da told a tale it changed—always in Da's favor. When he was still wet behind the ears, Hugh resented his father's boisterous and gregarious manner. But now he'd come into his own as a man, he admired his father. Regardless of how the chieftain relayed a story, Alasdair MacIain MacDonald wasn't only a descendant of Angus Og, progenitor of the Lords of the Isles—he was a legend in his own time.

Growing up in the shadow of a great man taught Hugh many things and set an example. No, his youth wasn't particularly comfortable. Da had been a hard task master issuing bruises most days and bloody noses when Hugh erred too far. At the age of five, under threat of birch branches taken to his bare buttocks, Hugh roused before dawn to collect firewood, no matter the time of year, no matter the weather. Och aye, a swatting with a clump of thin birch twigs made welts rise that wouldn't ease for three days.

Aye, he was Alasdair MacIain's heir, but Da firmly believed being born to power didn't mean shite. A lad had to prove himself over and over again—take a beating, then get up and take another. Damn good thing Hugh towered over the other lads his age, because after the wood had been chopped, the lessons learned, the cows milked and put to pasture, the real training began—training to become a man. A Highlander. A warrior. A defender of women and children and protector of the lands acquired by fire and sword centuries past.

Da made sure all his sons could handle a sword, dirk, musket, bow and arrow. He'd say, "To take up the sword pledges your oath to die for your kin, to die for your honor so that our clan will prosper."

Then he'd make the boys race to the river with buckets and poles, fill them and race back, the poles across their shoulders with a bucket at either end. The winner—the first to arrive with full buckets was rewarded by a sparring lesson with Da himself—not necessarily a reward given the arse-beating Da would dish out, but the losers had it worse. After they sparred for hours, Da gave them the disgusting detail of emptying all the waste buckets for the chieftain's house as well as the servant's quarters.

Hugh made a point of receiving his arse-kicking from Da near every eve and left the shite detail to his younger brothers.

Da stopped his story for a moment and took another drink from his silver cup. "I've been blessed to reach the ripe age of two and sixty, and over the years I've seen my share of battles. I've defended my home, I've raided my enemies, and I've fought for king and country. One of the greatest honors of my life was when my sons Hugh and Og flanked me as we faced the dragoons in the battle of Killiecrankie. Bonnie Dundee may have lost his life, but he died with a sword in his hand, well aware he had Glencoe men beside him, fighting for the right of the Stuart line..."

Hugh's gaze traveled across the room to Ma's face. Rosy cheeked, she always sat peacefully listening to her husband while working on embroidery or knitting, her fingers constantly moving, creating something from a skein of wool that would become a piece of art.

Beside her, Sandy held his wife's hand with a half-cocked smile on his ruddy face, listening to Da expound upon his tale with ale and a wee bit of whisky influencing his heroism. Beside Sandy, Sarah moved not at all. She kept her stare completely expressionless as if the story had no impact on her good or bad. Even her cheeks were pale—white like an unblemished canvas. She looked up for a moment, her gaze connecting with Hugh's. He hid his face behind his dram of whisky and observed.

Her stare was starker than the paleness of her complexion. Was it the dimly lit room, or were her eyes really cold as grey slate kissed by Glencoe's mist?

Hugh shuddered.

"What?" Da asked, coming out of his story. "Is the fire not warm enough for you, lad?"

Ma's fingers paused. "Oh dear, I hope you're not coming down with the influenza."

Hugh raised his cup, directing a pointed look to Sarah. "I've never felt better. My best times are sitting with kin listening to the old tales of clan and sword. It gives us all a sense of our history. Something to remember with pride."

Sarah glanced away and shifted in her seat. Och aye, it would be a cold day in hell afore Hugh grew to trust that woman—a shift of the eyes and frown might seem a trifle, but it spoke volumes about her character. Had Sandy not made his Campbell wife happy? Hugh vowed to find out.

Then he grinned at his father. "You were just coming to the best part. Please. Carry on."

And continue he did.

But Hugh didn't hear the rest. He stared into his cup as a wicked ache stirred in his loins. Aye, he'd gone too long without bedding a woman. The only problem? Just one woman filled his thoughts—a fair lassie he absolutely must block from his dreams.

God's bones, he was a rouge. True, he probably shouldn't have kissed Miss Hill in the window embrasure, but in that moment, temptation had taken ahold of his cods and ignited a raging fire that hadn't eased since. If only he could make an excuse to see the lass again. One more kiss might quell his lust—as long as she didn't press those succulent breasts to his chest. Och aye, the woman's flesh could put a hex on any man. To prove his point, thoughts of her practically made Hugh want to sign on with her da.

Again he shuddered. He could never, not ever, not on his life turn his back on clan and kin. 'Twas exactly why he must push his errant thoughts to the back of his mind and lock them away for good.

Thinking, dreaming, yearning for Charlotte Hill would only see him standing on the gallows with a noose around his neck. The sooner he forgot her honeyed tresses, the sparkle of innocence in her violet eyes and the way an unfettered smile could play across her succulent lips, the better.

THE NEXT MORNING, HUGH TOOK HIS MUSKET AND knocked on the door to Sandy's cottage.

After a bit of rustling, Sarah opened the door, arched an

eyebrow, and leaned on her birch-twig broom. "You come to call with your musket in hand?"

Hugh shrugged off the cool welcome. "I thought Sandy might enjoy a wee hunt this morn."

Said brother appeared behind his wife, red locks disheveled, dimples in his boyish face. "Och aye, I caught sight of an eight-point buck a sennight ago. The whole clan would feast for certain."

Sarah stepped aside and gestured into the cottage—dirt floor, the air thick with smoke from the peat fire. "You'd best come in out of the cold and eat breakfast with my lazy husband."

"Pardon me?" Sandy sauntered toward the table while his wife frowned after him.

Her fist moved to her hip. "Look at you, barely out of bed, whilst your brother is up with his boots on."

Hugh shrugged and sat on the bench. "Aye, but I haven't yet had a bite."

"Counting on my hospitality, were you, brother?" Sarah rested the broom against the wall.

"Of course he was," Sandy said, pulling the simmering kettle from where it hung above the fire. "And I'll brew up some of that newfangled coffee for us."

The woman gasped. "Och, I'm saving that for when special guests come to call."

Sandy pulled the stopper off a stoneware pot, the heady aroma of coffee filling the air. Hugh hadn't oft had the opportunity to smell it, but the powerful scent made his mouth water. Dumping a cup full of black granules into the pot, Sandy grinned. "If the heir to Clan Iain Abrach is not a special guest, I do not ken who is."

Sarah slapped a wooden plate of oatcakes on the table without a word. Hugh crossed his arms and ankles while pretending to watch his brother brew the coffee. "My thanks, brother. 'Tis a rare treat, indeed."

Sarah took a seat on the bench opposite and Sandy placed three cups on the table. Odd state of affairs—not that Sandy shouldn't help a bit, but his wife seemed none too eager to lift a finger.

"There's six feet of snow in the hills, if not more. Why would you be hunting when the smokehouse is full of meat?" she asked.

Hugh studied her for a moment before he replied. Her features had softened since he'd entered. Was the lass having a bad morning, or was she as gruff-natured as he'd deemed her to be last eve? "A man cannot remain cooped up in his cottage all winter." Hugh leaned forward and snatched an oatcake. "Besides, roast venison on the spit will please the old man for certain."

"Too right it will," Sandy agreed, pouring the coffee through butter muslin to catch the grounds. "I'll enjoy the sport and its spoils, too."

"Suit yourselves. I'll not be venturing out in the bitter cold to hunt." Sarah tugged her arisaid closer around her shoulders. "Make sure you watch the sky. I wouldn't want you men to be caught in those hills in a blizzard."

"Och," Hugh said. "Sandy and I were raised in the Coe. Not many men could survive in her hills in the thick of winter, but I reckon the pair of us would manage." He gave his brother a wink as he took a swallow of coffee. Lord in heaven, the brew was bitter enough to make his hair curl. He raised his cup and grinned. "A man could grow accustomed to this."

Sarah picked up the stoneware pot containing the unused grounds and replaced it on the shelf. "This came all the way from London—a gift from my Uncle Robert."

Hugh hid his displeasure with another sip of coffee. He

needn't ask. Her uncle Robert was a government-loving, arse-kissing Campbell for certain. Hell, it didn't matter if he and Sandy bagged their buck. He'd spend a carefree day with his little brother and spirit him away from this stuffy, smoke-filled cottage. He'd seen and heard enough. Sarah was as smug and pompous as her Campbell relatives. Och aye, Sandy would need to show his new bride her place sooner than later.

Ma says I need a wife? Bugger that idea.

Chapter Eleven

❧❧❧

A sennight later Hugh didn't take his own advice and dismiss Charlotte Hill from his thoughts. Oh no, that would have been too easy. He didn't care to be in such close proximity to red-coated dragoons, but his reason for letting a discrete chamber in a guesthouse in Inverlochy far outweighed the risks. And across the road was an alehouse where he was certain to find an old friend.

He'd seen Farley MacGregor on his visit to Fort William with Da. The Highlander might have proffered his tracking services to Colonel Hill, but secretly he remained a Jacobite to his very bones. With the times, a man didn't speak much about his political allegiances—especially after Hugh had watched his father grovel to the sheriff. The unspoken truth? Unless a Highlander's name was Campbell, he remained true to kin and king, even if that king was living on the continent in exile. Hugh didn't blame Farley for working for the government. He had a family. Eking out a living was difficult, and if you were lucky enough to be born in the Highlands, times were even tougher.

Once inside the alehouse, Hugh chose a table in a darkened corner and sat with a tankard of ale before him. Every time the door opened, he looked up expectantly, praying to the Almighty the MacGregor tracker wasn't away on some harebrained task for the governor.

Drinking slowly wasn't Hugh's style, and moreover, sitting idle nearly drove him to the edge of madness. Beneath the table his impatient leg never stopped moving. Above it, his eyes shifted at every sound. He should have brought his men, but that would have caused more suspicion to his precarious circumstances.

Not long after the midday bell rang, the door opened and in strode Farley MacGregor, dressed in green plaid swathed around his waist and draped over his shoulders. On his feet he wore a pair of brogues, laced atop plaid woolen hose and secured below the knee with bright red flashes. Puffs of frigid air swirled around the blue bonnet covering his mop of unruly brown hair. Holy mother, the man's unkempt beard came to the center of his chest.

Hugh pushed back his chair and stood. "Bloody oath MacGregor, are you part bear?"

The tracker squinted through the alehouse as he ran his fingers down his beard. "Och, what the bleeding hell brought you off your dung pile Mac—"

"Donald," Hugh finished. True, he was Hugh MacIain MacDonald, but nary a friend tacked on the MacDonald bit. That part was understood—moreover, the MacIain name instilled fear in the hearts of his enemies. No point in causing a stir when trying to lay low.

Farley's eyes shifted before he grinned. "You're wise to use your clan name around these parts."

"I reckon so." Hugh gestured to the chair opposite. "Would you have an ale with me, old friend?"

"What's this? Alasdair's son giving rather than taking?"

Hugh clutched at his heart in jest. "You wound my pride." He caught the barmaid's attention and held up two fingers.

Farley snorted. "It would take a lot more than a wee rib to cut through that thick skin of yours."

"My skin?" Hugh asked with feigned exasperation. "I reckon your skin is tougher than hog's leather."

That drew a hearty laugh from the burly tracker. "Och aye, just like any Highlander hailing from the Gallows Herd."

Hugh grinned. "'Tis good to see the redcoats haven't addled your brain."

"Bloody hell." Lowering his voice, the man threw a look over his shoulder. "Not for want of trying. With every lot of new troops, there're more bastards who come thinking we're a mob of useless savages. If you ask me, there's not a hospitable dragoon in the lot."

Hugh rubbed his hand over his wrist—where his manacles had worn him raw during his time in the pit. "My experience is the same." Farley might be a friend, but he saw no use in telling him about being a prisoner of war. The only person in the fort who knew he'd been their guest was Charlotte and Hugh wanted to keep it that way.

The barmaid placed two tankards frothing with ale in front of them. "That will be two pennies."

Hugh reached into his sporran and placed the coins on the table. "Ta." Once the wench was out of earshot, he held up his drink. "What news of Fort William?" He'd test the waters for a wee bit longer before he mentioned the true reason for his visit.

A thick eyebrow arched. "Our winters are too cold for the English, that's for certain. The milk-livered dragoons huddle by their braziers until Lieutenant Colonel Hamilton cracks his whip."

Hugh ran his finger down the tankard's handle. "I've heard

of this Hamilton—sent here to take Hill's spot once he's retired. True?"

"That's what they say." Farley again lowered his voice. The man was jittery for certain. "I reckon he's been sent here by the Master of Stair to make a stir."

"With the governor?"

"Aye, and with the locals. Hamilton's a supremacist and a hater if you ask me. I loathe tracking for the blighter—don't trust him either."

"No?"

Farley took a long look behind, then leaned forward. "I swear he'd stab me in the back if no one was looking."

"Bastard."

"Too right." The big man sipped his ale. "So, why in God's name are you in Inverlochy, and where the hell are your men? 'Tisn't safe for a Highland gentleman to be alone—especially when his allegiances are so, uh, *well known.*"

Hugh leaned back and crossed his arms. "I've a matter of a more delicate nature to attend."

"I see." Farley's dark brown beard split as he grinned, revealing a mouth of crooked teeth. "Come to meet a woman have you?"

"A tracker you are." Hugh laughed. "Tell me, if a man were to pay a visit to Miss Hill, how would he best go about it?"

Farley slammed his fist on the table. "For the love of God, do not tell me you've come all the way from Glencoe to call on the governor's daughter."

Hugh scratched his chin. "Guess I'm a glutton for punishment."

"Did you ken Doctor Munro has been courting her?"

Thick skin or not, Farley's comment set Hugh's blood to boiling. "That pasty codfish? How on earth can she put up with the likes of him?"

"I reckon he's a mite better than Hamilton." Farley scratched his beard. "Have you even met the lass?"

"Aye." The corner of Hugh's mouth ticked up. "Kissed her once." *The first didn't count—not really.*

"Truth?" Farley rocked back and thwacked his chest. "Did she kiss you back?"

"Why in God's name would I be sitting here in the midst of a mob of government troops?" Hugh probably shouldn't have mentioned the kiss.

The tracker took a good swig of his ale, then reached across the table and swatted Hugh on the arm. "Don't know what a cultured Sassenach lassie would see in a Highland scrapper like you."

God's bones, Farley needed a long turn in the mountains. "I beg your pardon? Mayhap the redcoats have addled your mind after all. Does my inheritance count for nothing with this lot of Williamite zealots?"

"Och, unless you have 'earl' attached to your name like Breadalbane, the redcoats would still consider you a scoundrel —especially hailing from the Coe." Farley stared at the wall for a long moment. "You'd risk your neck for the lass?"

"Aye—already have, I suppose." Ballocks, this conversation made his leg under the table jittery. For centuries the MacDonald septs had been at odds with the Campbells, and now the Earl of Argyll and the Earl of Breadalbane sat on the Privy Council, deliberately passing laws to destroy Clan Iain Abrach's reputation—just has they had the MacGregors not so long ago. "Nothing like being treated like a criminal in a man's own country," Hugh spat out.

Farley guzzled his remaining ale, then looked Hugh in the eye. "You ken I'm your mate. But bloody hell, you have to be daft to come here seeking an audience with the colonel's daughter."

"Probably am, but that doesn't change things." Hugh planted his palms on the table. "Can you slip me inside?"

"If there's no talking you out of it..." Farley glanced over his shoulder. "My lady wife happens to be Miss Hill's chambermaid."

Hugh nearly fell off his chair. He hoped Farley might help him steal into the fort—mayhap arrange a meeting, but his wife was the lady's chambermaid? Hugh grasped Farley's plaid and crushed it in his fist. "I must see her. Please."

With a squint to his eye, Farley glanced down. "Holy Mary, you do have a hankering for the lass."

"Aye." Hugh released his grip and forced himself to sit back while his foot tapped beneath the table. "Can you help me?"

"Don't ken. I refuse to put the colonel's daughter in a compromising situation. No, no. Emma would lose her position for such a misstep." The tracker drummed his fingers against his tankard.

Hugh's entire leg rattled the table. "There must be some way I can see her without causing a stir."

"Tell you what, I'll ask Emma to mention your presence in Inverlochy to the lass. Then we'll see if she even cares to see your ugly face." Farley shook his head. "I cannot believe it. The prince of the Gallows Herd kisses the princess of the Fort William Dragoons. Now I ken why bloody wars are fought."

⁊❧

HUDDLED UNDER HER CLOAK, HER HANDS WARM IN A FUR muff, Charlotte sat beside Emma in the coach. Though the snow was packed down, they ambled slowly to the chapel tucked away in the wood. She still couldn't believe Hugh was in Inverlochy—and Emma had been the one to tell her about it.

How devilishly exciting. Though Emma had repeated a hundred times Charlotte needn't bother herself with the likes of Hugh MacIain MacDonald, Charlotte would hear none of it. Emma said that Hugh was a loyal friend of her husband's, but the chambermaid thought Doctor Munro to be a better match. Charlotte had tried to tell Emma how utterly dull she found the physician. Though her words fell on deaf ears, Emma still arranged the meeting, bless her. Charlotte's insides danced as if she were soaring like a bird, or being introduced at court for the very first time. She patted her velvet hood. "Do I have any flyaway locks?"

"You look lovely as always," said Emma. "Though I should have taken a bit of coal and drawn a wart on your chin."

Charlotte nudged the chambermaid with her elbow. "You would do no such thing."

"No? I still do not have an inkling as to why I'm going along with this charade."

"Because you are a kindly and loyal servant." Charlotte gave the woman a pointed stare. "And I've sworn you to secrecy."

Mr. MacGregor pulled the horse to a stop outside the chapel, sitting alone in the midst of overarching trees. Only the narrow path just wide enough for the wagon was bereft of trees—some fir, but mostly sycamore and birch that had lost their leaves for the winter.

Charlotte's breath billowed in the cold. Her hands trembled. Goodness, her entire body trembled.

After tying the reins, Mr. MacGregor helped her alight. "You mustn't worry, Miss Hill. We shall be waiting for you right here."

"I'm not worried."

"Are you sure you don't wish for me to accompany you?" Emma asked. "I would feel so much better about this."

"Oh please." Charlotte held up a gloved palm. "'Tis God's house in which we'll be meeting. I'm sure Mr. MacIain will behave the perfect gentleman."

Emma took Farley's hand and hopped down from the cart. "I cannot believe I am going along with this. Your father will take it out of my hide if we're found out."

Mr. MacGregor gave his wife a pat. "Not to worry, my dear. Hugh's a good man. I trust when the time comes, Colonel Hill will see it."

Emma looked skyward. "Afore we're both dismissed, let us pray."

Thus far, they had proceeded in utmost secrecy. Charlotte had even been so bold as to tell her father she planned to pray at the chapel in the wood, though she hadn't mentioned anything about Hugh. A girl was entitled to a secret or two, was she not?

A twinge of guilt tightened her chest.

Mr. MacGregor offered his elbow. "I'll see you inside."

"Thank you."

Together they proceeded to the thick double doors, studded with blackened iron nails.

"Do you think he's here?" Charlotte asked, looking for a horse.

"If he's not, he'd be a greater fool than I thought possible." Mr. MacGregor pulled on the latch. "I'll be right outside. If I hear one squeak, I'll be upon MacIain in the blink of an eye."

Charlotte patted the kindhearted man's arm. "I'm sure that will not be necessary." Stepping inside, she blinked in rapid succession to enable her eyes to adjust to the dim light.

His head bent in prayer, Hugh knelt before the altar. A ray of light streaming from the stained glass above made him look like the archangel of war. Enormous, broad shouldered, dark hair cropped to his nape, the man could be none other than Hugh MacIain.

The door clicked shut behind her.

Charlotte's mouth went dry.

She took a step forward, her skirts rustling. *Should I interrupt his worship or wait?*

Her question was answered when he crossed himself, stood and faced her, his eyes more intense and hungry than she'd remembered. "You came." His white-toothed grin brightened the entire sanctuary.

Taking another step, she returned his smile, her heart fluttering with arrhythmic beats. "How could I stay away?" Goodness, her voice sounded breathless.

He closed the distance, and rather than gather her hands in his palms as Doctor Munro would have done, his big arms wrapped around her shoulders. "My God, Charlotte, you've no idea how happy I am to see you."

Oh merciful mercy, he'd used her given name. It rolled with a deep burr like a brook spilling over a waterfall on a lazy summer's day. In no way could she resist an embrace that spoke more than words could possibly express. He pulled her tightly against his chest, the warmth from his body sending soothing tingles along Charlotte's spine while her breasts swelled, craving more friction. Allowing herself to rest her head atop that very hard, very protective chest, she closed her eyes and inhaled the spicy masculinity of his scent. If only she could remain cocooned in his arms forever. "Why does this feel so right, when I know it is wrong?"

"Because only God in heaven tells us right from wrong. He kens what's in our hearts—not kings or queens or government officers." Hugh lifted her chin with the crook of his forefinger. "Lord Almighty, you're more beautiful than a rose in spring."

Charlotte opened her mouth to speak, but before she could utter a sound, Hugh's gaze dropped to her lips. With her gasp, he pulled her tighter and gently plied her mouth with tantalizing brushes of his lips. Her heart hammered so erratically, Charlotte swooned in his arms as she fervently tried to match his kissing.

Hugh reacted to her efforts with a low growl, as he slipped his tongue inside her mouth and plied her with a tad more pressure.

Every inch of her skin grew alive as she closed her eyes. Oh how blissful his touch, taking her to a place of rapture she never would have dreamed possible. Helpless to resist him, Charlotte gave her all, matching each swirl of the tongue, each tiny taste.

With a throaty sigh, he trailed kisses along her jaw, and Charlotte shivered, reveling in pure ecstasy as he continued down her neck. "I've missed you ever so much," his deep voice rumbled ever so softly. Merely his tenor made her pulse race—her mind swoon.

"And I you," she replied breathlessly. Charlotte had so much to say and so many questions, but by the stars, she could scarcely gather a single thought. "Ah...I heard your father signed the oath."

He nuzzled into her tresses. "Aye, though not without difficulty."

"But it is done now." She smoothed her fingers across his chin—shaved so close it felt like Holland cloth. "How long do you plan to stay?"

"A fortnight if I'm lucky." A feral growl pealed from his throat. "I shouldn't be here at all."

Oh, how the scent of leather and spice made her insides ignite with fire. "Mr. MacGregor said you're staying at a guesthouse nearby."

"Aye, in Inverlochy—far enough away from Fort William's dragoons."

"Do you have business affairs here?"

He brushed a wisp of her hair away. Blast, she knew after riding in the coach she'd have flyaways. "Aye." His eyes grew darker and his tongue tapped the corner of his mouth. "Serious affairs, lass."

"May I inquire as to the nature of your, ah, *dealings*?"

He twirled one of her damnable flyaways around his finger, his warm breath caressing her forehead. "Aye, miss." The treacle in his dark eyes glimmered as his gaze met hers. "The object of my affairs is standing before me at this very moment."

Chapter Twelve

Hugh's inner thighs shuddered as he tried to control the torturous throbbing beneath his sporran. Clenching his bum cheeks didn't help either. God's teeth, if only Farley and his wife weren't waiting outside, he could take his time and savor holding Charlotte in his arms. Her full breasts plying his chest were practically enough to send him to the ragged edge of madness. He'd never wanted a woman this much in his life, never experienced a body so supple, a woman whose half-lidded gaze told him how much more she craved from him—how ready she was to experience the heights of passion. Och aye, and Hugh was the man to take her there.

God Almighty, he was hard enough to spill right now.

He sucked in a deep inhale, clearing his head ever so slightly. On the other hand, it was probably best for the lass to have a guardian angel beyond the doors.

Charlotte smiled, her breath coming in short gasps. Aye, Hugh had seen desire written on a woman's face before, and the focus of her violet eyes upon him made it all the more difficult to maintain control over the deep fire raging in his ballocks.

There wasn't a padded seat in the chapel, but the altar would do. How could God object to a love as pure and unfettered as theirs? Hugh licked his lips as he contemplated his harebrained idea.

Christ. She's no alehouse tart, and I'll not treat her like one.

"Hugh?" she uttered his given name for the first time.

The seductive breathlessness of her voice reignited his deep yearning to possess her in a carnal way. "Aye?" he rasped.

"I want to see you again."

A low growl rumbled in his throat. "Rest assured I'll find a way to hold you in my arms every day I am here."

"But how?" She bit her bottom lip. "'Tis terribly embarrassing to admit...ah...but my father has given his permission to Doctor Munro to court me."

Though aware of this fact, a vise clamped around Hugh's heart as well as his gut. He abhorred the thought of anyone placing their hands on his woman. If the physician had been nearby, Hugh would gladly challenge the cur to a duel of swords. He forced himself to lower his arms and step away. God's bones, she wasn't his—not yet. "Have you enjoyed Munro's...ah...affections?" Simply uttering the man's name made the blood pulsing through his veins turn to ice.

The curls at her temples bounced with her shaking head. "I've repeatedly told him no, but the physician is awfully persistent. And then..." Her eyes shifted aside.

"Yes?"

"My father insists it's a good match. But I—I." She cupped her face in her hands and murmured a sob. "My life is such an utter mess."

Hugh stepped nearer and again wrapped his arms around her—a wee bit less passionately this time. Damn, he was being selfish wooing the lass. Aye, he might be the heir to the chieftainship of Glencoe, but presently he lived in a long-house with a dirt floor and nothing but a few ramshackle pieces of furniture and a wee hearth with a rickety grill to cook upon.

He smoothed his hand up and down her back. "You are a fine woman—a delicate lady bred for a life of privilege. Would you prefer it if I left you be?" He felt as if he'd taken a dagger to his own heart, but Hugh forced himself to continue. "A man like Munro can support you in grand style—mayhap in a city like Edinburgh." The last place Hugh wanted to live was behind the walls of a city where humanity crammed into tiny apartments and tossed their shite out the window when the bell rang at one after the nooning hour.

But Hugh wanted her so goddamned badly, he was willing to risk everything to hear her confess the desire he knew she held in her heart. Too often their attraction had connected as if lightning arced between them. Never in his life had he experienced such a powerful need for a woman and, by God, he'd seen enough to know she shared the same passion. He held his breath and watched as he opened his arms and allowed Charlotte to step back.

She tipped up her chin, a look of determination in her eyes—so bloody beautiful, Hugh had to force himself not to place his palms to her cheeks and shower her with adoring kisses. Before she spoke, Charlotte inhaled deeply. "No. I meant what I said—I do want to see you again, ever so much," her voice trailed off as she crossed her arms and turned her back as if troubled. "But I cannot ask you to take such considerable risks. No, I could not live with myself if something happened to you because of me."

Jesus, the woman feared for his safety? Hugh placed his palm on her shoulder and kneaded. "You needn't worry about me, lass."

"My father is a reasonable man, but even he has his limits. And the times are so perilous. Papa is desperately writing to London every day to encourage the king's advisors to remain at peace, but there are officers in the fort who would undermine my father at their first opportunity."

Hugh squeezed his fingers. "Are you afraid?"

"For you?" Charlotte faced him. "Most definitely. You met Lieutenant Colonel Hamilton. He's a snake, that one."

"I recall." His eyebrows waggled with his grin. "But a man like Hamilton is not to be feared. He's the one who is afraid. I've seen it in other men. His own hatred eats away his insides." Hugh reached for the lovely hand. Bless it, the softness of her fingers nearly made him groan with his need to have her hands upon his flesh. "What harm would it cause if Hamilton found out about us?" His voice grew huskier with his every word.

The corners of her mouth pulled down. "I fear he'd find a way to use our *alliance* against my father. And Papa would be forced to do something rash—mayhap even send me away."

"For loving a Highlander?" He'd best tread with care or he'd lose Charlotte before he'd had a chance to woo her. Lord, the government party grew more unreasonable by the day. He led her to a pew and gestured to the seat. "Your father would do that?"

She took a seat and scooted along the pew. "If provoked by that dastard. Some of the men are haters and feed on the rubbish spewing from Lieutenant Colonel Hamilton's mouth. I cannot even allow myself to consider what he'd try to do to you as well."

Hugh rubbed his hand over his throat. They'd find an excuse to send him to the gallows especially if anyone figured out he'd been a guest in Fort William's pit—and all for loving a lass who was supposed to be in love with a physician. "Och, I did not come here to worry about a pack of miserable officers. I'll find a way to see you, no matter what." He slid onto the pew beside the lass and laced his fingers through hers.

She squeezed his hand. "It grows worse. I take the

evening meal at the officer's table, and you wouldn't believe the horrible things they discuss."

"Like?"

Closing her eyes, she drew a hand over her mouth. "I cannot utter it."

"Let me guess." He leaned close to her ear, nearly losing his thought for her heady fragrance attacking his senses. "They're none too fond of Highlanders or the Highland ways," he managed in a low burr.

"Yes," she whispered.

"They think all Catholics should abandon their religion and become Protestant because that's what the king commands."

"Yes."

"And I imagine they have nothing good to say about Clan Iain Abrach of Glencoe because our lands border with Argyll and Breadalbane." Hugh closed his eyes and inhaled. God, he'd heard all of these distorted biases a hundred times or more when taunted by the guards during his incarceration in the bloody pit.

She nodded, moving her hand over her heart. "The Campbells have the king's ear—and more so the Master of Stair."

A lump tightened in Hugh's gut. "Because they are earls."

"Yes, and they have embraced the Protestant faith." She cringed again.

"Do you think that's important?" Hugh asked, holding her hand tighter, lifting her fingers to his lips.

"I believe an individual's relationship with God is personal. 'Tis different for everyone." She leaned into his shoulder, a warm and loving gesture. "I know 'tis blasphemous for me to say, but I do not believe a person's religion can change depending on who occupies the throne."

A slow breath of air whistled through Hugh's lips. "If only

you were in John Dalrymple's place as Master of Stair, the times mightn't be so precarious."

She chuckled. "If only a woman could be allowed to hold such an esteemed office."

Hugh nuzzled through ringlets and the lace of her bonnet, and pressed his lips to her ear. "In all the world there is only one woman who has ever stirred my blood the way you have done, Charlotte. Let us speak of this no more and enjoy our moments together."

"Yes." Turning her head, she inclined her lips toward his. "I shall think of the evil lurking outside this sanctuary no longer."

As her eyelids fluttered closed, Hugh closed the gap and captured her mouth. A very fast learner, Charlotte returned his kiss with a wee moan while joining his tongue in a magical dance. It only took a wee tug to puller her onto his lap. She nestled atop him as if made to be there, combing her fingers through his hair. The soft cushion of her buttocks molded against his hardened thighs through layers of skirts and wool. Hugh slid his hand down to her hem and held it there, the idea of running his hand up a silken leg made him grow harder than the bronze cross atop the altar.

God's bones, the damned cross shining across the nave is worse than an accusing glare from Ma.

Hugh closed his eyes and deepened his kiss while letting the hem drop.

Taking in a deep breath, Charlotte rested her forehead against his. "I am powerless to resist you."

He slipped his hand across the back of her sultry hips. "Me as well—more than you know."

"I go to the market on Wednesdays. Will you be there?"

Hell, it was only Monday. "Aye." He winked. "And I'll find a way to steal a kiss on the morrow as well."

"But—"

He didn't let her object, sealing his promise with another claiming kiss.

❧

CHARLOTTE'S FINGERS TREMBLED AS SHE TRIED TO embroider perfect heather blooms on a kerchief she'd started to make for Hugh. Her insides still fluttered from the titillating liaison she'd had with the handsome Highlander in the chapel, though she hadn't seen him today as he'd promised. Regardless of her mild disappointment, she would venture to the market on the morrow and he'd definitely agreed to be there. Surely he would have had difficulty arranging another meeting so soon—not to mention persuading Emma to play along this time would have taken nothing less than a direct order from the colonel.

"You've appeared in good humor the past two days," said Papa from his writing desk.

Charlotte sat upright, her eyes popping wide. *Does he suspect something?* One of her shoulders ticked up as she feigned a bored expression. "Truly? One must make the best of Scotland's long winters, I suppose."

"Well, 'tis good to see someone happy in this damnable fort."

Charlotte gasped at the creak of a floorboard beyond the door. "What was that?"

Papa shrugged. "A servant, no doubt."

True, it could have even been Emma climbing the stairs to make ready for Charlotte to change into her nightdress. But then, Emma usually used the servant's stairs at the rear of the house. Oh well, if Papa wasn't bothered, she'd let it pass.

Reaching for a missive, Father perused the letter, his head shaking along with a low grumble.

"What is it?" She leaned forward as if she could peer over

his shoulder from across the room. Papa kept a tight lip about the missives that came from his superiors in Edinburgh and London—he even locked all of his correspondence in an oaken chest that sat in the center of the sideboard. As an additional measure, he carried the only key around his neck. Charlotte kept her nose out of his affairs. All her life, he'd made it clear that as an officer of the crown, he had a duty to keep confidential all information, disseminating details only when necessary to inform his subordinates of information consummate with their rank.

He frowned and folded the letter. "'Tis nothing to concern you, my dear."

"Is the Master of Stair happy with the number of clan chieftains who pledged the oath?"

"I doubt the Master would be happy if half the clans under my jurisdiction pulled up roots and sailed for the Americas."

"Why?" Charlotte set aside her embroidery. "Does he want to claim the land for himself?"

A rueful snort blew through Papa's nose. "I do believe that man would prefer to see sheep take over the Highlands."

"How awful. I do hope you are jesting."

"I wish I were." Da carried a handful of missives to the sideboard and opened the box.

"Is there anything you can do to make him see reason? Has he ever been up here?"

"Unfortunately, no. The Master relies on reports from his cabinet ministers who are all peers with vast estates. He even listens less and less to the pleadings of the Scottish Parliament, preferring Breadalbane and Argyll who have established residences in London to bend his ear."

Charlotte had heard of the two Campbell earls—they had a great many enemies, and Hugh's clan was in the middle of it. "Are they not to be trusted?"

Papa locked the strongbox and sighed. "They are powerful men, intent on growing their wealth. If I've learned nothing during my two assignments in Fort William, the clans and the men who lead them are more interested in their own lands and affairs than anything else. Anything that will help them increase their own wealth and power is appealing."

"But isn't that the way throughout Britain?" Charlotte asked with a sarcastic edge to her voice. "Is there an earl in the kingdom who is a true philanthropist?"

Scratching his grey-stubbled chin, Papa shook his head. "I cannot think of a one."

Though not surprising, the news left Charlotte unsettled, and she resorted to rephrasing her first question. "So, if the Master of Stair's missives reflect displeasure with the Highland chieftain's support for King William, is he planning retaliation? Is that why the number of troops at the fort have doubled?"

Holding up his palms, Papa crossed the room. "You are too perceptive, my dear—such observations must be kept mum." He pulled Charlotte to her feet, looking a tad disconcerted. "Let us say he's not taking any chances. If my letters requesting amicable encounters are heeded, the growing army in this region will only serve as a reminder that we will not tolerate an uprising like the one led by Bonnie Dundee. The king wants to make it utterly clear that all action against his sovereignty will be met with a wall of force."

Her stomach fluttered with hope. "So, those who signed the oath are indemnified?"

"I suppose they are, as long as they keep their noses clean." Papa led her to the door. "But I do believe it is time for you to retire, my dear. You mustn't let this worry you in the slightest. This is army business and I'm doing everything possible to maintain peace."

"And lift the embargoes?"

He chuckled. "One thing at a time, but yes, that too."

"Thank you, Father. It warms my heart to know you are not anxious to take up arms like some of the younger officers in your ranks."

He opened the door and chuckled. "Perhaps I should keep you from the dining table. It appears Hamilton has put fear into your heart."

She paused in the doorway. "Anyone would shudder when listening to his banter about snuffing certain clans."

Her father grimaced with a hiss. "With luck, mayhap the young officer will receive a transfer."

"Have you requested one on his behalf?" Charlotte crossed her fingers behind her back.

"More than once." Papa nudged her into the corridor. "But enough talk about that. I've already divulged too much and do not want to overburden you." He kissed her cheek. "Sleep well."

Charlotte stared at the closed door. *I must tell Hugh how much the clans are being watched.*

Chapter Thirteen

Hugh waited until dusk to make his next move. Dressed in a woolen doublet atop a saffron shirt with his hunting plaid belted around his waist and slung across his shoulder, he walked through Fort William's gate like any other Highland scout working for the government. To ensure not to be recognized, he'd shaved clean that morning and cocked his bonnet low over his brow, tying his hair at his nape. There were so many redcoats about intermixed with men in in plaid no one paid him any mind. At first, Hugh considered it odd he wasn't questioned, but then the dragoons were on the lookout for armed regiments of Highlanders, not individuals who looked like trackers employed by Colonel Hill.

Walking with purpose, Hugh strode to the governor's house, his gaze shifting all the while. Lamps flickered behind the curtain of the governor's chamber and, above, a dim glow illuminated lace curtains, decidedly feminine. When certain no one watched him, he slid through the close to the rear entry.

Holding his breath, he listened.

"That ought to do it for tonight," said a man with a lowborn cockney accent.

"Mayhap we can make it to the alehouse for a pint," said another.

"You're a man of priorities." The latch creaked. "I'll dump these slops and we'll be on our way."

Hugh barely had time to back away when the door burst wide with a showering of light. A red-coated dragoon with bow legs tottered down the two steps and into the darkness. Skirting around the side of the house, Hugh's toe caught an axe handle, making it scrape across the cobblestones.

"Barney, is that you?" called the man tossing the slops.

The door swung open "Huh?"

"What're you doing?"

"Waiting for you, ya bloody blighter."

Hugh peeked around the corner as the dragoon moved into the light and set his bucket down. He drew his dagger, pointing it in Hugh's direction. "I heard something over there."

"Probably a rat," said Barney.

Ballocks. Straining to see where he was placing his feet, Hugh dashed for a tree, and plastered himself against the far side, praying the white of his collar wouldn't catch the moonlight.

The two old dragoons crept around the back of the house with their knives drawn.

Keep going, you bastards.

"I swore I heard something—'twas larger than a rat, it was."

When they reached the front corner of the house, the one with Barney's voice stood and sheathed his dagger. "Well, whatever made the noise is long gone. Come, I need a pint afore you start chasing ghosts."

Hugh crouched by the tree until the dragoons were well

out of sight before he stepped out from behind the tree and slipped into the kitchen. Once inside, he waited for his eyes to adjust before turning the handle on the door and popping his head into the corridor. Muffled voices came from the direction of the governor's chamber. First Colonel Hill's reedy baritone, followed by the sultry pitch of Charlotte's alto. Gingerly stepping on the balls of his feet, Hugh proceeded to the steps.

Halfway up, a stair creaked under his foot—loud enough to wake the dead. Hugh froze, his gaze shooting to the line of light glowing beneath the governor's door.

"What was that?" Charlotte asked, her voice resounding up the stairs, rekindling Hugh's fire burning with his yen to again hold her in his arms.

His fingers twitched. *'Tis I come to make good on my promise, lass.*

"A servant, no doubt," came the colonel's reply.

Hugh grinned and continued up to the second floor where he'd seen the lace curtains. This whole charade was far easier to orchestrate than he'd imagined. Holy hell, he figured at the least he'd have to do some fast talking at the gate—and at the worst, he might throw a fist or two. But aye, he'd promised Charlotte he'd see her today, and a MacIain always kept his promises.

Opening the door, Hugh's breath stopped as Mrs. MacGregor whipped around.

"You?" her fists snapped to her hips. "What on earth are you doing up here of all places?" she chided in a loud whisper.

Foiled at the last turn, Hugh held up his palms. "I promised the lass I'd see her this day." And he'd thought slipping inside had been child's play?

Mrs. MacGregor emitted an exasperated cough. "In her bedchamber? Do you realize exactly how disgraceful this appears? Have you thought nothing of Miss Charlotte's reputation?" She snapped her hands to her linen coif. "You cannot possibly remain here."

Hugh would have rather fought a dozen dragoons with his fists than meet up with the sharp-tongued wife of a friend. How dull could he have been not to realize Mrs. MacGregor would be waiting for her mistress? "Please. I must see her if only for a moment," he pleaded.

"That might have been permissible if you had knocked on the house door and asked her father for an audience—"

"He would have refused."

Mrs. MacGregor pursed her lips and glared.

A door closed. Footsteps pattered up the steps.

"You miserable, bull-witted Highlander, I cannot believe I'm going along with this." Farley's wife grabbed Hugh by the arm and pulled him inside, careful to ensure the door closed without a sound.

His heart spiked with a volley of rapid beats. "My thanks."

"If this results in me losing my position, it is you who will make up my wages."

Hugh grinned—good thing the beef had sold well in Glasgow last summer. "Gladly."

Emma thwacked him on the shoulder. "Farley told me you were a wily sort."

He gave her a wink. "Och, matron, I like the word *determined* better."

When the door opened, Hugh and Mrs. MacGregor stood side by side, looking like a pair of children caught with their fingers in Ma's plum tart. Charlotte's eyes popped as she gasped. She quickly closed the door behind her. "Good heavens, was that you I heard in the passageway?"

"M'lady." Hugh slid his foot forward and bowed. "'Twas on the stairs, actually."

Pushing him forward, Mrs. MacGregor looked about as happy as a patient sitting in a traveling dentist's chair. "Now say your good days and I'll spirit you down the servant's stairs."

"He must leave so soon?" Charlotte moved toward him, reaching out her hands. Lord, he could go dumb looking upon such radiance.

"Not to worry, Mrs. MacGregor." Hugh clasped the lady's lithe fingers and warmed them in his much larger palms. "I managed to slip inside. I can show myself out."

"You cannot possibly tarry," the woman persisted. "First of all, the gates will be locked at half past seven, and then you will be trapped within."

Hugh glanced at the ticking clock on the wall and reluctantly released the lady's supple hands from his grasp. "That allows me an entire hour."

Charlotte looped her arm through his. "Yes, indeed it does."

Lord, the lady impressed him more and more.

Mrs. MacGregor shook her head, wringing her hands with a woeful scowl. "But he should not be in your bedchamber, miss. If anyone discovers him, it would cause a *mortifying* scandal."

"Who will find out?" the lass challenged—honestly the woman had so much more grit than her diminutive stature would ever suggest. "Papa's chamber is below, I've already bid him goodnight, and I've sworn *you* to secrecy."

"No, no," Mrs. MacGregor's face turned from pink to red. "I must help you change into your nightdress—and I cannot remain within the walls after half-past seven. My husband will be worried to death if I do not walk across home's threshold within the hour."

After unthreading their intertwined arms and kissing Charlotte's hand, Hugh grasped Mrs. MacGregor's elbow and started toward the door. "I'm certain Miss Charlotte will be able to cope without your services for a single evening."

Mrs. MacGregor yanked her arm away. "I will not hear of it."

"Emma," Charlotte said in a very assertive voice—bless her gumption. "Mr. MacIain is right. I can manage to fend for myself for one evening."

"But—"

"I have made up my mind," the spirited lass continued. "Mr. MacIain has acted as a complete and utter gentleman since our first meeting and I trust he will continue to behave as such." She eyed Hugh sternly.

"Ah—absolutely," he agreed, forcing himself not to wink. That's exactly what he'd sworn to himself before he'd left the guesthouse. He had every intention of keeping that vow—even if there was a bed across the room, so inviting he knew it had to be topped with a feather mattress.

Frowning, Emma looked between them and held up her finger. "Truly, I should run down the stairs and inform the colonel forthwith."

Hugh started forward with every intention of pleading with the woman, but she sliced her hand through the air. "If you promise to make for the gate as soon as the clock strikes seven, I will allow it this once. But if you *ever* show up in Miss Charlotte's chamber again, I will have no recourse but to inform the governor of your impropriety."

Barely able to contain himself from wrapping the matron in his arms and giving her a Highland hug, Hugh strode to the door and opened it with another bow. "My thanks, Mrs. MacGregor. I will nay forget your kindness."

"Aye? Well then you'd best heed my warning." She still looked madder than a wee badger defending its burrow.

Charlotte stepped in behind him. "I shall ensure he spirits out of the fort in time. There's no need to worry, Emma."

With one last harrumph, Farley's wife turned on her heel and headed off. Thank the Lord for small mercies.

Hugh let the door close, and for good measure, he bolted it. His heart suddenly hammered in his chest. Charlotte clutched her hands under her chin, biting her bottom lip. "I cannot believe you're here."

He released his sword belt and placed his weapon atop the dressing table. Then he turned and inched toward her, one corner of his mouth turning up. "I cannot believe Mrs. MacGregor didn't boot my arse down the servant's steps."

"If I hadn't stopped her, I believe she would have." Charlotte's cheerful face brightened everything, even his mood. Heaven help him, every time he saw the lass she grew more alluring.

With a low growl, Hugh sauntered toward her and tugged her into his arms. "'Tis good to ken you have a headstrong Highland woman who looks after you when I'm not here."

Charlotte's hands slipped around his waist, sending shivers coursing across his skin. She blessed him with a coy smile, her eyes bright with an intelligent challenge. "Oh? Do you think I need to be tended?"

She felt so damned good in his embrace. The bed across the room called like a ship's bell, but he closed his eyes and pressed his lips to her forehead. "Aye, especially with so many red-coated officers mulling about."

Her body shook with an adorable giggle. "Pardon me, but my father wears one of those uniforms."

"And he kept me in the pit for nearly two years." Remembering his manners and his vow to be a gentleman earlier, he held her at arm's length.

Charlotte cringed. "That *is* dreadful. I can see where your opinion might be tainted by such a horrible experience."

"A wee bit, for certain." Hugh's eyes strayed to the bed. Lord, only a flesh and blood man, how was he to keep from gathering the lass in his arms and...? Absently he reached up with both hands and tugged the pins from her golden tresses.

In a blink, thick waves cascaded all the way down to her waist. Sultry and a wee bit disheveled, she pushed her locks behind her ear as the honeyed wisps flickered with amber in the candlelight. God's teeth, must everything about this woman turn the hunger in his loins ravenous?

Perfectly bow-shaped lips curved up to him while Charlotte's eyes fluttered closed. Hugh's mind could no longer form a coherent thought. With a feral growl, he pulled her flush against his body and kissed her. This time his insatiable urges claimed his mind, and rather than softly brushing his lips across her sultry mouth, he plunged inside and joined with her, desperate for more.

With a wee mewl, Charlotte melted into him, her breasts plying his chest. Damnation, such perfection begged to be released from the cage of her stays. Connecting with her mons, Hugh's cock grew so rigid, with one more deep swirl of his tongue he just might spill. Christ, he'd never been so aroused in his life—and merely by a kiss. He'd always maintained a modicum of control—took charge of the woman in his arms. But by the saints, must her breasts be so damn enticing?

His fingers itched to caress them, cup them, tease the taut nipples hiding beneath her corset. Pulling away her lace privacy panel, Hugh ran the back of his knuckles over the tops of her pliable flesh.

Charlotte threw her head back and released the most fevered moan he'd ever heard come from a woman.

Mercy save him, his cock grew harder while he rubbed his hips into her. It wasn't enough. Too many layers of clothing separated them. If only he could strip her bare, be naked with her on the damned bed calling to him from across the floor. He could practically feel himself sliding into her, joining with her intimately—her hot, molten core surrounding him. Trailing his lips down her slender neck, his hand slipped to the back of her bodice and found the bow. With a tug, the laces released as her gown slackened.

Charlotte arched her spine as his finger slipped beneath the neckline and found a hard pearl ready to be suckled. "Hugh," she said breathlessly. "We must stop."

Stopping was the last thing he had on his mind. She knew he was but a Highlander—descended from the Lords of the Isles. Descended from the loins of men who lived hard—who found what they wanted and refused to let any man stand in their way until they'd conquered. Charlotte knew he was from Clan Iain Abrach of the Coe—the most feared and respected clan of the Gallows Herd, moreover, she knew he was heir. With his quick inhale, he sensed she liked the danger—it fed her—tore her from her bashfulness and ignited a fire in her loins just as it did his. Christ, he wanted to claim her as his woman. Now.

Ignoring her plea, he ran feathery kisses over that silken flesh. He couldn't stop until he released the tiny pearl from its corseted prison. "Please let me taste you."

A sharp cry caught in the back of her throat with her feeble attempt to push him away. Oh no, the lass wanted this more than she could allow herself to realize.

Ever so slowly, he pulled down her bodice, exposing her corset and shift. "No woman has ever looked so....so *delicious*."

She panted. "You've seen many women in such a state of undress?"

Behind her back, Hugh found the bow at the base of her corset and expertly pulled until the tension slackened. "None so entrancing as you, m'lady," he growled. "You have me completely and utterly bewitched."

Hugh tugged the ruffled linen until the rose of her nipple teased him. His knees trembled as he leaned down further to take the tip into his mouth. Gooseflesh spread across her milky white flesh as he teased her to a hard point. Och aye, she couldn't hide her desire from Hugh MacIain.

Whimpering, Charlotte further arched into him. "How can you make me feel so rapturous? My fingers ache to sink into your hard flesh."

He groaned while a bit of seed leaked from the tip of his cock. Did she have any idea what she'd just said? Breathing out a stuttered breath, he pushed aside his sporran and held himself against her. Though wool skirts and petticoats separated them, his cock honed in on her heat steaming through the layers.

Charlotte met his bold move with arousing whorls of her hips, wee gasps catching in the back of her throat.

His eager fingers felt like they'd grown five times thicker as he fumbled to work the laces free. Damnation, his hands were even shaking as he pulled the satiny ribbons loose. Finally releasing her from the cage of clothing, he cast aside both her bodice and corset. "Lord in heaven, do you ken what you're doing to me?"

"No," she uttered breathlessly. "But I cannot stop myself. My longing burns so deep within. It is you who are vexing *me*."

He could no longer stand in the middle of her chamber with his shaft seeping seed into the wool of his kilt. Lifting her into his arms, Hugh carried her to the bed.

When he laid her down, she swooned into the pillows, raising her arms above her head. God, her tresses framed her face like a goddess. With a sigh, her breasts strained against her shift, giving him an eyeful of the heavenly female figure beneath the thin linen. Such a delectable sight she posed—the lass could not possibly understand the depth of her allure. Hugh's palm perspired as he kneeled beside her and placed his hand over the decadent mound.

Jesus, Hugh had enormous hands, but her breast filled his

palm as he kneaded his fingers while he plied the tender skin at her scooped neckline with flicks of his tongue. God save him, she smelled of a field of roses and tasted sweeter than port wine.

Drawing her hands over her mouth Charlotte gasped. "Hugh. How did we end up on the bed?"

"I think we must have floated," he whispered.

Pushing herself up, she brushed the tangles of hair from her face. The woman could not possibly look more ravishing. Her mere gesture set his ballocks afire. "But we mustn't remain *here*."

"Why should we not?" Trying to regain a modicum of control, he rolled to his side and toyed with the lace on the front of her shift. "Are you still aiming to marry the surgeon?"

"No."

He slid his lips to her ear. "Then marry me, lass."

"Oh," she gasped. "Oh, help me. I've craved that since the moment we met. But goodness knows Papa would never grant his approval."

Yes, the colonel would need convincing for certain. "If I ravished you, it would leave him with little choice," Hugh said with a cocky grin, though deep in his heart he meant every word.

Charlotte eased back onto the pillows and combed her fingers through her untamed locks. "If you did, every dragoon in the king's army would be out for your blood."

He inched toward her, drew his arm across her waist, and nuzzled into her neck. "But I want you more than life itself."

She smoothed her fingers behind his neck and pulled him until their chests touched with the slightest bit of friction. "We mustn't." She closed her eyes with a wee brush of her fevered lips across his. "W-why are you so entirely irresistible?"

"'Tis the same question I've been asking myself since I opened my eyes and saw your bonny face in the surgery."

MUST HIS EVERY SULTRY WORD WEAKEN HER LITTLE remaining resolve? Charlotte couldn't understand why the man in her arms summoned an insatiable appetite so powerful, she could think of nothing but him—think of no other place she'd rather be than lying on her back, watching his devilishly enticing face. She should have been angry and outraged when he spirited into her chamber like a rogue—yes indeed, his behavior was nothing short of what she would expect from a rascal. In a moment of sanity she tilted up her chin. "I should send you away." Her naughty fingers moved down to the top button of his doublet and released it.

"Is that what you want?" Goodness, the rumble of his voice poured over her like honey.

"Mm hm." She released the next button.

His warm breath tickled her neck. "But I'm not ready to leave yet."

When the last button popped open, she shoved the coat from his shoulders. Raising up, Hugh shrugged out of the doublet then slid back down beside her.

Blocking the needling thoughts of impropriety from her mind, Charlotte rolled to her side and faced him, placing her palm atop his saffron shirt. By the saints, how could a flesh-and-blood man be hewn from pure marble? Her breath became shallow as her fingers meandered over his taut chest. She wanted to feel every ridge of him, every sinew. Her tongue slipped across her lips. The coarse mahogany curls of hair peeping through his neckline made her hands tremble—her insides ignite with a fire that burned from her lips to her breasts to that unspeakable place she must never mention.

Biting her bottom lip, Charlotte pulled the leather thong,

desperately wanting to see more of him. Hugh's breathing grew labored as she spread the laces and slid her hand inside his neckline. Her fingers brushed powerful flesh she suddenly had to taste, just as he had tasted her breast. Timidly at first, she slid down and pressed her lips to him, then trailed kisses along the solid chest until met with a tight bud of rose. As he had done to her, she swirled her tongue around it, shocked to have him harden with her kiss.

"Mm," he groaned.

The sound of his deep voice rumbling in his chest increased the yearning inside Charlotte's body until she feared she might burst. Inching toward him, she slid her arms around Hugh's waist, desperately needing more, but having no idea what.

As if able to read her thoughts, he tilted her chin up and covered her mouth with a fervent caress of his lips. How on earth a man as hard and powerful as this Highlander could be so incredibly gentle, she couldn't fathom. Casting aside all doubts, Charlotte melted into his chest as he pulled her breasts against him. Every inch of her skin alive with desire, she followed his lead—she met each new caress with one for him, wanting him to feel the same churning need building up inside as the desire consumed her mind, body and soul.

Hugh breathlessly ended the kiss, holding his hardness flush against her. Lord in heaven, his every movement took her higher until she thought she might shatter if the intensity grew more.

"Och." He sucked in deep breath. "If we keep on this way, I'll not be able to hold back."

She blinked, suddenly aware of exactly what he meant. Yes, yes, yes, she wanted him so much...but then retained enough good sense to shift her hips away from the rock-hard column jutting against her. "Am I tempting you?"

"Ever so much, lass." His eyes darkened with a devilish

grin. "You're enough to drive a man to utter, insatiable, gripping insanity."

She gasped. "I didn't mean—"

"*Mo leannan*." Before she could utter another word, he rolled Charlotte onto her back diving into a delicious, head-muddling kiss. "What I mean is...if we do not slow our pace, I doubt I'll be able to keep myself from ravishing you."

Chapter Fourteen

With a jolt, Charlotte sat up and crossed her arms over her breasts. "I cannot allow you to ravish me." No matter how much she wanted Hugh's hands on her, his kisses, his deep growls expressing his love, she must resist.

She must.

Her gaze darted around the chamber. She held her palm up to him. "There are too many things that yet must be done. I've tried to tell Doctor Munro my feelings for him run no deeper than friendship, yet he has not accepted my refusal." Charlotte leaned forward, placing her forehead in her palm. "And I must speak to Papa." Heaven only knew what his reaction would be.

Hugh slid up beside her, placing his hand in the small of her back. His hand was ever so warm and tender. Curses, how could Charlotte ever be able to explain how she felt to her father? Everything she'd been brought up to believe shouted the physician was the better match, but her heart could not be ignored. For once in Charlotte's life, her heart won the battle between love and reason.

Hugh leaned on his elbow, looking more tempting than

sweets at the market. "I should be the one to speak to the colonel and ask for your hand. I shall do so on the morrow."

"Oh no. I'm afraid that would invite an uproar of monstrous proportions." She vehemently shook her head. "I must face Papa first, help him grow accustomed to the idea, else you might not make it out of the fort alive."

Hugh chuckled, toying with the tie at her waist. "You think I cannot hold my own with your da?"

"'Tisn't that."

"Aye?"

She clutched her fist to her chest. "'Tis the army of five hundred dragoons you'd have to fight through before you reached Fort William's gates."

Hugh slid his finger from her waist up between her breasts where he lingered for a moment. His lips parted, his eyes so dark they appeared almost dangerous. Then with a devilish grin, he caught a lock of her hair and twirled it around his finger as his tongue slipped out and moistened his bottom lip. "Well then you must make haste, for I cannot wait much longer for you, *mo leannan*."

Lord in heaven, his low growl reignited the heat boiling in the depths of her most sacred place and out through the tips of her breasts. Following his lead, her tongue tapped her top lip as her gaze again dipped to the dark locks curling in the opening of his shirt. She ached to run her fingers through them once more. "I shall do so at my first opportunity on the morrow, and then I'll send word to you via Farley."

"If you believe that is best." Rising up, he pressed his lips to her forehead. Charlotte loved it when he did that. Softer than lamb's wool, his kisses made her heart swell with unabashed joy. Who would have thought that she'd find true love in the most remote part of Britain? And here she'd been planning to return to London. At least Papa should be happy to be released from supporting her, and in turn she would live close enough to Fort William to see him often.

A dong rang out through the chamber. Bless it, if only they had more time. There were so many things she wanted to say—to ask him about Glencoe. Charlotte held her breath and looked to Hugh. "It is time."

The clock struck again.

Hugh threaded his fingers through the hair at her nape and kissed her while the clock sounded twice more. "Och, I do not want this eve to end."

"Nor do I." Charlotte cupped his cheek, savoring the masculine scent of spice and leather that only Hugh possessed. She counted three more tolls while she melted into his delicious kiss. With a sigh, she sat up. "You must make haste."

One more odious dong pealed from the mantel clock. Her heart stopped as she gaped at the ticking timepiece, blinking to ensure her ears and now her eyes hadn't deceived her. "Oh my heavens, 'tis eight! How did we miss the seven o'clock tolls?"

"Mayhap we were a wee bit preoccupied." Hugh raked his eyes down her body, his eyes turning black as coal while they blazed with mischief.

But this was no time to throw all caution out the window. Looking at Hugh only served to make her completely forget her priorities. With a sharp inhale, Charlotte swung her legs over the side of the bed and paced, wringing her hands. "How on earth can you jest at a time like this? The gates are closed. You." She pointed in the direction of the gatehouse. "Are locked within for the *entire* night—the very thing Emma warned against."

Hugh scooted off the bed and strode to Charlotte. "Forgive me." He grasped her hands. "I did not hear the clock toll the seventh hour either."

"How could we have missed it?"

His accursed gaze meandered to the bed. "I was a bit too wrapped up in wooing a bonny lass to be distracted by anything else."

She tugged her hands away and pressed her fingers to her lips. "Now what will we do?"

He chewed his bottom lip, one eyebrow cocked up. "What about the key you used for the postern gate?" Lord his devilish grin set Charlotte's insides aflutter. "You spirited me out once, why could you not do it again?"

"Because Papa was out looking for you, which made it easy for me to slip into his study and borrow his key."

"Blast." Hugh held up a finger. "I don't suppose you could slip down and borrow it again?"

"Not unless you want me to take a chance on rousing him." She cringed. "Lord, we must keep our voices down," she whispered.

Hugh nodded and pulled her into his embrace. Charlotte's head swooned. Why the devil did that have to happen every time he wrapped his arms around her?

"You needn't worry about me, *mo leannan*. I can find a corner in which to sleep outside."

She rested her head against his chest, her fingers slipping up to those intoxicating curls just above his neckline. She was powerless to leave them be. Oh yes, such a virile man, yet his hair was softer than silk. "You cannot be serious. 'Tis *freezing* out there."

He moaned a bit and slid his palm up and down her spine. "I can take care of myself."

"While I worry into a dither?" Charlotte's gaze slipped to the bed...they'd just been there in each other's arms—and it was the most exhilarating experience of her life. Why did this eve have to end now? Why must he go when the gates were already closed? "I think no..."

A growl rumbled through his throat as Hugh smothered her objection with a kiss. Not a feathery, titillating kiss, but a joining of the mouths that staked his claim. Charlotte held on, digging her fingers into his back as he plied her with deep churnings of his tongue, his hard body flush against hers, rubbing side to side, ever so slowly, ever so erotically. She clung to him as if her very life depended on it, trying to match his fervor, his every lick, his every little suck.

Taking a quick breath, she regarded him. "Am I in danger of losing my virtue, sir?"

He gazed upon her with a heavy-lidded stare. "Aye, lass." He cleared his throat and looked to the ceiling. "I mean *nay*. I aim to do this right, *Miss Hill*. But I fully intend to enjoy your company until you boot my Highland arse out of your bedchamber." Grasping her shoulders, he stepped back, panning his gaze down to her breasts while his tongue again slipped to the corner of his mouth. Lord, he was too desirable for words. Did he have any idea what looking at her like that did to her insides?

Charlotte glanced down at her disgraceful state of undress and gasped. She'd forgotten she wore only her shift on top. Thank the stars her skirts remained safely tied around her waist. "I've no idea why I become so audacious and bold whenever I am in your arms, sir." Goodness, the thought of Doctor Munro seeing her in such a state tied her stomach in knots. But for some reason, she felt not a thread of humiliation with Hugh MacIain's eyes upon her.

"Och, lassie, I cannot deny how much I'm drawn to you." He kissed her cheek, then inhaled deeply. "I cannot breathe in enough of your scent." With a low chuckle he kissed the other. "Merely pressing my lips to your succulent flesh makes me hunger for more."

Such passionate words—*mercy*—and such liberties taken should make Charlotte force him out the door, but the searing heat deep inside forbade her from doing such a thing. She ran her middle finger over his shirt collar as gooseflesh rose across her skin. No more powerful, breath-stopping emotion had she ever felt. Truly, they were meant to be together forever.

Charlotte still had enough presence of mind to pose one question. "You will not change your mind...ah...about *us?*" She brushed her fingers over the coarse stubble on his chin as if touching for reassurance. Indeed, he *was* real.

The look on his face grew ever so serious, making him look all the more desirable. Taking her hand between his palms, he dropped to one knee. "Och, Charlotte, I've loved you since the first time I laid eyes on your bonny face. If you'll have me, I cannot think of any other lass in all the world with whom I'd rather grow old. Please, m'lady. Though I now live in a Highland longhouse, I can build you a fine manse with a thousand-foot fortress to surround you. I swear on my life you will never go without or know hunger. You shall have the finest gowns, and horses, a coach to take you to see your da."

Charlotte had never heard such a declaration of love uttered, and from a man on bended knee. All of her wildest imaginings were coming true. A tear leaked from the corner of her eye.

"Will you marry me?" he asked, his voice hoarse, his eyes focused on her as if she were the only woman in the entire world.

"Yes," she whispered breathlessly. "You have my solemn promise there is no other man I would be content to wed."

Hugh tugged her into his arms, pressing his cheek to her abdomen. "I must be the happiest man in all of Scotland."

Her heart fluttered with elation. "We are the happiest couple."

Rising to his feet, Hugh picked her up and twirled in her

in a circle. "I can scarcely wait to break the news to Ma. She'll love you. I ken she will."

Charlotte squealed as her feet flew out and soared through the air.

Footsteps sounded on the stairs.

Hugh set her down, his eyes wide. "Are we not supposed to keep quiet?"

She covered her mouth. "Quickly," she whispered. "Under the bed!"

He knit his eyebrows. "Mayhap now's the time to face him?"

"Lord, no!" She shoved him. "Do as I say. Hurry!"

Thank goodness Hugh didn't try to argue. After he scooted beneath the drapes of the coverlet, Charlotte faced the door, clutching her hands to her chest while Papa's footsteps grew nearer.

A knock came. "Charlotte?"

"Yes?" Curses, her voice shot up too high.

"Did I hear voices?"

She threw the latch and opened the door, peeking her head around it. "I was dancing and...and singing." She cringed. "Apologies if I was carrying on a bit."

Papa frowned looking past her—straight toward the blasted bed. "'Tis late. I suggest you take your rest."

"Yes, Papa. Straight away." She kept her body flat against the door lest he notice she hadn't changed into her nightdress. "Sleep well."

She started to close the door when he stopped its momentum. Her heart nearly stopped as she peered at him, unable to keep her eyes from popping wide.

Papa smiled, patting her cheek. "Oh, to be young and spry. Good night, my dear."

. . .

WHEN CHARLOTTE CLOSED THE DOOR, LATCHED IT AND LET out a long exhale, Hugh felt like the biggest rake who'd ever walked the earth. Hell, he loved Charlotte. She wasn't like any of the other women he'd wooed. In no way did he want to do anything to jeopardize things between them. The fact that she was Colonel Hill's daughter made their situation precarious enough. Hell, Charlotte was right to shove him under the bed. If the governor had discovered Hugh in her bedchamber, it would have been over and the colonel would have strung him up by his cods before dawn.

Charlotte waited until the footsteps faded before she turned and held out her hands.

Hugh slid out from under the bed and brushed himself off. "I should go."

Her breath caught as her gaze slipped down and focused on the unbound laces of his shirt. "Must you?"

"Aye." The word stuck in the back of his throat. The love of his life stood an arm's length away, and he was going to leave her virtue intact and spirit down the servant's stairs? Christ, if he'd had a severe blow to his head, he would have understood, but no, he was behaving like a lovesick simpleton. He was a reiver. A man who always took what he wanted and damned the consequences.

God's bones, Charlotte swished her saucy hips as she stepped toward him. "You cannot possibly leave now. My father would hear you." She reached her arms around his neck and raised her pouty lips.

Oh, Lord in heaven, there he was trying to be chivalrous and she had to turn that pert little mouth up to his, begging to be kissed? With a feral growl, he drew her in with a kiss to match all kisses he'd ever experienced. Och aye, the lass learned fast as she pressed her breasts against his chest— lusciously soft pillows of succulent flesh molded to him, flush against his chest, breaking down his every shred of defense.

He could have slipped outside the door—could have done the right thing if she hadn't been so bloody forward. Damn her, if the wickedly soft breasts weren't enough, she now pushed her mons against his cock.

God, he was so hard, all he could think of was the bed behind him and how easy it would be to throw her down and sink deep inside her. Aye, she was ready, too. Her breaths came in sharp whimpers, telling him what she wanted.

Hugh circled his hips crushing his cock against her—through her skirts—through her petticoats, he could feel her heat, the desire oozing from the soft flesh at her apex. He'd never wanted to take a woman so badly in his life.

Their mouths still joined, his hand slipped down and grasped those layers of skirts. Inching them up, he finally slipped his fingers under the hem. Slowly, he coaxed her legs apart.

Charlotte gasped. "Hugh?"

"Wheesht. We cannot rouse your father." He regarded her with two quick arches of his eyebrows and a cheeky grin. With an exhale, she nodded her assent, her violet eyes filled with trust. Using a feathery touch, he slid his fingers into the hot, moist core of her womanhood. God save him, she was so wet, he could slip into her in one thrust. His cock throbbed, grinding into her hip.

Charlotte arched against him—her hips sliding around his hand. "I think I'm about to shatter." She tensed and tried to pull away but Hugh nuzzled into her neck, coaxing her to relax.

"Let me show you pleasure." Aye, he might show the lady the depth of her passion, but he would not take her this night —not until they were properly wed. Och, he would do this right if it killed him.

"Do you trust me?" he asked.

"Yes." Her reply came with such breathlessness it was almost inaudible.

He first released the string holding up her skirts, then removed one, two, three petticoats.

She crossed her arms over her shift. "Not this."

He grinned. "Are you shy, lassie?"

"No—y-yes."

Hugh didn't mind. He could see every curve of her form through the sheer linen, and he gathered her in his arms and carried her to the bed. Charlotte sank into the pillows while he moved beside her and slipped his hand up her thigh and swirled his finger around the tiny nub just above her opening. With muffled gasps, she yielded to his touch, rocking her hips. Her wee cries drove his pulse to thrum faster.

Hugh rubbed his erection against her hip, teetering on the edge of losing control. He slid his finger inside, and she clamped tight around him. A bit of seed leaked from his cock. If he could only enter her, but he tightened his buttocks and ground his teeth. Damnation, this was for Charlotte—and it was up to him to keep it quiet lest the colonel blast through the locked door with a musket.

Forcing his hips away from her, Hugh kneeled between Charlotte's legs.

Shuddering she tried to sit up. "Wha...what are you doing?"

He placed a palm on her abdomen. "Trust me."

Completely open to him, Hugh gazed on her womanhood, the scent turning his cods to molten fire. He needed to show her pleasure—wanted her to know what it was like to soar with the birds and shatter with ecstasy. With one more inhale of a fragrance more intoxicating than honey, he licked her with his tongue.

A scream caught in her throat.

"Sh," Hugh warned as his tongue again swirled.

She crossed her arm over her mouth.

Sliding his finger into her core, he worked his tongue faster, slipping it over and around her pearl. Up and down Charlotte's hips bucked until all at once she arched her back. Her thighs closed around Hugh's head and shuddered. Muffled cries came from above, while her breathing panted.

Aye...she found heaven.

Hugh slid up beside her and kissed her hair, cradling her against his chest until her gasps eased.

"W-what was that?" she whispered, followed by a sharp inhale.

"'Twas only a sampling of what could be between a man and a woman."

Sighing, she snuggled into him. "That's why I want to be with you for the rest of my life. No man could ever take me to the heights of rapture like that. No man but you."

Chapter Fifteen

✦

Hugh woke before dawn and swiftly straightened his clothing. Sound asleep and curled among the pillows with a comforter pulled over her shoulders, Charlotte looked like an angel, her shiny locks framing her face. The picture she made was bonny enough for a miniature. In fact, Hugh would commission an artist in Glencoe to paint a newfangled miniature for him to carry in his sporran. Then he'd have a wee bit of Charlotte with him always.

They'd spent the wee hours of the night whispering, telling each other about their childhoods, their tutors. Hugh had even told her about his education in France, and Charlotte about her Irish violin instructor.

Hugh had described Glencoe in great detail, trying to bring its grandeur to life in her imagination. He told her about the shielings—the MacIain summer homes where they took their cattle for grazing up by Black Mount. He described the flat grazing lands of Rannoch Moor and why that bit of lush land was oft the focus of the feud between the MacDonalds and the Campbells. He could hardly wait to show her his home. It was far more beautiful than words could describe—not even a painter could capture the magic of Glencoe.

Rather than rouse her, he slipped to her writing table and inked a quill:

30ᵗʰ January, the year of our Lord 1692

My bonny lass,

'Tis Wednesday, is it not? And on this fortuitous day I ever so much look forward to carrying your basket at Inverlochy market. Until then, my heart is in your care.

With deepest adoration and love,

Hugh.

After sanding the parchment, he folded it and slipped it beside her. *Och to be able to sleep like a bairn as she does.*

Afraid he should tarry no longer, Hugh opened the door.

Bloody, miserable, bleeding hell.

Clapping her hand to her chest, Mrs. MacGregor sucked in a gasp so deep, Hugh feared the woman might topple backward.

"What the blue blazes are you doing here?" she hissed, pushing him back into the chamber.

Hugh shot a startled look to the bed and held his finger to his lips. "She's sleeping."

"'Tis a good thing she's the one in the bed and not *you*!"

Hugh cringed. He wasn't about to tell the matron he'd just spent the most erotic night of his life with the slumbering beauty across the chamber. At least Charlotte's virtue remained intact. He could own to that.

Mrs. MacGregor drove her finger into his sternum. "I knew I should have booted you out last eve. I never should have allowed you to remain within."

"Apologies—"

"Hear me now. This will never, ever, not on your life, happen again." She pressed her palms to her head. "Lord Almighty, if the colonel finds out about this, he'll not only dismiss me, he'll hang me from the gallows for certain."

"He would do no such thing," said a stern, high-pitched voice from across the chamber.

Hugh and Mrs. MacGregor snapped their gazes to the bed.

Charlotte clutched the comforter beneath her chin. "To my dismay, neither Mr. MacIain nor I heard the toll of the seventh hour. In fact, I'm quite certain the clock erred."

Farley's wife shook her finger at the timepiece ticking away on the mantel. "I ken what erred and it wasn't the clock."

Hugh bowed deeply. "If you ladies will excuse me, I'd best be on my way." He looked to Charlotte. "I shall see you anon."

Grabbing his arm, Mrs. MacGregor strode to the door. "I will see you out the servant's exit and you will promise never to visit my lady's chamber again. You are a disgraceful rogue if I have ever seen one."

Over his shoulder, Hugh winked at Charlotte, then nodded to his letter.

With a grin, she picked it up and held it to her breast.

Marshalled down the back steps by Mrs. MacGregor, Hugh didn't allow himself to lose his temper with the woman, though she spewed a line of bitter bile. "If I hear one word that you compromised my lady's virtue, I shall have words with the colonel at once."

"She is not compromised," he whispered. Before stepping into the close, Hugh grasped her hands. "I asked Miss Charlotte to marry me."

The woman swooned. "Lord save us, you are touched in the head. Even if Miss Charlotte doesn't marry the physician, Colonel Hill will surely find her another match." Mrs. MacGregor leaned forward and cupped her hands around her mouth. "Someone who's not a *Jacobite*," she whispered as if she were blaspheming.

Hugh narrowed his eyes. "Now that you are serving in a redcoat's house, do you think so little of our Highland ways? Do you think so little of me? Have you forgotten that I rode with your husband in Dunkeld and Killiecrankie when we fought behind Bonnie Dundee?" he could not contain his low growl. "And now *I* am unworthy in your eyes?"

Her lips formed a straight line with wrinkles at the corners. "No." She slapped his back. "Now off with you afore we're both thrown into the pit or worse."

As Hugh slipped through the shadows in the early dawn, a burden lifted from his shoulders. With one word, Farley's wife had reassured him. Emma would not go to Colonel Hill, and with a bit of luck, she would eventually support Hugh's proposal of marriage to her lady, especially once Charlotte revealed the depth of her love and Hugh gained an audience with the governor. His stomach twisted as he made his way to the gate. Having a word with Colonel Hill would be the most difficult part of winning Charlotte for his own.

Hugh stopped dead in his tracks. Riding through the arched gateway, Robert Campbell of Glenlyon propped atop a high stepping stallion. Looking smug in his red coat, wearing a long curly wig beneath his grenadier's hat, the aging "captain" led a regiment of two score and ten men.

The miserable backstabber.

Glenlyon was the worst sort. To serve his gambling habit, he'd raided Glencoe, stealing two dozen of Hugh's black cattle. When Hugh and his men rode past Glenlyon's after the battle of Killiecrankie, The MacIains took their opportunity and retaliated. Hugh stole Glenlyon's worthless stallion. The bloody animal had yet to produce a foal, yet Captain Campbell had lodged a complaint with the court in Edinburgh, to which Da chose not to give the honor of a reply.

Worse, now that a Protestant sat on the throne, Glenlyon had abandoned the Catholic faith and joined the army to support his taste for whisky and his obsession for cards. *At least the bastard has given up praying on the Coe in his old age.*

Of all the Campbells, Hugh trusted Glenlyon the least. The man cheated at cards, had a reputation for being a slobbering drunk, and had a soul as black as the soot in an unswept flue. Armed with every weapon imaginable from new muskets to pikes, shiny swords sheathed in well-oiled leather scabbards, his men rode through the gates like a mob of cutthroat dragoons ready for battle.

What the hell is that snake up to?

Hugh glanced over his shoulder, back toward the governor's quarters. If he alerted Charlotte, she could find out what the colonel had planned for the bastard. But if he dared show his face while the lady was dressing, Mrs. MacGregor would holler so loudly, the entire fort would be alerted to his presence.

Damn. He'd have to wait until he met Charlotte at the market.

As the last Glenlyon horse trotted through the gate, Hugh pulled his bonnet low over his head and hastened away.

❦

WALKING BESIDE EMMA, CHARLOTTE ROSE ON THE TOES of her overshoes to see above the crowd. Though light snow fell, it was a reasonably fine day considering the past month of bone-chilling wind and blizzards. The aisles of the market were filled with townsfolk and soldiers all purchasing supplies in anticipation of more hostile winter weather.

Though Charlotte had brought a list, she had her needs memorized: More lavender silk to complete the heather on

Hugh's kerchief, a packet of hairpins, and a brass button to replace the one Papa had lost from his waistcoat.

"Are you looking for someone or something?" asked Emma.

Her chambermaid had behaved so poorly that morn, Charlotte hesitated for a moment. "Mr. MacIain should be somewhere about."

"Disgraceful...," the woman mumbled with a scowl.

"You mustn't think ill of him." Charlotte peered around a large man who appeared to be planted in front of her, taking up the entire aisle between the tents.

"Hello," said a deep voice as someone tapped her on her right shoulder.

"Hugh!" Charlotte squealed, whipping around to see Doctor Munro's smile fade into a disgruntled frown. Gasping, she drew a hand over her mouth. "What are you doing here?"

"I should be asking you the very same thing." The man looked her over from head to toe. "And who is Hugh?"

Emma grabbed Charlotte's arm. "He's the old MacGregor bard—tells the most fanciful stories."

The physician looked between them, his eyes narrowing. "Oh? And where does this bard tell his stories?" He reached for Charlotte's hand. "Mayhap we should give him an audience."

Emma looked skyward. "Anywhere he can find an ear that will listen."

Charlotte glanced over her shoulder. Curses, the rotund man had moved, and Hugh strode toward them—and he sported an even fiercer scowl than the physician.

Please, Lord, do not let there be an altercation.

Doctor Munro moved his hand to Charlotte's elbow. "I think I'd like to hear this bard spin a yarn. What say you we look for him together?"

"No." Charlotte jerked her arm away.

The physician blinked rapidly. "I beg your pardon. But you seemed to be elated that I might be he."

"Ah, apologies." Charlotte rubbed her elbow. Lord, she hated it when Doctor Munro touched her. "I mean that should not be necessary. I-I...ah...Mrs. MacGregor was just telling me about him."

"He's probably not even around these parts," Emma said in a voice pitched much too high.

Charlotte didn't care. She had to convince the physician to move on before Hugh stepped in and did something rash. "Forgive me, Roderick," Charlotte tried to sound genuine. "But Emma and I have sensitive matters to attend—matters only suited for, ahem, *ladies*." She put it as delicately as possible—perhaps she might need to duck into the nearest dress shop—where ladies also purchased undergarments.

"I see." Doctor Munro turned almost as red as his coat. Removing his hat, he bowed. "Then I shall not impose upon you." Rising, he stopped at her ear. "Though with great anticipation, I will look forward to examining such *matters* on our wedding night."

Charlotte's back stiffened like someone had shoved a steel rod down her corset. As Roderick strode away, she shot Emma a panicked look.

Placing a hand over her mouth, Emma leaned in. "If you aim to marry the MacIain heir, 'tis best you let the doctor know sooner than later."

"I've tried," Charlotte whispered with a cringe.

"Miss Hill," Hugh stepped from behind the tent flap and grasped her hands.

"How did you—?"

He waggled his eyebrows. "When I saw the physician, I thought it might be prudent to step out of sight for a moment."

Thank the good Lord.

"You'd best not tarry," Emma warned.

Hugh gave Charlotte's fingers a squeeze. "I need to talk to you—someplace away from all these prying ears."

Looking around, soldiers mulled about everywhere. Charlotte had never really thought about it before, but the Wednesday market certainly was not a place for secrets.

"Oh no." Emma stepped between them. "I am not allowing you pair out of my sight."

"Only for a moment," Hugh said.

"Absolutely not."

Ignoring her chambermaid, Charlotte turned in place. "Where can we go?"

"Let us stroll to the end of the aisle and then across the street. Did I not hear you say you had *sensitive* matters to attend?"

Charlotte cringed. "What did you hear?"

In a blink, Hugh's face grew dark. "Enough to know I'd like to tear off that swine's horse hair wig and slam my fist into his pasty face."

"Mr. MacIain," Emma chided with a shake of her finger.

He bowed. "Forgive me, matron." Hugh stepped around the woman and growled in Charlotte's ear, "If I ever see him touch you again, I'll make good on my promise."

"I hope he never does." Charlotte placed her palm on his elbow. "Emma was right. I do need to insist the physician accepts my decision once and for all."

"Today would suit." His face still looking much too dangerous, Hugh beckoned Emma. "Come along, Mrs. MacGregor. Miss Hill mustn't be seen in public without a proper chaperone."

The matron shuffled beside them. "Miserable, ungrateful Highlander."

Hugh chuckled. Thank goodness he was in reasonably good humor. Charlotte feared Emma had overstepped her bounds when she returned to her chamber and reported about the scolding she'd given him.

Walking beside Hugh made Charlotte's heart flutter. He looked so strapping in his red plaid. A head or more taller than everyone else, he not only could make good on his promise to defend her from the meddling physician, he could keep her safe from any imaginable harm.

Hugh reached in and twisted the latch, ringing the bell above the door while they stepped inside the dress shop. Charlotte had never given it much notice before, but frilly lace adorned everything from the curtains to the petticoats and corset samples on display on the far wall.

"A moment," the shopkeeper called from behind heavy red velvet drapes. Even they were feminine, trimmed with strands of pink glass beads.

"No hurry," she replied, leading Hugh to the settee.

He turned to Emma. "Where is Farley?"

She shrugged. "On some important errand for the colonel, no doubt."

Gesturing to the seat, he stood and folded his arms. "I must then swear you to secrecy," he whispered.

Emma frowned at Charlotte, before she gave a single nod. Goodness, it was the first time the woman didn't share her opinion with winded bravado. She looked from Hugh to Emma. *He trusts her—and after the chiding she gave him this morn.*

He kneeled before them and leaning forward, he rested his elbow on his knee. "I saw Robert Campbell of Glenlyon ride into Fort William."

Gasping, Emma covered her mouth.

Hugh met the woman's gaze, then grasped Charlotte's hand. "Of all the Campbells, I trust him least."

"The *captain?*" Charlotte asked. She didn't know him well, but recalled the mention of his forthcoming arrival at supper last eve.

"Aye, if you can pin such a rank to a lush who dresses in a red coat and dons a grenadier hat, then captain." He leaned forward. "I need to ken why he's here, and moreover why there are so many more soldiers at the fort than a wee month past."

Charlotte folded her hands in her lap. "Papa says they need to ride on more sorties to continue to keep the peace."

"I hope to God you're right." Hugh looked to Emma.

The matron leaned forward. "There must be more to it than that. Even Farley said he's never seen so many government troops assembled in one place."

"War?" Hugh asked.

Emma spread her palms. "No one kens. Even the dragoons Farley is on friendly terms with haven't a clue."

Charlotte bit her bottom lip. She'd been at more than one meal where Lieutenant Colonel Hamilton and her father had exchanged heated stares. Hugh was right to be suspicious. "What do you need me to do?"

"Will you dine with the officers this eve?" Hugh asked.

"Yes, as is customary."

"Then it shouldn't be unusual for you to ask a few questions." With Hugh's beckoning fingers, everyone leaned in, until all three heads nearly touched. "Find out how long Glenlyon intends to be at Fort William, what are his plans— mayhap talk about how impressive his men looked when they rode in this morn. A bit of praise will make a man like that crow from the rafters."

Charlotte squeezed Hugh's hand. This was the first time any man had trusted her to do something other than to organize the evening's menu. Her heart thrummed a squeamish rhythm. "'Tis almost like being a spy."

Hugh straightened. "Are you comfortable with this? I would never ask you to do something against your will."

Emma placed her hand on Charlotte's shoulder. "Please.

'Tis only a tiny bit of information, and it would help ease the tensions of the locals ever so much."

Charlotte drew her hand to her mouth. Her maidservant supported the Highland cause. And why should she not? She was raised in the Highlands. Moreover, why couldn't all Britons live together in harmony? Wasn't that what King William and Queen Mary wanted? "You realize my father desires peace?"

Hugh nodded. "I believe he does."

"Even after—" Charlotte turned away. She'd almost mentioned Hugh's time in the pit in front of Emma. *Curses, spying is complicated.* "Let me just say not every officer in the fort agrees with Papa."

Hugh stared at her with the darkest, most intense expression she'd ever seen. Oh yes, he could be deadly when provoked. "That's what I fear most," he growled.

"Apologies for the delay," said the shopkeeper, pushing aside the red velvet curtains. "How can I help you?"

Chapter Sixteen

C harlotte sat stiff as a board in her new corset. Of course she couldn't leave the shop without *something* and now she scarcely could eat for the suffocating tightness of new stays. True, her shortness of breath might also be caused by beastly jitters hopping around in her stomach. Why on earth was she so nervous? She'd been around soldiers and officers all her life, but Captain Campbell sitting across the table made her fingers tremble, and not in a good way.

From the moment he'd walked into the officer's parlor, he stared at her with his steel-grey eyes. He reminded her of an executioner—cold and emotionless. And though he had a damning presence, he was a reasonably attractive man near the age of sixty. But more than his unsettling presence, he was loud. He swilled his wine as if it were ale, laughing and swatting the other men on their backs—behavior she expected within the ranks, not in the governor's dining hall.

"Are you confiscating arms?" the captain asked.

Papa stopped mid-chew, as if the captain's question didn't sit well with him. "I haven't seen the need to seize weapons since the battle of Dunkeld."

"Perhaps we should start," the captain continued. "It seems there is more plaid in Inverlochy since my last visit."

"If you ask me, Jacobites shouldn't even be allowed to carry a dagger," said Lieutenant Colonel Hamilton from the other end of the table.

Papa leaned back in his chair, a glass of wine balanced between his fingers. "Even those who signed the oath?"

Captain Campbell snorted. "Och, the only reason the Jacobites pledged their fealty is because the James ordered it from France—word is Spain refused their support, and France is already embroiled in our war in Flanders."

Beside her, Doctor Munro cut his meat with a surgeon's precision. "Well, I say we should confiscate their arms. I'd sleep better at night for certain." He leaned toward Charlotte. "I'd wager you would as well, Miss Hill." At least he didn't refer to her in the familiar in front of her father.

"But we have made so much progress." Papa seemed to be the only sensible officer in the hall. "With our sorties into the Highlands, we've firmly entrenched our presence. The locals have grown accustomed to seeing us, and I believe by the resultant peace, we have made much headway toward avoiding the threat of civil war."

Captain Campbell reached for a bottle of wine and refilled his glass—all the way to the top until it nearly overflowed. "Mayhap 'tis the calm before the storm."

Charlotte watched the men's faces—particularly the highest ranking officers. Papa shot a stern glare to the captain, who then turned his head and smirked at Lieutenant Colonel Hamilton. The sound of cutlery hitting plates ebbed while the room filled with tension that in no way was caused by Charlotte's new corset.

Well, she'd had enough of listening to these men discus how they would benefit from confiscating the Highlander's arms. Such an act would be akin to starving families to death, which was exactly why her father rarely resorted to it.

Dabbing the corners of her mouth, she cleared her throat and regarded the Highland chieftain dressed in the crown's red-coated uniform. "Do your men refer to you as Captain Campbell or Glenlyon?"

The man set down his now half-empty glass and ruefully smiled at the colonel. "Och, the lassie can speak for herself, aye?"

"My daughter is well acquainted with the officer's table, and the resultant gentlemanly conversation." Papa smiled her way. He'd often said having a lady at the table kept even the most unruly officers in line without the need for a pistol in his belt.

The captain leaned back in his chair. "To answer Miss Hill's question, my men address me as Glenlyon."

"Most interesting." She picked up her fork and rolled the handle between her fingers, noting Glenlyon hadn't made use of his. "And how long will you be with us at Fort William, sir?"

He slapped his belly and belched. "On the morrow I'll travel south to pay a visit to my niece afore heading home across Rannoch Moor."

Her blasted stays clamped around Charlotte's ribs, threatening to make her swoon. She rested her fork across her plate and pressed her palm on the table, willing her heart to resume a gentle rhythm. "Is Rannoch Moor the pass through Glencoe?"

"Och aye, the lassie kens a bit about the Highlands does she?" Again Glenlyon posed his question to her father, rather than directly across the table.

"A bit," she replied. Charlotte might be a tad shy, but loathed anyone who acted as if she were too daft to respond on her own volition. "So you'll pass through MacIain lands, then?" she pressed, having been given the perfect opportunity to pursue the conversation further.

Captain Campbell gave her a long stare before he raised his glass. "My niece married Sandy MacIain. Thought I'd pay her a visit to ensure those *thieves* are treating her well."

Charlotte feigned a yawn, tapping her fingers to her mouth while her heart raced. "Do you have any reason to believe they would not?"

Papa slapped the table, making all the wine glasses slosh. "Of course, Alasdair MacIain would not arrange a marriage for his son and then force the woman into slavery. Goodness, Charlotte, you're questioning the man as if he were on the interrogation chair."

She fanned her face. "Forgive me. I thought I was making light conversation." Lord in heaven, she needed an excuse to leave. *Hugh was right, Glenlyon is a snake, and the braggart plans to head directly to Glencoe. I must inform him straight away.*

The captain drained his glass and looked to the others. "What say you? We retire to the drawing room for a pipe and some cards?" He glared at Charlotte. "Or do young ladies associate with the officers there as well?"

"Not unless you wish to hear Charlotte play her violin," said Papa. "She's quite good."

"Oh no, you must excuse me." She pushed her chair back. "I believe I am far too tired to serenade your game this eve."

Chairs scraped across the floorboards as all the men stood —Glenlyon much more slowly than the others.

After a quick exchange of curtseys and bows, Charlotte hastened to her chamber and threw the door wide. "Emma! We must hurry." She ran to the wardrobe and collected her cloak and muff.

"Good Lord, what's happened now?"

"Glenlyon is heading to Glencoe. Says his niece is married to Hugh's brother."

"And you aim to warn him?"

Charlotte threw her mantle over her shoulders. "Of course I do. Would you have me sleep soundly while Glenlyon prepares his soldiers to ride?"

"Think about what it will look like if you hasten to a man who has let rooms in a guesthouse." Emma caught Charlotte by the wrists. "Allow me to pass the word to Farley, he'll deliver the message to Mr. MacIain this night."

She stamped her foot. "But then I will not be able to see him."

"Oh, Lord in heaven, do you have no regard for your reputation?"

"Please." Charlotte shoved her hands into her muff. "I must speak to Mr. MacIain and if you will not accompany me, I will have no recourse but to go alone."

"My word, what is it about that man? I say, Miss Charlotte, he brings out the lioness in your heart." Emma bustled after her. "When I first took this position, I thought you the most mild-mannered Englishwoman I'd ever come across— frail like soft-paste porcelain.

Charlotte hastened down the passageway, straight for the servant's stairs. "Well, now you know differently, do you not?"

❧

HUGH SAT WITH FARLEY AT A TABLE IN THE REAR OF THE alehouse. He kept his back to the wall for two reasons, the first, he could see the door. But most importantly, no one could sneak up behind him. This being market Wednesday, the hall was noisier and rowdier than usual, but that made it easier to have a private conversation. Hugh glowered across the table. "We signed William's bloody oath. So have the MacDonalds of Sleat, the Camerons of Lochiel, the MacDougalls, the Grants, and the bloody MacKenzies for

Christ's sake. Why the hell is the colonel building troops and what in God's name is Glenlyon doing in Fort William? The bastard should be in Inveraray drinking the Earl of Argyll's whisky. Hell, all the Campbells should gather in Argyll's hall, drink him dry, and swindle *each other* at cards."

Farley raised his tankard in toast. "*Sláinte*. Mayhap they'd slit each other's throats while they're at it."

"Och aye, and then we'd send the redcoats home for good."

"Too right." Farley winked. "Except I doubt you'd want Colonel Hill to take his daughter back to London any time soon."

Hugh took a long drink and slammed his tankard on the table. "Miss Hill will not be returning to London."

"No?" The older man arched a thick eyebrow.

There was no use hiding his intentions. "I aim to ask the governor for her hand."

"And if he refuses?"

Hugh tapped his fingers on his hilt. "I'll marry her anyway."

The old tracker leaned back and crossed his arms. "I thought you might say something like that."

The noise in the alehouse suddenly softened to a low hum. Hugh looked past Farley to the door and his heart flew to his throat.

Bundled in a cloak with her hood pulled low over her forehead and clinging to Mrs. MacGregor's arm, Charlotte peered directly at him.

Hugh stood and grinned. "We've visitors of the female variety."

"What the blazes?" Farley twisted in his seat.

As the crowd resumed its banter, Hugh hastened toward the women. "Your news must be grave for you to leave the fort at this hour." He snapped open his pocket watch. "You haven't much time before half past seven."

"I told her the same," said Emma, wringing her hands.

Charlotte pulled a hand out of her muff and shook her finger. "If I speak to the Officer of the Watch after curfew, he'll let me in. Goodness, he'd be thrown in the stocks if he did not." She grasped Hugh's hand. "I've much to tell you."

He glanced at the rowdy crowd. Hell, a brawl could erupt at any moment. "This is no place for a lady. Please allow me to escort you back to the fort. You can relay your news along the way. I imagine your father will want to know the reason for your absence should you miss curfew, and it wouldn't be wise to upset the colonel—yet."

When Hugh heard the news about Glenlyon's upcoming visit to Glencoe, he considered barreling inside the fort to confront the bastard. A Campbell never set foot on MacIain lands without intention to raid.

With Charlotte's hands again tucked inside her muff, Hugh took her elbow and walked on the outside of the foot-path to keep her from being splattered with slush from the passing horses. "He plans to pay a visit to his niece—Sarah?" Hugh should have bloody known Sarah was related to Glen-lyon. "Did he say anything else about why he'd ride into Glencoe in the midst of winter?"

Charlotte glanced up at him. Lord, she could make his heart melt even in the midst of mayhem. "All he said was that he planned to head home after, via the route of Rannoch Moor." The corners of her petite mouth drew down into a cringe. "I wish I would have been able to ask more questions, but Papa stopped me. Would it be possible for his regiment to make the crossing in the thick of winter?"

"Perhaps—weather permitting. 'Tis the most direct path, though it can be treacherous this time of year." Something didn't sit right with him. "Was there any discussion of planned hostility?"

"Father tries to keep the conversation light during the evening meal, but..." Charlotte looked skyward with a sigh.

"Yes?"

"Honestly, you know how soldiers act—always saying vulgar things they don't mean."

"They expand upon the truth?" He chuckled.

"Exactly. The officers jested about seizing arms."

Hugh didn't like the sound of that even if the men had been posturing. "Do you think they'll do it?"

"Papa dismissed their banter, thank goodness. Perhaps some believe the king should enforce such a measure as he has done with the Irish Jacobites, though Father firmly believes such stringent discipline is not necessary in Scotland. Moreover, he talked about how peaceful things were with so many chieftains coming forward and pledging fealty to the king."

Hugh stopped in front of a large puddle and held out his arms with a bow. "May I carry you across, m'lady?"

She glanced down at her hem, though she wouldn't have been able to see it for the darkness. "Why thank you, sir." She giggled as he lifted her. "I imagine my gown is already soiled."

"No sense in making it worse when I am here to provide assistance." Feather light in his arms, Hugh would carry Charlotte all the way to the fort if it were proper. Sighing, he set her down on the other side and resumed his questioning, "Could there be orders from London? Do you know why the number of troops has increased?"

"There are always orders coming—and there is always secrecy. Although..." Her voice trailed off.

"Yes?"

"There may have been more shifts of the eye at the supper table this eve."

Hell, he couldn't take that tidbit of news back to Da. He'd be laughed out of the Coe. "What do you mean?"

"The officers always do it. One says something and a pair of others carry on the thought with subtle arches of their brows—that sort of thing." Charlotte's shoulders shook with a wee shudder. "I hate it when they do that. It makes me think they're keeping secrets."

"I've no doubt they are. 'Tis the way of the army." Hugh could no longer restrain himself from asking, "Have you perchance read any of the missives coming from London—or Edinburgh?"

She stopped, raising the muff up to cover her mouth. "Oh no, Papa never discusses army business with me, let alone show me his correspondence. I do believe he's the most secretive of the lot—he even keeps his letters locked in a strongbox."

Hugh snapped his fingers. "I would assume no less. I'm certain he receives a great many confidential missives, many of which are not intended for public scrutiny."

With the stone walls of the fort nearing, Hugh led Charlotte off the path into the shadows of a sycamore tree where the snow wasn't too deep. "I fear I must cut my visit short and return home afore Captain Campbell arrives." He toyed with the collar of her cloak—if only he could take her with him, but such a cavalier move would bring the redcoats on Glencoe like flies to rotten meat. Rubbing his hand along her shoulder, he pulled her into his body. Mercy, she was shivering with the cold. He rubbed his hands briskly up and down her back, he inhaled sweetness and roses. "I must thank you for all you have risked to bring me this news."

"I only hope nothing comes of it."

"'Tis my wish as well." He closed his eyes and held her tight, memorizing how magically her body molded to his. "If only we were not on opposite sides of this."

"We are no longer opposing," she whispered breathlessly. "Ever since your father walked into Papa's study and asked to sign the oath, you have been with us."

Lead the size of a cannonball churned in the pit of Hugh's stomach. In no way would he ever consider himself a Williamite. Da may have signed the oath, but that was because of a direct order from the true king. "You ken I will always be a Highlander. I'm the heir of the Chieftainship of Clan Iain Abrach of Glencoe. I will never turn my back on my people—you understand that, do you not?"

"Yes, of course, and I'm ever so proud of you." Her fingers plied his back. "But you are on our side now—your father signed the pledge of fealty."

Hugh ground his molars, wishing he had more bloody time. "If only there were no sides." It would take Hugh all night to explain exactly what King William's oath of fealty meant, and that all clans were now watching how the king responded. None of the money promised the clans by Breadalbane had been paid—not a single farthing. Thus far, King William hadn't proved he could keep up his end of any bargain. Regardless, Hugh couldn't risk losing Charlotte. "You and I are an island among many factions. Always keep me in your heart, for our love knows no boundaries."

A sigh whistled through her lips. "I adore how you said that. We are above any army in all of Britain."

"My God, I love you, Charlotte." Tightening his hold around her, Hugh closed his eyes and kissed her, his entire body shuddering with the strength of the emotion welling inside him. Lord, his heart was about to burst, and he hadn't yet asked Colonel Hill for her hand. That task would now have to wait.

She rested her head against his chest. "I love you so much, it pains me to think you are leaving."

"I promise I will return as soon as I am able." He held her at arm's length. "If anything happens, send word with Farley."

Her lovely almond-shaped eyes blinked. "He knows how to find you?"

"He's the best tracker in the Highlands." Hugh kissed her again. "If only I could bottle your essence and keep it with me."

"One more thing." Charlotte reached inside her cloak and fished in the pocket hanging from her belt. "I finished this for you after I returned from the market." She held up a white kerchief with something embroidered around the edge. "'Tis too dark to see, but I've stitched it with a wreath of heather."

"For me?" Hugh held it to his nose and inhaled. Oh yes, honey, roses and woman—exactly the scent that sent him mad whenever he was within ten feet of his Charlotte. "I will have something of you with me after all. I shall treasure this forever. Thank you."

Closing his eyes, he bent his head and claimed her lips one last time. God save him, he wanted to stay. But dammit all, he had no choice.

Pulling away with a sigh, he grasped her hand. "Now come. I'll walk you to the governor's house."

"Oh no. You cannot be caught behind the gates now."

Hugh almost told her no iron portcullis would keep him inside, but she was right on this account. He must make haste to Glencoe, no matter how much he preferred to follow the lady to her chamber and enjoy a repeat performance of last eve's lovemaking.

Chapter Seventeen

Colonel John Hill sipped his sweet sherry, willing it to numb his mind for the evening. He detested both officers who'd joined him for his late night meeting. Campbell of Glenlyon was as pompous as he was a slovenly drunk and Lieutenant Colonel Hamilton had been nothing but a thorn piercing through the bottom of Hill's boot since his arrival nearly two months past.

The colonel would never understand it. He'd been hand-picked to come to Inverlochy after the Battle of Killiecrankie —at the height of Jacobite hostility. King William had granted Hill the governorship and commissioned him to build the fort and maintain peace. 'Twas a promotion Hill had earned from over forty years as a career solider. No living officer had gained as much experience with Scotland's Highlanders as Colonel Hill. And for the past two years he'd fulfilled his charter and had sustained order. As a result, relations had never been better with the Highland chiefs. True, there were a handful of outliers who hadn't yet pledged fealty to the king, but most were unable to make the journey to their respective shires due to inclement weather and deep snow.

Glenlyon reclined in an upholstered chair, tossing a die on the table as if mesmerized by it. Thank God, Hill had the wherewithal to prohibit gambling in the officer's quarters, otherwise Glenlyon would have turned this night into more of a sham than it already was.

Lieutenant Colonel Hamilton maintained his harsh mien. If he ever became Governor of Fort William, there would be a rash of daily hangings, no doubt. "I do not understand why you are stalling. The Master of Stair's missive was clear. We are to act swiftly."

Lord, the young man was a smug bastard, but Colonel Hill knew he needed to tread carefully. Hamilton's family had its tentacles embedded in too many areas of government. "I have a responsibility to act in accordance with my conscious," countered Hill. "As a senior officer to the crown, it is my duty to question the Master of Stair's orders when the king's name is affixed to them without a proper signature, *especially* when the king is fighting a war in Flanders." Hill leaned forward and looked over his reading glasses. "Last I checked, I *am* the senior officer at this fort, and I *will* receive confirmation before I act." *Bloody Christmas, I pray to God the Master of Stair erred.*

The clanking of the die stopped. "Do I march my men south on the morrow or nay?" Glenlyon may be clad in a Williamite uniform, but his burr was as thick as Alasdair MacIain's.

"You march as I commanded," Hamilton grumbled.

Hill clamped his lips shut. *Marching isn't the problem. Let Glenlyon march all he wants. That might keep him away from imbibing in too much spirit for a time.* "But you must do nothing until you receive further orders."

Across the table, Hamilton groaned. "I see no reason to wait. We've amassed enough men."

The colonel eyed him directly. "That is why you are the junior officer."

Glenlyon grabbed the sherry bottle and turned it completely upside down. A single red drop splashed into his glass. The man stuck his grubby finger inside and licked it. "I suppose I should call it a night."

Hill stood. "Thank you, gentlemen. We have our orders and I expect each of you to act accordingly."

Hamilton gave a thin-lipped nod. Hill didn't believe Campbell cared if he had to wait or not. Having been a nuisance to both the Earls Breadalbane and Argyll, the lesser laird's reputation was not far off the mark. Robert Campbell of Glenlyon had joined the king's army at the request of his cousin earls in an attempt to keep him sober and paid. Hill was well aware Glenlyon raided and prayed upon his neighboring clans as much as they reciprocated, but nary a raid had happened since Fort William had come into existence. In truth, the reason for Glenlyon's sorry state of affairs was his insatiable appetite for gambling.

Opening the door of the drawing room to see the men out, Colonel Hill choked on something—it couldn't have been the sherry. A bit of his dinner must have somehow lodged itself in his throat, because for a moment he couldn't breathe, nor could he believe that his daughter spun and gaped at him, wearing a cloak, her cheeks and nose red as if she'd been out in the cold.

With a sputtering cough, he quickly regained his composure. "My word, Charlotte, where have you been at this hour?" Due to the fact they lived within the walls of a fortress full of soldiers, it was the colonel's rule that she retire to her chamber above stairs after every evening meal.

"Ah..." She shot a surprised grimace to Campbell, then to

Hamilton. "I needed some air and took a stroll around the battlements."

Hill waved her to the drawing room. "Please await me inside."

Groaning, she brushed past him.

Captain Glenlyon snorted and swayed. Truly, he had consumed the better part of two bottles of sherry, and the colonel had lost track of the wine pouring down the man's gullet during supper. "Not to worry. I have two daughters of my own." He leaned in, his pickled breath making the colonel cough again. "The best thing you can do is to marry her off. That lassie's far too bonny. She'll be tapped for certain if she continues to live within the walls of Fort William."

Clenching his fists, it was all Hill could do not to slam a left hook across the sniveling maggot's jaw. "I believe you overstep your station, captain. The next time you have such an opinionated remark, I trust you will think through your delivery before you spew your crass drivel to a superior officer." With that, the colonel marched the two men to the door. "I shall see you both at dawn."

Taking a deep breath, Hill faced the door to the drawing room. The last thing he wanted to deal with this eve was Charlotte. And she was such an amenable child. What in God's name was she doing out alone? Turning the handle, he yanked the damned door open. "Please tell me you were taking a turn with Doctor Munro."

"If I said that I would be lying." Damnation, if her face did not possess the innocence of a cherub, he might have slapped her.

Colonel Hill almost would have preferred a lie at this hour. Did she have to look like an angel when she said something so irritating? "Charlotte, I know you are usually a sensible young woman, but I cannot possibly oversee your safety if you ignore my rules." Clutching his hands behind his back, he paced toward the hearth. "It is not proper for any woman to walk unescorted especially after dark."

"I wasn't alone."

Not with the physician and not alone? "I beg your pardon?"

Her chin tipped up. "I was escorted by Mr. Hugh MacIain."

"Of Glencoe?" The colonel spun on his heel, that damned piece of food lodging in his throat again.

"Yes," she said as if she often walked with rogues such as the heir to the Gallows Herd. "If you recall, he was here with his father not too long ago."

How could he forget? The whole sordid affair had his pen scratching missives for the past month. "Of course I remember that ill-fated night, but what the blazes was he doing here—and moreover why did he entertain an audience with *you*?"

Charlotte blushed the color of the red settee.

The colonel coughed, trying to dislodge the bloody piece of mutton. "Oh, Lord in heaven, do not tell me that *barbarian* has taken a fancy to you."

She removed her muff and placed it on the table. "I believe he has, and I quite like him. He makes me—happy inside."

"Lord no. No, no, no. This is preposterous!" He slammed his fist on the table. "You are supposed to be in love with Doctor Munro."

"But I feel nothing for the physician. And...and Mr. MacIain is heir to the Chieftainship of Glencoe—he's a man of property. That should make you happy." Charlotte twirled across the floor. "Do you not understand? Hugh makes me bubble inside."

This cannot be true. Bubbling? 'Tis worse than I thought. The colonel strode across the floor and grasped his daughter's shoulders. "Listen to me. You will block this man from your mind. Do you understand?"

"But—"

He shook her shoulders firmly. "I forbid you to ever see Hugh MacIain again. And I confine you to quarters until I have regained my good humor, which I imagine will be a *very* long time."

⚜

RIDING AT A TROT, THE JOURNEY TO GLENCOE TOOK FAR too long. Hugh stopped at the North Ballachulish ferry and pounded on the cottage door of Archie MacSorley.

The big clansman opened with a lantern in his hand and a sleeping coif atop his head. "Och, are you trying to wake the dead?"

Hugh thrust his finger toward the south. "I need to cross Loch Leven straight away."

The man straightened, pulling his plaid tighter around his shoulders. "Something's afoot. I can smell it."

"Aye, there is. And you'd best hide your weapons in the rafters as there's talk at the fort about confiscating arms."

"Bloody red-coated riffraff," Archie grumbled. "I recon you're looking to be ferried across to your da."

"This cannot wait. Robert Campbell of Glenlyon is heading this way with a full battalion."

"Campbell?" MacSorley stepped back and allowed Hugh to enter. "You cannot be serious. Is the rogue coming to be slaughtered?"

"Coming to visit his niece." Hugh still didn't believe it. "Regardless, be on your guard."

Archie belted his plaid and shoved a woolen bonnet atop his head. "There's a gale blowing. The crossing will be choppy."

"We'd have to find a way to cross even if the loch were covered with thin ice."

In no time they'd boarded the wooden ferry. Planting his feet wide on the flat bottom of the raft, Hugh held his garron's bridle while Archie's weathered hands tugged them through the white-capped swells.

After paying the man, Hugh galloped through the packed snow past the village of Ballachulish, their cottage windows dark for the night. But when he arrived at Da's manse, a lamp glowed in the parlor window.

Hugh pushed inside, well aware Da never bothered to bolt his door. The clock on the wall read quarter past twelve. By the ache in his bones, he thought it no less than the witching hour. Aye, he'd oft traveled faster from Inverlochy, but that had been in daylight and during spring.

Da sat in his overstuffed chair in front of the hearth, a book open on his lap, a smoldering pipe in the tray beside him. His head tilted back and a light snore rumbled through his nose.

"Da," Hugh said, moving forward and placing his hand on the old man's shoulder. "Da."

Sputtering awake, the book dropped to the floor with a thud. "Hugh? What is it, lad?"

"Glenlyon is riding his regiment from Fort William to Glencoe on the morrow."

Lumbering to his feet, Da shoved Hugh aside as he stood and drew his sword. "The bloody bastard. That miserable milksop is the most damnable, putrid swine of the lot of those scandalous Campbells." Da swung his sword through the air with two hissing strikes. "I'll sever his cods, I swear I will."

Hugh held up his hands and took a step back—Da could overreact a bit when awakened. "I'm not certain that is the right tact—though I'd be the first to offer my dirk for the task."

Lowering his sword, Da squinted. "What say you?"

"The captain is stopping in Glencoe to see his niece."

"Sarah?"

"Aye, and there was banter at the officer's table about confiscating weapons."

Da's face went stone blank. "Wait a moment. Who informed you of this?"

"Miss Charlotte Hill—the governor's daughter. Remember? She's the lass who filled our bellies afore we rode to Inveraray."

"I ken who she is." The old man shoved his sword in its scabbard and rested it against the stony hearth. "What I want to know is why was she spouting the king's business to the likes of you?"

"Ah...She's...Um." Hugh straightened, clenching his fists at his sides. "I have to admit I didn't go to Inverlochy for the fete."

Da's eyes grew round as silver coins. "Lord save us. You mean to say you're courting Colonel Hill's daughter?"

"Aye. I aim to marry her."

"Christ." Da threw up his hands. "She's a bloody Sassenach wench—and she's the daughter of the red devil himself."

Hugh folded his arms, raising his chin. "Hill's not the problem."

"You think not? Does he ken you're a courting his wee daughter?"

"Not as of yet."

"Well, you keep up with your harebrained notion, the governor's dragoons will be breathing down our necks for certain." Da clutched his chest. "Is Glenlyon paying us a visit because Hill suspects something?"

Hugh sliced his hand through the air. "Like I said, he doesn't even know I'm courting his daughter...yet."

"Bloody good thing." Gesturing to a seat, Da resumed his. "So if you had to place wager on it, do you think Glenlyon's visit will be a peaceful one?"

"With one regiment?" Hugh scratched his chin. "I reckon they may be merely passing through—may also be spying."

"Then we'll not give them anything to gripe about. What say you? Show them some genuine Highland hospitality?" Da picked up his pipe and lit it from a bit of straw he'd put in the candle flame. "Besides, we signed the oath. We may have been a wee bit late, but I just received word today the MacLeans signed after me—and the Clanranald MacDonalds have not yet come forward."

"Truly?" Hugh's spirits rose for the first time since he'd seen Robert Campbell of Glenlyon ride through Fort William's gates.

"Och, aye." A puff of pipe smoke swirled above Da's head until it dissolved into nothing. "At dawn, we'll inform the men to conceal their weapons in their thatch—aside from any daggers they can hide on their persons. Then I'll meet Glenlyon with arms open—prove to him I'm the most hospitable bloody host in the Highlands."

Hugh sat back and stretched his legs before the hearth. "As long as the men keep their weapons close at hand, I believe your plan is not only smart, 'tis sound."

Chapter Eighteen

❧

Charlotte's fingers flew over the strings of her violin while the horsehair bow strained and frayed from the stress of sawing the strings with vigorous exertion. She'd been screeching out scales and woeful arias since she'd arisen that morn and hadn't a mind to stop. If her father intended to imprison her, she would ensure he heard exactly how she felt about such undue overbearance.

"Miss Charlotte!" Emma hollered, stepping in front of the music stand and waving her arms.

With a shrill downward stroke on the high-pitched E string, Charlotte stopped. She'd been trying to ignore Emma's prodding, but having the woman wave in her face only served to infuse her anger. "What is so important, it cannot possibly wait until I am finished rehearsing?"

"Oh, is that what you're doing? It sounds more like you were calling all the house cats in the shire."

Charlotte straightened the violin under her chin. "Did you stop me to issue an insult? Because I'm fresh out of forbearance this day."

The woman gestured to the table in front of the hearth.

"I need to know if you are planning to eat your breakfast, or if I should remove your tray."

"Bloody Christmas," Charlotte cursed.

"Miss Hill! What happened last night? Did Mr. MacIain behave improperly?" Emma snapped her fists to her hips. "If he did anything to bring on your fit of anger, I'll knock—"

"*Mr. MacIain* behaved like a perfect gentleman as always. It is my father who is a complete and utter pig-headed, bombastic, unbending, maddening—" She stamped her foot. "Nincompoop!"

"Oh, my heavens." Emma drew a hand to her mouth. "Did Mr. MacIain talk to the colonel last eve?"

"No." Tears stung Charlotte's eyes, but she refused to cry. "I told Papa I wanted to marry Hugh and he put me under house arrest."

Emma gaped. "Can he do that?"

"Close enough. He's confined me to quarters. Next he'll throw me in the pit."

The linen coif atop Emma's head jiggled as she shook. "He would never do such a terrible thing."

Lowering her instrument, Charlotte wiped her eyes with the crook of her elbow. "Curses to him. All my life I've tried to be perfect, pious, obedient. I've served Papa as a daughter ought in every way." The accursed tears kept threatening, and streams from her nose oozed over her lips. She set the violin and bow on the sideboard and pulled her kerchief from her sleeve.

The chambermaid stepped beside her. "I'm sure once the colonel becomes accustomed to the situation, he'll see reason."

"I thought he was a reasonable man, but now I question everything about him." Every painful experience she'd had in the past one and twenty years had played in her mind since

Father's chiding last eve. Charlotte hid her face in her kerchief and wailed.

Emma gently grasped Charlotte's elbows and led her to the chair. "Come now, you must calm yourself. I'll order some chamomile tea."

"But I don't want to be calm!" She rocked back in the chair, her arm slung across her forehead. "D-do you have any idea what it is like to be that man's daughter?" Gasping, in a desperate attempt to regain control over her tears, she continued, "H-he was never home. W-worse, I was but ten years of age when Mama fell ill—and where was he?"

Sitting beside her, Emma's brow furrowed.

"He was in Ireland on some superfluous military detail whilst my *mother* died in her bed in..." She panted, trying to take in a deep enough breath. "L-London."

"Heavens," Emma whispered. "How awful."

Hiding her face in her hands, Charlotte wouldn't be able to stop her tears no matter how hard she tried.

"There, there," Emma's calming voice soothed in between Charlotte's sobs. "Everything will work out for the better, you'll see. It always does."

When Charlotte finally regained relative control, the blasted hiccups plagued her. "I—was sent to live with my—aunt and uncle—a—and never allowed to talk about it. Can—you believe it? I lost my mother, and was shut in the upstairs suite with a governess—until I turned six and ten."

Emma's palm stopped rubbing. "Did you not see your father at all during that time?"

"Seldom—an officer makes a living being a soldier, and that leaves little time for family." She finally could breathe and inhaled deeply. "This is the longest I've ever spent with him."

"Well that explains one thing."

Charlotte dabbed her eyes. "I beg your pardon?"

"I've said it afore—you were a quiet wisp of a woman when you arrived, and gradually you have burst from your shell. You ken, I do not believe you're shy."

Swallowing, Charlotte knit her brows. She certainly had been bashful as a child, and honestly, she hadn't thought much about her quietness as of late.

Emma grinned with fine lines crinkling around her eyes. "I think you have a great big heart under all that silk and linen—and being up here in the *wild* is opening your eyes to the iniquities around you." Then she shook her finger. "I have a wee idea you are cleverer than the males in this fort."

Charlotte snorted, wiping her tears. "Is that right? Look who's locked in her chamber." She grabbed the kerchief in her fists. "I've finally found true love and I'm being punished for it."

Emma kneeled beside her. "Aye, but you didn't fall for just any Highlander—it had to be the likes of Hugh MacIain."

"Pardon me? Mr. MacIain is educated, well mannered, and..." *Exceptionally good looking, and his kisses...* Charlotte sighed.

"The way you talk about him, he's the most affable lad in Scotland."

"I wouldn't be surprised if he is."

"He's also Alasdair MacIain's son, with a reputation for avarice."

"Oh? What about the Campbells? I understand they are the greediest clan of the lot."

"Aye, but the Campbells always side with whomever is seated on the throne. That seems to make their misdeeds more acceptable."

This conversation was entirely maddening. Charlotte shook her head at the ceiling. "And that's where the MacIains have failed?"

Emma again smiled, but this time with a faraway glint in

her eyes. "They've the blood of Angus Og pulsing through their veins. They're wild men. Aye, they are educated and know how to be gentlemanly, but when backed into a corner, they are ruthless. You ken Hugh MacIain cannot be bested with a sword in a fair fight—even Farley has a healthy respect for him."

"I had no idea." Though this news only served to cement Charlotte's respect for Hugh. So, he acted out in defense of his home? Who wouldn't do the same? She could not think of a soul.

"Mayhap there are a lot of things about Hugh MacIain of which you are not aware."

Lowering her hands to the armrests, Charlotte straightened. "Perhaps, but I've seen enough to know I'd rather marry him than a disingenuous man like Doctor Munro. Papa wants me to marry the physician? Well, I'll have none of it."

As she stood, the matron brushed her hands on her apron. "Are you certain?"

"I would marry Hugh MacIain this instant if he were here."

Emma looked to the bed, that furrow deepening in her brow again. "What happened between you pair two nights ago?"

Charlotte's face burned and she hid it by blowing her nose. "Nothing that a lady would reveal."

"Did you...?" Emma stood and strode to the bed and pulled back the bedclothes. "Thank God, my suspicions are unfounded."

Jumping to her feet, Charlotte dashed beside her. "Pardon me, but I do believe you are overstepping your bounds."

"I am your servant, hired to see to your care, including protecting you from certain rogues who appear in your chamber after dark." Emma raised her hands skyward. "Lord in heaven, regardless that you managed to keep your virtue intact, I was daft allowing that man to remain in your chamber. He's addled your mind and turned you against the physician."

"Stop!" Charlotte yanked the comforter from Emma's grasp and threw it back over the bed. "I have never cared for Roderick the way I care for Hugh. I *will* marry Hugh MacIain. Bless it, have you not heard a word I've said?" It was her turn to furrow her brow and affect an angry glare. "Whose side are you favoring?"

"Your father pays my wages." Emma thrust her finger toward the bed. "But I daresay not for long, especially if that man ever again sneaks into your chamber."

Crossing her arms, Charlotte eyed her chambermaid whilst a storm roiled in her chest. "With all due respect, I am the one who decides if you are to remain employed here."

Emma wrung her hands and paced the floor. "Oh, my goodness. Forgive me for being so outspoken, but life in Glencoe will not come easy for a well-bred English woman such as yourself."

"Can you not see that a life of comfort does not matter to me?" Charlotte chose to focus on the only thing to set this situation to rights. "Papa will have to see reason sooner or later, and in the interim, I *must* have your support."

"Of course, you have it." Emma picked up the tray and headed for the door. "But I fear we're all doomed."

Chapter Nineteen

❦

The morning of the 1st of February, Hugh and the family assembled in Da's drawing room along with the clansmen who supported Clan Iain Abrach. It was no surprise when the runner appeared at the manse with news Captain Campbell and his retinue had taken Archie's ferry from North Ballachulish and were now enroute to Glencoe.

Sandy leaned against the wall, sliding a dagger in and out of its scabbard.

"Are the weapons hid?" asked Da, though he knew the answer.

"Aye, stashed away in peat stacks or on the brae beneath piles of stones." Hugh humored him. "If the bloody dragoons are coming to disarm Glencoe, the only thing Campbell will find is a pile of rust."

Shoving the dagger up his sleeve, Sandy pushed away from the wall. "Regardless, our arms are close at hand should there be an attack."

"There won't be," said Da.

Hugh arched an eyebrow. "Why are you so certain?"

"Your mother had a dream last eve. Said she saw the

washer woman with two plaids—one Campbell and one MacIain—washing them in the same basin she was."

Hugh rolled his eyes. Ma always had a knack for allaying Da's trepidations, but he wasn't about to be convinced by a dream. He had muskets and swords hidden in the pile of snow along the path to the house. If Campbell so much as hinted at a threat, the bastard would be the first Hugh would kill.

"How many?" Hugh asked.

"Counted sixty-five," said the runner. "Mostly foot, but they all carried muskets."

"Regardless, Captain Campbell is a Highlander." Da took a puff from his pipe and pushed the smoke through his nostrils. "If they're here to parley, we'll extend our hospitality. Nary a man this side of the divide would turn backstabber when a welcoming hand is extended."

"But we'd best be on our guards when we watch them take their leave," said Sandy.

"That won't come soon enough," Hugh mumbled under his breath.

Sarah nudged her husband with her elbow. "Uncle Robert would never double back and slit the throat of a man who took him in. The Campbells are not as ruthless as you lot make us out to be."

"Of course not," Ma said from her chair nearest the hearth. Her knitting needles hadn't stopped clicking since she sat over an hour ago.

"Are you ready, Hugh?" Da drummed his fingers on his trews. "Though we have John Hill's letter of protection, your calm judgement is what I need standing at the forefront of my army."

"I'll make you proud, Da," Hugh said. He wanted it no other way. And by God, he wouldn't stand idle while his father met the snake head on. Oh no, such an err just might be too tempting for Glenlyon. Thirty years younger, Hugh was in far better shape to pose in his chieftain's stead.

Tension hung in the air while they waited in silence, the only sounds: the ticking of the mantel clock, Ma's clicking needles, and the occasional pop from the fire. Hugh's mind rifled through his weapons. He had a dagger up each sleeve, two in his hose and, for good measure, a dirk hidden in his plaid behind his back. Though he preferred to face his opponents sword in hand, his aim was as deadly when throwing knives.

Muffled hoofbeats sounded outside. Alasdair Og pulled back the curtain and peered through the window. "They're starting up the path now."

Da stood first. "May as well go out and meet them." He turned to Hugh. "My sword is in the drift?"

"Beside mine." Hugh looked at Sarah. "And Sandy's musket as well."

The woman gave him a sharp nod. Unsure if she was just going along with the precautions or if she approved of their plan, Hugh shrugged off the chill of her cold stare. He stepped behind his father and followed him out the door. Once they were outside, Clan Iain Abrach formed an impenetrable wall in front of their chieftain with Hugh in the center.

In the distance, Glenlyon rode at the head of his retinue, dressed in a red-coated uniform, just as did all the men behind him. A long, curly wig powdered grey beneath his tall grenadier hat, he looked no more the Highland chieftain than he did a barrister from London. He held up his hand and the battalion stopped a good fifty feet away. Clouds of breath swirled above the soldier's heads while their muskets remained pointed down, their pikes still.

Alone, Hugh marched forward, his chin tilted up in question while Glenlyon sent Lieutenant Lindsay forward with papers in hand. Hugh wished he hadn't promised his father he'd not be the first to draw blood. Lindsay had been one of the bastards under Captain Drummond who'd detained the MacIains enroute to Inveraray to sign the oath—the very man who'd laughed in Hugh's face, telling him they'd be too late for the king's mercy.

Bastard.

"Do you come as friends or as enemies," he asked, fingering the dagger in his sleeve, a twitch firing under his eye. *Give me one reason not to kill you first.*

"As friends," said Lindsay, pushing the papers toward him. "We require quarters."

Hugh took them and read. Bloody hell, they planned to stay. "For how long?"

"Until Captain Campbell's orders come."

Hugh looked past the lieutenant at Glenlyon sitting a thoroughbred mount. "You mean to say, your leader is not traveling through the Rannoch Moor path to visit his missus at Meggerine Castle?" Charlotte had said they'd aimed to pass through. *Odd.*

"Ah." Lindsay glanced backward. "No. Colonel Hill commanded us to await his orders."

Hugh's gut twisted as he glanced down at the quartering-papers, looking for a signature. Indeed, Charlotte's father's bold signature scrawled across the bottom of the second page. Hugh rolled the papers and stashed them in his belt. "Well then, may I extend you the hospitality of the Coe and Clan Iain Abrach. You and your men are welcome." The words tasted like bile in his mouth.

Da strode forward, his arms open wide, his palms turned to the heavens demonstrating a warm welcome. "Captain Robert Campbell of Glenlyon. To what do we own this honor?"

After closing the distance on his steed, the gentleman

dismounted. "I've come to visit my niece. She wed your son afore I had an opportunity to wish her good cheer."

Gesturing to Sarah, Da grinned. "I'm certain my new daughter would enjoy your company if you aim to stay for a bit?" he pressed for answers.

"Yes, indeed. I hope our presence here will not cause you undue hardship. But these are difficult times, and to impose ourselves upon you in such weather—unfortunately the fort is full. Have you heard?"

"No—word hasn't yet reached us." Da peered around Glenlyon and his officers. "How many men are in your retinue?"

"A small company—myself, Sergeant Barber, Sergeant Hendrie, Corporals Campbell, MacPhail and Kennedy." Glenlyon threw his thumb over his shoulder. "And I've fifty-seven foot in my ranks."

Da scratched the long whiskers on his chin, his gaze shifting to Hugh. "Not a problem. Of course 'tis the Highland way to provide bed and comfort to a gentleman and a friend. I have a chamber above stairs I hope will meet with your approval."

"No, no. I'd rather be a wee bit closer to my niece." Glenlyon pointed. "I'll stay with MacDonald of Inverrigan at the bend of the glen. However, I'm sure Lieutenant Lindsay will be quite comfortable with your chamber."

"Very well." Da ran his fingers down his long beard, his eyes calculating. "I suppose we'll have to split up the rest of the troops—two or three to a cottage?"

Bloody hell—let the bastards sleep beside our clansmen and women...in their cottages? Hugh nearly blew steam out the top of his head. *No dragoon is going to climb into the hills and make camp in my house.*

"Hugh, Og," Da hollered. "Go spread the word. Every

cottage must house at least two soldiers, more if they have the means."

Hugh's jaw dropped. So did his brother's.

"Go on now." Da flicked his hands at his sons and then turned to the captain. "I trust you're ready for your nooning. Bring your men indoors and I'll have Cook prepare a meal to melt the frost from your beards."

Funny, Glenlyon's face is shaved clean. Hugh tugged his brother's arm. "Come, we've accommodations to arrange."

Once out of earshot, Og threw up his hands. "Why the hell are they not pitching tents—I ken a tidal marshland that would suit—might even drown a few of them."

"Bloody right. But Da's onto something with offering Highland hospitality. Once it is accepted, there's no way one of them could raise a hand against us—even a snake like Glenlyon has some integrity and honor."

Og shook his head. "This still must be a first. Clan Donald has feuded with Clan Campbell since we ruled as Lords of the Isles."

Hugh knocked on the first cottage door with an image of Charlotte filling his mind. Lord, he'd never want her embroiled in the midst of a clan feud. "Mayhap 'tis time to hang up our spurs, brother."

In the fortnight that passed, the flurries eased, giving way to melting snow on the floor of the glen. Every morning a grenadier drummer tapped a rattling snare at dawn. The blaring noise echoed off the white-capped cliffs of the glen, rousing every living thing and Hugh, asleep in his house in the hills was no exception.

Every day the soldiers drilled until noon, the bray of sergeant's orders shouting above the relentless beat of the drums. "Pikemen take heed. Advance your pikes. Charge your pikes..." On and on the sergeants droned while Hugh and the clansmen and women watched from the corners of their eyes, grumbling Gaelic curses while tending to their chores.

Every morning Glenlyon walked from Inverrigan's house to take his breakfast with Sandy and Sarah. Though Hugh's younger brother voiced his unease to Hugh, the loose-tongued captain was made welcome. He gambled every night with his host, playing cards and backgammon, all the while swilling MacIain whisky and wine.

Two days past, Alasdair Og had led a hundred clansmen and women to Da's manse and asked him to drive the soldiers from the glen. Hugh, as much as anyone wanted to see their backsides as they rode north or south—anywhere to be rid of their uninvited guests, but he stood beside his father. The old man's face grew red with anger. "Glenlyon is a Highlander. His men are Highlanders. They have bowed their heads at our tables and have broken bread with our clan. Therefore no harm will be done on their part and we shall give them no offence." His words were not shouted, but they seethed through clenched teeth as he disbanded the mob.

The afternoons, however, were never without amusement. Campbell's men joined the MacDonalds in Highland games— wrestling, shinty, throwing the stone and tossing the caber, archery and sword dances with Clan Iain Abrach's pipers playing well into the night. Hugh even found Sergeant Barber and Drummer Cuthbert Hunter to be good sorts—men with good humor and always willing to lend a hand.

Unfortunate there aren't more like them.

More than anything, Hugh wanted to send the regiment on their way because he desperately needed to see Charlotte. Since Glenlyon's arrival, he hadn't even had the chance to dispatch a letter to her. He'd left with such haste. It was no way to say goodbye to the woman to whom he'd proposed marriage.

This eve, Hugh strode beside Og on their way to Brodie MacDonald's house in Inverrigan. Captain Campbell had invited them to play cards as he had done many times in the past fortnight. A gale whipped through the glen and even Hugh was forced to lean into it to keep from being blown down.

Og looked to the sky. "A storm's brewing for certain. The clouds are so thick I can scarcely see the light in the windows ahead."

"Och, we couldn't expect the fine weather to continue. We have but to look forward to another month of winter afore the snow in the glen melts for good."

After they knocked, Captain Campbell opened the door with a grin plastered across his timeworn face. "Gentlemen, the cards are waiting." The man's nose was already as flushed as his cheeks.

Hugh raised a flagon of whisky. "From my still in the hills. The spring water there adds flavor that cannot be surpassed. The spirit slides over the tongue like nectar."

Glenlyon took the bottle and slapped Hugh on the back. "You're a man of good taste."

Sitting beside Cuthbert Hunter, Sandy waved from the table. "Brothers, come and save me from this shark—he'd winning already."

"What? You didn't wait for us?" asked Og.

"Just a wee wager," Glenlyon said, handing the whisky bottle to Brody, acknowledging his host for the first time since Hugh stepped inside.

Hugh sauntered to the table while Brodie served drams of whisky all around. "Better you than I, little brother."

Glenlyon shuffled the deck, his long fingers plying the

cards like the efficient plucks of a harpist. "Shall we play All Fours?"

"Very well." Hugh arched his brow at Og. "Why not make three teams of pairs to mix it up a bit?"

The captain grinned. "I'm not overly fond of splitting my winnings."

"Who says you'll win?" grumbled Og. Of all the MacIains, he was the least trusting of their long-staying guests.

"Come, Uncle." Sandy raised his cup. "Side with me and we'll show this lot of rabble how skilled we are."

Glenlyon lowered his gaze to his hands as he shuffled the deck one more time. "Three pairs it is. I'll play with Sandy—Hunter and Hugh—Brodie and Og." he bellowed loud enough to be heard by the cattle outside. Then he threw his head back with a hearty laugh. "I'm feeling lucky this eve."

Hugh reached in his sporran and pulled out a handful of coins, slapping them onto the table. "Then let's have at it. When this pile is gone, I'm heading to my bed—there's a storm brewing, and I'd prefer not to sleep under Brodie's table as I did last eve."

"Me as well," said Og. "In the past fortnight I've had enough to drink to keep my head swimming until spring."

Cuthbert snorted. "I've never seen anyone match the captain like you MacIain MacDonald lads."

Og raised his cup. "Had a good teacher."

"Och aye," agreed Glenlyon. "Your da can put it away for certain. I'll be dining with him in the manse on the morrow."

Hugh knew that to be true. He and his brothers were guests as well—detailed by Ma's shaking finger. "You wouldn't want to miss a table prepared by Ma. She's even pulled the rhubarb from the cellar for a tart."

Everyone at the table responded with mms, and smacking lips. Glenlyon rubbed his belly. "I'll look forward to such a feast with great anticipation." He sipped his whisky, then his rheumy eyes popped. "Mm. You distilled this yourself?"

Hugh nodded. "Aye. A man needs a great many talents to survive in these times."

The captain dealt the first round. "Many talents, indeed."

On and on the game continued while Hugh's pile of coins grew rather than dwindled for a change. Until Brodie answered a demanding knock at the door.

"Captain Drummond with a missive for Captain Campbell."

Hugh's gut turned over as his fingers brushed the hilt of his dirk. And across the table Og ground his fist into his palm. Sandy set his cards down and slipped his hand into his sleeve.

Aye, the bastard who'd detained Da and his men on their way to Inveraray stepped inside, brushing a healthy dusting of snow from his cloak. Then he pulled a missive from the cuff of his gauntlet and handed it to Glenlyon.

No one spoke while Campbell sliced his finger under the red wax seal and read. Brodie stood beside Drummond without offering the man a seat or a tot of whisky.

All eyes watched Glenlyon.

A single eyebrow arched as he folded the missive and stashed it in his waistcoat. Looking up, he grinned. "At long last my orders have arrived." He looked to Brodie and stood. "The burden we've put on Clan Iain Abrach has been lifted, but I've much to do afore the sun rises on the morrow."

Every man stood and Hugh extended his hand. "It has been our pleasure to receive you and your men as guests."

"Aye," the captain belted in his usual loud voice. He shook Hugh's hand, though his gaze wandered sideways. "Thank you for your generous hospitality. My only regret is I haven't relieved you of that pile of coin yet this eve."

Remembering his manners, Hugh bowed his head to

Drummond, and to the tune of laughter, the brothers said their farewells. Then Hugh mounted his horse and headed the mile up the mountain for his bed. Lord, he was bone weary. At last, Glenlyon and his regiment of foot would be off to impose on some other poor Highland blighters.

Chapter Twenty

❧❦❧

C harlotte hadn't taken the evening meal with the officers in a fortnight. She'd hardly said a word to her father, and hadn't visited his study at all. Only twice had he popped his head in to her chamber—to see if she was still with the living, no doubt.

Well, she'd had enough of the present stalemate. Hiding in her chamber wasn't helping anything and only served to worsen her misery. Regardless if the colonel intended to keep her under house arrest for the rest of her days, this evening she traipsed to the officer's dining room with one purpose.

Deliberately she arrived ten minutes late, but upon opening the door, Charlotte gasped. "Where is everyone?"

Doctor Munro lowered his knife and looked up, his face somber. "All out on a mission. Left me here with a handful of stragglers."

"Is my father away as well?"

"No. I gave him a tonic to settle an upset stomach as well as something to help him sleep."

Charlotte let out a long breath and tapped her fingers to

her lips. At least she wouldn't have to wait until after the meal.

The physician stood and pulled out the chair beside him —the one where Charlotte usually sat. "I've missed enjoying your company during supper."

"Unfortunately, I will not be dining here this eve." Charlotte clasped her hands and squeezed. "Though I did want to have a word with you."

His face brightened, making her take two steps back, a knot between her shoulder blades clamping taut. *Just out with it.* "I'm afraid I must tell you that I cannot possibly consider marrying you." She hesitated, taking a deep breath.

His face fell.

The last thing she wanted to do was hurt Roderick, but the damage had been done. There was no use listing all the reasons she didn't think their union would work. "Forgive me."

She pushed out the door and dashed to her father's study.

John Hill sat in his chair with a near empty bottle of wine beside him. He looked up, his eyes red, his features grey and pinched to the point of anguish.

She wanted to run to him, but something in his expression warned her against it. "I've refused Doctor Munro's proposal of marriage."

Papa nodded and reached for the bottle, taking a healthy swig.

"Is something amiss?"

"Nothing that concerns you," he slurred, his gaze unfocused.

Charlotte had never seen her father so completely despondent. "Are you inebriated?"

"Perhaps." He swirled the wine in the bottom of the bottle, holding it to the lamplight.

Steeling her resolve, she stepped further into the study.

"Regardless if I have your blessing, I have made up my mind. I love Hugh MacIain. It is he whom I will wed."

Papa guzzled the remaining dregs. Slamming the bottle to the table with a belch, his gaze wandered to the hearth rather than to Charlotte. "No." He drew the word out and it hung in the air and chilled like death. "You cannot marry a corpse."

Chills fired across her skin. "What in God's name are you saying?" Charlotte clutched her trembling fists to her abdomen. "You cannot send a man to the gallows for loving a woman!"

Da pushed back his chair and stumbled to the door. "There's no need for me to do so."

❦

UNABLE TO BREATHE, CHARLOTTE STOOD ALONE IN THE center of Papa's study. How could he be so heartless, and then just up and walk out with no explanation? Clamping her hands to her crown she paced. Should she barrel into his bedchamber and demand answers? Heaven's stars, she'd never been allowed to enter his bedchamber. A flicker of brass caught her eye. The key to Papa's strongbox was still in the lock.

Why were all the men gone...and if they were on a mission, why had they marched without Papa? Her head swarmed with questions and her father was in no condition to answer a one.

"*You cannot marry a corpse.*" The words echoed in her head and crawled over her skin like slithering serpents. Never had she heard her father be so insensitive.

Charlotte's palms perspired as she moved to the strong-box. The key slipped in her fingers, but she tightened her grip and turned until the click echoed off the study's walls. She paused for a moment, listening to the whispering silence. Then she steeled her nerves and opened the lid.

Piles of missives stacked so high they almost spilled over the edge—and to the side a leather money pouch appeared to be stuffed with coin, a tag affixed to it read "dowry".

Aside from being surprised of its girth, she couldn't care less about the contents of the pouch. On top of it all was a map of Glencoe. To the east marked the Devil's Staircase with Hamilton's regiment. To the south, mountains. To the west was a mark showing Major Duncanson's battalion. North denoted Captain Drummond and his men, with Glenlyon's regiment marked with an X in the center of Hugh's home.

Lord in heaven, there must be a thousand men deployed.

Reaching in a trembling hand, Charlotte pulled out two missives bearing the seal of John Dalrymple, Master of Stair. Moving to the chair, she opened the first letter, dated 21st January, the year of our Lord 1692:

In response to your correspondence of 16th January, I have but one thing to say. The king does not agree that all is at peace in the Highlands....Pray, when anything concerning Glencoe is resolved, let it be secret and sudden...cut off that nest of robbers who have fallen in the mercy of law. They did not come forward in the time prescribed. This pleases the king, for now you are at will to take action...I apprehend the storm is so great that for some time you can do little, but so soon as possible you will be at work...Deal with them...and by all means be merciless.

Charlotte shook as she read the signatures at the bottom. Both the king and the Master of Stair signed with bold strokes of their quill.

Is this why Papa is so despondent? Charlotte looked to the window, snow still clung to the panes. It had hardly stopped snowing all winter.

Hands trembling out of control, she opened the next

missive, signed only by the Master of Stair and dated 26th January:

I reject your appeal to my letters concerning the dispatch of Glencoe. You cannot receive further directions...be as earnest in the matter as you can...be secretive and sudden...be quick...You are hereby ordered to proceed to put all under the sword under seventy before dawn on the 13th February. Ensure the old fox and his sons on no account escape your hands...Lieutenant Colonel James Hamilton has received a copy of these orders to ensure you do not undermine my authority yet again...This time you will not hesitate...

Choking back bile, Charlotte dashed to the strongbox, dropped the missives inside and filled her pocket with coins. Then she grabbed her father's cloak from a peg on the wall, dashed to the door, slipped into her overshoes and ran for the stables.

Chapter Twenty-One

By the grace of God, Charlotte found Farley at the alehouse. She hastened toward him only to be stopped by a vile, stringy-haired man with foul breath. "Where are you off to in such a hurry, lassie?"

Another blackguard grabbed her arm. "Aye, 'tisn't often we see a morsel as tasty as this come through the door."

Someone tugged on her cloak. "And she's wearing an officer's mantle."

"Did you steal it, lass?"

Charlotte tried to wrench her arm away. "Leave me be, you vile beasts!"

"Och, coming into an alehouse with a stolen cloak and demanding to be treated as a lady?"

"Stop!" a deep voice boomed from the rear. Farley stood with both palms resting on his table. "That there's the governor's daughter. You lay a hand on her and you'll have every dragoon for a hundred miles breathing down your neck."

When the grimy hands released her arm, Charlotte hastened forward. "Thank you, Mr. MacGregor." She clapped praying hands together. "I urgently need your help—Mr. MacIain is in trouble. We must leave at once!"

A rumbling laugh snorted through the big man's nose. "How would a wisp of a woman like you be able to help a scrapper like Hugh MacIain?"

"You do not understand." Glancing over her shoulder, she leaned forward and lowered her voice. "I am privy to confidential information—news I should not be aware of. I *need* you to take me to Hugh's cottage in the mountains immediately."

Farley swayed, blinking his red eyes. "Are ye daft?" he slurred. "Besides there's storm a brewing"

"Good Lord, is everyone in his cups this eve?" She wasn't about to allow this big bear to turn her away. Charlotte stepped around the table, grasped his doublet in her fists and shook. "You *must* help me," she seethed. "Hugh told me if anything went awry to send word with you...well, this is *life* and *death*."

He straightened and blinked. "You're honest to God scared?"

"Truly I am frightened down to the tips of my toes, now let us saddle your horse and be on our way." She tugged his arm, but he stood there solid as a stubborn oak. Curses, she'd beg if forced. "Please. I can pay you an entire month's wages."

"Now why didn't you say you had coin?" His eyes bugged wide. "What's afoot?"

She tugged with more force. "I'll tell you once we're outside. No use starting a riot."

"Riot?" He guzzled his remaining ale as if she were but a fly yanking on his arm. "Why didn't you tell me 'twas that grave?"

With a groan, she led the way out the door. Spouting the words life and death hadn't been grave enough? "Where's your horse?"

"Stabled out the back of my cottage."

Charlotte untied the reins of the gelding she'd borrowed. "Come then, we've no time to lose."

"We?" He stepped in beside her, taking her reins and leading her down a narrow close. "You won't be going anywhere but back to the fort."

She clutched her cloak tighter around her shoulders. "Is that so?"

"Aye, now give me your message and I'll decide if it can wait until morning."

"'Tis grave." Her gaze darted side to side as she hastened to keep pace with his long strides. "They're putting all of Glencoe to fire and sword—before dawn on the morrow. Captain Campbell is there now—other regiments are moving into place as we speak."

Farley stopped dead in his tracks and regarded her as if dumbstruck. "Holy Mary, Mother of God."

Practically jumping out of her skin, she grabbed his wrist and tugged. "There's no time to waste. I must warn Hugh forthwith."

"Och, no, lassie." He yanked his arm away. "You do not ride into the midst of fire, not when you're outnumbered by a thousand to one."

Stepping in she shook her finger at his big nose. "You cannot back away from this. If you do I'll...I'll have no recourse but to go alone."

"Bloody Christmas." He marched ahead, then lashed the gelding's reins to the post outside a small cottage. "Wait here whilst I go tell Emma I've a job to do."

Charlotte clapped her hands to her chest with a huge sigh of relief. "Thank you."

With a grunt, Farley slipped inside the ramshackle cottage. Charlotte clutched Papa's cloak tighter around her shoulders and looked back along the close. Their footprints had already been covered with snow and she could scarcely see but ten feet ahead.

The door opened and Emma stepped outside with a plaid wrapped around her shoulders. "Miss Charlotte, please return to the fort. Leave this to Farley. He'll warn Mr. MacIain for you."

She dug her heels into the snow. "I'm going."

Farley came out, pulling a woolen bonnet over his head. "You'll slow me down."

"I can ride as well as any man, and I'll pay you two month's wages." Bless it she would not back down on this.

"Bloody hell," said Farley. "Where did you come up with all this coin?"

Charlotte raised her chin. "'Tis mine." That's all he needed to know—besides there was much more where that came from.

With a sigh, the big man looked to his wife. Emma shrugged and removed her blanket. "The least I can do is give you a plaid to throw over your head and shoulders."

"Thank you."

Farley stuck his finger an inch away from Charlotte's chin. "If what you say is true, the perimeter of Glencoe will be crawling with redcoats. Worse, we've already seen an inch of snow in the past hour. That means our only chance at success is to skirt around Loch Leven and up the hills to find Hugh."

"Will we arrive before dawn?"

"I know not, but one thing's for certain."

"What's that?"

"If you're pulling my leg, I'll be needing more than two month's wages."

Though Charlotte wore her father's cloak, overshoes, and atop it all, Emma's thick woolen plaid draped over her head and clutched taut at her neck, she'd never imagined a human being could be so cold. Worse, Farley's "back way" taking them around Loch Leven added far too many miles and precious time to the journey.

They'd been riding for hours, and if she asked one more time how much longer their journey would take, she feared the big tracker would knock her off her horse and leave her lying in a drift of snow. He'd practically alluded to as much with his grumbling responses to her questions, so Charlotte had kept her mouth shut for what seemed like an eternity.

Ahead, the big man rode on, his hand gripping her horse's lead line as he trudged through abominable conditions—it wasn't only inky dark, the snow blasted on the wind in sideways sheets. Farley had insisted he take charge of her mount in case they hit heavy snow, all the while griping about her worthless sidesaddle. Charlotte watched the mane in front of her. About an inch had built up again, like it had a few times thus far—the white flakes would accumulate and then grow overwarm and slide down the gelding's neck. She could see a foot, mayhap two ahead, and could swear ice crystals formed beneath her nose with every exhale. Her hands were too numb to move—not to mention her feet. Goodness, even her eyelashes were incased in frost.

With no mantel clock to tell her the time, all Charlotte could do was pray. They must arrive well before dawn. She was so distraught, she wanted to slap Farley's horse's rump with her crop and demand a faster pace. *Curses, curses, curses!*

How could men stand to travel like this in the dead of winter? Were all of the officers in Britain out of their minds, ordering an attack in the midst of a blizzard? Lord, she couldn't decide what made her more miserable—the fatigue sweeping through her entire body, demanding sleep, or being so cold she could no longer move. She ground her chattering teeth and tightened her grip on the plaid. In no way would she utter one word of complaint. The MacGregor man should be abed with his wife right now, but no, Charlotte had insisted he ride at once and take her with him.

She would freeze to death before she uttered a word of complaint.

They *would* make it to Hugh's cottage.

They must.

With resolute fortitude, Charlotte shook her head and focused on the only thing she could now see—her horse's ears. How Farley could pick his way through this squall in the darkness of night, she had no idea, but she trusted the tracker. If Hugh trusted him, then she did, too.

"The fires are burning atop Signal Rock." Farley's grumbling voice came from the silent darkness.

Charlotte peered ahead, but saw not a thing. "How can you tell?"

"There's a faint glow up and to the left."

"Are we almost there?" Charlotte asked, straining to see anything with snowflakes clouding her eyes.

Farley cleared his throat.

Curses, she'd vowed not to ask a gain. "Apologies."

A low chuckle rumbled. "Hugh's cottage is about a mile ahead."

Her heart skipped a beat. They were so close! Hugh was right to trust the tracker—Farley was a good man, despite his gruff mien. "Do you have any idea what time it might be?"

"Afore dawn."

"I could have told you that."

"Then why did you ask?"

"I supposed if we're so near the cottage, you might have a better idea than I." Charlotte tapped her heels and urged her mount closer to Farley's. "We must arrive well before the sunrise."

His white-shrouded outline twisted and regarded her. "Aye, and how many times are you aiming to remind me of that fact?"

"Forgive me." She bit her lip. "I'm ever so anxious."

"Let's just hope we don't end up dead, diving into the midst of this mayhem."

"I don't know about you, but I'm praying we arrive soon enough to thwart the whole thing."

Farley tugged the lead line without another word.

Truth be told, I'll wager the tracker's as nervous as I.

The following mile took an eternity to traverse—probably because the visibility was so poor. Charlotte didn't even see the cottage until they stopped at the door. Lord, the tracker could have probably led them there blind.

With a rush of her pulse, she snapped from her frigid cocoon and dismounted without assistance. Dashing to the door, she hammered on it with both fists, ignoring the shooting pain of ice cold knuckles. "Hugh! It's me!" With no immediate answer, she turned the latch and pushed inside.

Coals glowed from a small hearth, casting a dim light. Charlotte turned, spotting another door. Racing through, she found him beneath a heap of bedclothes. "Hugh!" She shook his shoulder. "You must wake."

He sat up with a start, dirk in hand.

Charlotte skittered away, well aware of what a man could do when roused from deep slumber.

"Charlotte?"

"You'd best listen to her," Farley said from the doorway, holding an oil lamp. "We've ridden all night in a bloody blizzard."

Hugh lowered his weapon. "What the devil?"

"I-I-I read a missive from the Master of Stair. They're going to put all of Glencoe to fire and sword—before dawn!"

"My God."

"'Tis worse." She clutched her fists beneath her chin. "Orders are to kill the old fox and his sons—put everyone under seventy under the sword."

"You're certain of this?" Hugh swiped his hand across his face. "But I saw myself—Glenlyon received his marching orders only this eve."

Dashing to the bed, she grasped his hand, squeezing it between her palms. "He received orders to murder you." She sucked in a gasp. "Major Duncanson is moving in from the west, and Lieutenant Colonel Hamilton's battalion is climbing the Devil's Staircase to block the pass to the west."

"With the amount of snow building up, I doubt Hamilton will make it to the party," said Farley.

Hugh leapt from the bed, belting his plaid atop his shirt. "What about the south?"

"Just a wall of mountains," Farley said.

Hugh shifted his gaze to the wall clock. "Jesus Christ. 'Tis only two hours 'til dawn."

A shot rang out in the distance—followed by another and then a volley of fire.

He pulled a sword from a hiding place inside the roofing thatch and belted it across his shoulder. "Take Charlotte southwest behind *Meall Mòr*." Shoving daggers into his sleeves and hose, he continued. "There are a pair of ramshackle hunting shielings hidden in the hills."

Charlotte jolted as the musket fire increased.

Hugh snatched a powder horn from the wall and charged two pistols, shoving them into his belt.

"You must go with us!" Charlotte grasped his arm. "Do you not hear? 'Tis madness to ride down there."

His eyes blazed as he met her stare. "I cannot abandon my

clan." Hugh gripped the back of her neck, planting a fierce kiss on her lips. "Go with Farley. I'll meet you there."

She grazed her fingers over stubbled cheeks. "But you could be killed!"

"No. 'Tis nay time for me to die." With a clang of weapons, Hugh raced for the door. "Farley will keep you safe. God help me, I *will* be there."

Chapter Twenty-Two

Hugh opened the door to his cottage to the click of a flintlock. Diving back inside, the musket fired, splintering the door. "Snuff the lamp," he barked at Farley. "Charlotte—hide!"

Shoving their bayonets through the doorway, six dragoons filed inside. Hugh drew his pistols and fired. Two men dropped.

Casting the weapons aside, he drew his sword, advancing with a roar.

Farley took up the flank.

The stunned dragoons charged with their bayonets.

With an upward swing, Hugh advanced. "Campbell sent only six to cut me down?" He lunged for the kill. "Thought I'd be abed did you?"

Spinning, he took out the next.

Farley cut one down.

Hugh whipped around, looking for the last. "Where is the bastard?"

"Never thought I'd see the likes of Colonel Hill's daughter

hiding in a rat's nest," jeered a red-coated dragoon levering a dagger at Charlotte's throat.

Hugh lowered his sword. "Let her go. She has nothing to do with this."

"Is that so?" The man's gaze shot to Farley as he inched toward the door with Charlotte in a stranglehold. "My guess is she tipped you off."

"How can you murder these people in cold blood?" Charlotte struggled, unable to break free.

The soldier pushed his knife harder. "Orders."

Charlotte grimaced with a hiss. "Do you not have a mind of your own?"

"Shut your gob." The bastard tightened his grip. "I'd like nothing better than to run my blade across your neck and blame your death on MacIain."

Hugh slid a foot forward, raising his sword a bit. By God he'd kill the louse just for touching his woman. "Why not take me on—just us pair?" *Come, you maggot.*

"You?" the cur smirked. "I'm not planning to die this day." His feet slid sideways as he continued to inch toward the door.

Staring straight at Hugh, Charlotte's fingers clamped around the arm holding the dagger.

He tightened his grip around the sword's hilt. Och aye, she was the daughter of a soldier.

She blinked.

Hugh gave a subtle nod.

Before he drew another breath, she bore down and twisted. The knife fell.

Lunging for the attack, Hugh drove his blade through the bastard's gullet.

In a blink, he had Charlotte wrapped in his embrace. "I should have kent the daughter of a colonel would be brave. My God, you are amazing."

Clutching her fists beneath her chin, she shook like a terrified puppy, but Hugh meant what he'd said. Lord, he knew men who wouldn't have acted with such courage when facing a dagger held at the neck.

"I—I..."

Hugh kissed her temple. "Wheesht, lass. 'Tis over."

Down below, musket shots continued to fire.

"I'm afraid it has only begun," said Farley.

Hugh nodded. Lord knew what horrors he'd find in Glencoe. With one last kiss, he nudged Charlotte toward the tracker. "Go with MacGregor."

Her fingers clung to his waist while a tear slipped from her eye. "Why can you not go with us?"

If only he could spirit her away—but Hugh MacIain MacDonald was no coward. "I give you my word I'll be with you soon."

"Take my horse," said Farley. "He's already saddled."

"My thanks." Shoving his sword back into his scabbard, Hugh sprinted out the door, leapt on the pony, and dug in his heels.

Approaching Glencoe at a gallop, Hugh couldn't believe his eyes. Yes, he'd raided and had been plundered, but he'd never seen complete annihilation. Every roof was ablaze, and as he neared, his kinsmen and women ran in all directions without aim, some naked, some barely clad while snow fell atop them.

"*A Meall Mòr*," he bellowed, digging in his heels. He drove straight toward a dragoon chasing a Mary with a battleaxe. Before Hugh reached them the sick cur cleaved the woman— no older than Charlotte—in the back.

Infused with rage, Hugh barreled on course. Drawing his sword, he roared at the murderer and cut him down.

Surrounded by death and dying, Hugh spun his horse and swung at every red-coated devil in his path. Blood spewed across the snow. As he fought, he steered Farley's garron toward his parent's house. In the distance, angry flames leapt from Carnoch. Seeing no clear route to the manse without facing a mob of bloodthirsty dragoons, he headed for the river path. It might take longer, but with luck he wouldn't be shot for his efforts.

As Hugh clambered over the icy bank, bedraggled MacIains huddled and shivered. "*A Meall Mòr*," he repeated over and over as he dug his heels deeper into the horse's barrel.

At the path to Carnoch, Hugh reined his mount to a stop. Dragoons ran through the snowy paddocks, firing their muskets at livestock. Piles of black hide lay in contrast with the white ground.

Hugh dismounted and crouched in the foliage, creeping toward the burning manse.

His mother's wail shrieked on the wind.

The rear door swung open and creaked as if hanging from a derelict shack.

Sword at the ready, Hugh stepped inside the kitchen. Smoke oozed through the air like ghostly spirits, but there was nary a soul in sight.

Ma's wail came again.

Hugh sprinted for his parent's bedchamber.

Finding the door kicked in, nothing could have prepared him for the horror beyond its splintered timbers. Completely naked with blood streaming between her legs, Ma crouched over Da's lifeless body, weeping out of control. Beneath the old man's head, dark blood seeped, spreading into the plaid rug. By the gaping wound in Da's skull, he'd been shot in the head—there'd be no chance for him now.

"Ma." Hugh dashed to his mother, wrapping his arms around her, shielding her from her nakedness.

"The captain b-burst in here and s-shot him," Ma shrieked in a staccato wail.

Tears stung Hugh's eyes.

Curling into a ball, every muscle in her body tensed. "And they took a d-dagger to me."

"Jesus Christ." Hugh jumped up and snatched a plaid from the bed. "They were here a fortnight." He draped the blanket around his weeping mother. "Stayed under our rooves as guests under trust."

"I'll kill them all," a husky voice growled from the doorway.

"Og." Hugh protectively placed his palm on Ma's shoulder while his brother stepped inside, blood dripping from his sword.

"Sandy's dead. Sarah ran a dirk across his throat whilst he slept."

"Noooooooooo," Ma wailed, clutching her fists. "Not. My. Bairn!"

Hugh kneeled beside her, tears blurring his vision as he tucked the blanket around her. "Glenlyon, Hill, William, Stair...they've all declared war."

Og leaned on his sword, taking deep breaths. "When I saw six of them ride up the hill, I thought you'd be dead, too."

"Not likely." Hugh ground his teeth. "We must move Ma to safety afore they double back to bayonet the survivors." Hugh hefted his mother into his arms. "Campbell has orders to put all under seventy under the sword."

"They're doing a bloody good job of it." Og sidled toward the window and peered out. "If it weren't for the creak of the floorboards, I'd have been murdered in my bed by my back-stabbing *houseguest*."

"'Tis an abomination," Ma cried with a shudder.

"Come, brother, take our mother to the cottages behind Meall Mòr."

"Why not up the pass—we might be able to make it to the summer houses?"

"That route's blocked. Hamilton's marching his men up the Devil's Staircase."

Og blinked and strode back to the center of the room. "How do you know?"

"Miss Hill arrived with Farley MacGregor moments afore the shooting started."

"Hill?"

"I reckon she saved my life—and now she's fleeing for hers. Headed to Meall Mòr like the rest of us." Hugh placed his palm on Og's shoulder. "I've a horse tethered by the river. Take Ma. I'll stay and fight."

Mother grasped his arm and squeezed. "No. No more fighting."

"Are you mad, brother?" Og glared. "Those who haven't fled are dead."

Burning timbers crashed down, blocking the doorway.

Hugh raced for the window and levered it open. "Hurry, else we'll be burned alive."

Together, the brothers spirited their mother outside while tongues of flames chased them out the window.

With Ma hunched over the horse's withers, Hugh and Alasdair crept along game trails to the pass of Meall Mòr, the flat-topped mountain with its steep slopes. He prayed the government troops had discounted this route—treacherous, it was one he'd taken only when hunting mule deer in summer.

In the distance, the roof of his cottage was now afire. Hugh swore he could see Glenlyon's outline against the blaze, mounted on a horse, his sword raised, bellowing orders, no doubt.

His orders were to kill the old fox and his sons? I'll see to it he'll fail by half, and then I'll have my vengeance.

Chapter Twenty-Three

With daylight came more horror. Given the luxury of horseback, Charlotte and Farley arrived first at the two broken down hovels—one with its roof caving in due to rot and the weight of snow.

Charlotte had no idea how the horses made it through the rugged pass. Her mount had foundered thrice. There had to be at least three feet of snow on the ground and snow was still falling. She prayed they'd blazed a trail for those poor souls on foot.

Farley levered open the door to the shieling with a roof. Stepping inside, it was too dim to see anything, but Charlotte's overshoes skimmed atop dirt. "We'd best start a fire."

"I'll set to it."

She nodded. "Leave the door ajar to cast some light."

Once her eyes adjusted, she'd wished they hadn't. The place was a shambles. Broken pots and timbers, a single chair missing one leg, a moth-eaten blanket, so filled with holes and infused with dust it would provide no warmth whatsoever. Thatch from the roof piled everywhere, and rather than a hearth, there were rocks in a circle with an iron hook hanging down from the rafters for cooking.

At least they could use some of the timber for the fire.

Charlotte picked up the chair to move it aside when a rat scurried out from beneath a heap of thatch.

Squealing, she dropped the chair and skittered backward. Staring at the heap of debris, it moved as if there were a whole nest of rats under the rubbish. Wringing her hands, she slid back until she bumped into the open door. Nearly jumping out of her skin, Charlotte dashed outside. "Farley!"

The big man was nowhere to be seen. *Curses.*

Charlotte hated rats. The filthy vermin made her skin crawl. She set off through the thigh-deep snow, heading toward the hovel with half its roof missing, when an eagle called overhead. Heaven's stars, Hugh's people would soon be here. She could not look the coward in their eyes—and those damnable rats had to go.

Clenching her fists, she forced herself back inside. With rapid blinks, her eyes again adjusted as she glared at the pile of debris. "'Tis you or me, and I'm a great deal larger."

Carefully stepping nearer, she picked up a pole like those holding the thatch above. She gripped the weapon for dear life while her face stretched in a grimace. Levering under the pile, she flung the rushes aside. Rats scurried in every direction. With a yelp, Charlotte ran after the nearest, slamming the pole to the ground. "Be gone you vile beasts!"

Around and around the cottage she darted, bashing her stick down on anything that moved. "I hate rats!" She clobbered one before it escaped under the sod walls. "I hate them, I hate them, I. Hate. Rats!"

"Miss Charlotte?" Farley's voice droned behind her.

With a gasp, she stopped and turned, gripping the pole against her chest. "Rats," she said inclining her head.

The big tracker grinned. "I'll wager you put the fear of God in them beasties." Moving inside, he waved his hand.

Two scantily clad people stepped into the doorway—a man with a bare chest and a plaid tucked around his waist—a woman in nothing but a shift. And Lord, she had a babe in her arms. Neither the man nor the woman wore shoes, their feet bloodied and blue from cold.

The man looked to Farley, his eyes filled with fear. "*Sassenach?*"

The tracker gestured inside. "*Tha i Hugh's bean.*"

Gaelic? "Do you speak English?" Charlotte asked.

The couple crept forward, giving her a wide berth.

Goodness, how on earth was she to communicate with these people?

Farley dropped his armload beside the fire pit. "Most in these parts do—a bit."

Charlotte rubbed the outside of her arms. "I think there's enough wood here. Will you start a fire?"

"Aye." Farley pulled a flint from his sporran. "I've set some snares as well."

Still clutching her pole, she looked over each shoulder. "I think the rats have scattered."

He chuckled. "If we weren't in the midst of this mess, I would have had a good laugh watching you swing that stick of wood around."

Charlotte propped the branch by the door. "I think I clanked on an iron kettle. It'll come in handy for melting snow to cleanse wounds—and to drink." Thank goodness she'd been working in Doctor Munro's surgery. Her training might come to some use.

The couple still stood in the middle of the cottage looking dumbstruck.

Charlotte touched the woman's arm.

She yanked away, shielding her child.

"Forgive me." Charlotte drew her fist to her chest, nodding to a place by the fire pit. "Please sit. We'll have fire lit in no time."

The pair exchanged bewildered glances, then did as Charlotte asked.

As soon as they settled, the baby cried and the woman opened her shift, offering the wee one a teat. Turning its head, the infant suckled as its mother rocked in place, her face devoid of emotion.

"My word, we need food," Charlotte uttered.

"And there's more coming, mark me." Farley struck the flint against a pile of dried rushes. "You'd best pray my snares trap something—else we'll be praying to be shot—'tis a much faster death than starvation."

Her head spinning from her own hunger and fatigue from riding an entire night without a wink of sleep, she leaned against the door jamb—with a steeply pitched roof extending down to all but three foot, there wasn't a wall tall enough to lean against.

Please, God, bring us food—and please, please, please help Hugh arrive safely.

⁂

WHEN HUGH AND OG MADE IT TO THE COTTAGE WITH their mother, a fire was crackling. A cast iron pot dangled above it, a shroud of smoke hung in the air, making it appear as if he'd stepped into a dream. In fact, a hollow chasm expanded in his chest as if he'd spent the entire day in the worst nightmare imaginable.

The walls were lined with crouching refugees who'd escaped the massacre—his kin who the day before were vibrant and filled with life, playing shinty with Glenlyon's grenadiers. Not an eye looked his way, not a face registered anything but utter defeat.

"Hugh." Charlotte stood from where she'd been kneeling beside the fire. Strands of hair hung in her face, and she wore naught but her gown.

"Where is your cloak?" He blinked, hardly recognizing her. She seemed so out of place amongst his destitute, homeless kin. "Your plaid? 'Tis freezing."

She spread her palms. "There are many who are in far more need that I."

Lord, she'd given her cloak and her blanket to others.

"Come in and close the door." She beckoned. "It has only begun to warm in here."

"A moment." He turned to Alasdair Og. "Take Ma inside."

"We heard Glenlyon shot the chieftain," Gavyn said, using his Gaelic.

Hugh looked to Charlotte. Och, the Sassenach had no idea what they were saying—he'd use English—most everyone else could do the same. "'Tis true, Da's dead, and the miscreant Campbell fired the shot."

"You're the chief of the Coe now." Graham, the elder said, his weathered face looking like death.

Hugh didn't want to hear it. "There's nothing left. They've burned all the glen and killed all our livestock."

"I'm hungry, Ma," said a little lad—Lachlan, huddling with his parents.

As the clansmen and women made room for Og to lay their mother on the dirt floor, Hugh looked at the forlorn faces staring at him, all expecting him to make a miracle happen.

Christ, I'm fresh out of miracles.

He squinted to the dark corners. There were people everywhere. "How many are here?"

"There are a score and ten," Charlotte replied.

His tongue ran across dry, chapped lips. "Any supplies?"

"I've set snares." Farley stepped forward. "But we'll need more than a few rabbits."

"How many horses do we have?"

Farley scratched his beard. "Miss Charlotte and I rode in —hers and the one I rode—that's it."

Hugh threw his thumb over his shoulder. "And there's mine."

"You mean mine," said Farley. "And he's my ticket home. Now Miss Charlotte is safe, I'm aiming to return to my lady wife."

Hugh nodded. This wasn't the tracker's fight. He'd already done far more than he'd expect from someone outside his own. "And you'd best take Charlotte with you. The midst of a bloodbath is no place for a lady."

"I'm staying." Charlotte planted her fists on her hips.

"Pardon?" Hugh looked from Og to Farley receiving not an inkling of support from either man. He took Charlotte by the elbow and led her outside—snow still falling sideways with hard driving wind. "Bless it, woman. Do you know what you're saying? If your *father's* men figure out where we're hiding, we could have every dragoon on the west coast of Scotland bear down upon us. And this time, Stair's goddamned orders to exterminate the entire clan just might come to completion."

Charlotte rubbed her outer arms. "The people in there are suffering. Most have nothing on their feet. They fled with a few threads on their backs if they were lucky. Most are in such a state of shock they cannot string two coherent words together—even if I could understand what they were saying." She folded her arms and tilted up her chin. "That's the end of it. I'm staying. With Doctor Munro's training, I can be of more use to you than you realize."

"Aye, if my clansmen don't slit your throat whilst you're sleeping."

"I beg your pardon?" She stamped her foot in the powdery snow. "I am trying to help. Why would anyone want to do that?"

"Because you're the spawn of Colonel Hill—the man who ordered this madness."

"My father did no such thing!"

"You cannot tell me he didn't have a hand in it."

She clutched her abdomen and turned her back. "He tried to stop it."

"But he couldn't."

"No. And the Master of Stair copied James Hamilton on his missives to ensure Papa obeyed his orders."

Hugh reached out his hand, but couldn't bring himself to place it on her shoulder. The haunting screams of the dying echoed in his head. Bringing his cold fist to his mouth, he blew warm air on it. "You ken I'll protect you. When you helped me escape the bowels of Fort William, I swore I would give my life for you, but I cannot remain by your side at all times. You heard them. I'm chieftain now, and only God kens what's in store. Do you realize they've annihilated Glencoe? Every home, every lean-to...Christ, even fence posts were burned. Glenlyon left not one sheep, not one cow or chicken for us to survive. If—I said *if* we pull together and steer clear of those red-coated vermin infesting Glencoe's hills, it will be a long and painful road."

"I understand the risk." She turned and placed her hand on Hugh's arm. It burned through his shirt like she'd branded him. "I want to stay with you."

God bless it, Charlotte was not the reason for their plight. Hell, if not for her, Hugh would most likely be lying in a pool of his own blood, burning to cinders in his cottage. Clenching his teeth, he gathered her into his arms and pressed his cheek atop her head. If only he could allow himself a moment's respite, she felt so damn good—felt like home to a man who'd just watched his go up in flames. But keeping her there was too selfish, even for a rogue like him. "I want you beside me more than anything. You must know that. Go with Farley. After this is over, I'll find you and if you'll wait for me, we can start anew."

She pushed away. "What do you mean, *if* I'll wait? Do you think so little of my love for you? For goodness sakes, I rode all night though a blizzard."

Hugh's gut twisted—his mind flashing with the sight of flames licking his father's lifeless body. Would he ever rest until he had his revenge? How could he hold Charlotte in his arms while his clan stood by and watched? No. He must stand his ground with her. The lady's presence would only serve to make things worse. "Your father is the goddamned Governor of Fort William. His name must have been on the order to put my clan under fire and sword." He pointed a finger shaking with rage—not for Charlotte but for the atrocities he'd just witnessed. "I am responsible for the lost souls in there. My father has just been murdered. My own mother has had a knife taken to her—" He couldn't say it. The ghastly terror stretched across Charlotte's face silenced him. Hugh dropped his chin with his shoulders. "I fear she'll bleed to death, and I've all but a woolen blanket to bring her comfort."

Colonel Hill's daughter moved closer and took up his hand, her fingers cold like ice. Looking up into his eyes, she kissed his knuckles as a tear spilled down her cheek. "There are no words to describe how horrific this day has been. But I swear on my mother's grave, I will not walk away. Not now. Not ever."

Chapter Twenty-Four

Not long after Farley took his leave, Alasdair Og had killed one of the horses for meat. Charlotte watched while a half-dozen more stragglers arrived at the cottage nearly frozen to death and hungry. How many more MacIain's were out there who hadn't found shelter? The snow and the driving wind hadn't let up all day—not a soul would be able to survive for long in such weather.

A scratch and a whimper came at the door. One of the men opened it to a scraggly-looking deerhound.

"Cuddy?" Hugh asked.

The dog whined and sauntered inside. First he went to Hugh and stood for a scratch behind the ears. "I cannot believe you survived, old fella."

"Another mouth to feed," grumbled Og.

"Wheesht." Hugh gave the dog another pat, then Cuddy sauntered around the shieling, sniffing everyone.

When the dog stopped at Charlotte, he whined. She let him smell her hand before she petted him—his coat felt softer than it looked.

Then the dog lay down, pressing his body against her.

Across the fire, Hugh's brother looked at Charlotte with hateful eyes, so dark he left no doubt he'd rather be roasting her over a spit than horse meat. She tried to block the uneasy feelings from her mind, but she knew everyone in the cottage focused their anger on her.

And why should they not?

To them she was the daughter of the devil, and trying to tell them any differently would only worsen their contempt. Even Charlotte couldn't rationalize her father's actions. Papa could have walked away—though in doing so, he would be seen as a traitor of the very government he served. Still—one man's death over hundreds?

The mere thought turns my stomach.

She shuddered while she dipped her petticoat in the kettle of warm water and wrung it out. It was the only piece of cloth available. Lifting Mrs. MacIain's blanket ever so slightly, she reapplied the flannel to the wound—though Hugh couldn't utter it, the vile beasts who served Captain Glenlyon had taken a dagger to the poor woman's womb. 'Twas an abomination. 'Twas unforgiveable.

"I think the bleeding has stopped," Charlotte said, pressing the back of her hand to the woman's head. Hugh's mother shivered, though a fever had set in. The woman endured her pain, never saying a word. Her eyes vacant, she stared at the rafters while tear after tear dribbled into the dirt.

Hugh kneeled beside Charlotte and held out a bit of meat. "Eat."

She hadn't allowed him to send her away with Farley. Since, his words had been sparse, as if he were sinking deeper into his own world of terror and flames.

Though she'd lost her appetite, Charlotte rocked back on her haunches and took the meat. She bit down and tore it with her teeth—tough as leather, the bite landed in her stomach and sat there like one of her father's lead musket balls.

She cast her gaze through the dim light to the faces of the clansmen and women who sat on the dirt floor and lined the walls. They were stunned, freezing and silent, staring into the fire as if their very souls were lost. Aside from an occasional outburst from the baby, it was too quiet—eerie—as if they were all frozen.

"Is there anywhere we can take your mother for help?" Charlotte whispered.

Hugh shook his head. "I reckon the redcoats have infiltrated every byway in a twenty-mile radius of Glencoe." At least he'd strung an entire sentence together.

Charlotte's back straightened. "But the soldiers are cold, too. No one can make it far in this storm."

Hugh's eyes were as dark and vacant as the others'. "How many men did your father amass at Fort William afore they set out to annihilate us?"

Charlotte's cheeks burned. Was he, too, now blaming her? "The fort was bursting at the seams with a thousand men. That's why Glenlyon's grenadiers were sent to Glencoe." She hung her head. "At least that's what everyone was led to believe."

"And Captain Campbell kent about it all along—accepting our hospitality, eating with us, playing cards." Alasdair Og slammed his fist into the dirt. "And we let them—brought the slithering Campbell snake in like he was kin."

"He was kin," grumbled Hugh. "Until that black-hearted bitch drew her knife across Sandy's throat."

Silence again cast a pall throughout the cottage. The smoke burned Charlotte's eyes, but venturing outside for air was no longer possible. She might push through the door and walk about three feet before being completely stopped by a wall of icy snow.

Hugh's jaw twitched as he sat silently and stared at the fire. The howling wind made the cottage shudder. Even the flames flickered with the force of the storm outside.

Charlotte wanted to say so many things—the soldiers will have to turn back because of the weather—she hoped the storm would soon pass—was there no one to whom they could turn for help? How long did Hugh intend to keep these people in this insufficient cottage? What was next? But she held her tongue. Her every suggestion or question had been met with a wall of rebuttal—especially from Alasdair Og.

No. This was not the eve to solve problems. Tonight they would lick their wounds, but with six and thirty human beings to feed, the horse meat wouldn't last.

Ever so quietly, Charlotte slid beside Hugh and under his arm. Together they sat in silence, an island among a homeless crowd with nowhere to turn for help, their future as precarious as a ship at sea with a broken mast.

§

HUGH KEPT WATCH THROUGHOUT THE NIGHT. THE STORM made it impossible to post a guard outside the cottage, but he couldn't sleep anyway. Charlotte was right. No one could survive in this weather—even the soulless dragoons would be huddled beside someone's hearth—hopefully not a family they planned to butcher. Unfortunately, the fact that everyone must seek shelter gave him no comfort. How many of his clansmen and women were suffering in the cold? How many more would end up dead because of God's wrath?

Her head resting in his lap, Charlotte had given in to her fatigue—more unconscious from exhaustion than asleep. The lass should have gone with Farley, but bless her, she'd resigned herself to stay. She'd tended Ma until she could hold her head up no longer. Hugh peered around the cottage. Not even Og had managed to stay awake through the wee hours. 'Twas probably for the best. His brother's rage needed tamping, else he'd soon do something that would get them all killed.

Of the men, Breac, Tavis, Kenny and Gavyn were all stealthy warriors. Though they had not but a plaid wrapped around their waists, Hugh was glad to have them at his back. They'd make pikes from tree branches if forced. They, too, slept huddled with their wives.

Hugh needed the quiet to think and having his kin stare at him, waiting for him to pull a miracle out of his arse only muddled with his mind all the more. He'd spent the entire night trying to make sense of this mess. How could he have prevented the whole sordid butchering? He'd known Glenlyon to be a snake—a turncoat of the basest order.

Christ, Hugh had relieved the bastard of his prized stallion only three years past. Was that why Captain Campbell ordered an entire battalion to open fire on a clan who'd shown him nothing but affability for a fortnight? Not to mention a chieftain who'd treated the blackguard like kin?

An entire clan for a miserable, sterile stallion?

No matter which way Hugh reasoned, his hatred burned a hole in his chest. Glenlyon broke the Highland code of hospitality.

The man's soul will wander through hell and burn for all eternity.

It didn't matter that Glenlyon's orders had come down to him all the way from King William and his deranged minister, Viscount Dalrymple, Master of Stair. Captain Campbell had a mind of his own, and he acted on his orders with all the black-heartedness of his kin. Not a Campbell was to be trusted...ever.

Hugh should have insisted that Da's men watch them—regardless. How blind Clan Iain Abrach was to welcome back-stabbing redcoats onto their lands with open arms and open larders. Christ, the men Hugh had played shinty with were the same murderers who attacked his cottage.

At least those miscreants met their end.

Charlotte took a deep, stuttering breath.

Devil's fire, he'd be dead without her. He needed to keep reminding himself of that fact. Hate was ugly. Hate played irrational tricks on his mind, and if he let her, hate would eat him alive. The bitch of hate had already started eating away his heart.

Hugh pressed his palm against his head and closed his eyes.

How was he going to rescue his kin from this mess? When would the goddamned snow let up? Where were the redcoats now? Did they have every pass to Glencoe shut off? The horse meat might last two more days, and then what? A handful of rabbits wouldn't feed six and thirty lost souls.

God's bones, his head throbbed. Every time Hugh tried to think about the future, he saw Da dead on the floor. He saw the blood streaming down the inside of Ma's thighs—mindless dragoons shooting cattle and stabbing sheep with their bayonets. He saw the roof of his own cottage going up in flames, burning everything he'd worked to save over the course of his life.

Aye, he'd been born a Highland reiver, just like every other proud clansman in the Gallows Herd—proved his manhood preying on the Campbells. They preyed on his kin, too. But never like this. No one ever broke the trust of hospitality. No one was ever left to starve—murdered in cold blood with no place to run—naked, running on bare feet in a blizzard.

The black chasm of hate spread from Hugh's chest through every fiber of his body.

"Son," Ma called weakly from her bed on the dirt floor.

Hugh gently rested Charlotte's head on the ground, then kneeled beside his mother.

Ma reached for his hand, her fingers ice cold, her grip feeble. Nothing about his mother had ever been feeble. Never.

She smiled at him, just as weakly. "'Tis time for me to join your father."

A lump the size of a walnut stuck in Hugh's throat as prickles swarmed down the outside of his arms. "What are you saying? You are the matriarch of the family. We all look to you for wisdom."

"'Tis your time now, son."

"No—"

"I'll have my say." She gulped, her lips parched.

Hugh held up a chipped clay cup he'd filled with water. "Here. Drink."

"No." She closed her eyes. "Promise me you will never abandon your home. Promise me you will build a manse grander than Carnoch." She gripped his hand—much tighter this time. "Swear it."

"I promise, Ma...but—"

She opened her eyes and caught his gaze, beckoning him closer. "You will raise your bairns in Glencoe." Her breath quickened like she was running. "Never let them forget. Always remind them they are descended from Alasdair Ruadh MacIain MacDonald—a direct descendant of the Lords of the Isles..." She swallowed again, then pulled his ear down to her lips. "Never be ashamed of who you are."

Hugh drew in a sharp inhale. Her voice was haunting, her breath warm against his ear. Grasping her hand to his heart he regarded Ma's face. Oh, how her words rang true. The cold, hungry and destitute people huddled in this wee cottage were his kin. They were driven from their lands, but by God, he would find a way to take them home. No matter if it took him the rest of his life, he would see justice—demand it.

"Promise," Ma's voice grew reedy.

"I swear. With God as my witness, I swear."

A long exhale wheezed through Ma's throat, and then she lay still. The soul left her eyes as they stared at nothing, her mouth agape.

Hugh's heart stopped as he pressed his fingers to her throat.

Nothing.

"Ma?"

A cry caught in his mouth. "Please, Ma."

But she was gone—left to be with Da as she'd said. Life slipped away with her last exhale. His hands trembling, he closed her lids, then took her into his arms and rocked. God, he wanted to burst into tears and wail like a wee bairn.

No.

No.

No.

Clenching his teeth, his head shook as he fought back his anger, his tears, his rage. How much more death would he witness before this was over?

Og slid across and kneeled beside him. "I'll never forgive the government for this. They wanted to quash the Jacobites? Well, King William just declared war."

"Amen," said Gavyn behind them.

Glancing over each shoulder, it seemed everyone had roused and witnessed Hugh's promise to his mother.

"'Tis all her fault," said Nessa, pointing at Charlotte.

Without time to rub the sleep from her eyes, Colonel Hill's daughter scooted closer to Hugh.

Earie stepped forward, squinting at Charlotte like she was the devil incarnate. "We should run a dirk across her throat."

Nessa, with her babe in arms, nodded. "Aye, it would be one less mouth to feed."

Og pulled his *sgian dubh* from his sleeve. "You cannot trust her, brother. Look at what Sarah did to Sandy."

"Put her under the knife!" The taunts grew louder, as the lost souls took out their ire on the poor lass who had done nothing but try to help.

Hugh stood, taking Charlotte with him, clutching her fast to his body. "Sheathe your goddamned dagger!"

He panned his gaze around the walls until he'd made eye contact with every soul. "Did you not see Miss Charlotte tending Ma? Who else lifted a finger to cleanse the blood from between our mother's legs? I say *our* mother because she was just that to every one of you. She always had compassion in her heart—treated each and every one of you like her own."

"Aye—always being friendly." Kenny stepped into the circle. "Mayhap that's why we're cowering in a ramshackle cottage in the mountains in the midst of winter."

Og slid his dagger back into his sleeve. "I think the Sassenach woman should go back to Fort William. She isn't one of us."

"Aye," agreed Tavis. "She represents the bastards who put us under fire and sword."

Hugh glanced down at Charlotte's face. The lass looked stricken—as if they'd issued consecutive slaps to her face. Well, he was chieftain now. His word was law. "I'll hear no more of this. We are not the animals the redcoats are. Miss Charlotte has my protection until I can take her home. If anyone hurts her, 'tis the same as hurting me."

Hugh looked directly at Og. "Do I have your vow, brother?"

The anguish on his brother's face reflected the same pain in Hugh's heart. But taking his ire out on an innocent woman would solve nothing. Hugh pushed Charlotte behind him and took a step toward Og. "I need your word," he growled through clenched teeth.

"Aye. She did warn you." He folded his arms with an up-ticked chin. "No one touches the lass whilst under your protection."

Hugh turned full circle. "Does anyone disagree?"

A few shook their heads.

He slid his hand into his sleeve and fingered his *sgian dubh*. "Does anyone wish to challenge me as Chieftain of Clan Iain Abrach?"

Several men mumbled, "Nay."

"Very well." He drew in a deep breath. "'Tis a new day, and if we aim to survive, there's much to be done. First, we prepare Ma's body for burial. I need an account of our weapons. We need firewood. Farley MacGregor set snares. We need them checked and more set. If we're to stay alive, we must have a constant supply of food. Guards will be posted around the clock. As soon as the weather lets up, I want a volunteer to go to Appin to beg blankets and clothes from the Stewarts."

Alasdair Og held up his hand. "I'll go."

"Nay." The elder, Graham MacDonald stepped forward. "The request must come from the chieftain. The Stewarts might turn anyone else away."

Hugh nodded his agreement. But appointing himself to go —possibly sleep in a bed and eat at the high table in Castle Stalker while his people suffered did not sit well. Dammit, Graham was right. "Very well. A visit to the Stewarts will also enable me to send a missive to Donald MacDonald of Sleat. The baronet should be aware of this abomination to our clan."

Chapter Twenty-Five

❦

After three days of wind and snow, Charlotte thought they'd all die of starvation in that dank cottage. The experience had tested her to the limits of forbearance. Yes, she wanted nothing more than to work beside Hugh while he pulled his people out of this disaster, but she hadn't counted on being the brunt end of their ire. Even after Hugh had declared her under his protection there were persistent hateful looks and hushed murmurs of distrust.

Worse, Hugh had withdrawn. He never let her leave his side, but that was all. There were no fervent looks across the fire. He didn't reach out and hold her hand or draw her into his arms. He'd been as cold and frigid toward her as the icicles hanging from the cottage's eaves. Sometimes she thought he blamed her for the massacre. Perhaps he did in some illogical way.

Charlotte hated it—almost wished she had returned to Fort William with Farley. Goodness, she was only trying to help—trying to start a life with the only man she wanted to marry. Why did this have to happen to Hugh's clan? Had their love been torn away along with everything else he'd lost?

At least he'd brought her along on this journey to Appin.

Sitting in the saddle, she hunched over and clutched her arms close against her body. The snow may have stopped, but the wind blew a gale, cutting through her woolen gown as if she wasn't wearing a stitch of clothing. In no way could she have asked them to return her cloak or the blanket that Emma had lent her.

Leading the garron pony through the rugged terrain, using only discrete animal trails, Hugh wore only a shirt with his plaid belted around his waist, spread across his shoulders. At least he was one of the few with a pair of leather Highland boots on his feet.

"Why can we not ride double?" she asked, trying to keep her teeth from chattering.

"You want the old fella to founder?" Hugh didn't bother to turn around. His curt remark mirroring the other clipped responses he'd tossed her way over the past few days.

"I'm sorry to be such a bother."

"I would have left you at the cottage if I thought you'd survive."

Charlotte shuddered. Without Hugh there to protect her —curt or not—she didn't want to be left alone with them. Not when so much bitterness coursed through their blood. They all wanted revenge—were driven mad by it, and she was the nearest English person within reach.

But heaven help her, she wanted Hugh. Wanted the same ruffian who'd been so bold to visit Fort William with his father and kiss her in the window embrasure. She wanted the Highlander with the cavalier spirit who slipped into her chamber with hundreds of dragoons mulling about. Yes, Hugh had put on a stoic face and set everyone to task, but Charlotte feared he'd lost his spirit and thirst for life.

Once they reached the burn the going grew easier, and when they turned south on the road along Loch Linnhe, the horse didn't stumble at all. In fact, the snow wasn't nearly as deep as it had been up at the cottage.

"How much further?" Charlotte asked.

"Should be there by midday."

Hugh may have spoken the words in a monotone, but Charlotte's stomach rumbled. Half-starved like everyone else, midday meant one thing—a meal. Mayhap one with bread and cheese—perhaps a meat pie with fluffy pastry. Shivering, she closed her eyes and hugged herself tighter against the frigid wind blowing off the loch. *Am I being heartless for craving a good meal? If only I could take such mouth-watering delights back to Meall Mòr. Would they accept me then?*

When a castle sitting atop a tiny isle came into view, Charlotte's heart squeezed. "Is that it?"

"Aye."

"Are the waters shallow enough for the horse to cross?"

"Nay."

"Will we have to take a boat, then?"

"Mm hm." Nothing had changed since they'd left the cottage.

Charlotte shivered again. This time she wasn't certain if the tremor had been caused by the cold or by Hugh's aloofness.

&

SINCE MA'S DEATH, HUGH HAD FELT LIKE HE HAD A cannonball lodged in his chest. And dammit all, Charlotte kept trying to raise his spirits. Didn't she know to keep silent? Aye, his feelings for the lass hadn't changed, but he needed time. Over and over, he'd kicked himself that he hadn't insisted she return to her father.

His kin were right. She didn't belong in the shieling. Mayhap she didn't belong with him. If nothing else, the past few days of suffering with his kin had shown him a glimpse of the long and arduous road to rebuilding. He had nothing to offer the lass. Nothing. He couldn't even kiss her without an audience. Worse, marriage was the last thing he could think about with hungry mouths to feed, and the thirst for revenge roiling through his blood.

The one good thing? He hadn't spotted a single redcoat on the journey to Appin. Aye, he'd kept to the burn and the byways, aside from the last stretch, but even Glenlyon wouldn't attempt an attack so close to the Stewart of Appin seat.

Met by Sir Robert Stewart's guard, Hugh and Charlotte received an escort, boarding a skiff to ferry them across the water to Castle Stalker—the grand old keep rose out of Loch Linnhe like a warrior from the sea clad in age-old armor, ready to take on anyone who tried to breach her walls.

The guards led Hugh and Charlotte straight to the great hall.

Footsteps pattered down the stairwell until Robert Stewart's bonny young face appeared. Christ, Hugh felt like he'd aged fifty years when he saw the young chieftain grin. "My God, you did survive."

Hugh offered a clipped nod. "Aye, and I've now gathered near three score of clansmen and women. They're all freezing in the hills, too afraid to show their faces, lest they be murdered by any red-coated bastard who happens past."

Robert looked Charlotte from head to toe—in truth the ordeal hadn't been kind to her either. Her matted hair draped over her thin gown, made thinner by her lack of petticoats. "Have you no mantle, no bonnet?"

Remembering his manners, Hugh gestured toward her. "Miss Charlotte Hill and I were fortunate to escape with the threads on our back. Most of my kin were not so fortunate."

"Charlotte Hill?" The chieftain extended his hand, his eyes filled with question. "The governor's daughter?"

She shot Hugh a startled glance, then nodded.

"If it weren't for this lady's warning, I'd be dead." Hugh still couldn't smile. "I've come to ask for your charity. I've nothing to pay you with, nothing to trade, but my people are cold and starving, and I've no alternative but to stand before you with my upturned palms and beg." His gut twisted into a hundred knots as the words slipped through his lips.

Robert drew his hand over his mouth and glanced at his guardsmen. "Of course. With the season our stores are low, but you're welcome to anything we have to spare."

"Clothing and blankets?" Charlotte asked.

"I'll send word to the clan, requesting that every family contribute something." Robert gestured to the dais. "Please, would you share my midday meal?"

Hugh's knees practically buckled. "I am honored."

"I hope you plan to stay. I've had word from Donald MacDonald of Sleat—he's requested accommodations whilst he visits Fort William—intends to find out exactly what happened."

Hugh ground his teeth, though glad to hear the baronet and head of all septs of Clan Donald had learned of his plight. "I can give him a first-hand account."

"I'd like to hear it myself." Robert led them up the steps to the high table and raised his eyebrow at Charlotte. "Your father is anxious for your return."

She followed the chieftain, lifting her filthy skirts to her ankles as she ascended. "He should have thought about that before he condoned an annihilation of an entire clan." Aye, she did have spirit, but Hugh had been wrong to woo her.

He now feared he'd be set upon by Colonel Hill because of his misshapen love for his daughter. Too right, he should have sent Charlotte home with Farley—bless it, how many times did he have to kick himself over that dull-witted decision?

Once seated, servants filed into the hall with trenchers laden with food. Lord in heaven, Hugh couldn't stop his mouth from watering. He tried to hide his trembling fingers under the table while a servant placed two juicy slices of roast pork on his plate—after Charlotte and Robert, of course.

"Applesauce?" another servant asked.

He licked his lips. "I'll have it all." Parsnips, turnips, bread, gravy. Though it had been less than a sennight since he'd eaten a meal like this, it felt more like he'd been starving for a month. Even sitting in a chair was a luxury. Christ, Stewart set the table with forks.

Once everyone had been served, Charlotte picked up her fork and knife, cutting her meat as if she weren't famished. "So, Sir Stewart, where is your wife this day?"

He raised his tankard of ale. "Ah, m'lady, I'm but eight and ten."

Her eyes bulged as she delicately placed a bite into her mouth. "You've risen to such an esteemed rank for one so young." Oh, yes, her soft "mmm" didn't escape Hugh.

"My father died of consumption but six month's past." The young chieftain dipped his bread in a bit of gravy as if he had all day to eat.

Certain he had juice dribbling from the corner of his mouth, Hugh wiped it with the back of his hand. "Delicious."

Robert smiled. "Simple fare." He turned his attention to Charlotte. "Would I be too bold to offer you a chambermaid and warm bath above stairs, Miss Hill?"

She glanced down at her gown and cringed. "Heavens, that would be a kindness I could not allow to pass by. I'm afraid I must look dreadful."

The young buck smiled politely. "Not at all."

Hugh reached for the tankard and guzzled his ale, washing

down the mouthful of bread, pork, turnip—everything he could stuff in his mouth.

"Slow down, big fella." Robert sat back and folded his arms. "By God, you *are* starving."

Hugh could only nod.

"Once you've eaten your fill, we can retire to my solar for a dram of whisky—Glenlyon's abomination—" Robert eyed Charlotte and cleared his throat. "Well, it looks as if it may have breathed new life into the *cause*. If nothing else, we'd best put quill to paper and record all the sordid events whilst it's still clear in your mind."

Bloody oath, Stewart's words infused Hugh with a thread of hope. He'd lead the Jacobites raiding across Britain today if King James was ready.

❧

WEARING A WOOLEN DRESSING GOWN TIED AT THE WAIST, Charlotte sat on the edge of the bed wanting to drop to her back and sleep for a sennight. She hadn't been appointed with a chamber this grand since she'd lived in London with her aunt and uncle. The four-poster bed was enormous, yet it didn't even take up a third of the floor. A welcoming fire crackled in an enormous hearth, in front of which was placed a wooden bathing tub.

A half-dozen chambermaids efficiently moved about with buckets of water and armloads of everything Charlotte could think of from drying cloths to petticoats, to hairpins and brushes.

"This was her ladyship's chamber, God rest her soul." Mrs. MacCallum, the housemaid in charge, frowned woefully. She had grey streaks peeking beneath her coif and wore a black frock buttoned all the way up to her throat. She hadn't smiled since they were introduced by Sir Robert. In fact, none of the lasses had. "Sir Robert thought you might be able to wear her clothing."

"That is very kind." Charlotte gripped her hands in her lap and smiled at one of the girls who instantly looked away. Another practically hugged the walls as if she were afraid. Charlotte's knuckles grew white from clenching her fingers too tightly. After her stay at Meall Mòr, she should be growing accustomed to leery stares by now, but still their behavior was unwarranted. "Have I done something to upset you?"

Draping a petticoat over a wooden chair, Mrs. MacCallum glanced up. "Why would you ask that?"

"Because you're all looking at me like Judas."

The maid who kept to the walls gasped and fanned her face.

Then a fair-haired lass stepped forward, folding her arms. "The men say you're Colonel Hill's daughter. Is he not the one who ordered Glencoe?" She said it as if it were an event rather than a place.

They all stopped and stared at Charlotte as if they expected her to draw a flintlock pistol from her sleeve and fire it at them.

She tried not to cringe. "My father tried to stop it. He remained at Fort William while officers Hamilton, Glenlyon, Duncanson and Drummond fell upon the glen, far outnumbering the poor MacIains."

"He stayed at the fort?" asked the fair one.

Having tried to rationalize it herself, Charlotte gave the only answer she knew to be true. "Because the Master of Stair ordered him to do something he could not abide."

Mrs. MacCallum now folded her arms. "But didn't the directive come from the colonel?"

"I'm ashamed to admit it, but yes—the orders to mobilize the troops came from him." Charlotte couldn't lie—true her father had played his part, but he seemed to be the only person who realized the order signed by the Master of Stair and King William was pure insanity. She hung her head. "Please do not judge me in the same light as the government troops. When I learned of Papa's orders, I rode all night to warn Mr. MacIain."

The fair-haired maid stepped forward, her face inquisitive. "But you were too late?"

Charlotte nodded. Thank heavens someone showed a bit of curiosity before condemning her. "I arrived at his cottage only moments before the shooting began. Mr. MacIain fought off the six dragoons who were sent to murder him and burn his house."

The nice girl's jaw dropped. "He fought six soldiers all by himself?"

Still sitting with her hands folded, her fingers began to throb. "My guide helped."

"While you watched?"

"I hid in the..." Charlotte shouldn't say Hugh's bedchamber "In the rear room."

"Oh my." The maid actually looked as if she were sympathetic. "That must have been terrifying."

"Aye," said another. "You were in the thick of it?"

Charlotte looked down, her old shyness creeping up the back of her neck. "Yes."

Mrs. MacCallum clapped her hands. "We must leave Miss Hill to her bath before the water chills."

As the chambermaids filed out the door, Charlotte hopped up and tapped the friendly maid on the shoulder. "What is your name?"

"Alice, miss."

"Thank you, Alice. Not many people have had a kind word for me in the past few days."

She curtsied. "I figured there was a good reason Laird

MacIain brought you with him." The tension in the chamber eased with her grin. "Imagine that, Colonel Hill's daughter is a Jacobite."

Snapping a hand over her mouth to hide her gasp, Charlotte watched as the door closed and left her alone. *Holy Mother. If I'm in love with Hugh, I must be a Jacobite.* She paced in a circle. *I surely do not condone the king's orders, nor do I appreciate the way he's ignored my father since he took the throne.*

With her realization, she discarded the borrowed robe and sank into the bathwater. Charlotte had always loved baths, but this one sent her sailing with the clouds. Even the lilac soap smelled like a gift from heaven. She slid down until the water reached her chin. Her entire body reveled in soothing warmth for the first time since she'd left Fort William.

Chapter Twenty-Six

✦

After spending the day devising plots against the government troops with Robert Stewart, Hugh had accepted a change of clothes, washed and shaved. Seeing his reflection in a looking glass had been frightening. True, he'd gone without shaving many times before, but the dark circles under his eyes and drawn, hollow pitch to his cheeks was new. He could have passed for a beggar on the streets of Edinburgh.

How the devil had Charlotte put up with him? He not only looked like a rogue, he'd been treating her like thresh on the floor. Now cleaned up with a good meal in his belly, he scoffed at his behavior. The lass had done nothing but volunteered to help him and his kin, and they resented her for it. He'd resented her, too, but couldn't for the life of him understand why.

And now, he again sat in the great hall in anticipation of the evening meal. He wouldn't be so daft as to refuse Sir Robert's fare, but his throat thickened at the thought of his clansmen and women huddling in that miserable hovel up at Meall Mòr. If only Clan Iain Abrach of the Coe had a fortress like Castle Stalker none of this would have ever happened. No, the Master of Stair and the Campbells had singled out the MacIain sept of Clan Donald because of their close proximity to Fort William and their lack of a motte and bailey defense. Hugh clearly remembered telling his father Glencoe was both a fortress and a trap. God, he'd had no idea how right he'd been.

Beside him, young Stewart pushed back his chair and stood, a soft whistle blowing through his lips.

Looking up, Hugh sprang to his feet, the screeching the floorboards behind him.

"Holy Moses," Robert swore. "Why didn't you tell me Colonel Hill's daughter was as ravishing as a princess?"

Hugh clenched his fists as he watched Charlotte exit the stairwell and proceed to the dais. The talk in the hall ebbed to complete silence. "Devil's bones," Hugh mumbled like a simpleton.

The woman had a bloody bath and turns herself into a goddess? Smiling like a fairy nymph, Charlotte floated across the floor, every male chin dropping as she walked past, her red gown shimmering with every step. Bloody hell, the scooped neckline displayed too much of her milky white bosoms. She seemed oblivious to all the attention she commanded as her gaze focused on Hugh. Christ, the woman could win the heart of any man in all of Britain, and she thought she wanted him—a chieftain without a home?

Sir Robert clambered to the dais steps and offered his hand. "My word, Miss Hill you are a vision."

She blushed as if she'd never heard a man tell her she was beautiful. Blast it, the slathering pup practically drooled on her as he led her to a seat—not beside Hugh, but the one to Robert's right. That would be the way of it. Hugh would have to spend the entire evening watching a pup who hadn't even reached his majority fawn all over his woman.

And Charlotte smiled at him as if she enjoyed his adolescent drool.

"Mother's gown fits as if it were made for you."

Charlotte sat as Sir Robert pushed in her chair. "Thank you ever so much for lending it to me. The color is beautiful."

"It compliments your fair coloring." Sir Robert turned to Hugh. "MacIain, why didn't you tell me Colonel Hill's daughter was bonnier than a mountain of heather in bloom?"

Hugh plopped in his chair. "It took a bath for you to notice?" He leaned forward and caught her gaze. His damned heart leapt. "And your gown does bring out the blue-violet in your eyes—ever so much." There, let Stewart chew on that.

Robert's brow furrowed. "You do seem an unlikely pair. How in God's name did you meet? I doubt Colonel Hill would have been anxious to make the introductions."

"Mr. MacIain was—"

"Let's just say I was an unwilling guest at Fort William for a time." Though the prisoners from the battle of Dunkeld had been pardoned, Hugh still didn't want anyone knowing the reason for his incarceration or the fact that Charlotte had helped him escape. He was in enough trouble with the government. No use piling on more reasons for her father to send him to the gallows.

Sir Robert filled Charlotte's glass with wine. "Word from the fort is your father is anxious for your return."

She leaned forward and glanced at Hugh. "I should send him a letter."

"You should go to him," Hugh said. "Hiding in the hills of Glencoe is no place for a lady as fine as you."

"Did you think I would give up so easily? I cannot just walk away and return to my father as if nothing happened. I would be an utter hypocrite."

"MacIain has a point. You are far too delicate a lady to be suffering with a mob of refugees in the hills during the midst of winter." Robert held up his glass. "You are welcome to stay here, if you'd rather."

Hugh slapped his palm on the table a bit too hard, making wine slosh out of his glass. "She's either going back to Fort William or staying with me."

Charlotte leaned forward, arching those damnable eyebrows at him. "So now you're making decisions for me?"

"I will if you will not make the right ones."

"I beg your pardon?" She pushed her chair back. "I shall not dine with someone who thinks so little of my sensibilities."

Now he'd gone and shoved his foot in his mouth. "I didn't mean—"

"Please stay." Robert put his hand on her elbow—a far too familiar gesture. "I most certainly didn't mean to upset you with my remark. Perhaps you are right. You should pen a missive to your da. I'd be happy to have my runner deliver it on your behalf."

Looking at Hugh, she gave a curt nod. "That would be ever so kind of you, Sir Robert."

Wonderful. Hugh ground his fist into his palm. Now he'd been made to look an unmitigated arse to the woman he loved.

A servant placed a tray of sliced roast beef in front of Stewart and he promptly picked it up, offering Charlotte first choice. "The Baronet of Sleat will arrive from Duntulm Castle on the morrow."

She selected a small portion. "'Tis good to hear the head of all the MacDonald septs is showing his support."

"Aye," Hugh agreed, helping himself to a juicy cut—the largest on the patter. "We'll certainly know more on the morrow. 'Tis worth spending another day away from our kin in the mountains."

"You both are welcome to stay as long as you need." Sir

Robert reached for the salt cellar and used the tiny spoon to sprinkle his food—ever so civilized of him.

Hugh practically kicked himself under the table. *For Christ's sake, the man is opening his home to us.* "My thanks. Your hospitality will nay be forgotten."

"Indeed." Charlotte reached for her wine and sipped. "Do you often invite minstrels to play on your gallery?"

"Pipes mostly, though I do enjoy a good fiddle."

"Oh, so do I." She grinned vibrantly as if she hadn't ridden down from hell earlier that day.

Young Stewart's gaze dipped too low—where was her damned privacy panel now? "Are you musically inclined?"

She blushed like a wee maiden. "I play the violin some."

"Honestly?" Sir Robert looked like his mouth had burst with sweet flavor. "Why, there's a fiddle up on the gallery just waiting to be played."

Hugh cleared his throat and shoved a bite in his mouth. The wet-eared chieftain would have her agreeing to stay at the damned castle for an eternity soon.

"Would you do me the honor of serenading us? These halls haven't been filled with a merry tune since Christmas." Robert elbowed Hugh in the shoulder. "What say you, MacIain?"

It would be a very long time before Hugh was ready to kick up his heels and dance jig to a raunchy fiddle. Charlotte ought to know that. Hell, did the ride down the mountain wash away the horror of what *her* father's men had done to his kin? Bloody hell, a sennight had not yet passed.

Robert and Charlotte looked at him as if he were daft. Hugh flicked his wrist toward the gallery. "Go on then. If it would please our host."

Charlotte stood, casting Hugh a disapproving frown before she turned and headed up the steps. Hugh's gut twisted. Ballocks, he was acting like an arse—but what did everyone expect? Should he cast aside the cannonball-sized hole in his chest and make merry as if nothing had happened? He couldn't do it. He wouldn't rest until he saw justice—until Glenlyon got his comeuppance. He wouldn't rest until every Jacobite in Scotland pulled together and took a stand.

Damnation.

Robert leaned in. "She has eyes for you."

Och, by the hostility in her glare, Hugh seriously doubted it. "I owe her my life." Christ, where did that line of drivel come from? He guzzled his ale. He did owe Charlotte his life and he wasn't a damned bit happy about it.

Or was he?

Bloody hell, he needed air.

"You look a bit piqued," said Robert.

"I'm fine."

"Oh?" Robert pushed a bit too far.

"Bugger off." Hugh set his tankard down and shoved a cooked carrot in his mouth.

Robert leaned back in his chair. "Well, I suppose I'd be as sore-headed as you, given the same circumstances."

An eerie pitch sang from the gallery. One long, lonely note resounded and swirled throughout the hall as if an angel swept down and requested their silence.

Hugh's breath caught as Charlotte used the fiddle, not to produce a foot-stomping ditty, but the strings sang a ballad so melancholy, gooseflesh rose across his skin. Aye, he'd heard countless minstrels when they'd stopped in Glencoe to play, but he'd never heard anyone make a fiddle sing hauntingly like the entire world wept.

Not a servant moved, not a word was whispered while she moved the bow back and forth across the strings, her fingers never pausing. The notes rose painfully high and woefully low, louder and louder the song grew, until all at once a note rang out so low it could hardly be heard. After one last refrain of gut-wrenching sadness, complete and utter silence filled the hall.

A tear leaking from his eye, Sir Robert led the applause. "Did you ken she could make a fiddle sing like that?"

Hugh shook his head. "'Tis the first time I've ever heard her play."

€

AFTER CHARLOTTE HAD COME DOWN FROM THE GALLERY, Hugh was already gone. She'd politely excused herself and was met in her chamber by Alice.

The young maid stood and curtsied. "I hope you don't mind. Mrs. MacCallum assigned me to be your chambermaid whilst you're visiting Castle Stalker."

Charlotte smiled and took a seat on the vanity stool in front of the mirror. "I'm delighted. Mrs. MacCallum is too somber and I fear the others are worried I'll pull a pistol from my sleeve and shoot them."

Alice removed a hairpin. "Do you have one?"

"A pistol?" Charlotte chuckled. "Heavens, no."

"How long do you figure you'll be here?"

Well aware any information about Hugh that managed to seep through the castle walls could result in his capture—or worse, she shrugged. "Not sure. So many supplies are needed, it could be a long time before we're ready to go back."

"And you're planning to return to the mountains with him?"

"Yes."

"Why?" Now that Alice had removed all the pins, she took a brush to Charlotte's tresses. "You do not need to hide."

"I suppose that's the way with love."

Alice sighed. "I kent there had to be a fairy tale in the making."

"Yes, though presently it seems more like a nightmare."

A loud bang came from the next room. Gasping, Charlotte whipped around toward the noise. "What was that?"

"Not sure. 'Tis Mr. MacIain's chamber. Would you like me to go rap on his door?"

Hugh was in the next room? Charlotte's heart skipped a beat, though she feigned calmness. "No—that should not be necessary." She stood. "Please help me out of my gown."

Alice proved as efficient at unlacing as she was at lacing, and soon left Charlotte standing alone in her chamber, wrapped in the red dressing gown.

All the while there had been more noise—thuds, as if Hugh were pounding his fist into the mattress—or the furniture—or Lord knew what else.

A suppressed yowl rumbled through the walls. Was he hurt? Would he be all right?

Charlotte wrung her hands and paced.

Would he want my succor? He doesn't seem to appreciate anything I do. He hated my violin. I just know it. I cannot do anything to please him.

The yowl came again, wrenching her heart.

Should I return to Fort William and leave him to pick up the pieces while I wait in my father's house like a hypocrite?

She pressed the heel of her hand to her forehead.

Dear Lord, why did this have to happen?

Muffled grunts of pain seeped through the walls. Charlotte could take no more. Tightening the belt around her waist, she tiptoed to the next door and hesitated. If she knocked, he'd send her away for certain. With a burst of courage, she pulled up on the latch and slipped inside.

Lit only by a candle on the mantel, Charlotte blinked taking in the furnishings. Hugh lay curled on the bed, his fists hiding his face. His chest bare, he wore only a plaid around his waist. Tension radiated off him as if his every muscle were pulled taut. Deep growls came from his throat—expressing the agony she knew twisted his insides until they could not withstand another turn.

"Hugh," she whispered, keeping her back against the door.

Shuddering he looked up. "Leave me."

She moved closer, crossing her arms over her chest. "I want to help."

He sat up and slammed his fist into the bed. "Can you not see I need no help?"

"Please tell me what you want me to do. It seems my every action pushes you further away."

He shook his head.

"Please."

"Do you want to take on your father's army? Do you want to march against William of Orange?"

She bit her bottom lip and closed the distance until she stood before him. "I want to make you happy."

He didn't meet her gaze. "I fear a man with a black heart is incapable of happiness."

"But we have each other. Isn't that a place to start rebuilding?" Reaching out, she touched his cheek.

Hugh pulled away so fiercely, Charlotte recoiled as if he'd issued a slap. "Do you hate me?"

"Yes—no." Hugh stood and marched to the hearth. "It is not you I hate."

"Then what is it?"

"Can you not understand?" He remained facing the fire. "I have a clan looking to me for guidance. I have nothing, not even one piece of silver I can give you. Christ, Charlotte, you are a well-bred lass who's lived in comfort all her life. I cannot ask you to camp in the hills like a wild animal, and your willingness to do so only serves to make me feel like the basest scoundrel who ever walked the Highlands."

She clutched her arms tighter around her ribcage. "So you're pushing me away because you think I cannot take the hard times?"

"Dammit, Charlotte I cannot give you the attention you need when I have so many other mouths to feed."

"And I am consuming precious food that could sustain someone else." Dejected, she moved to the bed and sat. "Someone who does not have the option of a warm house inside a fortress like Fort William?"

"Exactly."

She again clutched her arms across her ribcage, curling over. "And here I thought you loved me. I thought we had something special. Bless it, you asked me to be your wife and I accepted because I fell in love with a man who saw what he wanted and let nothing stand in his way until he got it. I saw a man of power and strength, a man that could pull through anything."

She stood and skirted toward the door.

Hugh faced her. "Charlotte, I—"

"No. I see now that I was wrong. You are going to allow this tragedy to eat away at your insides until there is nothing left." With a stamp of her foot, she dashed the distance to the door. Grasping the latch, she pulled it open.

Hugh's gigantic hand clapped against the wood and slammed it shut. "If you think I'm giving up on us so easily, you are sorely mistaken." His lips brushed her ear, his voice but a low growl.

Chapter Twenty-Seven

Catching Charlotte's scent, Hugh scarcely contained himself from ripping off the dressing gown she had cinched tight around her waist. Her back still to him while his hands trapped her against the door, his cock thrust against her soft buttocks as he lowered his mouth to her ear. "You want a broken man for a husband? A man who can give you nothing—not even a farthing?" Heat rose up the back of his neck. Christ, he hated himself as much as he hated the disaster he'd been thrust into. "It is my responsibility to care for my clan. It is my responsibility to keep them alive while God Almighty pummels us with the worst snows the Highlands have ever witnessed."

"You think I need nice things?" Holy Mary, the woman bucked against him, shoving her pillow-soft buttocks into his erection. "I have slept on a dirt floor for you. I have tended your mother using my own petticoat. I. Have. Endured taunts and threats from those people you have sworn to protect." She jutted against him harder this time—her hips pure torture to Hugh's resolve. "Can you not push it through that thick skull of yours that all of it has been for you? I would give you my last crumb—my last thread of clothing because you are my *world*. Wherever you are, that is where I want to be."

"Char—"

She spun around and faced him, tears glistening on her cheeks—so goddamned bonny, his thighs shuddered. "If it would ease your burden to send me back to my father I will go, but know I will only do so out of my love for *you*."

Words caught in the back of Hugh's throat. He was such a goddamned dolt. He clutched her cheeks between his palms dipping his head to take what he'd coveted since she'd walked into the room. His mouth fell over hers with a deep, carnal moan. Thrusting his tongue between her lips, he slid his hands down her back and pulled her tight until her rounded breasts molded into his chest, her mons jutted against him and a deep moan erupted from her throat. How she could turn molten in his arms after he'd acted so barbarously, he couldn't fathom, but there she was, melting in his arms, and by God he would worship her this night. For days he had fought his urge to bare that creamy white skin and savor her long silken legs as they wrapped around him.

Every time he looked at her in the shieling, it tied him in knots. If he touched her, everyone watched. If he kissed her, the heat of Og's stare alone was enough to stifle even the most ardent of desires.

"I need you," he whispered. "More than the air I breathe, I need you."

She swirled her tight little hips right where he craved her most. "Then take me."

Mayhap the lass needed this as much as he. By the naughty pressure of her mons against him, he needed no more encouragement. With a rumbling moan he swept her into his arms and carried her to the bed. Settling into the pillows, Charlotte's hair sprawled everywhere like a temptress' mane. Lord, she even lifted her arms above her head with a heavy-lidded stare. She was ripe and ready, and God knew his entire being had ached to take her for far too long.

He leaned over her, supporting his weight on his arms. "You are mine, Charlotte."

She threaded her fingers through his hair, her lips shimmering with moistness. "I am. Truly, I am."

No, he could no longer deny the lust thrumming through his blood or his deep-seated desire to bury himself inside her. Hugh's breathing sped as he untied her sash and spread open the dressing gown, revealing a crisp linen nightdress. "When you came down for the evening meal I wanted to throw you over my shoulder and haul you above stairs."

"Mm," she chuckled, untying the ribbon and opening the neck of her nightdress. "I thought you were upset to see me clad in such finery when..."

He knew what she meant, though glad she hadn't uttered it. He captured her pink lips with a searing kiss. Presently, Hugh didn't want to think about anything but Charlotte— stripping her bare and running his tongue over every inch of her flesh. "My mind ran amuck with jealousy. Did you see the way Sir Robert looked at you?"

"Sir Robert?" She smoothed magical fingers over his shoulders. "Why on earth would you be jealous of him? He's not even yet a man."

Och aye, her words were like magic to his heart, the heavy burden in his chest not aching quite so much. With a low growl, Hugh kneeled between her legs and nuzzled into her tresses. The sweet smell of lilac nearly sent him over the edge. Trailing kisses up her neck, he again plunged in for another kiss. With a wanton moan, she threaded her fingers through his hair. He could feel her passion, her heat, her need. Her hips rocked beneath him with the same urgency shooting straight to the tip of his cock.

Lowering, he rubbed himself back and forth. His manhood stirred against her with only two layers of clothing between them. He could feel her soft flesh open for him—heating up with her dampness.

God, he wanted to raise her hem and plunge inside—take her now.

But this was Charlotte—the woman he'd put on a pedestal, the woman he worshiped.

With a frustrated grunt, he rocked back. "I need to see you bare."

Panting she nodded, sitting up and raising her arms for him.

Casting the nightdress aside, Hugh licked his lips as his gaze took in the most seductive sight he'd ever seen. Waves of blonde tresses cascaded across the pillows. He wanted it all. Her heavy-lidded eyes, full-just-been-kissed lips, long, elegant neck, curvaceous breasts tipped by rose, pert and ready to suckle. His tongue slipping to the corner of his mouth, he cupped the softest flesh on this earth and lowered to capture the perfect pearl.

A palm to the center of his chest stopped him. "Now you."

Gulping, he nodded, his eyelids growing heavy. Oh yes, he liked that she wanted to see him naked. Watching her face, he unbuckled his belt and let the plaid drop. Lord, the mere friction of the cloth sliding down his thighs made him harder.

Charlotte's breathing stuttered as her gaze slid down his abdomen to his cock. He'd never imagined a woman could make a man come with a look, but the way her eyes darkened, and her pink tongue slipped to the corner of her mouth made a bit of seed pulse. Hell, even her nipples tightened, her chest heaving. God, she wanted this as much as he did. Her hips rocked up. "Please, Hugh."

Devil's fire, the trust in her eyes nearly blew him down. He wanted to be worthy of that trust, needed to protect her with his being. He would do anything to care for her the way she deserved. "I vow I will make it right for you."

She reached for him. "I know. I believe in you."

How much he needed to hear those words. With her confidence, his own would burst free. "You make me whole," he uttered, realizing this for the first time ever.

"Please."

Her plea practically made him burst out of his skin. Kneeling between her legs he started where he'd left off and captured a succulent breast in his mouth.

Gasping, Charlotte bucked against him. Then she did something no woman he'd ever bedded had been bold enough to try. Her lithe fingers wrapped around his shaft and stroked him. Barely able to contain himself, he shuddered.

"You like that?"

"Too much." He gritted his teeth, forcing himself not to come in her hand. He sucked in a breath. "I do not want to hurt you."

She guided his tip toward her womanhood—the sacred triangle of dark-blonde curls demanding he plunge inside and take her now. But he wanted to savor the moment. Make it good for her.

"Emma said it only hurts the first time. Please—let this be our first."

CHARLOTTE WAS ABOUT TO BURST. HER EVERY NERVE trembled with ferocious desire. She held him in her hand—hard as bedpost. All she could think about was feeling him join with her. If she gave him her virtue, he'd understand the depth of her commitment. If she could just figure out how to guide him inside, it would set things between them the way they'd been before the world had shattered around them.

But he hesitated, his mouth parted, his eyes dark as coal.

"Join with me," she pleaded.

His lips quivered. Quick breaths stretching his muscled chest. "I need to make it good for you."

"You will." She arched up until his member touched her— so slick. "You make me moist like this."

"Holy Mary," he groaned. "I can't s...top."

"Don't." Barely able to breathe, she held herself rigid, waiting for the pain.

With a tilt of his hips, he rubbed himself along her womanhood, stopping at her opening. "I'll go slowly," his voice was but a growl.

Charlotte stared into those deep pools of treacle and trusted him with her entire being. She wanted this—had wanted it ever since he kissed her when she helped him spirit out of Fort William.

Her insides stretched as he entered and held himself there, kissing her neck.

"A bit more," he moaned as if the pace were killing him.

"Yes." Reaching down, Charlotte dug her fingers into his buttocks and urged him deeper.

With a sharp gasp, he slid further. It stung, but the pain did nothing to assuage the pure ecstasy of feeling him inside —joining with her like a man and a woman in love.

"Can you take a bit more?" he asked through clenched teeth.

"Yes," her breathless voice peeped as she increased the pressure with her fingers. Glorious, blessed, rapture, he filled her as her insides stretched to accept him deep within her core.

Groaning, shuddering, Hugh slid further until, just when

she thought she could stretch no more, he pulled back a bit and rocked his hips. Saints preserve her, this was even better than having his mouth...down there. She clung to his buttocks and matched his rhythm.

Unable to control her little gasps, she encouraged him to rock faster while tension again built in her core. Just when her body began to burst into glorious spasms, Hugh arched his back and stifled a roar through clenched teeth. Charlotte's insides quivered around him.

With a feral growl he thrust until he bellowed. In the next instant, he pulled out and spilled upon her stomach. Panting, Hugh pushed back to his knees. "By God, you will be the death of me."

Charlotte froze with her gasp. Looking into his eyes, the unease of his clan's plight lurked in his dark pools of brown. No, he wouldn't want to chance bringing a child into this world. Not now.

Swallowing back her disappointment, she understood. Hard times would not last forever. And he was right. After they were married, she would conceive.

Chapter Twenty-Eight

Hugh stood on the battlements, facing Loch Linnhe. He'd told everyone he was watching for Donald MacDonald's galley, but he needed time alone. He needed a cold wind in his face to clear his mind. He'd nearly convinced himself Charlotte didn't belong in Glencoe, but after last night, his resolution crumbled.

His soul be damned, he couldn't give the lass up. His kin would have to accept her. She wasn't like Sarah—that nasty wench had never done anything to help others like Charlotte had done. As a matter of fact, Hugh never heard the Campbell woman utter a pleasant word about Sandy.

His gut twisted as it had so often in the past sennight. Yes, Hugh mourned the loss of his father and Ma, but Sandy had so much life left to live. A more affable lad Hugh had never known. Sandy had a natural talent for everything, and though he seemed to know it, he never boasted. More than once Hugh had seen him let another man win at archery or cards just to keep things friendly.

Hugh looked up to the sky. "Lord, you'd best put wings on

Alexander. He's the best bloody Highland angel you'll ever see."

Charlotte would make a bloody good angel as well. Hugh raised his fist. "But you can't have her. She's mine."

A gust of wind hit him with such force, Hugh took a step back, thrusting his fist higher. "I mean it!"

He leaned into the wind and cast his gaze northward. Where was that damned *birlinn*? Hugh needed to get back to Meall Mòr before his people starved—or froze, and by the looks of the sky, another blizzard was brewing. God, he hated waiting for anything.

Ahead, Robert exited the stairwell, rubbing his shoulders. "Bloody hell, with the wind 'tis colder than a dip in an icy loch up here."

"Aye. 'Tis at that." Wearing nothing but his shirt with his plaid draped over his shoulders. Hugh refused to let the cold vex him—dammit, if Robert thought it was miserable atop Castle Stalker, he should spend a couple nights in the mountains with his kin.

Stewart waved his thumb over his shoulder. "You'd never believe who just rowed across from Appin."

Hugh glanced over his shoulder at the southwestern corner of the keep. He hadn't visited that side of the wall-walk at all. *Was it Hill?* Lead sank to the pit of his stomach. "Who?"

"The Earl of Breadalbane."

Ballocks. "I thought you said I would be safe within these walls." Hugh started toward the stairwell. Hell, he couldn't risk being arrested and detained in the Inveraray Tolbooth at a time like this. "Where can I hide?"

Robert grabbed his arm. "He came alone."

Hugh pulled up short. "What say you?"

"Aye, left his retinue waiting in the snow in Appin. Says he only wants to talk. Says he'll surrender his weapons if necessary."

"Bloody hell. What the blazes does he want with me?"

"Not sure, aside from a private audience with you."

Hugh scratched his stubbled chin. Grey John Campbell, the Earl of Breadalbane was close to his age, but much shorter. Nonetheless, Hugh wasn't about to take any chances. "No weapons?"

"Aye."

"Very well." Hugh might leave his sword and dirk behind, but he'd keep his *sgian dubh* hidden inside his sleeve as insurance. He'd never again be able to trust one single Campbell backstabber.

"He's in my solar. You can meet with him there." Robert chuckled. "My men have already relieved the earl of his weapons."

When Hugh stepped into the solar, the earl was warming his hands at the fire, his brown horsehair wig curling well past his shoulders. He turned swiftly, raising his aristocratic nose. "MacIain." He walked forward and held out his hand. "I cannot tell you how much it pleases me to see you escaped this heinous crime."

Hugh looked down at the extended palm—white skin, smooth as a bairn's arse. After a moment's hesitation, he took it, crushing the bastard's fingers until Breadalbane's face turned scarlet. "To what do I owe this *honor*, m'lord?"

Reclaiming his hand, the man rubbed his knuckles and sat at the head of the table. "When news of the massacre reached me in London, I quickly sailed for home." He gave an exaggerated shake of his head. "'Tis an abomination of the worst sort."

"Aye." Taking a seat at the other end of the table far enough away so he wouldn't inadvertently strangle the cur, Hugh arched an eyebrow. "Word surely arrived in London with haste if you've had time to sail this far north in our tempestuous weather."

Breadalbane pursed his lips, stretching his neck out of the cravat knotted tightly at his throat. "There is a faction of us who are concerned with the way the Master of Stair is conducting the king's affairs during his absence in Flanders."

"Oh? I have it from a good source the king's signature was on the orders to put my entire clan under fire and sword." Hugh drummed his fingers atop the table, watching the earl's expression. "All those under seventy, I'm told."

The man blanched. "Your sources are credible then?"

"Very." Bless Charlotte Hill a million times a million.

Breadalbane sliced his palm through the air. "Be it known I had no hand in this."

Hugh believed that as much as he believed in fairy shite. "Aye? You were completely unaware—unable to stop it?"

"By the time I uncovered the Master of Stair's plan, it was too late."

Hugh shrugged. It no longer mattered if the earl was lying through his teeth or not. "So, why are you here?"

Removing a kerchief from his sleeve, the earl dabbed the sweat beading on his upper lip. "I have a proposition for you."

Hugh's gaze trailed to the fire in the hearth. This conversation grew odder and odder. "For me?"

"I want no hand in this affair." The kerchief disappeared from whence it came. "You are aware I tried to bring about Jacobite loyalty to King William peaceably."

"Pardon?" Hugh could have hurled his breakfast atop Stewart's fine walnut table. "Are you as full of shite as you sound? My father waited for days to sign the oath in Inveraray —when finally Campbell of Ardkinglas managed to show his face, Da signed it with as broad a signature as yours I'll wager —and all while you sat beside your hearth with your countess."

The earl's Adam's apple bobbed.

Hugh leaned further forward—another foot or two, and he'd be able to strangle that neck. By God, he would have his say. "As I recall, you offered payments to buy the highest ranking chieftain's loyalty." Hugh pushed back and rapped his knuckles on the table. "Except no compensation was offered to my father, nor were any payments forthcoming from London to compensate those who trusted you, *m'lord*."

Breadalbane again tugged on his cravat. The codfish should have loosened it a bit before requesting an audience. Hugh had no intention of kissing his pasty arse, earl or no.

"The king's coffers have been bled by the war in France."

Hugh didn't care about that either. The bloody war in France is what had prevented James II and VII from gaining support from King Louis. "Still, I do not see what that has to do with me or the fact that my kin are hiding, freezing. Damnation, most have nothing but a blanket on their backs."

Sitting back, the earl regarded him down the length of his nose.

Hugh smirked. "Not one cow or sheep, or even a chicken was left in Glencoe. We were murdered by *your* cousin for God's sake. Is there anything you can do to feed my starving kin? Cause if you cannot, this parlcy is over."

"Good God, you're as arrogant as your father." The earl gave a woeful shake of his head. Aye, a philanthropist he was not.

But Hugh refused to play the bleeding heart. "I'll take that as a compliment."

Breadalbane placed his palms on the table. "I did not condone Glenlyon's actions nor would I ever agree to such an abuse of Highland hospitality. Sir, I have come to you with a proposition."

Bloody oath, how long did Hugh have to sit there before

the earl spat it out? He rolled his hand through the air. "I'm listening."

"If you will swear and write under your hand that I am innocent of the slaughter, then I will use my influence to secure a full pardon and restitution for your clan."

Hugh's eyes nearly popped out of his head. "What the blazes do *I* need a pardon for?"

"I-I agree—your father signed the oath, though six days past King William's deadline."

"Not for want of trying. Christ, he had the missive from Hill explaining that he'd gone to Fort William first." Hugh's nostrils flared as he took in a deep inhale. Devil's bones, the man had a gargantuan set of cods. "And what could make me believe King William would give Clan Iain Abrach of the Coe a farthing or retract his order to annihilate us all? He hasn't made good on a one of his promises to pay monies due. Even Colonel Hill has had difficulty securing back pay for his bloody dragoons."

His gut twisting in a million knots, Breadalbane's proposal scraped against every nerve in Hugh's body. Would he sell his soul to give his people the money they needed to start anew? Hell, yes! But he would *not* sign his name to aid a known backstabber with a history of making empty promises.

Hugh stood and opened the door. "You want exoneration from my father's blood on your hands?" He made an exaggerated bow. "Then I suggest you seek one of your Protestant priests."

Looming in the hallway beside Sir Robert, Lord Donald MacDonald removed his feathered bonnet. "Lord Breadalbane, what a surprise."

The earl brushed past him with a scowl. "It was the Master of Stair and my worthless, wayward cousin. I had nothing to do with it. I told him this would come to no good!"

Hugh grinned for what felt like the first time in a decade as he watched the man stomp through the passageway to the stairwell.

The baronet held out his hand. "It looks like you made Breadalbane a wee bit hot under the collar."

"Bloody oath I did." Hugh gestured to the table. "Thank you for coming, cousin. We have much to discuss."

When Hugh looked at the two faces staring at him across the table, he felt like a grandfather. Bless it, the Baronet of Sleat was only three and twenty—a year or two older than Charlotte. But these two young men had plenty of clout not only with the Jacobite cause, but with the Privy Council in Edinburgh. Taking his seat, Hugh told them about Breadalbane's offer and his refusal.

Lord Donald ran his fingers through his thick, black tresses. "I understand your reasons, though it would have been good to sway him to our side."

Robert snorted. "He's a king's man no matter who's sitting on the throne. Bloody oath, after his uncle was beheaded by Cromwell, he's afraid to piss without asking the king's permission first."

"Well then, we've more important matters to discuss." The baronet flicked his wrist at Stewart. "Robert, have some ale sent up."

"'Tis on its way."

"Very well." Eying Hugh, Lord Donald shook his head. "The western clans are infused with rage over this abomination. Hell, the Camerons are ready to take up arms and march on Fort William."

"As am I," said Hugh.

"But not while they're expecting our retaliation." The baronet looked between them, his hawk-like gaze emitting maturity well beyond his years. "While you were chatting with the earl, Robert showed me your account of Glenlyon's heinous act. We need to ensure copies are made and they fall into the right hands."

"Absolutely," agreed Sir Robert. "This is news—the story needs to be told in every gazette across Europe—expose William for who he really is."

Hugh nodded. "Fair enough. I say we send an original to King James in France."

"Agreed," said Donald. "And our allies in Edinburgh will see to it a copy is placed before the Privy Council. Not a Jacobite will rest until we gain restitution."

Hugh pursed his lips. Breadalbane had just used the same word. Could there be hope? The clamminess spreading across his shoulders told him no. The government had declared war. "We must unite the clans. If we cannot gain support from the French, we have to build our forces within."

Lord Donald slid his hand down his chin. "'Tis tricky, especially now William has made allies with Spain."

A servant entered with a tray and Robert gestured to the table. "Leave it." He reached for the ewer. "We must prepare. Be ready at all times."

Hugh took a tankard and held it up for Robert to pour. "We have to meet—I want every clan chief to know what happened after my father traveled seventy miles in a blizzard to sign the bastard's bloody oath."

"Nay." The baronet shook his head. "'Tis too dangerous to bring us all together at once."

After he'd taken a swig, Hugh slowly placed his tankard on the table, his eyes narrowing. "How about under the guise of competition?"

"You look like you have an idea." Lord Donald leaned forward on his elbow.

"For centuries clans have met to compete in Highland games. Why not hold an annual fete bringing all the western clans together?"

"At least those who support James." Robert held up a tray of oatcakes, offering them to Lord Donald.

"My thanks," said the baronet. "Once a year is not enough."

Hugh threw up his hands. "Och, first you say 'tis too dangerous, and now an annual fete is not enough?"

Robert bit a bit of crunchy cake. "Quarterly?"

The baronet sipped his ale and eyed Hugh over his tankard's rim. "Quarterly could work."

Och aye, Hugh would soon have all the Jacobite clans in his palm. "We must meet straight away."

"Are your men ready to compete?" Robert asked.

Hugh knew they weren't. Hell, *he'd* been weakened by hunger. "I am. Og, too."

The baronet leaned back in his chair and crossed his arms. "Let me think on it—Ewen Cameron will have something to say for certain."

Oh no, Hugh wasn't about to let this pass without setting a date. "Duntulm Castle. As soon as the snow melts."

"April?" suggested Robert.

Donald shook his head. "Beltane."

"Too late." Hugh clamped his fingers around his tankard's handle. "Easter is in early April this year. Tie it in with the holiday."

"Holy week?" The young lord swirled the drink in his cup, his black eyebrows knitting.

"Why not?" Robert took another oatcake. "We could start the Monday after the ascension."

"I like it." Donald's face lit up. "I do believe we have a plan, gentlemen."

Hugh polished off his ale. "Hand me a quill and a bit of parchment."

Robert complied. "Another statement?"

"Something I've been thinking of since the Battle of

Dunkeld." Dipping the quill into the inkwell, Hugh drew two dirks, making a square cross. "Any man bearing this sign branded on the underside of his forearm is with us."

Robert flinched. "Branded?"

Hugh shoved the parchment toward him. "Are you milk-livered, or are you of true Highland stock?"

"A brand will serve to separate men from lads. I'll have my smithy make the molds—one for each clan." Raising his tankard, Lord Donald grinned. "We'll see it done in April."

Hugh and Robert followed suit, toasting in unison. "*Sláinte!*"

Thank God. Hugh and Charlotte could return to Meall Mòr with supplies from the Stewarts of Appin and news that the Jacobite cause had been rekindled.

Chapter Twenty-Nine

C harlotte traveled back to the mountains with Hugh under cover of darkness. He could take no chances, and with the order for his death still fresh with ink, the threat of being killed by government forces was too risky. He had made every effort to be inconspicuous, wearing a dark blue mantle draped across his shoulders and an English three-pointed hat Sir Robert had given him. Through the darkness, Charlotte rode cradled in his arms while he led a milking cow and six pack mules laden with supplies—again due to the kind generosity of Sir Robert and Clan Stewart. Goodness, he'd even insisted on giving Charlotte the violin, saying that with fingers so deft, she should never go a day without making the instrument sing.

How the gentry in London could think so poorly of High-landers, she would never understand. Ignorance was the only excuse. If only the Master of Stair could spend a sennight in Castle Stalker, he'd realize how mistaken his beliefs.

Still Charlotte could not rationalize Hugh's plight—a fugitive in the mountains, unable to return to his own lands along the River Coe. The order for his death still hung over his head like a black cloud. Only the good Lord knew when any exiled refugee from Clan Iain Abrach would be free to live in peace again.

As the pack mules ascended the hills toward the shelter, warriors stopped them in a narrow gully with sheer cliffs on each side. Their shadowy figures faced them and in their hands they held branches fashioned into pikes—the weapons might be crude, but would be deadly all the same.

Hugh reined the horse to a stop. "Og has done a good job securing the pass."

Tavis MacIain's teeth shone through the darkness. "Both entrances are blocked." He pointed to the cliffs above. "And we've plenty of boulders lined up to drop on the enemy's heads."

Charlotte cringed. The enemy could be her father, or any of the other men she knew from the fort.

"How are things?" Hugh asked.

"The same. Og shot a deer, but that used the last of the powder." Tavis leaned on his pike. "Another half-dozen stragglers came into camp—had been hiding in the caves."

"Good to hear." Hugh inclined his head over his shoulder. "The Stewart gave us supplies. It'll help some."

The warrior peered around at Charlotte. "I see Miss Hill has returned for more misery."

"I'd have it no other way," she said before Hugh could speak for her. "I am a Jacobite now." She'd never forget Alice's words. Always the proper young lady, Charlotte never would have thought she'd become a rebel—but she had. Yes, indeed, she'd joined with the most notorious clan in Scotland.

*

TWO WEEKS AFTER THE MASSACRE SAW THE END OF February, but no end to the bitter cold and blustery snow. Hugh had become withdrawn again, snapping orders and working like a dog from dusk until dawn. Nearly everyone busied themselves caring for the most basic of human needs. The men had put a new roof on the second shieling.

Trees had been felled, and lean-to's hastily erected to give families much needed accommodation. The supplies of grain from the Stewarts quickly dwindled, and they lived mostly on broth made from rabbit meat simmering in the big cast iron pot suspended over the fire in the man cottage. Thank heavens for the small varmints, as most had fashioned rabbit pelts for shoes. Lord, Charlotte felt grimy, cold and downright miserable, yet she refused to complain.

The days droned on with little privacy and little compassion. Charlotte tried to work as hard as Hugh, tending the sick, hauling in snow to be melted, taking her turn cooking, serving, cleaning, mending, gathering firewood—the list of chores seemed endless as one short winter day blended into the next.

The clansmen and women ignored her, mostly. Hugh did, too, during the daylight hours. At night she'd sit beside him as they told stories around the fire in the main cottage. Hugh spoke of times of old, of their clan's roots and Highland pride. And though the initial shock of what had happened to them had ebbed, there was never any laughter. The people sat quietly staring into the fire with hopelessness in their eyes, and Charlotte couldn't do a blasted thing to help them.

To add to her frustration, every night she lay beside her man, his body spooning hers for warmth—spooning, but not really touching. The epitome of frustration. Since they'd returned from Castle Stalker, Charlotte and Hugh had not spent a single moment alone together.

In the witching hours when snores pealed through the

cottage, his hand would slip over her waist, or tickle her neck while he fingered her hair. Oh, how she wanted him to kiss her, to hold her hand, and heaven help her, to again show her the depths of his love whilst joining with her in the throes of passion.

Charlotte could only hope for such blissful intimacy to return.

Darkness came so early in winter. It seemed they were always huddling on the dirt floor, waiting for a new dawn. This evening, after Hugh told the story of his capture at the Battle of Dunkeld and the horrors of living in the pit prison, he turned to Charlotte. "And because of this lassie, I'm sitting here today. If it hadn't been for her spiriting me out of the sea gate, I would have succumbed to the bloody flux for certain."

She looked down to hide her smile. Over a year had passed since she'd helped him.

Hugh nudged her. "Does anyone ken she can make a fiddle sing prettier than a meadow lark?"

"Didn't I see a fiddle come with the stores from Clan Stewart?" asked Og.

"Aye." Hugh brushed his fingers over the back of her hand —a simple gesture, but it made gooseflesh rise across her skin. "I reckon my kin would appreciate a wee tune."

She looked up with a cringe. "'Tis not too early?" She'd wanted to play for them, but feared some would be resentful, and curse her for making merry.

A few grumbles rolled from the crowd. Then Gavyn stood. "I'll fetch it."

"Are you sure?" Charlotte whispered.

Hugh turned his lips to her ear, his warm breath caressing her—Lord, his whisper made all her trepidation ease away. "Play a ballad—something soulful."

Charlotte knew exactly the song. When Gavyn returned, she swiftly tuned the violin and began a Celtic air she'd learned from her Irish instructor in London. She'd never heard the song sung—never heard it played aside from her playing, but it was expressive and perfect. Closing her eyes, she let the bow take over, drawing out each note as the tune swirled and danced through the air. Gooseflesh again sprang up across her skin as she threw everything she had into her performance. Her love for Hugh, her growing love for this sorrowful group of outcasts, the violin sang for her father—a pawn used by the king to carry out something he knew was morally wrong. Heaven help her, she could express so much with her music—say things from the deepest recesses in her heart that she could never utter or form into words.

When the last note faded and curled with the smoke, winding its way up through the small hole between the thatch, Charlotte lowered her bow and panned her gaze across the faces. Earie and Tavis wiped their eyes. So did Alasdair Og. Not a soul clapped, but she'd expected that. It was still too soon.

Beside her, Cait tugged Charlotte's skirt. "Thank you."

Blessed be music. She'd found a way to touch them at last.

§

IT WAS MID-MARCH WHEN HUGH WIELDED A RUSTY OLD axe, trying to carve out a hole in the frozen ground to sink another pole for the lean-to. Yet another family with four children wandered into their camp a day ago. He had no way of knowing how many clansmen and women had survived, but he knew of a hundred and three. Some had found refuge with friends or relatives outside the clan, and had sent messages of support up through the narrow pass guarded by his men. In the foothills of Meall Mòr, two and seventy souls were now under his protection.

If only goddamned spring would come.

He swung the axe again. His arms jarred like he'd slammed into a wall of iron. The axe handle shattered in his palms. Devil's fire, if it wasn't one thing, it was the next. Could nothing be easy?

"Hugh," Og strode across the clearing. "You'll never believe who's here."

Glenlyon? The Master of Stair? Lieutenant Colonel Hamilton? William of Orange? Hugh could think of a hundred enemies who would fall upon him at any given moment—kick him at his weakest. Wasn't that the art of war? Weaken your opponent and then attack? Hugh looked at the shattered handle in his palm, opting to ignore his brother. "I'll need to fashion a new shaft afore I can set this post."

"'Tis Colonel Hill."

He let the handle drop to the ground. *Miserable, bleeding, bloody hell.* Hugh reached for his sword, but it wasn't belted to his hip. "With a full regiment?"

"We stopped him and only Farley at the pass. Hill says he wants to talk. Alone."

Charlotte stepped out of the cottage.

Hugh beckoned her. "Did you hear?"

"Yes."

"Can I trust him?"

"He's the only man in the entire Williamite Army I would trust." Aye, those violet eyes were as steady and assured as he'd ever seen them. Still true to his first impression—Miss Charlotte could never lie.

Hugh turned to Og. "Did he state the nature of his business?"

"He asked if you wanted your lands back."

"Holy Mary." Hugh removed his bonnet and combed his fingers through his hair. Could he dare to hope?

Charlotte placed her palm on his arm. "Let me go with you."

"The colonel said he'd meet with me alone?" Hugh planted his fists on his hips. "Is he willing to come up here?"

Og scratched his beard. "I reckon he would if we offer the hand of hospitality."

Hugh almost laughed. Almost. He turned to the others and raised his voice. "Governor Hill from Fort William is visiting us. We will grant him safe passage and listen to what he has to say." With that, he nodded to Og. "Bring him and make ready the shieling. I'll meet with the colonel in there."

By the time the governor was ushered into the cottage, Hugh and Charlotte sat on the dirt floor as they had been doing for a month. Across the fire they'd placed a blanket for the colonel to sit upon. Though they could have dragged in a log for the old man's arse, Hugh refused to make any accommodations.

Charlotte gasped when the door opened and her father stepped inside. The man had dropped at least a stone since Hugh had last seen him, and his face was grey and gaunt.

Hugh stood and bowed. "Colonel. I wish I could offer you more comfort, but as you see, we have nothing but a plaid for you to sit upon."

The man's eyes shifted to his daughter. "I thank you for inviting me in. I know it must be difficult." He stooped, his old bones creaking as he dropped to his knee. "'Tis pleasing to see my daughter in good health—though you do resemble a guttersnipe, dear."

"Forgive me," Charlotte quipped. "There are few opportunities to bathe here in exile."

"But your exile is self-imposed." The old man chose to remain on one knee, crossing one arm atop the other.

"Tell me." Hugh tossed a log onto the fire. "Why are you here?"

"Aside from taking Charlotte home?" The colonel arched a brow at his daughter. "I've a proposition for you."

Hugh threw back his head and laughed. "Aye? Do you want me to exonerate you from responsibility for the murder of my father, my clan? Cause that's exactly what Breadalbane did, tooting a song of restitution out of his arse."

The colonel took in a deep breath and watched the smoke curl up to the roof. "I understand the earl has not a history of being forthright."

"Aye."

Charlotte placed a gentle hand on Hugh's arm. "I trust Papa's word."

Hugh's da had always trusted the colonel, too. But the old governor had a hand in the killing. Waiting a bit before he spoke, Hugh scratched the beard that had grown in since their return from Appin. "How can I trust you after you betrayed my father?"

"My actions for king and country are misdeeds that will haunt me the rest of my days."

"We have nothing. We're cold and starving. I cannot even return to my lands for fear of reprisal. I have no livestock, no grain to plant come spring. Our homes are but empty stone shells with walls blackened by fire. All of this was due to *your* command, sir."

"True." The colonel stood and paced with his hands behind his back. "The Master of Stair has offered you and your kin free passage on a ship to America. There you could work the plantations, mayhap come into some land of your own."

Ma's final words rang loud and clear in Hugh's head. "*You will raise your bairns in Glencoe. Never let them forget. Always remind them they are descended from Alasdair Ruadh MacIain MacDonald—a direct descendant of the Lords of the Isles...Never be ashamed of who you are.*"

"No." Hugh's entire body shook with the strength of his conviction. "No, no, no. My people have been wronged, and I will not rest until I see them set to rights. I will not compromise land which for hundreds of years my people have tilled with their own hands, their own sweat and blood. By God, I was raised in the Coe. My father was raised in the Coe, and his father and his on and on down the line. No!"

Colonel Hill faced him with a quirk to the corner of his mouth. "I thought that would be your response. I would have expected the same from your father."

Puzzled, Hugh looked to Charlotte.

"What are you saying, Papa?" she asked.

"I've already written a missive rejecting Stair's proposal. I just needed Mr. MacIain's blessing before I dispatched it."

Hugh flicked his hand through the air. "Tell the cur to call off his dogs while you're at it."

"I'll do more than that."

"How?" Hugh stood as well, towering over Hill.

"I'll push for a pardon." The Colonel stepped in. "News of your calamity has spread, and it has drastically sullied King William's reputation. Stair may think otherwise, but there could very well be anarchy in Highlands if you do not receive some sort of recompense—including the return of your lands."

Charlotte stood and moved beside Hugh. "Do you think the king will grant us a pardon, Papa?"

"Us?" Hill cleared his throat. "I will push for Hugh MacIain and his clan to have his lands reinstated, to have the crimes waged against him heard by the Privy Council in Edinburgh, but..."

Hugh narrowed his gaze. "Aye?"

Hill pointed at Hugh's sternum. "You have to swear to me you will keep your nose clean."

"Bloody hell." Hugh threw up his hands. "Do you expect me to gather my kin and rain fire and sword on Glenlyon?"

"That's exactly what you must not do!"

Hugh wasn't about to tell the bastard there were only a handful of weapons between his men. "Agreed."

"I *can* gain you a pardon. I can seek amends for your kin and make your clan whole again. And unlike Breadalbane, I am a man of my word. Though it may take time, I will not rest until I see this done."

"You would do that for us?" Charlotte asked.

The colonel's eyes turned dark. "I have one condition."

Standing with his feet wide, Hugh moved his fists to his hips. "That is?"

"Charlotte returns to Fort William with me."

"Are you jesting?" Charlotte grasped Hugh's hand. "We are to be married."

"This is no place for a well-bred English woman." The colonel began to pace. "Bless it, Charlotte, you're living like an animal!"

Hugh pulled her behind him. A pardon for the entire clan? An alliance with Fort William? No longer living in fear of another massacre? There had to be some way to negotiate this without losing Charlotte. "If my lands were to be reinstated. If I built a fine home to offer your daughter—would you give your consent for us to marry?"

Dashing forward Charlotte kneeled before her father, holding her hands up in prayer. "Please, Papa. Help us. 'Tis the least you can do after your part in the MacIain Clan's demise."

"Rise, daughter. Begging does not become you." Taking Charlotte's hands and pulling her up, Colonel Hill gave Hugh a stare devoid of emotion. "I might agree to that. *If* your lands and title are reinstated and you have a proper home—one that suits her station as the daughter of the Governor of Fort William—the fifth son of an earl, *and* you attempt no retaliatory action, I will consider your suit."

Charlotte yanked her hand away. "Consider? I refuse to—"

"Stop," Hugh shouted.

She whipped around and faced him, fists clenched at her sides. "I beg your pardon?"

Hugh gestured to the door. "Colonel, if you will please excuse us, I need a word with your daughter."

Chapter Thirty

❧

C harlotte couldn't believe her father had the gall to come to Meall Mòr and demand conditions. Standing inside the shieling, she thrust her finger toward the door. "My father owes you a new home, and he thinks he can place terms on his offer to help?"

Hugh regarded her with too much intensity in those dark eyes. "He hasn't condemned my proposal for marriage."

"But what if it takes years for you to regain your holdings? Are we to put our lives on hold for an indeterminate amount of time?"

"No." Hugh took her in his arms for the first time in days. His strength, the power in his body surrounded her like a wall of protection from all the evil in the world. His big hand slid up and down her back. "Och, Charlotte. If only I weren't in this predicament."

She slid her arms between them and tried to pull away, but he kept her wrapped tight. "What are you saying?"

"Would it be so awful to go back to Fort William, even just until the end of winter?"

"Are you serious?" She stamped her foot. "Snow still covers the ground—spring may never come."

"Bless it, Charlotte, I cannot even touch you. Have you any idea how much it twists me up inside to have you lay beside me each night, your scent filling my nostrils and yet I cannot pull you into my arms and make love to you?"

Oh yes, she knew very well how frustrating things were. Some nights she could jump out of her skin for wanting him. "At least we're still together. It isn't right for my father to use me as a bargaining chip to help you or not."

"Nothing is free, *mo leannan*."

Curses, she hated it when he lowered his voice and rumbled his Gaelic endearment. Well, she only hated it this once, but Hugh could weaken her resolve merely with a few words. "I don't want to leave you."

"Nor do I want you to go, but we need your father on our side. *I* need him."

She groaned and finally broke free. Pacing, she shook her fists. "This is so unfair."

"But you said yourself you could trust him." Hugh caught her arm and pulled her back into his embrace. "I need allies—the snow will soon melt. You ken how short the growing season is. If we can head back to the glen and rebuild afore the autumn winds start howling, it would be a blessing."

"And what happens if Papa is unable to bring about a pardon?"

Hugh's jaw hardened. "I shall give your father my word there will be no retaliation whilst he sends his missives and represents our cause."

"If he fails?"

"I do not believe there is a need to utter it."

Charlotte knew Hugh would take up the sword and fight alone if he had to—but he knew as well as she, the Highland clans were in no position to wage war. If Hugh took the path of vengeance now, he and his men would not live a sennight. She slipped her hands around his waist and rested her head on his chest. The drum of his heartbeat served to calm the jitters firing across her skin.

"Go with your da," he whispered.

"Will you come to Fort William?"

"With a price on my head?"

Every dragoon in the Highlands knew who Hugh MacIain was now. There'd be no slipping through the gates in disguise. "I'll not go without your promise as to when I will see you again."

"With so many uncertainties, how can I make such a vow?"

She stood back and ticked up her chin. "Before the autumn winds."

"I—"

"Swear it!"

He nodded and took her hands in his palms. "Sooner, God willing."

Her eyes filled with tears. "I hate this."

"As do I, bless it." His gaze lowered to her mouth. "Come here."

The Highlander had shown her how to kiss, could set her loins afire with a look. With the slow tilt of his head, he claimed her lips and gradually increased the pressure. Cradling her tight in his arms, Hugh showed her the depth of his love for her. Charlotte watched his eyes as they closed with the deep pinch of his brow. Lord, he was hurting so much, yet he must ignore his own desires and put his clan first.

With a ragged inhale, he touched his forehead to hers. "I love you more than the air I breathe."

"And I you." She cupped his cheek with her palm. "We

shall weather this, just as we have everything else that's been thrown our way."

"Now that is what I like to hear. You're the strongest woman I know and I will not rest until you are again in my arms."

A lump the size of her fist formed in Charlotte's throat. As tears streamed down her cheeks, all she could do was pull him close for one more raw, passionate kiss.

※

CHARLOTTE SPENT A TOTAL OF ONE DAY LOCKED IN HER chamber feeling miserable about her lot in life. However, as soon as her tears dried, her head also cleared. Come to think of it, as she'd ridden down the mountain with her father, the snow in the valleys had melted. Spring indeed was on its way.

Infused with a brilliant idea, Charlotte sprang from her bed with purpose and hastened to eat the breakfast Emma had brought.

How could she be so dim-witted when the buzzing village of Inverlochy lay just beyond Fort William's gates? And what did they have there? Just like any town west of Scotland's Great Divide, Inverlochy was full of Highlanders.

She'd witnessed Sir Robert's generosity, and Hugh had told her about the Baronet of Sleat's reaction to being "*Glencoed*". Yes, Highlanders had actually started using it as a verb. She'd even heard Emma say, "The clans are scared. No soul in all of Scotland wants to be Glencoed."

Well, Charlotte would harness that generosity. "Emma, I need your help."

"Oh no." After tucking in the bed linens, the chambermaid held up her palms. "You've only just arrived. Your father would murder Farley if he took you back to Meall Mòr."

Charlotte groaned. "My, you are unduly preoccupied with that."

"Well, 'tis the only thing I can imagine you'd need help with, considering how you carried on yesterday."

Charlotte rested her spoon beside her bowl. "This morrow is a new day and there is much to do."

Emma wiped her hands on her apron. "Och, I do not like the sound of that either."

"Hear me." Charlotte hopped up and held a chair for Emma.

The chambermaid arched her eyebrows, then gave the bed a thump and tottered over. "This must be quite a scheme you're plotting."

"It is." Charlotte slid back into the chair opposite. "I'm going to set up a stall at the market. Papa will give me a table and canvas for a tent."

"Are you planning to sell something?"

"No." Charlotte smiled—oh heavens, did it feel good. "We'll paint a sign that says: *Help the Glencoe Victims*."

"Collect alms for them?"

"Alms would be nice, but they also need everything from shoes and clothing to cookware, tableware, tools and seed to plant come spring." Charlotte left out weapons on purpose— if she even hinted at supplying the MacIains with arms, her father would hear of it and then her plan would be foiled.

Emma drew a hand to her chest. "Ooo, I do like it, Miss Charlotte. And what a good use of your time whilst you wait for responses to your father's letters."

Charlotte rose and clapped. "We must start straight away. First I'll ask father for the supplies we need—and I know exactly where I can find a board and a bit of paint for the sign."

"And I'll ask Farley to spread the word through town. Everyone can part with *something*."

Charlotte clasped Emma's hands. "Make sure he stops at the churches—I'd love to hear the reverend preach about it on Sunday."

Emma grinned, her eyes dancing with excitement. "I do believe you've come up with a brilliant idea to help those poor souls."

Chapter Thirty-One

❧❧❧

Easter week came quickly as the snow in the mountains began to melt. Again slipping to Loch Linnhe under cover of darkness like the scourge of the Highlands—an outlaw on his own land, Hugh and Og met Sir Robert Stewart and boarded his galley. They sailed through the Sound of Mull and up the west coast, all the way to the tip of the Isle of Skye.

The grand fortress of Duntulm Castle loomed atop a rocky promontory with sheer cliffs on three sides. Better yet, its remote location ensured it was out of sight by all but the government-arse-kissing MacLeods. Though that mattered not at all. Tents bespeckled the foreground, giving the impression of a grand fete including Highland games. Nary a ship sailing past would suspect an Easter celebration to be a gathering of Jacobite forces—unless they knew Hugh and Alasdair Og MacIain were present.

Unsure whom they could trust, Hugh and Og kept to the shadows without participating in any games. Lord Donald MacDonald wanted nothing to appear suspicious, thus the festivities took place while Hugh waited. His brother seethed angst out his pores as together they sat on the hill looking down on the games. All the while, Hugh rubbed his fingers over the kerchief Charlotte had made for him. The heather she'd embroidered reminded him of her eyes.

God, he ached for her.

Hugh made use of his time, sizing up the contenders, making mental note of those who showed physical superiority. By all rights he and Og should have been competing. Hugh had never met a man who could best him at wrestling, or Og at the caber toss.

Hugh had just about spent his patience when on the second eve, the Baronet of Sleat called a meeting of the chieftains in the great hall. His guards bolted the door and guarded the entrances from the kitchens and the stairwell. Not even a single henchman was allowed inside—not even Alasdair Og.

All the men sat around the table on the dais with Lord Donald at the head. Hugh took note of those in attendance. Christ, he'd been watching them for two days. He knew who was worth their salt and who needed an army behind him.

The baronet pounded on the table with the butt of his dirk. "We all know why we're really here."

"Aye to plot against the Williamite bastard who Glencoed MacIain." This came from Ewen Cameron, the oldest man in attendance—even older than Da had been. He didn't partake in the games, but his son and heir, Kennan, had been the best marksman of the lot.

"I say we all fall upon Glenlyon and eliminate his entire line of Campbells," said Ian Grant, a knife thrower, with hair black as coal. He very well could be the deadliest man in all of Britain.

"Attack every red-coated stronghold from here to the border—that's where we should set our sights." Och aye, if Hugh wanted anyone to have his back it would be Coll

MacDonald of Keppoch. A mammoth beast, the man had won the wrestling tournament—might even be as good as Hugh himself.

Shouts of outrage rose to the rafters as Lord Donald pounded on the table demanding silence. "Meeting the government troops on the battlefield is all well and good, but I'll not take up my arms until I'm sure we can win. My father buried enough of our kin after Killiecrankie and Dunkeld and, presently, I need some lads to come into their majority afore I march into battle."

"What do you propose?" asked Lachlan MacPherson. Hugh didn't know the ruddy chieftain from Newtonmore very well. MacPherson hadn't won a single game, but had placed in them all.

The baronet must trust him, otherwise, his birlinn would not have made it ashore.

"We need organization," said Lord Donald. "You all have armies at your disposal. How many men can we pull together at a moment's notice?"

After going around the table, Hugh tallied three thousand. "We need ten times that."

"What about the Earl of Seaforth?" asked Allan MacDonald of Clanranald. The bonny young lad by rights should still be a squire at the age of ten and six, but his father's untimely death left him with responsibility far exceeding his years.

Hugh scratched his chin. "Indeed the earl would bring a sizeable army—and the MacRaes would follow for certain."

Donald frowned. "I sent Seaforth an invitation to our gathering, but received no response."

"Mayhap if you pay him a visit," suggested the old Cameron chief. "An earl needs his ego stroked a bit."

"Very well." Donald pointed to Robert Stewart who sat

with parchment, quill and ink before him. "Our first entry will be to recruit more Jacobites to our cause."

As the victim who had been "Glencoed", Hugh thoughtfully listened while the banter continued through the night— every man expressing his objections to King William and sharing widespread misdeeds by government troops. Though none of them had been put under fire and sword, they'd all had a gut full of red-coated dragoons taking their livestock in the name of the king, as well as countless other transgressions.

It was far past the witching hour when Lord Donald asked Robert to read the creed the Jacobite chieftains toiled to compile that night. The most important tenet listed at the top of the final slip of parchment: *To protect Highland families and their lands*. This was followed by things that all free men would expect: *To support free trade. To rise against tyranny. To demand justice and equal rights for all*. And finally, the last entry, the one by which every chieftain held up his tankard and pledged his oath: *To support the reinstatement of the Stuart line on the throne of Scotland*.

In the wee hours they formed a secret society. They agreed to meet four times per year under the guise of Highland games. After everyone had sufficiently liquored up with whisky, the baronet opened a long wooden crate in the center of the table and pulled out the brands. "Hugh MacIain designed the sign of the Jacobite warrior. Every one of your fighting men will bear this brand."

"And each of us will be the first to be marked," shouted Ewen.

"Och aye." Hugh held up his tankard. "Every Highland Defender shall be branded. No missive will be accepted except from a Defender!"

"Sláinte!" bellowed every man at the table, including young Allan.

The Baronet of Sleat placed the brands in the fire and the men shared another tot of whisky while they waited until the iron turned flame red.

Hugh stood and handed the brand to Donald. "I'd like to be the first."

"Agreed. 'Tis proper for the son of Alasdair Ruadh MacIain MacDonald to be the first to pledge his oath."

Hugh removed his doublet and rolled up his sleeve.

"Place your arm on the table." Donald held the brand so close, the heat singed the fine hairs on the underside of Hugh's arm. "Do you swear to uphold the creed of the Highland Defenders, inscribed this night by the chieftains who live by its doctrine?"

"I so swear." Hugh gnashed his teeth as his flesh sizzled under the agonizing pressure of the brand. Sweat dribbled from his brow as his entire body shook. But he uttered not a sound.

One by one, each of the two and twenty chieftains in attendance presented their arms for branding. There may have been a few restrained grunts, but every single man bore his pain with stoic determination.

With the sun's rise, pounding resounded from the hall door. Lord Donald nodded to the guard who opened it to a runner waving a missive. "I've a copy of the Paris Gazette sent up from our allies in Edinburgh."

The baronet beckoned the man forward and read the article. Then he looked up and grinned. "If this does not light a fire under William of Orange's arse, I fear we'll all be damned."

Sir Ewen picked it up and read aloud, translating the French:

"The Liard of Glencoe was butchered several days ago in the most barbarous manner, although he was amenable to the present Government..." The article went on about Glenlyon's involvement and

the men, women and children who were murdered and how such barbarity made all nations see what little trust could be placed on those in power. Unfortunately it named Governor Hill as an accomplice in the massacre—the very man Hugh was counting on to help him gain his lands back. Nonetheless, it was a black mark for the Williamite Party—one that would sour the king's reputation across Europe.

Sir Donald spread his arms and faced the table of chieftains, now sallow with pain from their seeping brands and a night without sleep. "This is a fortuitous day, indeed. With our new alliance and with the strength of this message from France, we shall be heard."

"Sláinte!" the men bellowed.

"Information is our strongest ally. I will ensure every Scottish town crier receives a copy of the Gazette."

A STORM TOSSED THE BIRLINN THROUGH CHOPPY SEAS ON the voyage back to Appin. After they sailed through the Sound of Mull and into Loch Linnhe, Hugh looked to the north. His heart twisted into a goddamned knot. Hell, looking up toward home hurt worse than if he'd had his entire body branded.

As they approached Castle Salker, Hugh's mouth watered. Eight miles up the coast was the outlet to Loch Leven. And around that bend was home.

Moreover, twenty miles further up was Fort William and his Charlotte. God, he'd missed her in the few weeks of her absence. He missed the subtle calming brushes of her fingers, her ever present, stalwart support as he battled with his men to provide for the survivors. If only he could sail there now.

But he was still a wanted man.

Would he ever be free from the shackles that kept him

from freedom? Would the words of the Gazette and letters from Colonel Hill be enough to exonerate him?

Thousands of times he'd told himself Charlotte was better off with her da. She could sleep in a warm bed, bathe in a proper tub. She had Mrs. MacGregor to tend her and beautiful gowns as any woman of her station should be clad. Charlotte wouldn't have her food rationed and she could warm herself by a hearth of stone on cold nights.

If only Hugh could have provided her with enough warmth.

But he was still living in poverty. The plaid on his back had worn and hung on his limbs like a rag.

What was Charlotte doing now? Had the physician resumed his pursuit of her hand?

That bloody, pasty codfish. I'll wager he never put in an honest day's work in his life.

"Are you coming ashore, or are you aiming to stare northwards for the rest of your days?" asked Og.

"Huh?"

"You haven't moved since we sailed into Loch Linnhe. Everyone's stepped ashore except you, brother."

Hugh cleared his throat and straightened his sword belt. "Then there's no time to waste. We've supplies to haul up the mountain afore daylight on the morrow."

Chapter Thirty-Two

❧

Regardless of the weather, Charlotte worked in the tent not simply during Wednesday markets, but she manned her stall every day, asking people to extend their generosity. "Please. We will accept anything to ease the suffering of the victims of the massacre," she repeated so many times the words filled her dreams. She would have preferred to dream about Hugh, but he only managed to consume her every waking thought.

After the circulation of the article from the Paris Gazette implicating her father in the "butchering", things in the market became uncomfortable.

"You *should* help those poor souls," a woman snapped as she shoved a pair of knitted stockings into Charlotte's hands. "The sooner they tear down the walls of Fort William, the better."

Charlotte bit her lip while heat burned her cheeks. Indeed, her father's association with the whole abominable affair was unforgiveable. But with the ever present dragoons, she couldn't voice her disapproval too loudly, else they just might gripe to her father and her alms collection service would be shut down. On the other hand, the locals' taunts were but whispers for the same reason—berating the colonel's daughter with soldiers looking over their shoulders could earn them a day locked in the stocks.

At least Emma stood beside her faithfully. The MacGregor woman was of tough stock and she could take the whispers as well as dish them out. "At least Miss Hill is doing something to help them." She looked the woman up and down. "I don't see you clambering to stand out in the wind and rain to set up a tent and collect alms for the poor souls hiding and freezing in the mountains."

Charlotte offered a polite smile to the woman. "Thank you ever so much for the stockings. Your generosity will be rewarded handsomely come Judgement Day."

Together they stood shoulder to shoulder while they watched the woman walk away, basket in hand. Emma chuckled. "I like the bit you added about Judgement Day."

Charlotte covered her grin with her fingers. "A pair of stockings? Bless it, they're nearly worn through, and by the looks of her mantle and overshoes, it would have made no difference to her purse to put five pounds in the alms chest."

"Even a few guineas would have been nice."

Rubbing her fingers over the wooden box, Charlotte sighed. "A few guineas from anyone would be wonderful. When I counted last night we had a score of farthings, two guineas and five and ten pennies."

Emma shrugged. "At least we've been given plenty of blankets."

She had a point there. They'd been given the odd petticoat and a few shirts—mostly rags, but Charlotte set herself to task mending holes and seam tears in the evenings.

The chambermaid picked up a blanket and refolded it. "We ought to be able to take these things up the mountain soon."

Charlotte's stomach squeezed. "Papa wants to wait until he can deliver good news."

"I'd sooner believe pigs would fly than the Master of Stair back down."

Charlotte refused to allow doubt to cloud her mind. "Fortunately, King William ranks above Lord Dalrymple—if it were up to the viscount, the government troops would have butchered all Jacobites, rather than making an example of one *notorious* clan."

Emma cringed like she'd tasted something bitter. "Did your father say that?"

"Yes."

"I thought no less." Emma picked up the stockings and put them in the burlap bag for safekeeping.

"My dear Charlotte, how goes the benevolent collection?" Doctor Munro stopped in front of the tent and regarded the sign.

Her hackles prickled at the back of her neck, but she forced a smile. "We've collected nearly fifty blankets and numerous pieces of clothing."

The physician used his pincer fingers to lift the corner of one of the far-less-than-new plaids. "I suppose even a dog needs a blanket to lie upon."

"How dare you?" Charlotte quipped.

Tipping up his chin, Doctor Munro advanced toward her. "You, madam, are lacking in the good sense to stay away from matters that shine you in an ill light."

"Oh?" Moving her hands to her hips, Charlotte looked the braggart in the eye. "I am quite assured of my choices."

"Giving up a life of privilege for one of misery?" The physician sniffed. "You are a fool and I am fortunate not to have made the folly of marrying you."

Charlotte snapped her hand to her chest. "Well, I've never been—"

Pushing between them, Emma shook her finger. "Miss Charlotte is the only English speaker in the Highlands who has a heart—something I would think a physician would know a thing or two about."

"The insolence." Munro shirked from the insult.

But Charlotte wasn't about to allow his rudeness to pass without adding her own dig. She'd listened to his jibes at the officer's table enough times to know him to be truly black-hearted. "Yes it is quite evident your studies are lacking when it comes to matters of the heart—or compassion of any sort."

He tugged up his gloves. "That clan is nothing but a mob of thieves."

"You know this?" Charlotte's fists moved to her hips. "You've visited them and broken bread with them? Accepted their hospitality for a fortnight as Glenlyon had?"

"I do not need to listen to this drivel."

"Then show you do have a heart!" She jammed her finger atop the alms box. "Donate to their plight. For goodness sakes, they're flesh and blood people just as we are."

"Och aye, Miss Charlotte," Emma cheered, then leaned toward the physician. "May the pox be upon you and your spawn!"

He sneered like a rogue. "Your insolence is abhorrent." Thrusting his hand into his purse, Doctor Munro did something completely unpredictable. He slammed a handful of guineas on the board. "Damn you. Let no man say I haven't a capacity for benevolence." He glared at Emma. "And I spit on your forked-tongued curses, madam."

Charlotte stood arm-in-arm with Emma while they watched the physician storm away until the crowd swallowed his red-coated form. "Was it my plea for a donation or your curse that persuaded him to give?"

Emma grinned as wide as a tot with a plum tart. "I've no idea, but I think we make a good team."

"We surely do." Charlotte picked up the coins. "This coin will buy grain for certain."

"If only they can plant it afore 'tis too late."

CHARLOTTE SAT IN HER FATHER'S STUDY AND WHIPPED stitches in her haste to mend numerous pieces of clothing. She hadn't yet forgiven him for insisting she return to Fort William, but the best way to pick up tidbits about recent events was to force herself to sit with him in the evenings has she had always done.

Papa threw a tabloid on his writing desk, then leaned forward, cradling his head in his hands.

"What is it?" Charlotte asked.

With a grunt he nudged the paper toward her. "Read for yourself."

She prayed it was something from the Master of Stair admitting his guilt in being the mastermind behind Glencoe. The paper had been clipped from the Edinburgh Daily Record, the title: *Colonel Hill is a Murderer*

Sitting, she read while her stomach tied in knots. "They're blaming only you."

Papa moved to the sideboard and poured himself a brandy —something he'd been doing a lot of as of late. "I had a hand in the whole abominable affair."

"But you only carried out the extent of Stair's orders once he'd copied Lieutenant Colonel Hamilton. In fact, it is quite evident to me now that James was placed here only to undermine your authority and insure you acted on the Master's orders explicitly."

"Thank God that ambitious young man is off to Ireland." Father leaned his backside against the sideboard, his hand trembling as he sipped.

"'Tis good he's gone, indeed, but what will you do about this?" Charlotte replaced the paper on Papa's desk.

He smirked, his shoulders shaking. "There's not much I can do that I have not already tried. I kept copies of each missive to every man of influence from London to Edinburgh with my pleas against an uprising. Now, only God Almighty will judge me."

"Yes, he will." Charlotte's gaze trailed aside. There were no shades of grey with this crime committed by the crown. There was only right and wrong.

"I know." Papa shook a gnarled finger at her. "You believe I am guilty of this genocide, but no soldier hath ever tried more diligently to prevent it than I."

Ah, but you could have refused and then resigned yourself to face the consequences. "Do you truly believe that?"

"Yes, I do. And if I hadn't relayed my orders, Lieutenant Colonel Hamilton would have carried out the deed in my stead."

She pursed her lips and crossed her arms, standing firm. "You could not have stopped Hamilton?"

"Charlotte, I am a soldier of the king. My orders were signed by William himself. Stopping Hamilton would have made me a traitor to the country I have served for two score and four years of my lifetime."

She flung her arms to her sides, leaning toward him. "But your actions were wrong."

"Silence!" Papa carried the bottle and the glass to his desk. "You spent too long in the company of those heathens. Since you have refused Doctor Munro, I have no choice but to send you back to London, where I pray my sister will be able to find you a match now you've shown your propensity toward treason."

"What on earth are you saying? I have shown nothing but my propensity to act as a Christian woman. I am making an effort to help those poor souls." She stamped her foot. "We must soon take the supplies to them."

"Oh no, you will not be accompanying those supplies anywhere—"

"Dammit all," Charlotte cursed for the first time in her life. "Heathens? Treason for acts of charity?" Steam practically oozed from her pores as she stomped to his desk and leaned forward. "Tread carefully, Father. Your façade of superiority makes you appear weak and vainglorious—just like Breadalbane, or Stair, or Argyll, or any of the other men in power who conveniently turn their heads and do nothing but blow wind out their mouths!"

"You insolent child." Papa pulled out his chair, then slammed it back against the desk.

"I am not a child! If anything, I am brutally honest." Charlotte pointed to the strongbox. "You promised Hugh I could marry him. I want my dowry monies. They were Mother's and by rights are mine."

"Oh no." Papa strode around the desk and clamped his fingers around Charlotte's wrist. "Those funds are to go to your husband, if I can ever make a match for you, now you've spent the better part of two months with that rogue."

She yanked her arm away. "I *will* marry Hugh MacIain MacDonald, Thirteenth Laird of Clan Iain Abrach of Glen coe, and that fat pouch of coin should go to him!"

"Dammit, Charlotte, I didn't want it to come to this, but I *forbid* you to marry him. I may help him win his lands back, but he will *never* be good enough for you. You are a well-bred English lady and a Protestant to boot."

"I am a Jacobite," she seethed.

"That is sedition!" he shouted, the color in his face turning from red to purple.

"Oh no, Papa. I've seen the letters you have written on Hugh's behalf. You have uttered the Williamite lies for so long you believe them yourself. But you cannot fool me. I know what is in your heart. Those people hiding in the hills are no different than we are. They eat and drink and raise children, tell stories and play games just like us."

He vehemently shook his head. "But they are Highlanders and they follow an exiled king."

Charlotte crossed her arms. "Does it matter?"

"There can only be one king." His shoulders sagging, Papa slid into his chair and rubbed a hand across his brow. "I must depart for a visit to Lord Forbes in Inverness on the morrow. Upon my return, I will arrange transport for you to travel to London."

Chapter Thirty-Three

❦

Charlotte stood in her father's study and stared at his strongbox with a fork in her hand. She raised the tined implement. *How the devil did Hugh pick the lock?*

Unfortunately, Papa had left for Inverness with his key stowed safely around his neck. There wasn't one in his bedchamber—Charlotte had made sure of that before she opened her keepsake chest and removed the fork Hugh had returned to her. The base of one tine was kinked where he'd obviously bent it. The problem was it took a man hewn of iron to bend it again. No matter how much pressure Charlotte applied, she couldn't get the accursed thing to budge.

Turning full circle, she spied the hearth—and the fire poker. A bit of leverage might help. She took the fork and wedged it between the poker's hook and the shaft, then twisted with all her might. Stars crossed her vision, but with a loud grunt, the tine gave way and bent.

Lord, how Hugh managed to bend the blasted thing with his hands when he was weak with fever, Charlotte would never know.

Now to figure out how the pick the padlock. Tiptoeing to

the strongbox, she slid the tine inside and turned. Nothing. With flicks of her wrist, she jiggled it, but the lock held fast. Then she tried pulling it out by fractions of an inch and twisting.

When nothing she tried worked, Charlotte yanked the fork out of the lock and pounded the top of the chest with her fist. She growled through clenched teeth. "Curses. This must work!"

Thrusting the tine back inside she levered it up and down as fast as she could, rattling the blasted thing while her teeth clenched to the point of breaking. "Please, please, please!"

She twisted the confounded fork until her wrist burned from exertion.

Then something clicked and her hand turned over.

Charlotte gasped, her eyes popping. Turning the fork a bit further, the big blackened-ironed lock popped open. "Oh, praises be."

She lifted the lid and grasped the leather pouch of coin, careful to click the lock back into place. The dowry monies may be rightfully hers, but she didn't want to take any chances of having her father's correspondence fall into the wrong hands.

Then she took the bent fork and her coin and dashed up to her bedchamber. "Emma, we must make haste."

The chambermaid stood at the hearth, tongs in her hand. "Whatever are you on about?"

"We must find Farley and buy some sheep and hire some drovers." Charlotte inhaled deeply to catch her breath. "Quickly. This all must be done before Papa returns from Inverness."

Emma's gaze dropped to the pouch. "What on earth is going on?"

"Let us just say, 'tis time I took my dowry into my own hands."

"You stole it?"

"How could it be stealing if 'tis mine?"

"I suppose you have a point." Emma smacked her lips. "How much coin is in there?"

"I have no idea, but by the weight of it, we can purchase a herd of sheep and some grain." *Mayhap have some left to furnish a cottage.*

"And you expect the MacIains to shepherd the sheep in the mountains?"

"Why should they not? The snows are melting. There ought to be ample grazing—why Hugh even told me they had summer shielings up at Black Mount." Charlotte covered her mouth. "I shouldn't have said that."

"What would I care where their summer grazing lands are?" Emma clasped her hands together. "But what you propose will take a great deal of thought."

"'Tis Wednesday on the morrow. Surely there are a few men in Inverlochy who need a day's wages."

"And you expect Farley to help you?"

"I hoped he would." Charlotte tightened her fist around the bag of coin. "Honestly, I've never droved sheep before—or anything for that matter."

"I would hope not." Emma shook her head. "Your father would be mortified if you had."

Charlotte started for the wardrobe. "Please, I need Farley's services only once more. There's ever so much to do. We must make haste."

"I daresay, Miss Charlotte, I was completely wrong about your character when you first arrived at Fort William."

"Why do you say that?"

"You're about as demure as a badger—though you're as resourceful as a beaver."

Pulling her cloak over her shoulders, Charlotte chuckled. "I shall take that as a compliment."

Chapter Thirty-Four

"You've grown weak. Now come again," Hugh swung his sword in an arc and beckoned Tavis with a flick of his fingers.

"I'm not bloody weak, you blind bloodhound." Baring his teeth, the young warrior raised the old, two-handed sword and lunged in with a downward strike.

Hugh countered, their blades clanging with reverberating force. Locked in a battle of wills, the steel screeched until their cross guards met. "Now you're showing a wee bit of vim, you milk-livered swine."

"I'll knock you on your arse afore this is finished," Tavis grunted through clenched teeth.

Hugh sidestepped as they circled. Lord, it felt good to have a sword in his hand and expel his pent-up hostilities. "In your dreams, young pup."

"Hugh," Og's voice came from behind. "You'll never believe what's coming up the pass." Thank God the tone in his brother's voice was one of bewilderment rather than urgency.

He gave Tavis a nod, pressing him backward before

lowering his weapon. "I take it Glenlyon isn't leading an army to finish us off?"

"Come. There's a flock of sheep heading our way." Og swiftly led them up the crag to the northern lookout.

Hugh stepped to the edge of the cliff. Heading for their secret hiding place, the bleats from a mob of sheep kissed his ears like angel's bells. Thick wool covered their backs. Aye, the ewes and weathers would soon need to be shorn—a gift from heaven for certain. "I'll be damned."

"They're driving them straight up the pass," said Tavis, pointing. "Och, is that Miss Charlotte bringing up the rear?"

Lord in heaven, Hugh wouldn't mistake her outline for anything. His chest tightened until he could scarcely suck in a breath, his skin perspired, a hot bolt of longing made him instantly hard.

Damnation.

He'd tried to ignore his feelings of loss after he'd sent her away—tried to work harder, relentlessly driving his men, preparing them for the possibility of another attack. But seeing Charlotte sitting erect in the saddle looking up the hill while the sunlight caught her face hit him between the eyes like he'd been stunned. The vision brought more emotion than any raucous sparring session could have prepared him for—and he'd given Tavis a walloping. But onc glimpse at Charlotte and Hugh's knees buckled as if he'd been delivered a blow to the gut. His fingers twitched to touch her, to wrap her in his arms and inhale the heady scent of woman. God, he'd missed her, wanted her, craved her.

Blinking, Hugh shook his dazed head and regained a modicum of sanity. Why was she riding with a mob of drovers bringing sheep up the mountain? *Devil's bones, what has she been up to?*

"Aye, 'tis Miss Charlotte for certain," said Og. "But why the bloody hell isn't she leading a herd of cattle?"

Hugh thwacked his brother with a backhand. "If I hear anyone utter one spiteful word against her, I'll cut out their tongue and eat it for breakfast."

Og made a show of clutching his chest and shuffling backward. "Christ, Hugh. You're a wee bit sensitive about the lass, are you not?"

"Wheesht." He didn't need an opinionated brother's snide remarks. "Tavis, go tell the women we'll have guests for the evening meal. Og, we'll give them a Highland welcome—if you can manage to keep your off-color comments to yourself."

"I was just saying cattle would be preferable to sheep."

"Shut it." Hugh gave his brother another smack. "Damnation, we're in no position to barter, you bleeding milksop."

Climbing down the hillside, a tightness gripped his chest. Ballocks, why did Charlotte have to be his Good Samaritan? This whole thing didn't feel right. If any Highlander in Scotland had given him a small flock to help set the clan back to rights, he'd be kicking up his heels. But to see Charlotte riding behind the lambs didn't sit well. What the devil? Lord knew he would move heaven and earth to be with her, but as clan chief—hell, as a man, he needed to be the one to provide. He needed to make a proper home for her—not the other way around. Aye, it might take a few years, but he would regain his lands and rebuild Glencoe.

By the time they arrived at the pass, the entire clan had assembled, clapping their hands, their faces rapt with joy for the first time in what seemed like a hundred years.

Damnation.

"I can taste the roast lamb now." Young Lachlan smacked his lips.

Hugh frowned. "We do not yet ken if the flock is intended for us."

"'Tis ours." The lad pointed with more surety than he ought. "Miss Charlotte has brought them for us."

A twitch fired at the corner of Hugh's eye.

Bonnie clapped her hands and pressed praying fingers to her lips. "Aye, thank heavens for Charlotte Hill. Indeed, she is a saint among women."

"Och aye?" Hugh gaped at the woman. "And it wasn't so long ago you were telling her she didn't belong with us."

Bonnie's round face flushed bright red.

"Mayhap you've had a change of heart?" Hugh didn't wait for her to respond. The clan hadn't treated Charlotte well and now the lass had appeared with alms he expected from no man.

The children ran to the pack mules, squealing around Miss Charlotte, asking if she'd brought them any sweets. Hell, they surrounded her horse, making her stop. She grinned at every one of them. "I've brought blankets and clothing mostly. Perhaps there's a pair of shoes that might fit."

"Och, I don't need shoes now 'tis spring," said Lachlan— the cheeky beggar.

Hugh strode forward and reached for her gelding's bridle. "You all leave Miss Charlotte be. She's had a long ride and needs her rest."

His gaze strayed to her face. Blessed be Mary and all the saints, a pure rose never looked so radiant. How could she be more beautiful than he remembered? And Lord knew he'd remembered her as the bonniest lass he'd ever laid eyes upon. Her healthy smile brightened the entire world and the corner of Hugh's mouth tuned up like a simpleton. "What is all this?"

"My dowry." She grinned even wider. "At least a portion of it."

Hugh couldn't stop the concerned pinch of his eyebrows. "Pardon?"

"Help me down and I'll explain." She stretched her arms out.

Clumsy as a wet-eared lad, Hugh reached for her waist, so small, his thumbs touched. Why in God's name did he feel like a pubescent lad? Hell, his heart could stop its damned fluttering right now.

As soon as his hands held her firmly in his grasp, everything around them vanished. It took such little effort to lift her from her sidesaddle. Drawing her to his chest, his senses honed, awash with a scent more heavenly than lilacs. As she slid down his body, he groaned at the friction. Soft, exquisite breasts plied his chest and molded to it like a well-worn doublet. God, she felt so good, he could haul her into the rushes right there and then.

Hugh slipped his arms around her back, clutching her to his body. Pink, bow-shaped lips pouted only inches from his. "God, I've missed you," he growled.

Her sultry gaze dipped to his lips. "Not a moment has passed where I haven't longed to be in your arms again." Lord in heaven, her voice was every bit as honeysuckle sweet and soft as it had been the first time he'd heard it.

Heaven help him, she turned his entire body to fire and molten iron. Slipping a hand up her neck, he cradled her head and captured those delectable lips in a kiss. She tasted delicious—beyond delicious—warm and sugary like a hot apple tart overflowing with rich cream. God, he wanted to devour her. His hand slid down to her buttocks and pulled her mons flush against his cock. Holy Moses, he was already harder than an axe handle. He thrust against her—feeling her feminine parting through her skirts. The past two months of suppressing his need for the bonny lass came to a boil and Hugh had no intention of stopping.

With a gentle moan, Charlotte tugged her lips away. "A few more inches and my feet might touch the ground."

His knees buckled at the sound of her steamy voice.

Hugh blinked, the peals of laughter from the others rang in his ears. Had he really almost lost his senses in front of his clan? Bloody oath, he'd lived like a monk for too long. Letting out a nervous chuckle, he eased her down his body. "You feel too good to be real."

Her eyebrows shot up and a pink tongue slipped to the corner of her mouth. Devil's bones, did she know what that coy look did to a man?

"Perhaps we should take a walk?" he suggested before he really did something to embarrass himself. And bloody oath, the lass had learned fast. From the waggle of her brows, the lass kent exactly what she was doing. It only took a wee look to seduce him and turn him into a lovesick fool.

Regaining a modicum of control, he took her hand and addressed his men with a stern clear of his throat. "Offload the mules and portion the supplies to those most in need." He looked to Charlotte. "When must you return?"

Farley stepped up. "The horses need rest. I'd be much obliged if we could stay the night."

"Of course." Hugh's heart skipped a beat. He'd be able to hold Charlotte in his arms for an entire night afore they had to turn back?

"I intend to stay," she said, loud enough for everyone to hear.

Farley gaped. "But—"

"I believe Miss Charlotte and I have matters to discuss." What the hell did she mean about staying? She couldn't stay. Not yet. Nonetheless, Hugh could hardly wait to spirit her away and have her to himself. "Welcome to all and my thanks. Og, kill the fattest lamb. We'll roast it over the fire and feast this eve."

When Hugh squeezed the lady's hand, he wanted nothing more than to forget his lot in life and enjoy the cool spring day before the sunset. But her surprise appearance needed answers for certain. "Are you up for a wee climb?"

She nodded. "Anything to stretch my legs after an entire day in the saddle."

Holding her hand brought on another stampede of raw emotion. Lord, he'd forgotten the silkiness of her skin, and how fine-boned she was. Like a well-bred filly. Hugh's palms perspired, his tongue went dry—if only he'd known she was coming, he would have cleaned up a bit. "I cannot believe you're here."

"'Tis wonderful to be back." She blessed him with a smile —one that reflected the same restlessness making his heartbeat thrum across his skin.

Leading her up a steep path, he held tight to her hand and grasped her elbow in the jagged places. He took her to a pool that had only recently thawed. Surrounded by trees, water trickled into it via a burn from the mountain above, and flowed out with the tinkling harmony of a waterfall. And across, his most recent project—a shieling he hoped to share with her one day—though it only had the makings of stone walls and a frame for the roof.

Mossy green tipped the trees with leaves that had only begun to bloom. But green moss hung from their dormant limbs, giving them a bit more privacy.

"This is beautiful." Her eyes brightened when she peered across the pond. "Are you building?"

Hugh slapped a dismissive hand through the air. "'Tis only a ruin." He didn't want her to know he'd thought of her while he set every single stone in place—while he'd stripped the timbers of bark and lashed them into place with strips of hardened leather he'd made from the hides of the animals that had kept his kin fed.

Moving behind Charlotte, Hugh slid his arms around her

waist and nuzzled into her slender neck. "I will not be able to drink in enough of you afore you leave on the morrow."

She turned her head toward him, those violet eyes enormous as she peered up at his face from under long lashes. "Did you not hear me? I have no intention of returning."

"Your father agreed?"

"No." She looked away. "But by the saints, I am a woman full grown. I should be allowed to make my own decisions."

Hugh's back tensed. "Should I expect an attack?"

"Heavens, no." She stepped away, wringing her hands. "Papa is in Inverness. We...we argued and he said he would send me back to London upon his return." She spun around and faced him. "I've been collecting alms for your clan for weeks at the Inverlochy market. I told him we must soon deliver them to you, and he launched into a tirade—said you are wrong for me." With a gasp, she hid her face in her hands.

Lord knew, the colonel was right, but that still didn't give her father the right to crush her dreams. *Thank God she still loves me.* Hugh swirled his palm across her shoulders. "Everything will work out for the best. I ken it will."

She shook her head and faced him. "He said that I am a ruined woman and my only hope to be saved is to find a husband in London." She shook her fists. "I hate him for that."

A chasm in Hugh's heart stretched wide. Dammit all, her father was right. There she stood, wearing a fine gown and cloak—the likes of which he might never be able to afford. How could he provide for such a jewel? Aye, he wanted Charlotte more than life itself, but that didn't make it right. She would suffer. He could never ask her to give up her fine things, her life of luxury for him—a fallen man. "And the sheep? Where did they come from?"

"As I said, I paid for them with money from my dowry."

He frowned. "Charlotte, aren't fathers to decide how dowry funds should be used?"

"Yes—but to whom should be *my* choice. Not his."

A thick ball formed in Hugh's throat as he shook his head. No matter how much he wanted Charlotte to stay, he couldn't let her spend her precious coin on his clan. So much remained uncertain and unresolved. They still lived in fear of being attacked by government troops—especially the Campbells, the Menzies, hell, even Colonel Hill could fall upon them in the dead of night. But now she'd purchased the sheep and driven them all the way from Fort William, there was little point in sending them back. "I must repay you." That was the only answer.

"Repay?" Her mouth dropped open with a wee gasp. "Do you retract your proposal of marriage?"

"I wish—I wish." God, the disappointment and misery reflecting in her expressive eyes was more than Hugh could bear. "Damnation! I must have your father's approval afore we can wed."

He tried to take her hands, but she jerked away. "Why? Is not my love enough for you?"

Christ, he'd rip out his heart and hand it to her on a platter if she asked. He spread his palms, desperate for her to understand. "For me, your love is all I want in this world, but you ken I have a clan to protect. Your father is the *only* government officer in all of Scotland who gives the slightest damn about us. If I off and marry you without his blessing, I am condemning my people to a life as fugitives. We might as well sail to the Americas to be slaves on tobacco plantations —just as the Master of Stair offered."

Shaking her head, she clapped a hand over her mouth. "But if I return to Fort William, Papa will send me away on the first transport."

Bloody hell, he didn't want that. "You must try to stall."

This time Hugh didn't allow her to shirk away. He pulled her into his arms. Closing his eyes, he savored every inch of her small frame. God, why did she have to be the daughter of the Governor of Fort William? Why could she not be a simple lass from his clan. "Och, *mo leannan*, what am I to do with you?"

She took in a stilted gasp. "Love me."

"I do." He squeezed his eyes against the pain in his heart and kissed her forehead. She had no idea how difficult it was for him to send her away. "On the morrow, you must ride with Farley."

Two big, violet eyes bore into his soul. "There must be some other way."

There was only one alternative—and Charlotte was the only woman for whom he'd give up the fight. "We can give up and go to the Americas. Do you want that?"

"Of course I do not. Glencoe is your home and I want it to be my home, too." She rested her head against his chest. "A pardon will come. I know it in my heart. The king is being severely criticized about his brutality toward you. He must do something soon to bolster his reputation."

A bit of tension eased from Hugh's shoulders as he slid his hand along her spine. "Then that makes my position more resolute."

"My father's letters have already been sent. Surely it is only a matter of time."

He cupped Charlotte's cheeks with both of his hands. "'Tis exactly what I'm trying to say. I want it all, my love, and if we do it right, we will have it and our bairns will grow up in the valley of Glencoe, just as they have for generations past. Please, this is my mother's dying wish, and the only woman in the world I want to share it with is you."

She bit her bottom lip, worry creasing her brow. "Even if Papa sends me to London?"

He met her gaze with every shred of determination in his soul. "There is no place in this world I will not find you."

❧

THE BONFIRE ROARED WHILE CHARLOTTE STARED INTO THE leaping flames. How could everyone around her be so merry? Farley had brought a cask of whisky and people were laughing like she'd never heard before—it was as if they had taken three months of misery and let it go with the smoke from the fire.

So many things had change during her absence. Sima—Breac and Nessa's baby could now sit up. Lean-to shelters had been built around the edge of the clearing, allowing the families more privacy—there were even more new faces.

It seemed everyone appreciated her efforts aside from Hugh, showing each other their new blankets (belting them as arisaids for the women or kilts for the men) or shirts that Charlotte had mended or shoes or stockings. Hugh hadn't taken a single thing for himself. He just sat beside her staring into the fire and sipping his whisky. Didn't he know how much she'd labored to please him? Didn't he know she'd stolen her dowry funds for him?

I stole from my father.

Heat spread across the back of her neck along with a sinking in the pit of her stomach.

But the money was mine. Curses, I would do it again if given the chance.

She peeked at Hugh out of the corner of her eye. He just continued to sit there and gaze into the fire. They only had one miserable night together and he was completely ignoring her. *Blast him.*

Then he looked her way. Charlotte quickly averted her eyes so he wouldn't notice her staring at him.

He pointed to her trencher. "You hardly ate a thing."

She shrugged and pushed the lamb away. "Not hungry."

"Charlotte, I—"

"Slàinte to Miss Charlotte," Gavyn hollered.

Hugh raised his cup. "Slàinte," he chorused with the others, but the smile on his face strained. Why was he being so difficult? Didn't he know if she returned to Fort William now her father would do everything in his power to prevent their marriage?

A drum sounded.

On the far side of the fire, Breac beat a hollowed log with a hide stretched across it. The drum thumped in a rousing rhythm.

Alasdair Og beckoned his brother. "I challenge our leader to a sword dance!"

The clearing erupted with boisterous cheers and applause. Lachlan hopped up and danced a jig. "I want to dance, too!"

Hugh glanced at Charlotte with a bit more vim in his eye, then smirked at his brother. "You reckon you can leap higher than me?"

"I ken it."

"No," shouted young Lachlan. "Our chieftain is the brawest man in all the Highlands."

Hugh grinned. "I like your spirit, lad. But Og is a worthy opponent." He bowed to Charlotte. "If you'll pardon me, m'lady."

She nodded. Now everyone around the fire was in good spirits except her. Cuddy sauntered over and plopped down in the spot Hugh vacated, laying his head in Charlotte's lap. She scratched the deerhound behind the ears. "You wouldn't send me away, would you?"

He yowled and licked her hand—at least the dog understood.

When the laughter died down, the drum beat a steady

rhythm while the crowd parted for Hugh and Alasdair Og. Side by side they marched forward, each holding two rusty swords with blades crossed. They bowed and placed them in a cross on the ground.

The drumbeat sped as the men danced, their plaids swishing with every athletic leap. Hugh's predatory gaze focused intently on her as he danced. He may have been despondent when sitting beside her, but now embroiled in a contest of fineness and strength, his stare captured Charlotte in his web and she didn't dare look away. The powerful muscles in his calves flexed and bulged with his every step. Indeed, he did leap higher than his brother. With every jump, Hugh grew stronger, his grin growing broader while the amber firelight flickered over his powerful form as if the flames heightened his performance.

Blast his incredibly desirable physique. Must he be so intoxicatingly alluring? And why did everything about this day have to turn out all wrong? She'd been so excited to return with the flock that they so badly needed—and she'd been able to acquire it for them. But why did she feel as if she'd committed a crime? When Hugh sat beside her, he was despondent—unbending in his decision to send her back to Fort William and her father's wrath. Now, across the fire, he didn't even blink, seducing her with a dance—a display of masculine skillfulness.

Charlotte's face grew so hot, she pushed to her feet. Hugh drew his brows together in question. Did he not understand? Watching him only brought torture. She'd done everything she could to make him happy—to help him gain a new foothold, and all he could do was insist on her returning to Fort William? How many more months of separation must she endure? Years? For all she knew, it could be forever.

She blindly ran into the forest, desperate to flee the celebrations. Yes, she wanted the clan to revive. Yes, more than anything she wanted Hugh to be happy, but he was sending her back to a life of misery. Didn't he know how much she hated Fort William?

Was Papa right? Should she have settled and married the physician?

No.

Tears burned her eyes and spilled onto her cheeks. She'd been so thrilled—thought her efforts would make Hugh happy, too. *Blast his pride!*

After climbing and falling and running to nowhere, she raced into the clearing with the pool. Still as glass, it took on an inky void in the moonlight—a void as deep and wide as the abyss in her heart. Charlotte fell to her knees and buried her face in her palms as she wept. Her stomach convulsed as if it had been ripped inside out. Her heart ached. Lord in heaven, nothing would ever be the same again. She would return to Fort William and Papa would force her into a convent or worse. Mayhap he'd even send her to the Americas alone as a slave to the tobacco trade. Oh no, Hugh would never find her there. She'd be lost forever.

"Charlotte!" Hugh burst from the foliage and dashed to her side. Dropping beside her, he wrapped her in his embrace.

"Nooooo!" She pushed away, but hadn't the strength to fight his powerful arms as they encircled her. Curses, must his body be so incredibly warm? Must he smell like wood smoke and spice? Why couldn't he be vile and vulgar like the monster the Master of Stair had painted him to be?

Between stuttering gasps for air, she found enough strength to take in one deep gulp. "Go away!"

"Please, Charlotte. Did you not see the happy faces around the campfire? Do you not know how much they appreciate all you have done for them?"

"For t-them?" Sucking in staccato breaths she tried to speak. "'T-tis all f-for youuuu."

Pulling her into his lap, Hugh cocooned her in his enormous arms, rocking back and forth, whispering into her hair. "I ken my love. Please don't cry."

On and on he rocked, whispering in an accursed, soft, male, wonderful, damned voice while Charlotte bawled, completely unable to bring herself under control. There she was, a worthless, blubbering mess, too distraught to push him away.

"Hush now," he whispered as her breathing slowed to a cadence of hiccups.

"You do not...appreciate....meeee." She tried to fight again but failed, blast his iron grip. "You say you love me but you do nooooooooot." A new bout of wails gripped her stomach.

His hand smoothed up and down her spine, feeling too darned good. "I do love you. I do love you." Hugh repeated over and over again. "I promise we will solve this. I swear on my father's grave I will not rest until we are together again. Can you not allow me a wee bit of time?"

She nodded, not trusting her voice to speak. She didn't want to agree, but what else could she do? She couldn't stay when Hugh didn't want her there. Lord, upon her return, Papa would launch into the worst tirade ever.

Hugh's arms relaxed as he let out a long sigh. "Our time will come soon, my love."

Charlotte wanted to believe him. If only she could convince Papa to allow her to stay on at Fort William through the summer. But she'd ruined her chances there. Her heart squeezed. By taking her dowry, she'd lost his trust, and though she knew her father to be a just man, he would punish her disloyalty severely.

Chapter Thirty-Five

Saying goodbye to Charlotte was always one of the hardest things Hugh had ever done. But this time it was worse. After mounting her horse, she scarcely gave him a look. Last night, he'd repeated a hundred times that he loved her. But she continued to push him away. Dammit, Hugh knew she didn't want to go. He could only pray that, in time, she'd realize this was for the best. Until things settled and he got back on his feet, she'd live in comfort. This separation was necessary for the clan, for the return of his lands, but she seemed so distraught, as if she truly believed they'd never be together again. It didn't matter how much he tried to reassure her, she sank deeper into melancholy until her cries muted into deafening silence.

Hugh stood in the pass and watched her horse fall in behind Farley. She didn't wave. She didn't even turn around.

"Why the blazes are you sending her away this time?" asked Og—Lord, even his brother couldn't see reason.

"Didn't want to." Hugh regarded Og as a pounding started in his head. "Her father is our only hope for restitution."

"And you think sending her back after she used her dowry funds to purchase sheep is going to make everything all right? What do you think the governor will do when he discovers she's defied him? Jump for joy? Och, if I were her da, I'd give the lass a good hiding and then send her to a convent for the rest of her miserable life."

Hugh froze. Had he once thought about the repercussions for Charlotte? No. He'd only been concerned about the clan and his fight to get his lands back.

"Hugh!" Breathing heavily, Gavyn ran from the south pass, waving a letter. "A missive has arrived from the Baronet of Sleat."

He snatched it. "Did the messenger have the brand on his forearm?" Christ, must everything happen at once?

Gavyn handed him the letter and shoved up his sleeve. "Aye, just like mine."

"At least something is working as it should." Bloody hell, Hugh hardly had time to read. "Og. Saddle my horse."

"What the—?"

"Do it, I say!" Hugh ran his finger under the red wax seal.

My Dearest Cousin, Hugh Maclain MacDonald, Chieftain of Clan Iain Abrach of Glencoe,

It is with raised spirits that I take quill to parchment this day. I have solicited the good graces of his lordship, the Earl of Seaforth, imploring him to take up your cause with the Privy Council in Edinburgh. This day I received notice that the esteemed council has initiated an inquiry into the horrendous crime committed against you and your kin. We are forthwith pulling out every stop and using every influence to persuade decision makers to invoke justice.

This is a grand step in the achievement of our quest.

Long live the true king.

Your servant,

Lord Donald MacDonald, Baronet of Sleat, Chieftain of Clan Donald

Without another moment's hesitation, Hugh ran into the shieling and snatched his quill. Hastily dipping it in ink, he scrawled a letter to Colonel Hill.

"What are you waiting for? Christmas?" Og's voice bellowed from outside.

Blowing on the parchment, Hugh hastened outside and leaped onto the back of his garron. "My thanks, brother."

He dug in his heels and galloped after Charlotte, praying he'd reach her before they moved into the valley of Glencoe.

❧

A GROUP OF REDCOATS PATROLLED THE GLEN AHEAD—so small in the distance, they looked like ants. But Charlotte and her party was nearer. Hugh took a chance and whistled.

Farley pulled up and pointed.

Hugh pushed his horse faster, wanting, needing to reach her now. She reined her horse and turned. As their gazes connected her face glowed bright as a ray of sunshine. "Hugh!" she dismounted and ran to him.

His horse skidded and before the garron stopped, Hugh leapt down and closed the distance. Enveloping the love of his life in his arms, he spun in a circle. "I am such a fool. I cannot bear to see you leave me again."

"But what about your clan? What about your lands?"

"It will be all right. I know it. I will no longer play the role of victim. Aye, it may take longer than I'd like, but I will see justice." Even if he hadn't received word of the inquisition from Lord Donald, he wouldn't have been able to let her go.

"I'm so happy."

Hugh gently set Charlotte on her feet. Taking one hand, he dropped to his knee. Yes, he'd posed the question before, but it needed asking again. Before, he'd been a wealthy man. Before, he'd been heir to a vast estate. And now? He was a fugitive hiding in the hills. "I have absolutely nothing to give you but my heart. I promise on my life that I will work hard every day to provide you comfort—a home in which you will be proud, and to provide a fine upbringing for our children. I love you more than the air I breathe or life itself. Will you marry me, Miss Hill?"

Her hands trembled as a tear dribbled from her eye. But this time, she smiled so warmly, heaven had opened the gates and surrounded them with angels and sunshine. "I never thought you would ask again."

His gut twisted—so precarious his situation, he had to ask, "Is that your answer?"

She rapidly tapped her lips with her fingers as she smiled and cried at the same time. "No—my answer is yes, yes, a hundred and fifty times, yes!"

Rising to his feet, Hugh pulled her into his arms and kissed her. God save him, he didn't care who might be watching. He had his woman in his arms and would never again let her go. He savored her soft body against his hard, overjoyed that he would hold this woman in his arms for the rest of his life.

A throat cleared behind him. "I guess we'll be off then?"

Hugh forced himself to step back and regard Farley. He drew the missive from inside his doublet. "Please deliver this to Colonel Hill."

"What is it?" Charlotte asked.

"An invitation to our wedding one sennight hence. That should give me enough time to put a roof on the shieling I've been building for us." He gave her a lopsided grin. "The ruin at the pool is nay a ruin—I'd hoped we could one day use it as a summer shieling."

"Us?"

"Aye." He cupped her cheek with his palm. "But I'll build us a fine manse in the Coe as well."

"A shieling of our own sounds marvelous—more than I'd hoped."

"Och aye, lassie. In time you will have everything you've ever dreamed of and more."

Chapter Thirty-Six

C harlotte had packed her best gown for this day—just in case. A sennight ago, she'd thought all was lost but now, she stood in the main cottage while the MacIain women curled her hair and primped her ribbons.

"Have you seen inside your new shieling yet?" asked Bonnie.

"Hugh hasn't allowed me near it."

"It should be something special," said Nessa. "The laird worked day and night. Breac told me he made the furniture out of logs."

"Wheesht." Bonnie shook the hairbrush. "'Tis supposed to be a surprise."

Charlotte chuckled. "I must admit 'tis a bit difficult to keep secrets with all of us being so close-knit."

"Have you seen it then—I mean the bed?" asked Nessa.

Goodness, she must be blushing to her toes. "Heavens, no —but I guessed he'd made a few pieces from all the timber the men were carting inside." She had a few surprises of her own as well. Charlotte had decided not to tell Hugh about the gold and silver coins that remained from her dowry until well after their wedding. Oh no, she'd already wounded his pride by showing up with a flock of sheep—regardless if they'd been much needed.

The door creaked open and Lachlan poked his face inside. "Are you ready yet? The men said they're all growing old."

"I beg your pardon?" scolded Nessa.

Charlotte snapped her hands to her veil. "How does it look? I feel ever so awkward without a looking glass."

"You're prettier than a sunrise," said Bonnie.

"Thank you." Charlotte nodded to the lad. "Very well. Are you giving me away then?" A pang of sadness passed through her for a moment. The only thing this day lacked was Papa's presence. Everything else had come together like a song. Sir Robert Stewart had brought a chaplain from Appin along with some needed supplies as his wedding gift—bless him, and for some reason Hugh had no qualms about accepting alms from another chieftain.

"Come along." The boy beckoned. "I cannot wait to eat the sweet cake Sir Robert brought."

Charlotte glanced at the kind faces of the women she'd come to know. True, they feared her at first, but now they knew she would be a part of their clan, they treated her as one of them. No longer an outsider, she looped her fingers around Lachlan's elbow. "Lead on, young squire."

"Do not forget your posy." Bonnie had collected some yellow primrose earlier that morn and tied them with a pink ribbon.

Accepting the bouquet, Charlotte bowed her head. "How could I forget such a perfect bouquet? Flowers from the garden of Glencoe." Her voice trailed off with a sigh.

When Charlotte stepped outside, the crowd gradually parted, making an aisle until all she could see was Hugh standing beside the priest. He wore a new plaid and doublet she'd never seen before. She leaned into Lachlan as her knees wobbled. Hugh had tied his dark tresses at the nape with a white bow. He grinned with his broad smile—the one that made her heart soar. White teeth, a clean-shaven chin, and eyes of liquid treacle. Oh yes, this was the man with whom she wanted to spend the rest of her life, even if they had to live in their mountain fortress—though the news of the inquisition was the biggest step to emancipation yet. But even that didn't matter. This day, she would marry the man of her dreams—a Highlander from the most notorious, most rugged clan in all of Scotland—a man with a heart as large as Glencoe.

Slowly she walked forward with little Lachlan beside her while she tried not to the crush the fragile stems in her fist.

Not once did Hugh's gaze stray from her face until finally he stepped forward and took her hand from the lad. "There are no words to describe your loveliness, *mo leannan*," he whispered so only she could hear.

The priest held out his stole. "May I have your hands?"

He chanted the outlawed Catholic mass in Latin while he bound their wrists together, then looked to the crowd. "Is there anyone present who can attest to any reason why Hugh MacIain MacDonald and Charlotte Elaine Hill cannot be lawfully united in marriage in accordance to God's Word? If so, you must now confess it."

A moment of dead silence passed.

"Then I shall continue—"

"Stop!" a man hollered from the back of the crowd.

Stewart guards muscled Papa down the aisle and pushed him toward Hugh. "We caught the colonel trying to spy."

Papa brushed his hands down the front of his uniform, looking a tad flustered. "How many times do I have to tell you the bride is my daughter, you sniveling maggots!"

With one wrist still bound to Hugh, the primroses

dropped as Charlotte reached for her father. "Papa, you came."

He gave her a thin-lipped nod.

"Are there others?" asked Og.

"I came alone." Papa reached inside his coat.

The guardsmen clamped onto his elbow. "Watch yourself."

"If I may be permitted, I have in my possession a proclamation from the Master of Stair."

Charlotte's gaze shot to Hugh. He looked like he couldn't breathe either.

Clearing his throat, the Chieftain of Clan Iain Abrach inclined his head toward their bound wrists. "If you would please do the honor of reading it aloud, sir."

The colonel pulled out a missive and unfolded it. "I shall eliminate the master's colorful language about the forthcoming inquisition and drive straight to the point."

"*The king hath rescinded his directive to extirpate all those under seventy who occupied the territory of Glencoe. His majesty has granted pardon to allow the Glencoe men to return to the Valley of the Dogs providing they agree to live peaceably under the oath sworn by their father in the presence of the Sheriff of Inveraray.*"

Hugh bowed deeply. "Honorable sir, this news is exceedingly favorable, and I swear the Government shall nay have cause to doubt our loyalty by the favor you have shown us on this blessed day. I shall never forget the courtesy you have shown me or the respect you owed my father. This is a wonderful day, indeed."

Charlotte watched her father's face while Hugh spoke the words that so clearly raised him up to be a responsible, upstanding chieftain. Yes, he would always remain a Jacobite, but he would own up to the oath he'd just sworn.

Og stepped in, anger written across his hard features. "What about compensation? What about the Privy Council's hearing?"

Papa dipped his head politely and drew his hand away from Hugh's grasp. "To answer your questions, the inquisition will still proceed. I have been ordered to present my testament. Unfortunately, there was nothing in Viscount Dalrymple's missive suggesting recompense."

"'Tis a start," said Hugh, his gaze panning the expectant faces. "My kin can return to their lands and, in time, to plant and rebuild." He again bowed. "My thanks to you, sir."

"Though I would have chosen differently for my daughter, I believe we have a wedding to finish." Papa stepped forward and kissed Charlotte's cheek. "I wish you happiness. 'Tis all I ever wanted for you, the rose of my heart."

Lachlan picked up the posy and handed it to her. "Can we get on with the wedding now? I'm starved."

Hearty laughter pealed from the crowd.

Charlotte's heart swelled as she gazed into Hugh's eyes, barely hearing the priest as he chanted the ceremony that would bind them as man and wife forever.

Chapter Thirty-Seven

Though the clan had pulled out all the stops and managed a grand feast for Hugh and Charlotte, he had never been so happy to spirit away from them. He carried her all the way up the hill to their new shieling beside the pool. The gentle music from the babbling burn welcomed them.

"I was planning to cut a path with steps, but with your father's news, I suppose that will have to wait," he said, taking the last few steps before they reached the door.

"'Tis a grand reason to wait." She curled against him, running her finger over his new cravat. "You looked ever so handsome tonight. I've never seen you in such finery."

"Thanks to Sir Robert. He delivered a suit of clothes befitting a Highland chief—said it was his wedding gift."

Hugh pulled the latch and crossed the threshold, kicking the door closed behind him. He thought of setting her down on the bed, but that wouldn't be right—not for his wife. He must give her time to grow accustomed to their surroundings. Gently, he set Charlotte on her feet in the middle of the one-room shieling. "At least 'tis warm. I stoked the fire afore the ceremony." He gestured to the fireplace. "And I built a proper stone hearth so the smoke doesn't hang in the air. I ken how much it can bother your eyes." He stood awkwardly for a moment—then realized they could barely see a thing. "I've a lamp."

"Thank you." Her voice sounded as nervous as he felt.

Like a lad, he hastened to the fire and lit a twig. He'd made an oil lantern out of an old wine bottle. Lighting that and a pair of tallow candles, he tossed the twig onto the fire and turned.

Lord, he'd married the bonniest lass in all the world. She smiled, her hands clasped in front of her gown. Made of silk and edged with lace, it was embroidered with violets that matched her eyes—even had violet silk roses gathering the cuffs at her elbows. Hugh had noticed how perfectly the gown formed to her feminine shape as she walked toward him during the ceremony. Aye, she remained a well-bred Sassenach from London.

He gestured to the walls with uncertainty twisting his gut. "'Tis a bit rustic."

"'Tis perfect." Her genuine grin made all trepidation slide from his shoulders. He'd worked like a dog to make this night comfortable for her, the whole time thinking it wasn't good enough.

She glanced around him to the hearth and walked forward. Wrapping her fingers around the handle of a cast-iron pot, she lifted it. "Where on earth did you find this sturdy cookware?"

Och, she was indeed an angel. Hugh grinned. "Ever since you brought the sheep, I've been slipping to my old cottage at night and digging through the rubble—it hasn't been looted like those in the glen, and some things survived the blaze—like these." He and Og had scrubbed them with pumice to remove the creosote stains and they looked almost new.

Charlotte set the pot down and brushed her fingers over

the well-oiled mantel Hugh had hewn from an oak. Slowly she walked around the cottage, past the big bed he'd built with its straw mattress—he'd have a feather bed for her soon. She stopped in the center of the chamber and placed both her hands on the back of a chair he'd fashioned from birch wood. "Only two chairs at the table?"

"Aye." Hugh chewed his lower lip.

"We shall need more once children come." Lord, her cheeks took on a rosy glow.

Hugh chuckled and crossed the distance, taking her into his arms. "Och, you have no idea how much it warms my heart to hear you utter those words."

"I've waited far too long for this day, my love," she whispered, her eyes awash with joy and tears.

Reaching up, he gently tugged off her veil. "I still cannot believe you are mine."

She untied his cravat, her breathing suddenly shallow. "Believe it, husband. Believe it."

Fighting his urge to haul her to the bed—like he'd dreamed of doing so often, he removed the pins from her hair, running his fingers through angel-soft tresses. Oh yes, this night would be far more memorable if he took his time—savored removing every stitch of clothing, every bit of lace. Peering over her shoulder, Hugh twirled the ribbon of her bodice around his finger, then caught the end and tugged.

With every piece of her dainty clothing, Charlotte unfastened one of his. After the cravat sailed to the floor beside her bodice and corset, she unpinned the plaid at his shoulder and held up the brooch. "Is this your clan badge?"

"A likeness, aye." It wasn't Da's—the one Hugh was supposed to inherit, but the near-perfect copy had been his since his parents had given it to him when he reached his majority.

"'Tis yours?"

He nodded. Later he'd tell her his treasure box buried beneath his longhouse survived. Since two nights ago, he hadn't been as destitute and poor as he'd thought. "Charlotte, I've so much to say."

She held her finger to his lips. "We have a lifetime to reveal our secrets."

In a bold move, she took his hand and led him to the bed.

Ever so eager to follow, Hugh's mouth suddenly went dry. Hell, he couldn't even manage a swallow. "Are you ready, my love?" he croaked.

Licking those delectable lips, she nodded. "I want you more than the air I breathe."

No words had ever been so arousing. "You've made me so incredibly happy." He stepped behind her and swept her tresses aside, caressing her neck with fluttering kisses.

With a wee gasp, she shivered and rolled her head back. "That feels divine."

It only took a tug to untie her overskirt, sending it whooshing to the floorboards. Two flannel petticoats remained over her shift. Hugh placed his hands on her hips with a rolling snicker. Would Charlotte ever cease to amaze him? "I never would have thought a gentlewoman would be one to sport a red petticoat, m'lady."

A wee laugh curled from Charlotte's throat, so sultry it sent his cock rigid. "Red's the latest fashion in London."

"Aye?" He slowly unlaced the first bow. "Mayhap English women have a bit more spirit than their male counterparts."

Her stately profile regarded him over her shoulder. "Mm, I would definitely agree to that."

As the petticoat fell away from her body, Charlotte turned, placing her palm on his chest. "I do believe it is your turn."

"Och, but you are wearing so many more layers."

"Mm hmm." She trailed a finger down to the deerskin

sporran suspended from a chain around his hips. "What do you keep in there?"

When she tapped it, the intensity of his shuddering inhale surprised even him. God, he might not make it onto the bed. "A few coins," his voice strained. "A wee dagger, a handful of musket balls, and a flint."

When he reached to unclasp it, Charlotte slipped around him and brushed his hands away. "I'll do it."

"I hoped you'd say that." Mercy, his voice had grown as husky as the smithy's rasp.

Being undressed by Charlotte ratcheted up his desire even higher. Though he stood still, his breathing sped as if he'd run up a flight of stairs. After she placed the sporran on the bed, she smoothed her fingers around his leather belt, sauntering around him until she arrived at the big brass buckle. "Now this."

Hugh hoped she'd say that, too. If she grew any more assertive with him, she might just drive him to utter madness. "Once you remove my plaid," he growled. "I'll be completely and utterly naked."

"'Tis what I want." Her tongue snuck to the corner of her mouth, her fingers had a slight tremor as she tugged his belt and the plaid cascaded to the floor. Hugh didn't move while she stood back and raked her gazed down his body. Only Charlotte had ever stopped to drink him in like that, stare at his abdomen, his thighs, his rock-hard cock. It made him desperate to rip off her final petticoat and shift and do the same to his wife.

He took in a sudden inhale when she brushed her lithe fingers along his length. "Every inch of you is sculpted as if hewn from marble. Is there no part of your body that isn't hard?"

"Nay, lass." He thrust his hips forward. "More than anything else, this is hard for you."

Grinning, Hugh took a swaggering step and clamped his hands on her shapely hips. Lord in heaven he wanted to go slowly, but she'd pushed him to the ragged edge. "I've yet to unlace your last petticoat." His gaze traveled down her body and stopped at her waist. "May I?"

Closing her eyes, she nodded and stood perfectly still while the last flannel petticoat slipped away from her waist. Standing in nothing but her linen shift, Hugh ran his finger around the lace neckline. "Now this."

Lids fanned with honeyed lashes gradually opened and she raised her hands.

"Are you nervous?" he asked.

"Not anymore."

Within a blink, he had her completely disrobed. Charlotte's arms flew across her body. Hugh slid his fingers over her wrists. "Let me gaze upon perfection."

She looked away with a shake of her head. "I'm not."

He coaxed open her arms, ever so slowly. "Aye, but you're wrong, lass." God save him, he could scarcely take a breath. It had been so long since he'd seen her disrobed and now he swore she'd grown more beautiful. "I have to be the luckiest man alive."

He could restrain himself no longer. Wrapping the love of his life in his arms, he covered her mouth with a claiming, heart-stopping, bone-shattering kiss. Lord, the woman knew how to please him in every way. Even if she had a wart on her nose, he could love no one else in this world as he loved Charlotte Hill MacIain. He ground himself against her, his cods afire—demanding relief from the pent up desire he'd ignored for months.

Before he completely lost his head, he lifted her into his arms. As he rested Charlotte on her back, he kneeled over and kissed her, their mouth's joining in a dance that had now become enticingly familiar. Trailing kisses down her neck, he moved his hand to her breast and caressed the most succulent flesh he'd ever had the honor of touching. Charlotte arched into him and bucked. "Please, Hugh. I cannot wait much longer."

"Mm hmm." But his mouth didn't stop. He ran kisses all the way down her body, lingering for a moment over her nether parts, his hot breath teasing her, drinking in the ambrosia of her sex.

Moaning, she circled her hips for him. "Pleeeease. I need you now."

He slid back up her body and pushed between her legs, ready to explode. "I, too, can wait no more."

Charlotte opened her eyes, so incredibly dark. Her lips swollen and seductive, his entire body shuddered as if he might spill his seed right then. He ground his hips against her core, his cock catching at her entrance. Heaven help him, she was so wet—so ready.

With a gasp catching in his throat he slid inside heaven.

Charlotte's fingers gripped his buttocks. "Faster. Deeper."

All Hugh could do was hold on and thrust. The world became a shower of starlight as together they rode the wave of passion. Her high-pitched mewls sent his mind into utter oblivion. All he could think of was how good this felt and how lucky he was to have this woman as his wife. With a cry catching in the back of her throat, Charlotte shattered into a thousand trembling shudders. The friction blew his mind as with two more deep thrusts he met her at the peak and roared with the potent force of his release.

When he recovered his breath, he pushed up, staring at the most unbelievably fantastic woman of all his imaginings. "My God, I will love you forever."

She cupped his cheek and smiled. "You've no idea how happy you've made me. I am fulfilled in every way."

Chapter Thirty-Eight

❦

The sun shone for Clan MacIain Abrach as together they marched down the pass and into the glen with Colonel Hill riding his horse behind them. Og and Gavyn rode the ponies, while Cuddy helped them herd the sheep to the valley where the grass had grown lush and green. Hugh clutched his bride's hand, while both excited and hesitant to take her there.

To Hugh there was no place on earth as stunning as Glencoe. The best thing about leaving was always returning home again. No matter what time of year he crossed the valley, it took his breath away. Emerald green, majestic mountains towered above, their precipices stern and rugged, warning of the dangers brought by sheer cliffs and piled rocks.

During his exile, Hugh had glimpses of home from a distance but with dragoons infesting the glen, it had been too risky to go there. As the crags of their hiding place behind Meall Mòr gave way and sloped to the valley, Hugh stopped, holding up his hand.

Beside him, Charlotte gasped. "Papa?"

A group of black cattle stood in a makeshift pen, and rows

of white tents cut through the landscape as if the army had moved in. "What the devil?"

Hugh turned around to see his father-in-law cantering toward them. "I figured you'd need temporary accommodations until you could put new roofs on your cottages." The old colonel dismounted and led his horse while he walked beside them. "The six heifers and bull are my wedding gift. Should give you a start."

Charlotte grasped his arm and hugged it, resting her head on his shoulder. "Oh, Papa, thank you, thank you ever so much."

"Aye, sir," Hugh stretched his palm forward and shook the old man's hand. "Your generosity exceeds all expectations."

Colonel Hill wiped his eyes. Perhaps the stern colonel had a gentle side when it came to his child. "Nonsense. I would have my daughter well looked after." He handed Hugh the reins and grasped Charlotte's shoulders. "Does anything of your dowry remain?"

She met Hugh's gaze before answering. "Most of it."

"Then I expect you to put it to good use." He pulled her into his embrace. "I shall miss you ever so much. You are the sweetest thing ever produced in this weary soldier's lifetime."

Then Charlotte held him at arm's length. "We will see you often," her voice trembled as if she were staving off tears. "'Tis only twenty miles to Fort William."

"I will hold you to that." The colonel smiled, his teeth stained yellow. "I expect to see grandchildren within the year."

Hugh chuckled. "We're working on that, sir."

Charlotte covered her mouth, her eyes shocked. "Hugh!"

The old man extended his hand. "Take care of her. She's more precious than all the king's gold."

Hugh grasped the offered hand and held it firm. "I will, sir."

After the colonel and his men took their leave and the clansmen and women set to cleaning the burned shells of their cottages, Hugh led Charlotte to Carnoch. Black creosote scorched the manse's stone walls with upward lashings, posing as a testament of the devastation of that fateful morning on 13th February, 1692.

Charlotte squeezed his hand. "I pray the inquisition will rule in your favor and compensate you and the clan for all you have suffered."

Hugh still would have rather taken up the sword and fought until he ran William of Orange out of London, but as Donald of Sleat had said, times were changing. The Jacobites needed the support of France to be successful. In time, perhaps there would be another rising. When that time came, Hugh would be at the forefront of the first line, leading the army of Clan Iain Abrach. But for the time being, he must play the game of the ruling aristocracy. Aye, there would be an inquisition in Edinburgh and, aye, he would testify and repeat the truth over and over—as many times as it took for the peers who lived lives of luxury to understand the extent of the heinous crimes committed against his family and his people.

Moving his arm around Charlotte's waist, he clutched her to his side. "As I said before, our lands have been returned to us. At least that is a start."

"Yes it is."

They stood in silence for a moment and stared at the burned shell of the place of Hugh's childhood memories—of Da and Ma—of an era that somehow had passed and faded into the earth.

"It will be a quite a job to rebuild such a large manse," Charlotte whispered.

Hugh shook his head. "We will tear down these walls."

She looked up at him in question.

"Here, I will build a memorial to my parents as testament to their lives and their brutal deaths. Never shall anyone who passes through this place forget what happened here."

"Yes." Charlotte rested her head on his shoulder. "You are right to honor them."

Swallowing back the thickness in his throat, he took her hand. "Would you like to see where I will build your house, m'lady?"

She grinned. "You mean our house?"

He mirrored her smile. "Aye."

Taking her hand, he led her along the path to the mouth of the River Coe. They stood on a curved peninsula high above the river where it would be free from floods. Hugh spread his arms wide and looked across Loch Leven. "The hills of Glencoe will be our backdrop, the river of the Coe will be our music, and our galleys will sail through the waters of the Leven to Loch Linnhe and out to sea. Mark me, my love, Clan Iain Abrach will rebuild, and will once again rule these lands."

He looked into her eyes and saw joy there. "And you will be my queen."

Epilogue

✦

It was mid-July, the year of our Lord 1695—three years since the massacre of Glencoe. Hugh and Charlotte had pooled their treasures and built a fine manse at the mouth of the River Coe where Hugh had taken her the day they returned to the valley. The lintel above the door bore their initials inscribed in stone. Every time Charlotte crossed the threshold she regarded it, proud to be the matriarch of the new generation of MacIain MacDonalds.

The Jacobite chieftains continued to gather under the guise of their Highland games. And with their every meeting their forces grew stronger—both in brawn and more so, their web of clandestine activities. Nonetheless, Charlotte prayed every night for peaceful resolution of the differences between the Williamite and the Jacobite parties.

Warmed by the sun, they sat on the verandah awaiting Colonel Hill's arrival. Charlotte held three-month-old James in her lap while Hugh rocked two-year-old Alexander. Two healthy sons had been born to carry on their legacy—the eldest named for Sandy, the youngest for their exiled king.

A single rider approached in posting trot, wearing a tell-tale red coat. Charlotte grinned. "He's here."

Together they stood and said their hellos. Papa's back had stooped more since the last time she'd seen him. The inquisition hadn't been easy on Hugh, but it had been even harder on the old man.

Charlotte gestured to a chair. "Please sit with us and share a cup of ale."

"I don't mind if I do." The colonel grunted as he sat—Charlotte could almost hear his bones creak. "My, the boys are growing too fast."

"That they are," Hugh agreed. "Have you news?"

After pouring, Charlotte resumed her seat, her stomach squeezing. They'd had word that the Scottish Parliament under direction of the Privy Council had drawn up its address to the king.

Papa took a drink, then pulled a missive from inside his coat. "Indeed, parliament has condemned the slaughter as 'Murder under Trust'." He handed the missive to Hugh. "Thank God for justice."

Both elated and concerned for her father, Charlotte placed her palm atop Papa's hand. "And you? What are the findings regarding your role?"

"Innocent." He hung his head and shook it. "Only because of all the appeals I made against Stair to begin with."

"Oh, praises be." She bit her bottom lip. "And the king?"

"Of course, they couldn't convict William without inciting a rebellion." He regarded her with sad, rheumy eyes. "The Master of Stair was named as the original cause of the whole sordid affair. Robert Duncanson was convicted as well because his order to Glenlyon exceeded the directives I'd given him."

Hugh folded the parchment and tapped it. "Captain

Campbell of Glenlyon and Captain Drummond were also accused."

Papa raised his tankard. "At least it recommends full reparation for your loss."

Hugh smirked. "I doubt we'll ever see that. The king never did make good on the promises he made through Breadalbane."

"I wish I could admit differently, but with the war in Flanders, payrolls are oft overlooked at Fort William." Papa took a long pull of his ale. "It seems there are never enough funds to cover all the expenses."

James awoke and yawned, his tiny mouth turning toward his mother. "The wee one will need to suckle soon."

Hugh stood and stretched, setting young Alexander on his feet. "Thank you for bringing this news, colonel. We shall have a gathering to share the resolution with the clan." He bowed to Papa. "You're welcome to join us."

"It would be my pleasure."

The lad toddled over and raised his arms to Grandad. "Up."

Papa chuckled and pulled Alexander onto his lap, his eyes growing moist. "You and my grandchildren are the only joy left in this old man's heart, my dear."

At last their plight had been resolved. Charlotte stood with James on her hip and kissed her father. "I am blessed with so many men to look after me." Looking to her husband, she straightened. "Tonight's gathering shall be the grandest the Coe has ever seen. Let us revel in our good fortune."

Hugh moved beside his wife and smoothed his hand around her waist, tugging her close. "And celebrate a new era for us all."

Author's Note

Thank you for joining me on this fictional journey that encompasses the Glencoe Massacre. Hugh MacIain MacDonald was fashioned after John by the same last name, the son of Alasdair MacIain MacDonald, murdered 12th Chieftain of Glencoe.

Though Charlotte is a fictional character, the record does mention that Colonel Hill supported two spinster daughters who lived in London.

Robert Campbell, 5th Chieftain of Glenlyon indeed had a reputation for drinking and gambling his estate away, and became the oldest captain in the king's army at the request of his earl cousins Argyll and Breadalbane. As an officer, he received pay and work that his cousins hoped would keep Robert from their coffers. It is said that after the massacre, Glenlyon could be found in an Edinburgh alehouse, nursing a tankard as he sat against the wall in a dark corner with a haunted stare on his face. People would come to observe the spectacle of that crazed, aging man. "I would do it again!" he reportedly would holler. "I would dirk any man in Scotland or England without asking cause if the king gave me orders."

Some reports said, "MacIain hangs about Glenlyon day and night." Indeed, the man's soul was haunted.

The missive to Captain Campbell ordering the massacre was written by Major Robert Duncanson in Ballachulish on 12th February, 1692, and was said to have been passed down through Glenlyon's kin until it ended up in the possession of the National Library of Scotland in Edinburgh where it resides today. It reads:

You are hereby ordered to fall upon the Rebells, the M'Donalds of Glencoe, and putt all to the sword under seventy. You are to have a special care that the old fox and his sones do upon no account escape your hands. You are to secure all the avenues that no man escape. This you are to putt in execution ate five of the clock precisely and by that time, or verie shortly after it, I'le strive to be att you with a stronger party; if I doe not come to you at five, you are not to tarry for me, butt to fall on. This is by the King's special command, for the good and safety of the country, that these miscreanis be cut of root and branch. See that this be putt in executoine without feud or favour, else you may expect to be dealt with as one not true to King nor Government, not a man fit to carry commission in the King's Service. Expecting you will not faill in the ful-filling hereof, as you love yourselfe, I subscribe these with my hand at Balicholis, Ffeb. 12, 1692.

R. Duncanson

"To Capt. Robert Campbell of Glenlyon."

"ffor their Maties service."**

Interestingly, five o'clock was two hours before dawn, and Colonel Hill's original missive stated seven o'clock. That Major Duncanson wanted no part of the killing was clear, for when he did arrive with his battalion at seven that ill-fated morning, the killing had been done and the survivors were fleeing into the hills in the midst of a blizzard.

Though three years later, the Privy Council did conduct an inquisition and found the Master of Stair, Glenlyon,

Duncanson and others guilty of murder under trust, John (Hugh) MacIain MacDonald and his clan never saw a penny of recompense. Further, though convicted, penalties were not enforced, and not one "murderer" spent a single minute behind bars.

Today Glencoe is a thriving place of awe-inspiring landscape and is home to an abundance of wildlife. In the town of Glencoe there is a lovely museum displaying remnants of the early life. A memorial still stands giving ode to Alasdair MacIain MacDonald, the fearless old laird. Up the A82, the National Trust for Scotland has built an impressive visitors center with something for everyone. Glencoe truly is one of nature's grand fortresses, one well worth a visit.

*The missives from the Master of Stair included in this story are adaptations from historical papers reported in GLENCOE, by John Prebble, Published by Penguin Books, 1966.

**The order from Major Duncanson is a reproduction of the missive sent to Captain Campbell on February 12, 1692. The original handwritten order resides in the National Library of Scotland.

EXCERPT FROM THE VALIANT HIGHLANDER

Chapter One

❧

Castleton, Isle of Skye. June, 1694

With a deafening crack, the musket ball missed the target by a furlong. Mary cringed, perhaps she'd exaggerated the distance of the miss, but after an hour of instruction she expected her little brother to show *some* improvement. With a sigh she cast her gaze to the puffy white clouds sailing above. Would the lad ever catch on?

She pulled the stopper from the powder horn with her teeth. "Give it to me," she said out of the corner of her mouth.

"Och, Mary." Rabbie inclined the musket her way. Goodness, the thing was longer than the nine-year-old was tall. "I lined up my sights just like you said."

She snatched the barrel and inclined it away from her face to ensure the gun didn't grow a mind of its own and misfire. "Aye? Then what went wrong?"

The lad rubbed his arm and winced. "Don't ken. But my shoulder feels like Florence stomped on it with one of her wooden heels."

"Then it's the kick. 'Tis forcing you off sights." Mary

poured in the powder and jammed a lead musket ball down the barrel with the ramming rod. "You need to push your shoulder into the butt like so." She demonstrated, lifting the wooden stock and taking aim. "Then close your left eye and line up your sights with your right."

"I did all that." Rabbie clapped his hands over his ears as she pulled the trigger and fired.

The ball smacked straight through the center of the bullseye painted red on the straw target. Mary lowered the weapon and gave her little brother a nod. "Ready to give it another go?"

"Aye, and I'll top your shot this time for certain."

He'd been saying that since yesterday at the evening meal when they'd discussed doing some target practice. The lad was keen to prove himself with a musket. After all, before sunset this day every Jacobite chieftain in the Highlands would be arriving at Dunscaith Castle for the games—hosted by the MacDonalds of Castelton for the first time since the secret meetings had begun two years past.

"Just try to hit the target first." She again charged the barrel with powder.

Rabbie held out his hand. "Give me the ball. I'll ram it myself this time."

"Very well." After dropping the piece of lead in his palm, she passed him the musket. Then Mary stood back and folded her arms, saying a prayer he'd have some luck this go round.

Pulling back the cock, he lined up his sights. Then her freckle-faced brother gave her a cheeky grin. Gracious, if Mary had been a lad, she would have looked just like him. "Are you ready?" he asked.

She tipped up her chin. "The question is are *you* ready?"

"Och aye, sis."

She held her breath.

The musket fired and recoiled with a ferocious boom. The scrawny lad tottered backward while Mary waved her hand in front of her face to clear the smoke. "Merciful fairies, you hit it!"

Rabbie slung the musket over his shoulder and ran to the target. "I told you I'd do it."

She chuckled. At least he'd hit the outer edge of the target.

"Hey you pair," Lilas hollered, running over the hill with Florence in her wake. "A *birlinn* has landed and there are more sailing in behind it."

"So soon?" Mary regarded her attire. *I'll have to slip in the postern gate.*

"I hit the target," Rabbie yelled, pointing.

Ignoring him, Mary eyed her younger sisters. "Do you ken what clan?"

"Nay." Florence caught up and planted her fists on her hips, giving Mary an exaggerated onceover. "Heaven's stars, why are you wearing trews?"

Mary had actually borrowed the whole get up from Da—bonnet and all. "I cannot very well teach Rabbie how to shoot wearing a kirtle and arisaid, now can I?" It was the same hunting costume Da had worn when teaching her how to handle a musket—in the years before the Battle of Dunkeld when he lost his leg.

"Why not?" The lad came up behind them. "You always wear a dress."

"Aye, but you couldn't see my feet. After the last disaster, I thought it would help some and it did." Mary glanced to her sisters and pointed to the target. "He hit it. Did you see?"

"I saw," an incredibly deep voice said from behind. "Having a bit of target practice afore the games are you?"

The nape of Mary's neck tingled while she spun on her heel. The guests were expected to begin arriving after the midday meal—three hours hence. She bit her bottom lip. The voice belonged to a very tall man, grinning from ear to ear and carrying a musket under his arm. He wore a proper Highland bonnet covering tawny tresses, tied back with a ribbon. Goodness, the nearer he came, the girth of his shoulders grew ever so much wider. His sporran swung to and fro atop his dark plaid while he walked—sword in his belt, dirk at his hip as if he were ready for battle. Mary's chin dropped. The muscles in his legs flexed like nothing she'd ever seen before.

At seven and ten, Lilas cleared her throat and nudged Mary's arm. "*Holy Moses*," she whispered as if she were gazing upon a god.

Giving her sister a subtle elbow, Mary prayed she hadn't turned as red as Lilas. She threw her thumb over her shoulder in the direction of the target. "Teaching the lad how to shoot."

The big man gave Mary the most quizzical look. His stare was most unnerving. Aside from being perhaps the most handsome man she'd chanced to regard, his dark blue eyes made it difficult to breathe. Aye, as dark as midnight those eyes. His gaze started at her man's bonnet and meandered down to her trews before he looked to Rabbie. "Is that so?"

"Och aye. I'll be joining the rebellion soon." The lad never lacked in self-confidence for certain.

The man glanced behind as one eyebrow arched. "You'd best keep your voice down when uttering such fervent words."

Mary stepped in. "Why? Have you not come for the games?"

"Aye, lad." He studied her with a pinch to his brow, as if she posed a confounding sight. "But I spotted a camp of redcoats not fifty miles down the coast."

Mary pursed her lips with a brisk nod. "That would be Lieutenant Balfour MacLeod and his regiment of upstarts."

She groaned with a huff. "He's a spineless weasel if you ask me." The officer always looked at her like a starved dog. Worse, he hated everything Jacobite, and insured everyone on her part of Skye suffered in the stocks if they were but a day late with their taxes.

"Aye, he's vile." Lilas batted her eyelashes at the Highlander like a harlot. Heavens, the lass was incorrigible.

"Then I suggest you stay well away from the likes of him." The man raised his powder horn. Odd, he didn't give Mary's flirting sister a second glance. "Care for a wager?"

"With me?" Mary's jaw nearly hit the ground.

He again regarded her from head to toe. "Thought you said you were teaching the lad to shoot."

"Aye—since our da cannot." Mary took the gun from Rabbie. "A farthing?" Good heavens, she'd never placed a wager in her life.

Frowning, the big Highlander scratched his chin. Merciful fairies, his eyes were an intriguing shade of blue—not like the sky, but more like the sea made angry by a winter storm. "How about a crown?" he asked as if it were a trifle.

Her gaze shifted to the target. She'd hit the bull's eye five times today—missed by an inch once. Odds were she'd win... and if she lost, she had a few crowns tucked away in the chest in her bedchamber. But those were intended for her future. No, she'd best not lose. She bit down on the cork and pulled it from the powder horn like she always did. "All right. You first."

Florence caught Mary's eye and mouthed, *a crown?*

Mary knit her eyebrows and batted her hand through the air. "Wheesht," she said so quietly, the shush was barely audible. "Go back to the keep and tell Da the guests are arriving." The last thing she needed was her two sisters giggling behind her and ogling the Highlander.

Nonetheless, Lilas made googly eyes at him. "Do we have to?"

"Yes. And now," Mary said, shooing them away.

"Best of three?" The man still appeared oblivious to her sister's antics.

Mary cringed considering his question. *Is that what men do when they place a wager?* "Certainly."

"Laddie, go fetch us a bit of charcoal. You can mark the shots so we will not lose track."

Rabbie's eyes sparkled as if he'd been commanded by King James himself. "Straight away, sir."

Aye, the man looked dapper with his hair the color of burnt honey neatly tied back with bow at his nape—his silk waistcoat was of fine tailoring as well, but he couldn't be a chieftain. *Could he?* The man's laird must have alighted the birlinn and headed straight to the keep to greet their da.

By the time they charged their weapons, Rabbie returned, grinning from ear to ear. Mary wasn't sure if his excitement was because her brother wanted to see her bested, or if he was happy to have a brawny man there to learn from.

"Do you mind if I fire off a practice shot?" he asked with a hypnotic burr. "I'm afraid my legs think they're still at sea."

Mary gave a polite nod. "By all means." Then a wicked grin spread across her lips. "But only one."

She swayed a bit, watching the man line up his sights. He planted his feet firm, closed one eye, his bold forehead angled down to the barrel. Dear Lord, his concentration was as impressive as his bonny countenance. A tic twitched above his eye just before his finger closed on the trigger. The blast cracked with a puff of smoke.

Mary hardly flinched. "Did you travel far?"

The man peered at her over the musket's stock. "Glasgow."

Goodness, he had come quite a long way. "Was the sea calm for your journey?"

He lowered his weapon. "Och, you're awful chatty for a lad." He squinted at her. "How old are you?"

Mr. Handsome thought her a lad? *Just as well.* Mary cast a thin-lipped glare at Rabbie, sending him a silent message to keep his mouth shut. "Forgive me for talking too much," she said, avoiding the question about her age and looking down. Ah yes, her breasts were concealed beneath her father's over-sized waistcoat. Then she hastily gestured to the target. "Carry on."

He again charged his musket and lined up his sights. This time she pursed her lips to prevent her mouth from distracting the man whilst he fired.

With a thunderous boom, his musket kicked more than hers ever had.

Mary's gaze snapped to the target. He hit the outer edge of the bullseye. "Nice shooting."

"My thanks." He grinned, seemingly satisfied with his mark.

Palms perspiring like never before, Mary stepped up to the line. Curses, even her hands shook a bit. She wiped them on her trews and took a deep breath. She wasn't about to lose a whole crown—a farthing mayhap, but not a crown. Positioning the butt against her shoulder, she eyed the bullseye. Confidence surged from her heart as her finger closed on the trigger.

When the smoke cleared, Rabbie was already running to the target. He marked both spots.

"Mine's a hair closer." Mary smiled.

The man squinted. "Perhaps, but there's two more to go."

After the second round, the contest was too close to call —even for Mary. The man had a keen eye for certain, but so did she. By the looks of his attire, losing an entire crown would make no difference to his purse. But it would mean a great deal to her.

His last shot hit the bullseye much like his first.

Mary blew on her palms. This was it. She had to win. Rabbie gave her a nod. With a subtle nod back, she raised the musket, lined up her sights and took a shallow breath. Before she blinked, her finger closed on the trigger.

"Lord in heaven," the man said. "Spot on the middle."

Grinning, Mary held out her palm. "Would you like another round?" Only the fairies knew what prompted her to say that. Holy Moses, she needed to hasten to her bedchamber and change into a kirtle. For heaven's sake, she was the lady of her father's keep. Thank goodness no one important had arrived as of yet. She'd be mortified to be discovered wearing a pair of trews by someone like the Baronet of Sleat.

He ignored her outstretched palm. Those hawkish eyes focused on her while he sauntered forward, rubbing his palm over the pommel of his dirk. "You have no other weapons?"

She took a wee step back. "N-no."

He smirked. "Are you ready to fight for *the cause* should you be called?"

She nodded.

His eyes shifted aside.

The hairs on the back of Mary's neck prickled.

With her next breath, the world reeled. Hands as powerful as a vise clamped on her shoulders, spun her around. Before she knew what happened, her arms were trapped, his dirk leveled at her neck. He pressed his lips to her ear. "Nay, laddie, you'll not be ready for battle until you build a bit o' muscle...can take on a man like me." The deep tenor of his voice rumbled through her entire body—made gooseflesh rise across every inch of skin.

Mary shook right down to the tips of her toes. Mercy, his

back was warmer than a brazier, and the arm clamped around her torso like iron. She chanced a glance at him over her shoulder. "Yes, s-sir."

Who was this man? And how dare he manhandle her, even if he thought her a lad.

With a rueful chuckle he released his grip. "I suggest you wait until your beard comes in afore you join the wrestling competition."

"She's not going to wrestle." Throwing back his shoulders Rabbie dashed forward and kicked the man in the shin. "Never touch my sister again."

"Ow." The man's jaw dropped. "Sister?" His gaze snapped to Mary's face. "Bloody, miserable bleating hell. You'd best don a proper gown afore you trick anyone else out of a crown."

Crossing her arms, Mary scooted away. "As I recall, you were the one who placed the wager."

"Aye," said Rabbie. "And I haven't seen your coin, mister."

The man looked at Rabbie as if he could shoot daggers through his eyes. With a growl, he dug in his sporran. "Do not tell me your father is John of Castleton?"

Mary's stomach turned over. Da wouldn't be happy if he found out she was wearing his trews, let alone placing wagers. But she raised her chin and held out her palm. "What if he is?"

"Good God." The man slapped the coin in her hand. "I would have thought more from his offspring."

Please, this cannot be someone important. "Pray tell, what is your name, Mr....?"

"MacDonald." He turned on his square-toed shoe and headed toward the keep.

She smoothed her fingers over the coin while studying his retreating form. Holy Moses, he posed a sight—tall, well-muscled, well-dressed. She bit her bottom lip. Aye, Mr.

MacDonald had to be someone important for certain. *He called Da by the familiar*.

With luck, he'd soon forget this morning's events. Looking to the wispy clouds sailing above, Mary clapped her hands together and prayed it would be so.

Da had never allowed her to attend the games before—and growing up in Castleton on the Isle of Sky didn't give her much of an opportunity to meet anyone interesting. And goodness, nearly everyone in these parts was named MacDonald. Several of the clans who'd be here for the games were MacDonalds as well...and Camerons, and Grants, and MacDougalls. Her mind boggled. She'd best hurry. Dunscaith Castle kitchens would need oversight for certain—and she didn't want to be caught by any of the great men due to arrive this afternoon.

§

MARCHING TOWARD THE KEEP, SIR DONALD MACDONALD, the Baronet of Sleat clutched his musket under his arm. Bloody oath, the castle looked as if it were crumbling. And he'd just been bested by John of Castleton's *daughter*? Covered with freckles, a Highlander's bonnet pulled low over her forehead, the lass looked more masculine than her little brother. Damnation, he kent something was amiss when he wrestled her into his grip. Not only did she smell like a garden of lilacs, she weighed no more than seven stone. 'Tis why he asked his —rather—*her* age.

Don shook his head. He would have bested the wench if he hadn't been navigating a birlinn through the rough swells of the North Sea since dawn yesterday. He needed a good meal and a healthy tot of whisky to regain his land legs.

Bloody hell, he'd been looking forward to this jaunt to the Highlands? He didn't need a parcel of children in his way. He had serious matters to discuss with the Defenders—the Jacobite chieftains who had pledged their fealty to *the cause*. Aye, one day they'd see King James returned to the throne and oust the usurper, William of Orange. To add insult, the false king's wife, posing as Queen Mary II was James very daughter. No greater backstabber hath ever worn a crown.

-End of excerpt from The Valiant Highlander

Also by Amy Jarecki

Highland Defender

The Valiant Highlander

The Fearless Highlander

The Highlander's Iron Will

Highland Force:

Captured by the Pirate Laird

The Highland Henchman

Beauty and the Barbarian

Return of the Highland Laird

Guardian of Scotland

Rise of a Legend

In the Kingdom's Name

The Time Traveler's Christmas

Highland Dynasty

Knight in Highland Armor

A Highland Knight's Desire

A Highland Knight to Remember

Highland Knight of Rapture

Highland Knight of Dreams

Devilish Dukes

The Duke's Fallen Angel

The Duke's Untamed Desire

ICE

Hunt for Evil

Body Shot

Mach One

Celtic Fire

Rescued by the Celtic Warrior

Deceived by the Celtic Spy

Lords of the Highlands series:

The Highland Duke

The Highland Commander

The Highland Guardian

The Highland Chieftain

The Highland Renegade

The Highland Earl

The Highland Rogue

The Highland Laird

The Chihuahua Affair

Virtue: A Cruise Dancer Romance

Boy Man Chief

About the Author

A descendant of an ancient Lowland clan, Amy adores Scotland. Though she now resides in southwest Utah, she received her MBA from Heriot-Watt University in Edinburgh. Winning multiple writing awards, she found her niche in the genre of Scottish historical romance. Amy loves hearing from her readers and can be contacted through her website at www.  amyjarecki.com. Visit her web site & sign up to receive newsletter updates of new releases and giveaways exclusive to newsletter followers.

f y a BB

Made in the USA
Monee, IL
12 December 2020